THE BEARER

FRANK MCILWEE

'Beware the fury of a patient man.'

JOHN DRYDEN, 1631- 1700

CONTENTS

PROLOGUE

**Singapore
1979**

THE HUGE LIZARD writhed against the twine, its forked tongue still tasting the air even though swallowing was no longer possible. The noose around its neck was tightening as its tail was raised from the ground by a line that arched over the low bough of a tempinis tree.

The boy grinned as he pulled at the apex of the elaborate rope-work. He was pleased with his hanging rig. He'd tried it on small lizards before, but nothing this big. This reptile was as long as his arm and weighed much more than his wheelbarrow, even when it was full of sand. He had executed his plan well, using the netting that was kept at the back of the greenhouse and the jute twine the gardeners used for planting their neat rows.

He had captured the lizard at the bottom of the long garden, near the lake that stretched westwards for at least half a mile, almost into Fort Canning Park. He'd scoured the area patiently, working his way methodically through the vegetation surrounding the big lawn, pushing aside the giant agave leaves and the fronds of banana plants. His sandals protected his feet from the sharp twigs and spiked fruits that had fallen to the ground but only a pair of brown shorts and a checked short-sleeved shirt protected his body. His bare arms and legs were heavily scratched.

Round and round the garden . . .

He had recited the nursery rhyme to himself as he'd searched.

Like a teddy bear . . .

He squirmed inside with pleasure as he imagined his mother's finger tracing a circle on his bare tummy.

One step . . .

Her cool finger touched his chest as her hand started to walk up his body.

Two step . . .

Her second finger purposefully stepped higher up his chest.

And a . . .

That delicious moment when he knew what was going to happen.

Tick-a-lee under there!

He yelped with delight and his shoulders shuddered as her fingers touched the sensitive skin under his chin. And then, as he grasped for her hands, she quickly changed direction and reached into his armpits for a vigorous tickle, mother and son shrieking and laughing as he pretended to escape and she leant forward to hold him closer.

His body was still tingling with the memory of her touch when he spotted the water monitor slowly walking down the slope towards a pool of shade near the bamboo archway.

One step . . .

He gathered the netting up in both hands as he hurried towards the unsuspecting reptile.

Two step . . .

He slowly positioned himself closer, ready to cast.

And a ...

He released the net in one smooth action. It arced into the shade and dropped softly over the lizard's hard back.

Tick-a-lee under there!

The lizard immediately thrashed and twisted in the netting, entangling itself still further.

The boy waited for the lizard to tire. He pulled a grubby handkerchief from a pocket in his shorts and dabbed at a cut on his shin. The dank smell of the dense tropical plants filled his nostrils.

The lizard was eventually still. The boy drew the sides of the net together and started to haul the bundle across the rough grass towards the top of the garden. The lizard inflated itself inside the net and renewed its writhing. Its tongue flicked through a square in the mesh that had closed around its mouth.

The boy pulled the net up to the tempinis and positioned the creature over two large loops of twine that he'd set out on the ground earlier. He pushed one loop over the lizard's head and brought the other loop over the tail and hind legs. As the lizard thrashed, both loops drew tightly against its dry skin, cutting into its neck and thorax.

He tugged the net away, stepped back, and pulled hard on the doubled-up line. One end extended from the rear end of the lizard over the branch and back to the pulling point at the apex. The other end ran from the noose around the neck down to the ground and then through the croquet hoop that he'd driven into the ground earlier that morning. The line angled back to the boy's two-handed grip.

When he had pulled as hard as he could, he tied the twine around a nail he'd hammered into the tree's hard bark and stood back to admire his handiwork.

The giant lizard hung helplessly a few inches from the ground, its tongue hanging from its mouth. The boy jumped into the air and slapped his bare knees. He let out a whoop of joy as he landed.

'Where's my little man?' a woman's voice called from the house. 'Darling, where are you? We're coming to find you!'

He glanced in the direction of his mother's voice before slowly turning his attention back towards his prey. There was nothing to worry about—after all, she hadn't stopped him before, even when he'd cut the wings from a sunbird to see how far it would be able to run before toppling over. Mama would be proud of him, he was sure. She always was. And he had trapped the monitor for her. It had no right to be in their garden. It should have stayed in Fort Canning Park, where it belonged. It was getting what it deserved.

Earlier, he'd carefully whittled the end of a stick to a sharp point with the penknife his father had given him for his sixth birthday, and he picked the stick up now from where he'd placed it in the shade of the tree. The penknife, with its mother of pearl handle and two folding blades, was his favourite possession.

'I know where you are,' the voice sang, 'and I'm going to squeeze you so hard when I find you.' She was getting close now. 'So hard you'll beg me for mercy.'

She was laughing as she spoke and he could imagine her pretending to scan the horizon as she made exaggerated, plodding steps down the garden from the big double doors at the back of the house.

He had watched her do this many times before. Usually, he'd be hiding in the thick foliage lining the expanse of lawn and she would pretend not to know where he was for several minutes before suddenly homing in on him. She'd scoop him up in her arms and carry him back to the house for lunch as he kicked the air, his play screams muffled first by her chest and then her abdomen as she twisted him upside down and ran. That was the best he would feel all day and although he had not yet reached the magic age of seven that his father kept telling him about, he knew what made him feel good.

'We're getting closer, darling. Kim Ying has her broom and she will beat you with it!' Her voice was closer now, behind the thick screen of Lillypilly.

He threw the stick under the tree. If Kim Ying was part of the game, then he would have to be more careful. Even though he knew she loved him as much as Mama, she could get angry very quickly. Just a couple of days ago, she had given his outstretched palms three sharp strokes with her black rattan cane and that was only for taking a jackfruit muffin from the kitchen larder without permission.

He glanced at the lizard, to check that it had not worked itself free, then stood tall next to it, hands clasped behind his back. He faced the gap in the Lillypilly where the crazy-paved path came through from the lawn. He was proud of his catch and he knew that they would be too.

His mother burst through the gap in a cloud of sweet vanilla perfume and freshly laundered cotton. Her cheeks were flushed and her mouth wide in a victorious smile; her teeth were sparkling white and her dark eyes flashed. He felt that familiar electric jolt shoot through him that only she could produce, a rush of reassurance that rooted him to the spot.

'There you are, mischief. I told you we'd find you!' She knelt down and wrapped her arms around him, pulling him close and resting her chin on his shoulder. She was facing the hanging lizard, but her eyes were closed, the moment of bliss as she hugged her son all-consuming.

'Let's have some lunch, darling. I think Papa might be able to join us today.'

The rush of reassurance drained away as quickly as it had come. Any talk of his father filled him with an unpleasant shaky feeling. He did not want to hear that loud voice today. Especially if it made Mama quiet and scared-looking. Nor did he want to hear about the age of reason again. Or the big grey school in England that he would be sent to soon. That made him feel heavy and cold.

'That will be nice won't it, darling? He's going to take some time off from helping the Army this afternoon. The Tanglin's closed for repairs so he said he would be home for lunch with us.' Her eyes were still closed. 'Let's just hope he isn't still angry about those silly Israelis doing his job for him,' she whispered, as if he wouldn't understand but she was telling him anyway. 'I just don't think I can cope with it anymore.'

Kim Ying followed her mistress through the gap and he tensed. She would see the lizard right away, he was sure. *Amah* never missed anything.

He was right. She saw the lizard immediately and stopped short, her mouth dropping momentarily before she regained her poise and stepped dutifully beside her mistress, smiling beatifically down at her charge. He looked up at her and smiled back. She always smiled at him when Mama was around and he liked that. Her round, smiling face made him feel strong. Or it had. Until the day he had seen her face squashed up against his father's. It had not been smiling then. Father was squeezing her against the kitchen wall and making her cry. Just like he did with Mama. That made him feel like catching a big spider and pulling off its legs. One by one.

Kim Ying was always dressed the same. Black trousers and white shirt, shiny black hair in the same knotted pattern down her back, the pattern he had copied with the rope that pulled up the hammock strung between the trees at the bottom of the garden. He thought again about his lizard and that made him feel better. They would both be proud of him.

'C'mon little big man. Let's have some lunch.' Mama pulled herself straight and lifted him up to her chest, turning towards the house.

Kim Ying followed hesitantly and then looked back at the lizard.

'Ma'am,' she said quietly. 'I think little man want to show you something.'

He smiled to himself as he detected the *amah's* discomfort.

'Show me what, Kim Ying?'

'Big gecko. On rope.'

'Gecko? Where?'

She turned and froze as she saw the hanging lizard. She let the boy slip slowly down to his feet. He looked up at her chin. She would smile again soon, he knew. She would give him one of her big smiles that showed how much she loved him and how clever he was. Her chin was moving now, up and down very quickly, like when she was cold.

He looked across to Kim Ying. She was staring at the ground. He moved away from his mother and went closer to the lizard, which had stopped scything to and fro. He prodded its stomach with his finger. It was soft, like his bed pillow. He prodded it again and this time it moved. He smiled. He could make the lizard wriggle again just by touching its belly. He prodded it a few more times but the wriggles started to slow down.

He looked back at Mama and Kim Ying. They were now sitting on the bench next to the big hedge. They were pleased with him, he could tell. They hadn't told him off and they were watching him play. Mama looked white now, rather than flushed, and Kim Ying kept looking at the ground, but they were enjoying watching him play. Mama was staring at the lizard. She must want him to play with it.

He glanced at the sharpened stick he'd thrown to the ground, then back at the two women. They were still silent. Time to play. He picked up the stick and pushed the pointed end against the lizard's scaly back. The creature revolved slowly and he stopped it when the yellow-brown skin of its underside faced him. He traced a circle around its stomach with the point of the stick. All thoughts of being sent to England melted away.

Round and round the garden . . .

He traced another circle.

Like a teddy bear . . .

He looked up at his mother to see if she was joining in. She was smiling at him now and he knew he could carry on. Kim Jing was smiling as well. He knew they wanted to be part of his game.

The point of the stick jumped a couple of inches down the lizard's belly towards its head.

One step . . .

Another jump of the stick. He pressed on the stick, which stretched the pale skin. There was no movement from the lizard.

Two step . . .

He mouthed the words of the rhyme for Mama's benefit. Her
smile was bigger now and he could see her sparkling teeth again. He
could feel her warmth crossing the grass to him and her fragrance
filled this special corner of the garden. It was *their* part of the garden.
Just theirs.

The point of the stick was pressing into the area between the
lizard's neck and the bottom of its lower jaw. He pressed harder and
the skin stretched into a deep indent. He gurgled in pleasure and
took another look at his mother.

She was still smiling, an elbow on her knee and her chin cupped
in her hand. She was looking straight at him with an intensity that he
liked. He knew he was at the centre of her world. She was not
thinking about anything else, not about the house or the servants or
father or anything. She was staring straight at him and she was so
proud of him. But he knew how to make her even prouder.

And a . . .

Her eyes were flashing brighter now, which told him that she
loved him more and more and that they would protect each other
forever. With their eyes locked, he thrust his makeshift spear hard
into the lizard's soft flesh. The skin made a popping sound as it punc-
tured and he turned to see how he had done. Blood gushed down
towards the bone-hard tip of the monitor's jaw. He watched it flow,
spellbound. The red drops fell to the grass.

He pulled the stick from the wound and ran the point gently
through the blood.

Tick-a-lee under there!

1

AS MIKE BRENNAN took his seat at the meeting room table he also took the temperature of the room. The streets outside were shimmering in the mid-summer sunshine but a frost had permeated this small corner of Covent Garden.

The presentation had finished just before he had entered. An impromptu lunch with Sarah had delayed him but that hadn't concerned him too much. After all, he was just going to be sitting in. It wasn't his meeting.

Sarah had brought Cara into the office and after all the usual oohing and aahing from his two assistants, he had taken his wife and their three-year-old for lunch at Joe Allen's. It wasn't often that Sarah could get away from the domestic routine, but Brennan appreciated it when she could. They were his world. Just them. And the agency, of course.

From the look of the faces around the table, he could see that the presentation had generated zero excitement. The three-strong creative team of Brennan Matterling sat opposite Craig MacQuarrie, founder and CEO of Kinross Air and his Commercial Director, Helen Withers. At the head of the table was Brennan's business partner, Doug Matterling.

Both sides were looking at each other blankly. Brennan had opted for the empty seat next to Withers to even things up and make it seem like they were all on the same side. He pushed business cards along the table to the two directors as he settled in. The print on the cards was a simple grey copperplate:

Michael J Brennan. Creative Director. Brennan Matterling plc

He had not met these clients before and he quickly assessed them. MacQuarrie was a large man in his late fifties, with sandy hair in a military-style crew cut. Probably lived and breathed his business. Withers was small and thin, large black-framed glasses padding out her face, black hair scraped back hard against her scalp. Her no-nonsense tough look, he supposed.

MacQuarrie's face was reddening by the second as he stared up at the closing slide still being projected onto the white wall. It showed the proposed new company logo—a purple flying thistle set against a stylised skyline of three mountain peaks. Underneath, in lurid orange, were the words, *'Freedom Redefined. Flying for All.'*

Brennan's heart sank. *What was this shit? Charlie wouldn't have let this get airborne, surely.*

He looked at the team responsible. In the centre was Alan Boman, the new account manager who'd only started at the beginning of the week and would have had only minimal input into this offering. It was Boman who'd suggested Brennan attend this meeting. He had taken over this campaign from Charlie Walsh, who'd left the company for reasons that Brennan was still trying to understand. Charlie wouldn't have involved Brennan at this stage, but Boman obviously had concerns about what he was taking over.

The meeting was what Charlie would have called a tissue meeting—back in the day, New York agencies sketched out their rough ideas on tracing paper so clients could see that nothing was set in stone yet. It was a way of gauging a client's reaction to an embryonic campaign. Brennan discouraged them because he felt they blocked true creativity and led ultimately to the client being sold short, but some clients insisted on being involved at such an early stage. Someone here must have succumbed.

The other two creatives were young, both with floppy dark hair and both dressed in tight dark suits. They were known as Gilbert and George around the agency and Brennan had forgotten their real names. But they came as a pair and were usually pretty reliable. Except for this time. And Doug Matterling was overseeing proceedings.

Brennan looked at his business partner. He was met with an icy stare. A warning to keep out of it.

MacQuarrie looked fit to burst. Brennan needed to bide his time.

When MacQuarrie did speak his voice was steady, controlled. A soft Scottish burr.

'That's a lot of information, Alan,' he said. 'A lot about the fleet, about legroom, about smiling flight attendants and strong-looking coffee. Even guff about managing to land on tarmac.' He paused. 'But nothing that relates to the brief that was discussed at the outset.' His tone was hardening and he nodded towards the head of the table. 'Nothing about family. That is what we wanted to get across. We're a family-run company with family values. Whether they are off on holiday, or whether Dad—' he glanced at Withers, 'or Mum—are travelling for business. It's all about family.'

He scanned the faces opposite him and looked up again at the message emblazoned across the wall. 'And what the fuck is *that* supposed to mean?' He stared at its creators with a mixture of wonder and pity. '"*Freedom Redefined*"? My team back in Aberdeen will think I've gone off my nut if I let that kind of crap be associated with our company.'

Family values? Brennan thought. MacQuarrie didn't seem to fit that particular mould. He certainly didn't use family language.

'Doug,' MacQuarrie said. 'I think we're owed some kind of expla-nation here. Not just for the complete disconnect, but also for the time we've wasted because of your company's arrogance in refusing to pitch to us like the others did. I never did understand that. Are we supposed to sit back in awe and wait for you guys to don your black cloaks and pull a rabbit out of a hat? If we'd known at the start the angle your young geniuses were going to come up with, we could have saved ourselves a lot of time. And money.'

Everyone followed MacQuarrie's gaze towards Doug Matterling. He leaned back and returned their gazes steadily. Brennan studied him hard. They were of a similar age but Matterling was usually taken for the older of the two. His hollow cheeks, thin lips and light hair contrasted with Brennan's rounder face and what his mother used to fondly call his 'black Irish looks'.

Matterling was slighter than Brennan and he wore a slim-fitting charcoal suit, white shirt and navy-blue tie. No wacky ad agency frip-pery for him. Just a straight-down-the-middle, meat-and-potatoes kind of exec, dedicated to his clients' success. That was the look, at least. But evidence to the contrary was starting to build in Brennan's mind.

They'd founded the agency together eight years ago. After working together for just a year at one of the big internationals. It had been an astonishing eight years of meteoric growth that had taken Mike Brennan from humble copywriter to doyen of the London advertising scene. He had even been asked to write a book about it and *The Art of Persuasion* had just been published to widespread acclaim.

It had been eight years of a seemingly solid partnership. Until now.

Brennan wanted to intervene, to take the heat out of the situation and shift the focus. But Matterling was looking straight at him. Still telling him to keep out of it. Still warning him. Brennan could tell something was coming but he had to let it happen. No point in trying to get his retaliation in first. He had to let Matterling talk.

'I understand your concerns,' Matterling said, 'and it's a policy that I profoundly disagree with.' He stared calmly at Brennan. 'I feel that clients should see from the outset whether an agency is going to be the right choice for them.'

Brennan stared back. Not only was Matterling implying that this trainwreck was somehow the client's fault, he was also blaming company policy for letting the train leave the station. And not just company policy—Brennan's policy. It had been his conviction that the agency should not give creative pitches to potential clients. Their showreel stood on its own merits and the client either trusted them to come up with the goods or they didn't. Brennan certainly wasn't going to spend time and effort giving away ideas for free. That was for less experienced agencies, not for Brennan Matterling, the award-winning tinder box of fizzing creativity.

'That's not what the policy is about,' Brennan cut in. He could see where this was leading. 'And you know it.'

Matterling ignored him. 'The no-pitch policy was certainly an attention grabber when Mike was learning his trade under the tute-lage of the greats. But the world has moved on since then and clients now place great value on, on . . .' He paused and looked around the table, biting gently on his lower lip.

Brennan could tell that he was playacting, pretending to search for the right word—the word that would simultaneously flatter his client and shift the blame for this fiasco.

'On perspicacity.' He pronounced the word slowly, savouring its effect. 'Modern clients value perspicacity over illusion.' He smiled at MacQuarrie knowingly and fluttered his fingers in the air as if touching the forcefield around a suspended crystal ball. He raised his eyebrows and turned back to Brennan.

So, this was it. Not only was Matterling accusing him of delib-erate obfuscation, he was also crudely implying that he was out of date and probably a bit touched. Time to jump in.

'The policy has nothing to do with lack of perspicacity,' Brennan said to the Kinross directors. 'It has everything to do with originality.

That is what we strive to provide.' He stopped there but the unspoken sequitur hung over them. *Just not in this case.*

MacQuarrie and Withers stared back at the closing slide as if to verify what they had just seen.

Brennan had to give them a moment. They were not finished yet. And what exactly was Matterling doing at this client meeting anyway? His role was rainmaker, a business introducer rather than a creative provider. That was the yin and yang of their partnership. Since when did Matterling get involved with the early stages of campaign planning? He looked after the business side of things; Brennan was the creative maestro. That was how they had set up the agency at the outset and that was what had worked so far. Matterling was head of schmoozing and Brennan was head of magic.

MacQuarrie looked momentarily bewildered and then leaned towards Matterling. 'Effective communication is what I value.' His voice was low, warning Matterling to listen carefully. 'We only have a limited budget, Doug. I don't care about all this perspi-crap. All I want is to get the message across, to tell the customer about what a great little airline we are and get him to give us a go. Once he flies with us, we have a customer for life.' He looked across at the creative threesome then back at Matterling.

'There was nothing in that . . .' he pointed helplessly at the last slide, '. . . in that steaming brown pile of mediocrity that would excite anyone to fly anywhere. I really feel we've been duped here. You used a mutual friend to get to me, a close friend who I trust implicitly but whose judgement I am now calling into question. I feel that you saw us coming. A bunch of bog-trotters from the frozen north who you could palm off with something these bozos probably put together in their coffee break, while they saved their best work for your 'important' clients.' He inscribed the quotes in the air with his fingertips.

He glared across the table. The bozos in question looked suitably downcast although Brennan thought they seemed marginally more hopeful now. After all, wasn't MacQuarrie acknowledging that they did have talent? He was just bemoaning the fact that none of it had been deployed in his direction.

'So, I cannot see any reason to stick around.' MacQuarrie stood and started gathering his papers together. Withers also rose and scooped up some of the visuals that had been handed out during the presentation, key images to build up a table-top mood board. Brennan stared emptily at the glossy ten by eights as she diligently slid them into her leather meeting folder. Too polite to throw them in the bin straight away, he guessed. But that's where they would end up.

One of the images caught his eye as she was pushing it into the folder. A stock photograph of a boy's face, a young fresh-faced kid with an open mouth and wide eyes. Eyes that could easily be filled with wonder.

The air was heavy with disappointment and everyone was now making moves to leave. Matterling was staring up at the ceiling, a bored look on his narrow face. Brennan couldn't believe that he wasn't even going to stand up to say goodbye to his client, no matter how badly the meeting had gone.

Brennan looked down at the boy's face in the photograph and thought about what MacQuarrie had said. A switch flicked in his brain. Outside the cone of his focus, time slowed down, giving him an opportunity to process the options. Clearly and steadily, he was homing in on his target.

'Mr MacQuarrie and Miss Withers,' he said. 'Can I just express how sorry I am. I take full responsibility.' The two directors turned to him then looked down at the business cards in front of them.

'As creative director of the agency I do feel your disappointment.' Neither spoke. 'May I?' Brennan reached across and picked up the image of the boy's face. He turned it towards them.

'Perhaps I could offer another angle that we could develop,' he said. Another pause. He had their attention. 'Imagine, for a moment, this boy playing at his grandfather's knee. Somewhere in the Highlands. Grandad's sitting on the porch of a small wooden bothy. The sun is shining and the rolling hills in the background are a rich green. God's own country surrounds them.'

He looked up towards the ceiling. 'The sky is a translucent Wedgewood blue and as the camera pans across, we see a single puffy cumulus cloud forming above a valley behind them.' He spoke dreamily, to no one in particular. MacQuarrie and Withers slowly sat back down.

'Cut to the boy,' Brennan went on. 'This boy. He is appealing to his grandfather: *Please, Grandad, please, please! Just do that trick you told me about. I can't wait. Please!* Grandad smiles affectionately at his grandson but is reluctant to grant him his wish too easily. Grandad is a gentle soul, bearded with a kindly weather-beaten face. At each cut, we come in closer to the faces of the boy and his grandfather. The boy pleading to see the trick again, the old man playing him along, coaxing the boy's eagerness.'

That eagerness was starting to seep into the room. Brennan had everyone's attention. He glanced at Matterling whose eyes were now black slits. His lips were pursed and his fingers were steepled, the tips of his forefingers tapping against his chin.

'Then, Grandad smiles an indulgent smile and turns sideways to the boy. He rounds his lips and starts to blow out a long silent breath. The breath is visible against the sky and it merges into the single cloud that hangs over the valley. The boy's eyes widen in wonderment and when we cut back to the billowing cloud, we see something appearing through the vapour. It is an aeroplane. A Kinross Air jet, which we follow as it swoops through the glens and skims low across the lochs. Stunning scenery is reflected in the deep blue waters of the sea and then again in a cabin window. The boy's face with its saucer eyes appears in the reflection and we see that he is a passenger in the plane. We see the view through his eyes. We see the spectacular scenery of your destinations.'

Brennan smiled at MacQuarrie and Withers, acknowledging their role in creating such a world. 'We experience the wonder of flying for the first time. We remember what it was like to be that boy, to have that magical experience.'

He let them savour that experience again for themselves.

'Big awestruck eyes drawing us in. Crystal-clear photography. Powerful scenery. Reflections and clouds. Smoke and mirrors. Visceral music that grabs our souls and takes us from one world to another. The sheer wonder of childhood. The sheer excitement of flying. The sheer beauty of a world we can reach with your help.' He looked straight at MacQuarrie, whose jaw was starting to unclench. 'Kinross Air can transport us. Your company can make it all possible. You make the excitement possible.'

He let the concept sink in. He was introducing crude flattery, but he had to gamble everything in this last-ditch attempt. They had been about to walk out so there was nothing to lose. He looked at his creative team. Boman was scribbling in a pad as though he were still involved in the process. Gilbert and George were downcast, still embarrassed at their own efforts. And not used to a client being so direct about their shortcomings.

Doug Matterling's expression hadn't changed. He was staring straight at Brennan. It was a cold, forensic look that made Brennan even more uncomfortable than he'd been when he first came into the meeting. That look told Brennan their professional relationship was nosediving.

They would have it out later. There were other questions Brennan had besides Matterling's involvement with the Kinross Air account. He wondered how many other client meetings Matterling had gate-crashed. How many other embryonic campaigns were heading for stillbirth? And, client matters aside, there was also the status of their investment in that venture capital outfit in California to explain, as well as the lack of progress with the Hong Kong acquisition. They needed a meeting. Urgently.

But for now, he had to attend to the matter in hand.

'No statistics,' he said to MacQuarrie and Withers. 'No facts and figures. No prices. No offers. Just atmosphere. Just a feeling. A powerful story simply told. No wheels on tarmac runways, but a soft touchdown on the beach airstrip at Barra.' An appreciative smile flicked across MacQuarrie's lips at the mention of the Barra airstrip. 'Any image that will help the strong emotional connection that we will build between your customer and Kinross Air. Shared values. Family values. The bond between the boy and his grandfather. The trust the boy has in the magic that Grandad can perform. And the shared experience of flying over some of the most stunning scenery in the world.'

MacQuarrie looked at Withers and Brennan sensed a tacit agreement pass between them. The tension had gone. The mistrust in the room seemed to be dissipating.

Timing now was essential. Brennan knew he had to strike before anything else was said. 'It would be a completely different approach,' he said and nodded briefly at the offending thistle projected onto the wall. 'We would concentrate on the simple thrill of flying. Nothing would get *redefined.*' He smiled at his new clients and kept his eyes firmly on theirs. 'We would only *rediscover.*'

Helen Withers turned to Craig MacQuarrie to let him respond. MacQuarrie leaned back and folded his arms across his chest. For the first time since Brennan had met him, he looked interested. Excitement would have to come later.

Brennan felt Matterling's stony glare boring into him as he waited for MacQuarrie to speak.

'I think, Mr Brennan,' MacQuarrie said slowly, 'that your rabbit may just have started to poke his ears out of that hat.'

2

London
June

CARA'S tiny fingers pushed hesitantly at the keys.

'C—C, G—G,' Brennan sang next to her on the piano stool. His right hand covered hers. He moved her right-hand pinkie along one key. 'A—A.' Then back one. 'G.' Another handful of notes completed the melody.

Her face lit up with pleasure. 'My turn, my turn!' She pushed his hand away and this time played the notes without assistance. She sang as she played.

'*Twinkle, twinkle, little star. How I wonder what you are.*' She looked up at him. 'Next bit, Daddy. Next bit.'

He pressed her fingers onto the notes for the next two bars.

'*Up above the world so high,*' they sang together. '*Like a diamond in the sky.*'

She looked at the sheet music intently and then back at the keys. Brennan lifted his hand away.

'And now back to the beginning.' He pointed at the sheet and she played the final four bars herself, Brennan clapping each beat to help her with the rhythm.

'*Twinkle, twinkle, little star. How I wonder what you are.*'

At the final beat, his clapping turned into applause.

'Well done, darling. *Bravissima.*' She joined in with the clapping for a few seconds and then hugged him, her arms wrapping tightly around his middle, her blonde curls pressed against his chest.

He bent over and gently kissed her hair.

'We'll do the left hand as well tomorrow. You'll soon be playing the Albert Hall.' He hugged her close. 'I think it's time for bed soon. Mummy's coming to get you ready.'

He looked up as Sarah came into the room from the kitchen, carrying a set of Garfield pyjamas.

'Come on, my little genius,' Sarah said. 'I heard you play. Now let's get you changed.'

Cara slipped off the piano stool and ran across the room to her mother. They sat on the sofa and Sarah started to pull off Cara's clothes. Brennan shifted around on the piano stool to watch them. Sarah was tall, with a flat athletic frame, like a long-jumper. Her blonde-brown hair was tied back today. Narrow face, delicate aquiline nose, bright blue eyes and a wide mouth that turned up at the sides. Definitely the ex-model type. Which she was.

They had met at one of the agency's shoots, at a studio some-where near Old Street. Sarah had been sitting patiently in a bath, half-naked, cupping a bar of soap in front of her breasts and waiting for the photographer's assistant to adjust the lighting. That bar of soap had to look just right. Brennan had playfully offered to boil a kettle to keep her water warm. She said that she would prefer a coffee. They'd hit it off straight away.

Sarah scooped Cara into her arms in one easy movement.

'Now, kiss Daddy goodnight and we'll twinkle our way to bed.'

She tipped Cara over so that Brennan could kiss her and as she did so he reached for the top of the piano and pulled a small black jewellery box from behind the music stand. 'This was my mother's. She would have loved to see you play.'

He opened up the box and took out a gold chain bracelet with a single charm attached to it—a golden grand piano. He looped it carefully around Cara's left wrist and she beamed with pleasure. She touched the miniature piano with her free hand and then slipped the chain off her wrist and held the whole bracelet in her palm.

Brennan folded his hand over hers and looked into her bright eyes. 'Keep it safe, darling. It will keep you safe, too. It's your *No Harm Charm.*'

Cara turned her head into her mother's neck and wrapped her arms around her, still clutching her new bracelet.

'That's a surprise,' Sarah said. 'Where did that come from?'

'I've had it forever.' He smiled. 'Never suited me, of course.'

After the final goodnight kisses, Brennan watched them climb the stairs. As they turned onto the landing the familiar questions clawed at him again. How could he be the best father to her that he could be? How could he make sure that she had the best life possible?

He swivelled slowly back to the piano, shook his arms, adjusted his seat and put his hands on the keys. His right hand dawdled over a slow introduction, building the tension within a dominant seventh chord while he let his hands decide which way to go. He cocked his head, listening for any crying from upstairs. No bedtime tantrums, apparently.

His hands started banging out a Meade Lux Lewis classic boogie-woogie as loudly as he dared. After the third chorus, he finished the twelve-bar with a neat ending that he'd recently put together and added a couple of glissandos, running his right-hand fingernails up the keyboard and his thumbnail all the way back down.

After this quick shot of blues adrenaline, Brennan headed into the kitchen and pulled a bottle of Oyster Bay Sauvignon Blanc out of the fridge. He pulled out two glasses from a cupboard and poured generous measures into both, gulping down one glass and refilling it. The Kinross meeting continued to bug him—Matterling had disappeared as soon as it had finished. Brennan needed to talk about it with Sarah.

He took the glasses and the bottle into the conservatory. The room was hot; it had been a blistering summer day and he could hear birdsong in the garden. When they'd first moved in all those years ago, he'd spent a lot of time clearing that little garden and then used all the design tricks he knew to make it seem larger than it was. Now it had become overgrown again and he knew that it needed more of his time. He swallowed another glassful of wine and put it out of his mind. He had other things to worry about. He refilled his glass.

Sarah reappeared and looked sharply at the half-empty wine bottle.

'She's loving it, isn't she?' Sarah said. 'The piano.'

'Seems so. At least I can help her with that.' He handed her a glass. 'How was your afternoon?'

'Great thanks. After lunching with a charming man who said he worked in advertising I left my daughter with a friend while I went to taekwondo. Good session.' She touched his wrist and kissed him on the cheek. 'How about you?'

'Not so good.' He finished his wine and went for another refill.

'Thought so,' she said quietly.

They stood silently, looking out over the garden.

'I got the tickets,' she said eventually.

'The tickets? What for?'

'The sprint finals. At the Velodrome. On the 6th — like you asked.'

'Oh right, right. Thanks.'

She looked at him expectantly. He stared into his glass.

'No run tonight, then?'

'Not tonight, no.'

Another pause.

'As well as getting to see some of the Olympics this summer I've been thinking about holidays.' She smiled brightly. 'We haven't been away together for ages. There are so many places where we've had a fantastic time. And we can take Cara anywhere now.'

'Sounds like a great idea.' It came out flatter than he'd intended.

Sarah's smile disappeared.

'What's wrong, Mike? Is it work?'

'Mm.' He waited for another prod. It was just the way they worked. He had to make sure she was ready to get into it.

'Staff problems?'

'Bigger than that. It's Doug.' He looked into her eyes. 'I've got some concerns.'

'Doug? What's wrong with him? Is he ill?'

'Not that. I'm not sure what's behind it. But he's kind of *turned.*'

'Turned?' She gave a short, awkward laugh. 'Into what?'

'I know it sounds crazy, but he seems to have turned against the business. He's getting involved with clients in a destructive way. I saw it for myself this afternoon. And he's turned against me.'

'Against you?' Sarah sounded incredulous. 'That's impossible. Without you, there would be no business.'

He smiled at her. 'That's not the way he sees it. He thinks my policy on pitching is holding it back.'

'But you've both got the same objectives, haven't you? You're both working towards the same goals.'

'That's what I always thought. Money, power, love and glory. That pretty much covers it.'

Sarah looked away. 'I thought business was booming.'

'Not in the last few months. We've just had our first quarterly loss. I was given the accounts this morning.'

'A loss? How?'

'That's what I'm trying to find out. I've asked for more analysis but cash flow has suddenly become a problem.' He put his glass down on the coffee table and slipped his arm around Sarah's waist. He could feel how tense she was. They never talked about the financial side of the business, only campaigns, personnel and awards. Never the nitty-gritty.

'I'm sure it's just a temporary blip,' he said. 'There'll be an explanation.' He smiled weakly. 'Sorry, I didn't mean to worry you. It's my problem and I'll deal with it.'

Sarah pulled away. 'If Doug is posing a threat, then that needs to be dealt with. Straight away. You can't let it get worse. There's too much at stake.' She glanced around at their home. '*Everything's* at stake.'

'I know, I know. But it'll sort itself out. After I've seen the details, I'll cut costs where necessary and we'll get through it.'

'What exactly is he doing? When he was round here last year, you two were toasting each other to the moon. There was no stopping you. The work was flooding in and the champagne was flowing. Even the wives got a look-in.' She laughed weakly. 'At least that's still happening.'

'Yeah, we'd had a strong run, then. We'd hit a critical mass.' He frowned at her. 'What do you mean by 'look-in'? You've always been a key part of it.'

Sarah chewed at her bottom lip. 'Hasn't Doug discussed it with you, yet?' She hesitated. 'He should have done by now.'

'Discussed what?'

'The wives' salary scheme. I know Doug's not married, but he said that he was paying his to his sister.'

'Sister? I didn't know he had a sister.' He picked up his glass but didn't take a drink. 'Anyway, what payment? What are you talking about?'

'The salaries being paid to the directors' wives. Or sister, in his case. Her five-year-old twins both have cerebral palsy. Asphyxia at birth. He said the accountants had recommended it as a way to save tax. That's when he asked for my bank account details.'

'Your bank account details?' Brennan tried to sound casual. What scheme was this? He had never raised this with the accountants.

'You'd gone out to pick up a takeaway. From that new Thai place on Willesden Lane. He had quite a long chat with me about the iniquities of our corporation tax system. I tuned out after about twenty seconds. Anyway, the monthly payments have been coming in like clockwork since then.' She hesitated, then said quickly, 'But I haven't been spending it. Doug said to treat it like holiday money, so I haven't touched it. That's why I mentioned a holiday. I've been waiting to talk to you about it for weeks, but you always seem too busy to think about having time off. Doug said to keep the money as a surprise until after your year-end. He said you'd deserve a decent break by then. He was going to talk to you when the time was right. I thought that he would have done that by now.'

'Our year-end? That's just gone.'

'Exactly. So let's plan something. It would do you good. Even if we just go back to that cottage in Skibbereen for a couple of weeks. County Cork is so beautiful in the summer. Give you a chance to get back to your roots.'

He laughed. 'My roots are Neasden. Born and bred. No matter what my parents wanted to believe. Anyway, I don't think now is the right time. Much as I'd like to get away.'

'We can go anywhere in the world with the twenty-eight grand we've got in the holiday pot.'

The glass jerked in his hand and he put it down carefully.

'Twenty-eight thousand?' Matterling was dishing out more than pocket money. This was serious stuff.

'And it's building up every month, so I can't see that your cash flow is that bad. Perhaps the accounts you were given are wrong. Doug seemed to want to do everything he could to save some tax for us. I doubt he'd willingly do anything to harm the business. He'd be losing out as well, wouldn't he?'

'Of course.' Matterling was in charge of the financial side. Staff remuneration was the largest expense in the accounts and he could easily have hidden these extra payments. But why would he?

'Something has changed,' he said. 'I'm sure of it. I thought money was his main motivation, but I think it's something else now.'

Sarah looked puzzled. 'Power, glory or love.'

'What?'

'According to your four categories,' she said. 'If it's not money, it must be one of the other three. So, if he is jeopardising the business, I can't see it bringing him much love. Or glory.' She gave him a hard look. 'If he even *is* putting the business at risk. Perhaps you're just being paranoid. Over-reacting to that blip.'

'Perhaps I am,' he said. 'Or not. Either way, it'll sort itself out. I'll get a better handle on the figures and we'll get back on an even keel.'

Sarah started picking up a couple of items of Cara's clothing that had been shed on the conservatory floor.

'Or there's power,' she said. 'As his potential motivation. Perhaps he feels threatened by you.' She dropped to her knees and folded a pink flowery skirt across her thigh.

Brennan shook his head. 'We've always been very careful to separate our roles. I've never intruded into his.' But perhaps he should have. Perhaps he should have kept closer tabs on what Matterling was doing. Especially now the business had expanded to its current size.

'Just you telling me this means it could be serious. It doesn't make sense, but you could be looking at the symptoms. Not the real problem.' Her fingers tightened around the material of Cara's skirt. '*We see what we want to see.* Isn't that what you've always told me?'

There was no reply to this. She was absolutely right, of course. He was the last person who needed to be told that. After all, hadn't he built his bloody career exploiting that simple truth?

She was worried, though. He had hoped that by sharing his concern they could make it go away and carry on as normal. But now he'd burdened them both with it. His duty was to shield Sarah from work problems—she had enough to worry about looking after Cara every day. In many ways, she was the strongest woman he had ever met, but she had an underlying vulnerability that he had to protect. He also had to make sure that she never felt she had to return to what she called 'the puppet theatre'—the world of modelling that she'd worked so hard to leave behind.

'Remember, Mike, sometimes things don't just right themselves. Natural justice won't solve everything.'

She retrieved a toy medical bag from beside the sofa and repacked its contents, which were scattered around it: stethoscope, syringe and thermometer were put away for another day.

'I trust in you, Mike. I know you'll do the right thing. And make the right choices.'

Brennan swilled the remaining wine around in his glass and stared into it. He would tackle Matterling in the morning. First thing.

3

London
June

BRENNAN HEARD the clanking of weights hitting their stops as soon as he opened the small gym's door. It was six in the morning. He hadn't expected anyone else to be here. There never was. Usually, he had all the machines to himself. He liked it that way. He felt a ripple of annoyance that he'd have to share the facility with someone else.

That annoyance turned to surprise when he saw who was sitting astride the pull-down machine. The white vest was already dark with sweat, as was the thick flannel headband. Brennan had planned to talk to Doug Matterling this morning, but the opportunity had arrived sooner than expected.

'Morning, Mike,' Matterling said with a welcoming smile. 'Hope I'm not encroaching on your personal gym time. You're an inspiration to the rest of us with your early morning work-outs.'

An inspiration? What was Matterling doing here at this time? He'd never shown any interest in the new gym before.

'Really?' Brennan said. 'That's good to hear.'

Matterling allowed the pull-down bar to slowly rise; behind him, the slabs of weights descended. 'Here. Do you want this one? I can switch.'

'No, Doug. Thanks for the offer but I'll warm up first.'

He went over to one of the exercise bikes and started pedalling. He looked at the floor as he built up speed. He imagined he was cycling along a country road. He could smell the early morning dew on the verges and hedgerows.

He closed his eyes and he was eleven years old again, heading out to another fight. On the village green at four o'clock. A fight arranged by the other kids at school. He was happy to oblige—he enjoyed the notoriety of being 'that new Irish kid' who would take on anybody.

Most of the fights only lasted a few minutes. They were scrappy affairs with few punches landing cleanly and usually ending up with the two boys rolling around on the grass until one of them got the other in a headlock. Then the pummelling to the head would begin and the one taking the battering would give in. Brennan was never the one who surrendered and the after-school fights became just another part of his daily routine.

When he reached grammar school, he channelled his aggressive instincts into boxing and he was about to make the school team when the sport was discontinued. He was guided towards gentler, more creative activities by his teachers and he didn't resist. But he had never lost that fighting instinct. An instinct that hadn't always served him well.

After ten minutes, he slowed. He saw Matterling go over to one of the running machines. Brennan dismounted and stepped onto the adjacent treadmill. He hit the start button and broke into a gentle jog. This would give them the opportunity to talk.

He needed to know what was going on with the Hong Kong acquisition and also the Californian investment. Then there were the wives' salary scheme and the Kinross meeting to discuss.

Brennan soon matched Matterling's pace and they glanced at

each other in the wall mirror ahead. Matterling was breathing easily. He was obviously fit.

'Good to see you here, Doug.' Brennan had to start the conversation, but Matterling being in the gym at this time was no coincidence. He knew Brennan's schedule. Perhaps he wanted to apologise, but that wasn't his style and Brennan dismissed the thought immediately. 'I was hoping to catch you sometime this morning,' Brennan continued. 'I've got a couple of questions.'

Matterling did an exaggerated eye-roll and shook his head. 'I know, Mike. I know. I owe you an explanation for yesterday. And a big apology. As well as a massive thank you for coming to the rescue. We'd have lost them if it hadn't been for you.'

Brennan didn't respond. This was a very different Matterling to the one that had stared at him so coldly in the meeting yesterday. Perhaps they weren't heading for a bust-up after all. Thank God for that. The tension drained from his legs and he kicked harder to keep up the pace.

'I'd specifically asked Boman to give me a thorough briefing beforehand,' Matterling said, 'but he never showed. I hope he's up to the job because he hasn't started well. We don't want another Charlie Walsh, do we?'

This confirmed Brennan's fear. There must have been some kind of barney between Charlie and Matterling. Charlie had refused to be drawn on why he was leaving; he'd simply cited family reasons for the move. But Brennan had sensed that there was something else going on.

Matterling's expression flicked from concerned to delighted, like a switch had been thrown. 'But your picture of the granddad and the boy was just brilliant. Good old *magic Grandpa*. Works every time.'

This was more like the old Matterling. A barb in every compliment.

'That boy didn't look like he was going to be abandoned any time soon,' Matterling continued. 'There's no wonder when that happens.'

Matterling's reflection bobbed up and down in the mirror. *Abandoned?* Where had that come from?

'The bog-trotters lapped it up,' Matterling said. 'I've asked Gilbert and George to work it up and they're going to ditch that crap they were going with. I did tell them Boman was still the account manager.' He smiled at Brennan in the mirror. 'Loyalty is everything, isn't it?'

Brennan smiled politely back. 'I like to think so, Doug.'

'After all, look at us now, eh? In our own company gym. The gym of a multi-award-winning agency.' He took his hands off the treadmill grips and held them, palm upwards, in front of him. 'This is our destiny, Mike. You and me. Masters of our own universe. All this was meant to be.'

Brennan did not reply. He looked hard at his business partner. On any other day he might have agreed. But not today.

Matterling grinned broadly and turned back to the treadmill dashboard. He tapped the screen and his pace quickened.

Why the line about destiny? Brennan increased his treadmill's speed. He hadn't associated Matterling with that kind of hyperbole before. Their business partnership had been based on pragmatism. Matterling got the clients through the door and Brennan created their stories for them, the stories that they couldn't necessarily see for themselves. Even though most of the time they were at the centre of them.

Brennan Matterling was a symbiosis that had worked well for both parties. And Brennan couldn't see why it should not continue to work. As long as they both stuck to their roles, appreciated what was at stake, and kept communicating.

'So you weren't upset yesterday?' Brennan said. 'You seemed a bit pissed off at the Kinross meeting.'

Matterling threw his head back and laughed. 'God, yeah. Of course I was pissed off. At Boman. But nothing was directed at you. You're the one who got his arse out of a sling. You rode to the rescue. It was payback time and I appreciated it.'

Payback time. Brennan gripped the pulse-measuring handles at the front of the treadmill. That again. Matterling was never going to let it go.

'So did the boy and his granddad resonate with you, Doug?' Even though he felt that he knew Matterling well enough on the business front, he had no idea about his family life. That had always been a closed book.

'Not at all. I never had a granddad. I only had Mama and Papa.' He stabbed at the screen to up the pace.

They ran in silence for a couple of minutes, back in step. Brennan knew that there was more to tell.

Eventually, he said, 'Did you experience the wonder of flying at a young age?'

'I did fly. But there was no wonder about it.' Matterling stared straight ahead at his reflection. 'There was no wonder in being abandoned. Flying meant being sent to incarceration. It's when the misery began.' His voice dropped away. 'And I couldn't look after her anymore.'

Matterling switched his attention back to the screen and checked his stats for the workout. That conversation was over.

Nor did there seem to be much more to say about the meeting yesterday. Matterling had dismissed it as a problem with Boman, nothing to do with him. He didn't seem too exercised by the client's perception of him. He was above those kinds of detail—even if the agency's reputation was at stake.

'How's Hong Kong going? Any progress yet?'

'Funny you should ask.' Matterling looked up from his stats and smiled at Brennan. 'I'm flying over later today. Got a meeting with PwC, who want to run through a target list with me. Looks promising.'

'Any names I'd know?'

'Not sure yet. They didn't want to disclose much over the phone. Insisted on a face-to-face.' Matterling grinned. 'It's our future, the East. You should come over with me.'

'Next time, perhaps. When we've got something to get our teeth into.'

Matterling prodded the screen again and his pace increased yet further. He was sprinting now. The change of speed indicated that the conversation about Hong Kong was also over. Brennan touched his own screen to keep up.

'Sarah told me about the wives' salary scheme.' He was breathing hard now. 'We should have discussed it, Doug, you know that. It's a board matter.'

Matterling looked hurt. 'Ah come on, Mike.' He was breathing hard as well. 'It was meant to be a nice surprise. A little bonus for all the hard work you've been putting in. I thought you'd be pleased.' Several deep breaths. 'And I'm sure you would have earned a few brownie points with Sarah. I bet she's been on your back for all the long hours you've been putting in lately.' He reached for the screen again. 'And it's not a lot of money, in the scheme of things.' He started slowing his pace. 'It's what you deserve.'

Matterling pulled a towel from the holder at the front of the machine and mopped the sweat from his face. 'You'll have a great time away with the family. That's what it's all about, isn't it? No point in doing all this if you can't enjoy the fruits of your labour.'

'What about you?' Brennan slowed his treadmill. 'Sarah said that your share was going to your sister. I didn't realise that you—'

Matterling cut him short with a wave of his hand. His eyes were closed as if in pain. 'Not now. I'll tell you all about her another time. It's a tragic story and I just do what I can. Which is way too little.' His treadmill had slowed to a gentle walk and he continued mopping himself with the towel. 'I'm only away for a few days. We'll catch up when I get back.'

He stepped off the treadmill and gave Brennan an approving look. 'You're going well, Mike. These workouts are doing you the world of good. We need them, don't we?' He touched the side of his head. 'To stop us going doolally tap.'

He flashed a big smile and turned towards the door to the

changing room. Brennan was slowing down as well. He needed to ask one more thing.

'What's happening with the Olson investment? I haven't heard anything since we made the transfer.'

Matterling stopped and turned.

'All good. I sent you their report. The money's fully invested now.'

'What report? I didn't receive anything.'

'Last week sometime. I'm sure I sent a copy as soon as it came through.'

Brennan shook his head. He'd received nothing regarding the investment they'd made six months ago with a venture capital fund in San Francisco. The fund specialised in tech start-ups and at that time BM had a lot of spare cash looking for a home. After all, didn't everyone want to invest in the next Apple or Oracle?

'Not to worry.' Matterling turned back towards the changing room. 'I'll send it again.'

He opened the door and flung his towel over his shoulder. Brennan's treadmill came to a halt.

'Adios,' Matterling said as the door closed behind him. 'Keep at it.'

Brennan took a long swig from his water bottle. Matterling hadn't provided any answers. None. And now he was off to Hong Kong.

Brennan looked at his reflection. He'd been running for ten minutes and got absolutely nowhere.

4

Hong Kong
   July

EVEN THE BOATMAN was finding it difficult to hang on. The
rolling and pitching made his footstool slide across the wooden
boards, smashing into one side of the broad-beamed junk then the
other.

Victor de Souza looked up at the sign telling occupants in
Cantonese and English that they were in a *Passenger-carrying
Sampan Licensed to Carry 12 Persons (Including Crew) Within
Aberdeen Typhoon Shelter*. But this was a private charter and there
were only three of them being carried today. He was the first, the
skipper was the second and the third was Doug Matterling. The only
one smiling was Matterling.

It had been a long day of investor meetings at Heilong Investment Corporation and this trip around the harbour was supposed to
round things off. *A little down-time,* Matterling had said. *To give us
both a chance to ensure that our objectives are aligned.*

Victor had come to learn that this meant only one thing. It meant that Doug Matterling's objectives were being aligned. Aligned with Doug Matterling's objectives. The problem was that these objectives had changed. Changed radically.

Victor felt sick. The violent rolling was churning his stomach. He could feel the steamed shrimp dumplings and the chicken congee slurping around together like the contents of a washing machine. He had to keep control of himself as well as the conversation. Matterling had pushed two threadbare seats opposite each other so that they could talk. The legs of the chairs were held in place by ropes attached to the supports of the benches running down each side of the junk.

'Feeling okay, Victor?' Matterling said. 'Thought you'd enjoy this outing on the water, with you being a long-time boat owner.'

Victor smiled weakly. 'I've only been out in it once.' He pushed his right hand against his mouth to keep it closed. There was a short stump where his ring finger had once been.

'I know,' Matterling said, grinning at Victor's discomfort. 'Shame that. Not everyone's born with sea legs.' The junk pitched and yawed past the gaudy lights of the multi-layered Jumbo Kingdom Floating Restaurant and Matterling nodded towards it. 'Thought we might pay a visit there, later on.'

Victor resisted following Matterling's gaze. He had to concentrate on anything other than food. He removed his hand from his mouth and took a deep breath through his nose. He refocused on their conversation.

'What's wrong with our current arrangement, Doug? Why do you suddenly want control over Heilong? You're making a fortune on the commissions from the investors.'

'I set up Heilong, Victor. It's my creation. A bigger idea than yours. You just got lucky with the way complementary technologies have developed.'

A bigger idea? What the hell was he talking about?

'But the share structure was your idea,' Victor said. 'You were the one who wanted to ensure that I wouldn't lose control of these voting rights. For the sake of my family.' He was battling hard to keep control of his stomach but he managed to lean forward defiantly. 'That's why you got the deal on the commissions. So what's changed? Why not just sit tight and let me carry on growing Elba? Your investors will get what they want. They seemed pretty happy today with progress . . . though obviously, they're not aware of the full picture on the commissions.'

The engine roared louder as the junk headed between the rows of high-rises that lined the harbour, twisting and turning around the moored fishing boats and other craft jostling for the same patches of ink-black water.

Matterling ignored Victor's questions. 'Your priorities are different now, aren't they? I'm not so sure your family ranks highly anymore. You're not exactly the model family man these days, are you?'

Victor's head was swimming, but he wasn't going to let Matterling use this to force a capitulation. He hadn't relished the idea of this jaunt, but he was determined to stand up to him. Matterling thought he could take anything he wanted. Not only was he taking obscene levels of commission from the Heilong investors, he now thought that he could take the controlling share from Victor.

'I know I've made a mess of certain things. But I know what I've done right, as well. And I know that selling my share to you would not be the right thing to do. Not for me or for Carmel and the family. If you get control of Heilong, you'll want my family's shareholding next. It's not going to happen.' He looked out at the harbour as it flashed by. 'Now, let's tell our man here to ease off the throttle, turn this tub around and get back to *terra firma*. Isn't there a speed limit around here?'

Matterling went over to the man on the tiller and gestured for him to slow down. The skipper grinned a gold-toothed grin and the junk slowed. Victor's stomach settled as the motion steadied. Matterling returned to his seat and pulled out an envelope from inside his jacket. He handed it to Victor.

'You need to reconsider.' Matterling leaned forward, put his elbows on his knees and steepled his hands together. 'Let me put it another way. Let me tell you that you *will* reconsider. Inside that envelope is my final offer. My final offer for the bearer share. I can assure you that I will find it. So, you can either be paid for it . . . or I will simply take it. It's your choice. It's a generous offer. And I'm just protecting my long-term interests.'

Matterling turned back to the skipper and pointed upwards. The engine roared even louder and the junk sprang forward. The footstool jumped out from under the skipper's foot and resumed its clattering across the boards.

The sudden acceleration shunted the two rickety chairs together and Matterling's head came within a couple of feet of Victor's. Matterling grabbed the lapels of Victor's jacket with both hands and pulled him close. He stared hard into Victor's eyes, looking past his squashed, boxer's nose.

'You know I believe in family, Victor. Without that strength we're nothing. I was the one who had to suffer when my father went down the same road as you. So, make sure I'm not the one who has to explain matters to your poor wife, the delightful Carmel.' He twisted the lapels in his fists. 'When your name is called.'

He twisted his fists back again and brushed the rumpled lapels flat.

'Your decision of course. But all decisions have consequences.'

'Don't lecture me about consequences.' Victor pulled himself away. 'You're getting greedy. And we both know where that will end.'

The oily stench of burning diesel drifted through the cabin and Victor's chest started to heave. He staggered to the side of the junk. The fresher air at the side of the open boat helped, but it was too late. He saw the row of tyres which lined the outside of the junk below and his body folded over the guardrail. A stream of vomit bounced off the tyres and sprayed into the water.

After disgorging the contents of his stomach, he sucked in a few lungfuls of clean air then straightened himself and turned back to

Matterling, who was leaning back in his seat, grinning and seemingly enjoying the show. Victor pulled himself a couple of feet along the rail and regained his poise.

'Sorry about that,' he said. 'The last thing I wanted to do was add to the pollution around here.'

5

London
  August

MIKE BRENNAN KNEW that there would be fireworks at the meeting. His stomach tightened at the prospect.

It was due to start in a few minutes. Neil Travers had proposed that they call this meeting of creditors of Brennan Matterling plc for four o'clock in the afternoon, on the Friday before the August Bank Holiday. After all, he'd argued, what would any creditor gain by showing up? There was no stock, hardly any assets, and the goodwill —which had once been valued in the millions—had evaporated within weeks. But Brennan knew that feelings were running high and such a crude ruse would only stiffen the resolve of those creditors determined to attend.

As he took his place at the table in the Somerset Room of the Great Westway Hotel in London, he felt bruised and nauseous. Part of him had been ripped away. Shock had given way to quiet fury. The vortex which had sucked him to the bottom over the last couple of months had been remorseless. Now there was nothing left for the creditors to fight over. Just enough cash from debtors to cover the liquidator's fees. Beyond that, nothing.

This meeting was going to be hell. He knew that despite the timing, many of the senior staff would show up. Some of the suppliers would also make the trip. And Lisa Richards, of course. It didn't matter what time the meeting was scheduled for. They'd all still want to vent their collective spleen.

Travers had offered them the route of a pre-pack administration, explaining that they could set up a new company, use it to purchase Brennan Matterling's assets and carry on trading. At least the creditors would get something for their old debts, and new business if they wanted it. It could all have been settled by now and the creditors would have accepted the new reality.

But Matterling had flatly refused to countenance such an arrangement. He'd argued that there was no reason for them to pay anything to the creditors. He'd proposed that a new company should be formed after the creditors meeting, which would then buy the BM name for a song and take over the office lease and most of the employee contracts. This phoenix company would rise from the ashes and be back in business with the necessary working capital provided by a consortium of Hong Kong investors that Matterling had put together. Existing creditors would get nothing.

Brennan favoured the pre-pack but Matterling had dug his heels in, saying that his Hong Kong investors were insisting on the phoenix company route so that all the new money would go into expanding the business rather than paying off old debts. Brennan had finally agreed after seeing photos of Matterling's two disabled nephews. The pictures were heartbreaking. It seemed Matterling had been supporting them for years and if the company survived, then not only would many of the employees still have jobs, but Brennan and Matterling would be able to continue providing for their families. The only losers would be the companies that had supplied goods and services to BM in good faith.

It was those creditors that he was about to face.

The green padded seats were filling up but Brennan couldn't bring himself to look up and see who was there. Sarah had wanted to come but he'd managed to dissuade her. It had been difficult enough for her to comprehend the company's precipitous financial collapse over the past couple of months—he didn't want her to witness this humiliation too.

He stared at the printed notes in front of him. They contained the statement of affairs, the list of creditors—showing how much each of them was owed—and the all-important company history. He reread them. For the umpteenth time. Eight years of his working life summarised and dissected and then summarised again. Probably his best years, he thought grimly.

He had written the first draft himself for Neil Travers, the insolvency practitioner advising them on these final rites and the man who would, if all went to plan, be nominated as liquidator at the end of the meeting. Neil had edited the draft for popular consumption, taking out the emotion. It would not help proceedings for Brennan's seething anger to be laid out so crudely in front of an already hostile audience.

Brennan looked up as Travers took his place at the middle of the table. He was accompanied by an assistant who busied himself with stacking half a dozen thick buff files on the table in front of him. Brennan did his best to return Travers' encouraging smile.

Doug Matterling entered the room and took his place at the other end of the table. He placed a slim leather briefcase on the floor next to his chair, grinned broadly at everyone present and leaned back, crossing his legs at the ankles. He wore a crisp grey flannel suit and conservative blue tie. His dark hair was gelled to his scalp, parted in the centre. Brennan stared hard at his business partner. The past couple of months had tested their relationship to the limit but they were still in it together. They were still on the same team.

The latest testing point had been the news that their investments via the Californian venture capital fund had come to nothing.

Despite Matterling's previous assurances that all was going to plan, the two start-ups that BM had invested in had both hit the buffers. This had been verified by a Statement of Nil Value issued by the American auditors. Matterling had been mortified and was now saying that the appropriate due diligence procedures had not been undertaken. A class action against Olson Associates had already started.

As four o'clock passed the quiet buzz around the room subsided. Travers stood up, looked around wearily and then started to speak.

'This is the first statutory meeting of Brennan Matterling plc, convened pursuant to Section 98 of the Insolvency Act, 1986,' he said before continuing with the opening formalities. He spoke with an affected air of boredom as if to say that no one really wanted to be here on the eve of the bank holiday weekend and they should just get it over with and all go home.

As Travers spoke, Brennan finally let himself take in the audience. About fifteen members of staff had turned up. Plus a similar number of creditors whom he recognised immediately and a few sober-suited individuals he assumed to be representatives of other creditors. And, sitting at the very front, was Lisa Richards.

Lisa caught his eye and gave him such a cold look that he could not free himself of it for several seconds. Hatred or disappointment? He couldn't determine which, but he shuddered inwardly.

Travers referred the attendees to the statement of affairs of the company. He had started explaining that this was a summary of its assets and liabilities when a large man stood up in the centre of the audience, his bloated face flushed crimson. Brennan recognised him immediately as Ron Eddings, a long-term supplier.

'Never mind these figures, sir,' he said. 'They're probably made up as well.' He paused and there was an uneasy quiet from the rest of the audience. 'But could you tell me—you being a professional man used to dealing with these matters—could you tell me how this company could place a print order with me for over thirty thousand pounds, to be delivered within two weeks, collect the money from its client and then tell me that there was nothing left to pay for the order?' He swung his gaze to Matterling and stared at him aggressively. 'My company had to organise weekend overtime and call in favours from our own suppliers to get this job out. And we won't see a penny from it—or the other forty grand owed from before that.'

Travers sailed in smoothly. 'I was just about to say that there will be an opportunity for questions after I have read out the directors' statement relating to the history of the company and the reasons for calling this meeting.' He paused and nodded at Eddings. 'At that time, I will ask all contributors to identify themselves to the rest of the meeting as bona fide creditors of the company, in accordance with the list you all should have in front of you.'

Brennan stared at the worn carpet under his feet, a gold fleur-de-lys pattern on a dark blue background, in which he sensed a timeless solidity. It offered him a sliver of reassurance.

All things must pass, he thought. *Including this ordeal.*

He liked and respected Ron Eddings. Ron's small family company had been supplying the agency with top quality print at what Brennan knew must have been wafer-thin margins for years. He was reliable, conscientious and heavily dependent on the volume of work that BM supplied. And now his own company might go to the wall as a result of all this.

Eddings was in no mood for Travers' sidestepping. 'Bastards!' he shouted. 'You're just a couple of bloody crooks.'

Brennan flinched. But he couldn't blame the man. Eddings was breathing hard, his chest heaving under his ill-fitting suit and Brennan met his burning gaze.

'Sorry Mike,' Eddings said. 'I know a bit of the background—I know who's really to blame.' He glowered at Matterling again. 'At least, I know who bought a seventy grand Merc the day after losing his biggest client. And I know who promised me, hand on heart, full payment would be made on delivery for that last job. But you're both responsible. You're both—'

Travers jumped in. 'Please, please. We must have some order if we're going to accomplish anything this afternoon. As I said, there will be time for this type of contribution later in the meeting. And I can assure you that if any creditor wishes to draw my attention to any aspect of the company's trading, I will be giving my contact details at the end of the meeting.'

Eddings snorted and sat down. 'Bastards,' he repeated and looked around defiantly for support. A concurring murmur went around the room.

Brennan struggled to contain a reply, but he had been coached by Travers before the meeting to say as little as possible—and preferably nothing.

He looked at Matterling with undisguised contempt, hoping the audience would pick up on it. He relaxed slightly, now that the focus of the meeting was squarely on Matterling, who looked ahead steadily, cheeks hollow, lips drawn tight. No visible response.

Travers read the prepared statement, which outlined the history of the advertising agency he and Doug Matterling had founded all those years ago. As Travers gave a dry history full of facts and figures, Brennan reflected on the real business.

They'd started it with the ten-thousand-pound loan facility each of them had on their Amex platinum cards. Their Covent Garden offices became the new temple to *advertising works*. They were in *Advertising Age* every week. Their campaigns were bright, contemporary, challenging and effective. Clients needed to connect consumers and products quickly and clinically. Brennan Matterling did this. They rapidly built up a reputation for highly-concentrated qualitative research and ruthless campaigns.

Clients knew they were at the limit. They knew that they weren't missing out. And *it worked*. That was the agency's slogan, though they would never have used such a trite term in a campaign: *It Works*. The words were everywhere, scrawled over the Floral Street entrance, across every email and every slide of every presentation; it was on every invoice, laminated onto every meeting room table and desk, on every screensaver, mug and mouse-mat. *It Works.* It was even the pattern of the office carpet.

It Works. And don't you ever forget it, Mr Client.

Travers started ploughing through a summary of the company's assets and liabilities.

A movement at the front of the table caught Brennan's eye. Lisa Richards was slowly getting to her feet. She was petite with smooth Oriental features and coal-black hair cut sharply into two symmetrical crescents around her high cheeks. She wore black jeans and a black sequinned jacket over a white T-shirt.

She stood still, not interrupting, waiting for Travers to stop. The rest of the audience seemed to sense that she was someone who had to be heard. They waited expectantly. Travers, reading intently from his notes, must have felt the sudden change in the mood of the meeting. He looked up and saw her standing. He stopped talking.

Lisa smiled at him, a brief but direct smile that told him it was her turn now. He acknowledged it by promptly sitting down. Matterling looked surprised.

'Thank you, Mr Travers,' Lisa said. 'We've all had an opportunity to digest the figures over the last few weeks and contemplate the sudden demise of Brennan Matterling.' Her sceptical tone drew a rumble of approval from the audience.

'It has not, of course, been all that sudden,' she continued. 'A great business like this does not just go down overnight. And all that verbiage about the change in market conditions and global factors is just plain insulting.' Her voice was gaining strength but it was still steady.

'Hear, hear!' came a shout from the back followed by other angry noises of support. Eddings roared his own affirmation.

'I know that this is an attempt at some kind of ending,' she said and gestured at the meeting in general. 'I know that a conclusion is needed in order to pick up the pieces.' She paused and looked at Travers hard. 'But there's one thing I—and everyone here—has to know.' She looked around at the captivated audience as her voice rose. 'And that is: *who* exactly is to blame?'

Travers recoiled at the ferocity of her tone.

'I invested over one hundred thousand pounds of my family's money into this company in its early stages,' she said more calmly. 'I gave my backing to a fast-growing business that needed working capital. The business was sound. Good clients, good reputation.' Her gaze swung from Travers to Brennan to Matterling and back again.

Brennan could only stare at her. His nausea was subsiding. Perhaps this was what he had been fearing—her approval . . . or the lack of it. Now that it was happening, he felt calmer. She certainly wasn't going to pull any punches and he was squarely in her sights.

'And somehow,' she said, 'these two directors managed to screw it all up. They managed to lose all their investors' money and lead their suppliers up the garden path. They kept their employees in the dark. And yet they still sit here like a couple of innocent bystanders who didn't have anything to do with it.'

The meeting erupted. Several creditors jumped to their feet and joined Eddings in hurling expletives at the top table. Lisa's speech was greeted with enthusiastic applause and she remained on her feet, awaiting an answer.

Brennan stared at the tabletop. He felt that these people might kill him if they could. What could he say that wouldn't fuel their anger further? The measured responses, the quiet contrition and the *mea culpa* attitude weren't going to work. So he decided to say nothing. Any sound would draw the mob onto him.

After what seemed like an eternity, Travers got to his feet.

He and Lisa looked at each other for several seconds. Everyone in the room fell silent, although many were still standing. Travers took his time over adjusting his notes. He took his glasses off and put them back on. Brennan knew he was buying time, allowing the temperature to cool.

But as Travers tried his tricks, Matterling also stood up. He had taken a bright red wallet folder from his briefcase and put it on the table. He walked out from behind it and took a couple of steps towards his audience. He stretched both arms towards them and waved at them to calm down.

Travers sat down again as the room quietened. There was nothing Matterling could say that would do much good. Brennan felt more apprehensive than ever.

'I can fully understand your feelings,' Matterling said. His rich brown voice was deep and smooth. 'You have all lost something. Mike Brennan and I deeply regret that. But we cannot do anything now to get that money back. It was lost in a commercial venture, a venture which for many years was extremely successful and promised much, but which then hit difficult times.' He paused, as if to search for his next thought.

'As I am sure many of you will appreciate, when a business grows quickly it requires expert financial management. Well, Brennan Matterling—or BM as it came to be known—grew more quickly than most. I am sure you will all agree with me that it is no fault of Mike Brennan's that he is not a corporate accountant.' He smiled broadly at the B of BM.

'He is an advertising man, through and through,' Matterling said and Brennan's gut twisted in anticipation. 'And generally, he's considered to be a pretty good one.'

Brennan felt the blood drain from his face at this attempt to focus the meeting's anger on his own abilities—or lack of them. What the hell was Matterling doing? What about Travers' plan to ride out the storm and then put their efforts into the new company?

'He's won awards,' Matterling went on. 'And no one can ever take that away from him. He was always an inspiration to his staff and I'm sure that we all learned a lot from him.' Matterling reached into his briefcase and pulled out a hardback book with a bright yellow cover. 'He even wrote what is fast becoming the bible for the industry.' He held the book aloft and showed it to his audience. 'It's called *The Magic of Persuasion* and it's a masterclass in modern-day advertising.'

This was getting worse. Although the book was now receiving a good deal of acclaim, he couldn't see its relevance here. It would only serve to antagonise those who were struggling to understand how they'd lost money.

Matterling said, 'And we all hope that the future brings him better luck than he has had in the recent past.'

He paused, as if to gauge the mood. It was still hostile but Brennan sensed they were keen to hear him out. Matterling turned back to the table, put the book down and picked up the red file. He solemnly handed it to Travers, who looked surprised, but accepted it instinctively. Brennan saw the label: *Radix Research Ltd.*

Radix Research? Brennan had never heard of them.

'However, at least he will be financially secure.' The room fell silent as Matterling gave the audience his full attention. 'Or at least he thought he would be.'

The audience looked towards Travers and the red file he was holding.

'I have just handed Mr Travers a file containing documents related to the activities of a company called Radix Research. This company is owned by Michael Brennan through a network of nominee shareholdings. It is a company that has billed Brennan Matterling a considerable amount of money for market research. In the file are all the relevant invoices and details of payments made by Brennan Matterling to Radix. Some of the money received by Radix has already gone out in expenses. Expenses such as a salary to a Sarah Brennan. Who happens to be Mike Brennan's wife.'

Brennan struggled to his feet. He didn't know what he was going to say, but he knew he had to be standing to say it. His chest was tightening. What the hell was Matterling playing at?

'The problem,' Matterling was saying, 'is that none of these supposed research services was ever performed. The whole arrangement is completely fictitious. Radix Research has never done any research. It was a scam. A scam that has just come to light. But it has led directly to the demise of Brennan Matterling plc. I am sure that once Mr Travers has digested the contents of the file, the relevant authorities will be informed.'

There was a stunned silence in the room and then a wave of protesting voices started to build. Brennan swayed on his feet as he looked at Matterling with disbelief.

Stay calm, he told himself. *Whatever this is, you can deal with it. But stay calm.*

He reached for the mental switch that would compartmentalise Matterling's accusation and let Brennan assess the options. But his anger was too great, the sense of injustice too raw. The switch was jammed.

Matterling stepped towards Brennan and leaned over the table. Brennan registered the noise in front of him as a pink blur. Matterling's face loomed into focus, only inches from his own. He was smiling, the even white teeth bared in triumph, the dark brown eyes remorselessly driving home the victory.

A few things rapidly fell into place.

The secrecy around the wives' salary scheme suddenly made sense. *A nice surprise,* Matterling had told him. So this was the surprise. A bogus company with bogus activities. Matterling had set up Radix Research in Brennan's name and created the whole charade. Paying Sarah's salary from the company was the final telling detail.

And then there was Matterling's resistance to a pre-pack administration. He could see now the real reason for Matterling's veto. It was nothing to do with money. Matterling had needed a hostile audience. A baying pack of wolves, hungry for red meat.

Finally, showing *The Magic of Persuasion* had led the audience to the conclusion that Mike Brennan believed he could pull the wool over anyone's eyes. No longer the brilliant communicator, but a slippery charlatan. A real reptile.

Game, set and match to Doug Matterling.

'You see, Mike' he said slowly, as the protest reached a crescendo behind him, '*it works*. Every time. *It works*.' And then, as if an afterthought, 'You taught me that.'

'What the hell is this about?' Brennan said and squared his shoulders. 'Why are you doing this? Think about your sister and her boys.'

Matterling smiled a tight smile and said nothing. He didn't need to. Brennan suddenly realised. There was no sister. And no stricken nephews to provide for. Another lie, to keep him on board. Another elaborate confection.

He had to do something. He could either protest his innocence to the meeting or take the attack to Matterling.

A picture of Sarah scooping Cara into her arms zipped across his brain. He had to protect them against the torrent of injustice that was threatening to drown them all. But this was just one single aberration and Matterling's lies would soon be exposed for what they were and the reasons behind them would be understood. Natural, logical justice had to prevail.

Brennan didn't feel himself swinging the punch, but he saw his fist connect solidly with Matterling's mouth as if in slow motion, knocking his jaw sideways and sending him to the floor. The feeling of the punch was familiar. Instinct had taken over. The crunch of his knuckles against bone gave an immediate surge of satisfaction. He was that boy again. Then the pink blur rushed in, surrounding him, cushioning him. There was a sudden second of silence and then the braying noise of the pack resumed, deafening him as he was surrounded by dark suits and his arms were roughly grabbed and twisted behind his back.

6

London
   September

CARMEL DE SOUZA gently closed the half-door behind her and sunk into the seat of the ornate confessional box. She pulled the curtains across the opening and sat back against the panelling. Beyond the box, the muted sounds of tourists echoed around Westminster Cathedral as she acclimatised to her timeless surroundings. What legion of human sins had been confessed in this tiny space over the past hundred years? How bad could one more be?

The small partition to her left opened and she slid forwards onto the padded kneeler. She could hear the sound of the priest's patient breathing. She closed her eyes, crossed herself and took a deep breath of her own.

'Forgive me, Father, for I have sinned.' Her voice was quiet and she paused nervously. 'It is twenty-eight years since my last confession.'

She listened for a reaction but there was no change in the priest's breathing. She wondered whether it was his turn to speak or if she should just plough on. She chewed at her lip and decided to wait a few seconds.

'Go on, my child,' the priest eventually said. 'There is no need to be afraid in the presence of the Lord.'

It was not a voice she was expecting. It was the voice of a young man. He sounded younger than her. Was that right? How would he understand?

'I have sinned against God and I am contrite.'

'God has sent the Holy Spirit amongst us for the forgiveness of sins. Contrition is the first step to receiving absolution. Tell me your sins.'

'I am frail, Father, and I have been punished.'

'Do you feel that God has punished you?'

'My husband is an adulterer, Father. He commits the mortal sin of adultery as punishment for my own weakness.'

'A mortal sin is such that it leads to the sinner being separated from God's saving grace. So confess to me your sins.'

'My sin is a mortal sin of the same grave matter. I have committed it with full knowledge and deliberate consent.' There was a long pause and she wondered if he was surprised that she knew exactly what defined mortal sin.

'I have committed adultery.'

Another pause.

'I see. Was that as an act of revenge? Do you feel wronged by your husband?'

It was an obvious conclusion and she could see why the young priest had asked the question. But it was far from the truth.

'The reason for my adultery has nothing to do with my husband.'

'Please help me understand why you told me about his sins.'

'Because I understand punishment. I understand why I have been punished throughout my life. I understand why God has chosen to punish me.'

The priest let out a long breath. 'God is forgiveness. God does not punish.'

God did not punish? How could he say such a thing, when her life had been such a sacrifice?

'It is natural to seek revenge by committing the same sin,' the priest said. 'An eye for an eye and a tooth for a tooth. But by coming here and making your confession before the Lord, you have chosen a different path. A just path.'

'Is it that easy, Father?' She forced herself to call him that, but it was part of her role and she was determined to play the scene out with sincerity.

'It is not easy for you to be here,' he said. 'You must have thought long and hard about it. Twenty-eight years is a long time without guidance. But remember that only God can seek revenge.'

'Is that not punishment, Father? Is it not God's will that sins have to be punished so that justice can be done?'

The priest cleared his throat and through the musty screen, she could hear his breathing quicken. She no longer felt nervous; she even felt sorry for this young priest, being put on the spot. But did he believe that he was the voice of God? Did he believe that the wafers he dispensed at communion were the flesh of the Lord? Her own indomitable faith could not always stretch this far when she asked herself those questions.

'Justice is God's will and His alone,' the priest said. 'Ecclesiastes tells us that God will bring into judgement both the righteous and the wicked, for there will be a time for every activity, a time to judge every deed.'

The flicker of doubt was extinguished as quickly as it had sparked. Her belief was total again.

'And the role of confession, Father? How will such a judgement view a wicked deed whose perpetrator has confessed his sin?' She paused and then added. 'Or *her* sin?'

'You have confessed your sin and professed your contrition. I can now pronounce absolution in the knowledge that you have recognised your errant behaviour, and by seeking God's forgiveness, you have understood His discipline and will seek a different path.'

'But I won't,' she whispered into her cupped hands. 'I will not give up my life for God's discipline anymore. I will continue. I have to.'

'Have strength, my child. Do not countenance weakness of intention. God is by your side now and will help you find the right path. He will give you the strength you need.'

'But I have committed a mortal sin.'

'And you fully recognise the gravity of such a sin. You also told me that you are contrite. You have confessed your sin to God. You are here with me and in God's care.'

Carmel closed her eyes and lowered her forehead onto her palms. She felt the strength of faith flooding into her body. She now knew that coming into the Cathedral had been the right thing to do. She had needed this charge from above, just when she was faltering. She knew exactly what she had to do and how to deal with the consequences. God, after all, was on her side. And the young priest had told her what she had needed to hear.

Only God could seek revenge.

She knew that the priest would soon pronounce the penance and she would diligently kneel in the pews outside this box of absolution and say her Hail Marys, or whatever he decided upon. She was looking forward to cleansing her soul and experiencing the joy of renewal.

She was looking forward to a lot of things now.

7

London
   December

THE SINGLE METAL handcuff clunked onto the Formica counter as the young policewoman handed a sheet of paper to the uniformed man on the other side. Brennan's left hand followed hers. It had to.

The court official looked down at the paper then up at Brennan before transcribing the information into the register. He wrote a number on the sheet of paper and handed it back to the policewoman. Brennan saw that his name, address and date of birth had been entered into the register alongside his case number. He'd entered a world of ledgers and big, bound books. No place for computers here.

The policewoman looked down at the paper and led Brennan down a corridor to a small cell. She released the handcuff and stepped out of the cell. The metal door banged shut behind her and a hatch slid open in it at head height.

'It'll be sometime this afternoon that you'll know,' she said through the hatch. 'Then you'll know where you're going.'

She gave him a small kind smile and the hatch snapped shut. There was a loud rasping as the key turned. Every sound—the doors clanging shut, the keys jangling against heavy chains, gruff barking voices from the receiving area—seemed to echo endlessly.

He sat down on a wooden bench bolted to the wall and faced the door. There was nothing left now. No phone, no iPad, no messages or calls. No contact with Sarah. Just the wait. He was staring into the void. The rage of the last few months had emptied him. He'd been carried along by the tide of British so-called justice. A tide that had inexorably sucked him from the high water of a just and ordered world into the dark, shallow pools of duplicity and unjust convictions.

It could have been ten minutes or two hours. He couldn't tell. But the key in the door did turn again eventually and a large female officer brought in a brown box and a Styrofoam beaker. She put them down on the bench next to him and backed out.

'Best in Southwark, this grub. Talk of the town. Enjoy.'

'Thanks,' Brennan said automatically as the door slammed shut. His voice sounded hollow, like a bad recording.

He unfolded the top of the box. It contained a sausage, a rasher of bacon and a small mound of baked beans. The sausage was cheap, its wrinkled skin retreating from its filling at each end. The bacon was burnt and the beans were cold. There were a plastic knife and fork in a sealed wrapper taped to the underside of the lid.

For some reason, he hadn't been expecting food. He hadn't even thought about food. When he'd let himself think about prison, he hadn't considered the cuisine. Not that he was in prison yet. This was only the bowels of the Crown Court, halfway between the real world and the unknown underworld he was about to enter.

Sarah's expression kept jumping into his mind—her expression when the judge had made his pronouncement. Brennan could only hold her gaze for the briefest of moments before he was turned around and marched down the narrow staircase towards the cells. Her look had summarised the last six months. A look of utter astonishment; a look that asked what could have happened to so brutally capsize their lives. But he was glad that he'd been marched away. He hadn't wanted her to see his complete and utter shame.

He gnawed at the crisp of black bacon and the door swung open again. A short, stout male entered, hands on hips.

'You're off, Brennan. You'll have to leave that.'

Brennan stood up reluctantly. He wished he had been quicker with the contents of the box. Suddenly that withered sausage seemed appetising.

'You're off to Belmarsh.'

The warder waited for a reaction. When Brennan simply stared at him, he smirked and turned on his heel.

'Follow me.'

Had he heard that right? Belmarsh? Wasn't that Britain's hardest prison? A maximum-security jail for the worst criminals? Murderers, gunmen, rapists, terrorists? How could he be going there?

Brennan's legs were moving but he couldn't feel the floor under his feet. There was some mistake, surely. The officer must have meant Wandsworth, as he'd been told by the lawyers. The same lawyers who'd advised him to lodge a guilty plea to get a more lenient sentence. Guilty to the charge of false accounting. A crime he hadn't even known existed, never mind committed. The elaborate documentation involved in the creation of Radix Research, plus the falsification of the financial transactions, had drawn admiration from his lawyers for the thoroughness of their execution. Which had persuaded them that protesting his innocence would be counterproductive. They'd told him he'd spend a few days in Wandsworth and then a quick transfer to a rural open prison. That was if the worst came to the worst, in the unlikely event of a custodial sentence being handed down. As unlikely as being run over by a bus, they'd said. More likely was a fine and a short, suspended sentence. Certainly not two years.

How wrong they'd been.

Suddenly the future was very frightening. The cold December air hit him as he was led to a fortified white van. It was dark outside. The large van contained six compartments, like upright coffins. His coffin had a small ledge as a seat and a tiny slit window with dark reinforced glass. He could stand up but couldn't move. Although he had never thought of himself as claustrophobic, this tiny vertical space was making him nauseous.

Rain flecked the dark window as they sped through London. This was his city but he couldn't work out where they were; he couldn't even work out which bridges over the Thames they were taking. The streets went by without any sense of where they were headed.

Eventually, the van slowed and turned off the main road. Brennan saw a giant set of gates as they swung around onto the apron in front of them. The gates opened and they were quickly swallowed into the belly of an enormous complex of high walls, watchtowers and bright lights. The van drew up behind two others. The rain was lashing down, beating fatalistically all around him.

The van door finally slid open and he was released from his mobile cell. He was led, with the van's other five prisoners, into a large dirty room. An enormous steel gate closed behind them.

'Brennan,' barked a voice from behind a counter at the end of the room.

Brennan went over to the counter and in response to the brusque questions gave his name, date of birth and address.

'Over here. Take off your clothes.'

He took off his jacket, shirt and tie. A prison officer handed him a grey T-shirt and burgundy sweatshirt.

'And trousers, underpants and socks.'

Brennan hesitated and looked towards the nearest of the officers.

'Come on. We haven't got all night.'

He obeyed and pulled on the prison underpants and tracksuit bottoms. He was surprised at how comfortable they felt and pushed away all thoughts about their possible previous owners.

He looked around at the roomful of men being processed along with him. The same drill. Clothes off, bagged and catalogued. Possessions handed in, bagged and catalogued.

A young Asian to the left of him was protesting.

'Surely I can take in a pad of paper?' he was saying. 'That's hardly going to help with my escape, is it?'

'I said no.'

'But I'm going to write down my reflections, my thoughts.'

'No'

'So's I can think about where I've gone wrong in life.'

'No'

'To better myself, officer.' He laughed. 'Surely that's not against the law now as well?'

'Not my law, son. Talk to the Justice Minister about that. His orders.' He spat out the name and a couple of his fellow officers smiled their concurrence. The Minister of State was obviously not a popular figure with the prison officer class.

The reception officer counted out the banknotes from Brennan's wallet. He noted down a figure in the register and then pushed the wad of notes through an oblong security slot in the counter. This caught the attention of the prisoner standing to Brennan's right.

'Christmas Fund,' the prisoner sneered. 'I've contributed as well.'

'Shut up, Farley,' the officer snapped. 'Keep your chat for the nurse.'

Brennan looked sideways at Farley. He was short and stocky with a completely shaved head. His scalp was covered in blue tattoos of lightning bolts. Farley glared back at Brennan.

'You got a problem, rich boy?'

'I said shut up,' the officer repeated. 'You're done here. Stand over there.' He nodded toward a corner of the room where the prisoners were starting to gather for the next stage of the process.

Farley leant over and looked at the register on the counter.

'Brennan, eh? A bloody Mick. And a toff.'

Brennan pulled back. He'd said nothing to this man and done

nothing to provoke him. Just caught his eye. But that was obviously enough to set him off. Hopefully, they'd be sent to different wings.

Farley pushed his head towards Brennan's and shot a look at the Paul Smith suit hanging off the hook behind the counter.

'Reckon you're a cut above, eh? Better than us?'

'Move on, Farley,' the officer said. 'Leave the *gentleman* alone.'

Brennan shuddered inwardly and dropped his gaze to the floor. Any eye contact was dangerous. With anyone.

'Nonce,' Farley snarled and pushed past Brennan, heading for the far end of the room.

Brennan looked up at the reception officer who had been dealing with Farley and was met with a blank stare. The officer took a long suck on his e-cigarette and went back to his register.

'Okay, Brennan. All done here. Follow your new mate to the end of the room.'

Brennan did as he was told and joined the huddle awaiting the next part of the induction process. He stood as far away from Farley as he could. He stared at the concrete floor and as more prisoners joined the group, he was careful not to look up and catch anyone else's eye. Anonymity was vital here, he thought. Keep your head down and go with the flow. That was the key to survival.

8

HMP Belmarsh
    December

'EVER HAD SUICIDAL FEELINGS?' the nurse asked. She was a doughy middle-aged woman with a speak-your-weight-machine voice.

'No,' Brennan replied. Although the last few months had been a nightmare, he had never contemplated leaving life behind.

She scribbled the response on her form. She had rattled through a list of illnesses and conditions and Brennan had answered no to them all. His health was good—and he was determined to keep it that way.

'I should probably go for the Hep B jab,' he said and pointed at a notice on the wall offering Hepatitis B injections. 'From what I've seen so far.'

If the showers and cells were anything like the induction area, this place was a breeding ground for the virus and any scratch or cut could give rise to infection.

After the injection, he was led into a small hall where a food trolley had been wheeled against one of the white walls. Two men wearing green trousers approached him.

'I'm Chris and this is Will,' the smaller of the two said. 'We're Listeners. We're prisoners too, but we're part of the Samaritans. We're around for anyone who needs to talk.'

Brennan felt momentarily lifted. He didn't expect to need their services but it was good to hear a male voice that was not innately hostile.

'Do you want some food?' the larger Will said.

It had been a long time since the brown cardboard box at Southwark Crown Court. 'I'm starving,' he said and tried a weak smile.

'There's only chicken curry left.'

Chris spooned out a heap of congealed white rice and topped it with a thin, light-brown sauce containing tiny square pellets of yellow material.

'You can sit over there to eat. This is the induction wing and you'll be allocated a cell shortly. Grab some bedding after you've eaten.' Chris pointed to a heap of plastic bags at the side of the hall.

The two Samaritans moved on to the next inductee. Brennan looked around to check that Farley wasn't close by and sat on one of the padded benches that lined the room. He began to eat. The curry was tasteless. He wondered how the chicken pellets could have changed colour when no seasonings seemed to have been used. He sat in silence and tried to digest both the insipid meal and his new situation.

He needed to make a phone call. He needed to speak to Sarah. Her expression in court was haunting him. A mixture of shock and fear. He had to tell her that he was okay. That they were okay. That it was all going to be okay.

Prison guards marched past him, but no one seemed interested. At this moment, he could have been sitting on a park bench watching the world go by. The atmosphere in the hall was calming down. Not so much shouting as in the reception area.

Brennan saw an officer sitting behind a desk at the end of the hall, writing in another large ledger. He thought she looked approachable and walked over to her. She had neat, short-cropped blonde hair and a relaxed look about her, which none of the other officers had.

'I was wondering what the arrangements are for making a phone call,' he said.

She looked up, surprised. 'Haven't you been allocated yet? What's your name?'

Brennan told her and she looked at a print-out next to her ledger. 'Someone'll be fetching you in a moment. We'll approve your phone numbers tomorrow and you'll get your phone credit then.' She ran her finger down the list. When it stopped, she smiled a small smile. 'Seems you're off to Beirut.'

'Beirut? Is that good?'

'Not really. House Block Three. You don't look the type, but the Governor must have his reasons.'

He wondered what exactly 'the type' was and felt his stomach rolling again.

'Wait over there. You'll be collected soon enough.'

Brennan went back to his seat and waited.

A good half-hour later two prison officers came up to him and checked his name and paperwork. They escorted him through a labyrinth of green and white tiled corridors with iron-barred gates every fifty yards, all of which had to be unlocked and relocked when he passed through. The further they walked, the emptier he felt. There was little sign of life in the dimly-lit corridors and he guessed that most prisoners were asleep by now.

When they reached House Block Three, they climbed three flights of iron steps from a wire-meshed enclosure. At the third floor they turned right along a metal landing with a high guard rail. After about thirty paces the officers stopped and opened a cell door.

'You're in there, Brennan,' one of the officers said. 'Remember your cell number. Fifty-three. Fifty-three on the threes.'

Brennan entered the cell cautiously. A single metal bed on the left and a table, chair and washbasin on the right. In the far right corner was a toilet without a seat. The walls and ceiling were covered in graffiti. He was hit by the pungent smell. A mixture of stale tobacco, drains and human sweat.

'No feeding the pigeons,' one of the officers said solemnly. 'Otherwise you'll lose remission. Sleep tight.'

The heavy metal door swung shut. He pondered the bizarre warning for a moment and slung the bag of bedding onto the thin, stained mattress. He sat down next to it and cupped his chin in his hands. Despite the smell and the graffiti and the dusty threadbare mattress, he felt relief. Relief that he was in a cell on his own and would have a modicum of privacy. He had no idea how long he would have to spend here. But surely he would be moved on from Belmarsh soon.

He thought back to this morning when he had walked into Southwark Crown Court with Sarah and the lawyers. They'd expected to be in the pub by lunchtime, knowing it was all over and there was a fine to pay and perhaps a short suspended sentence. They hadn't expected this. He'd come up against a sentencing judge on a crusade and a surprisingly vehement tirade directed at '*the insidious poison of white-collar crime betraying the hard-working families of this country.*'

A switch had been thrown. Suddenly he was on the wrong side of the law. Society wanted its pound of flesh. He was in a real prison, surrounded by real criminals.

Not Doug Matterling, but Mike Brennan. It was Matterling who should be paying this price and Brennan vowed that he would make him pay. No matter how long it took.

He pulled the blankets from the plastic bag and spread them across the mattress. His body felt heavy. The light in the cell went out and dim moonlight cast a faint shadow of the bars on the window across the bed. He was ready for sleep. He crept under the top blanket, closed his eyes and thought of sitting with Cara on their piano stool, her tiny fingers guided by his. If only he had been able to make that call to Sarah. Just to say that he was surviving and he'd be back with them before they knew it.

The newly-laundered smell of the blanket camouflaged the clinging stench of the cell and Brennan was starting to feel comfortable. He was still alive. He would survive.

Then, like the slow rumble of a tube train approaching, a noise rose beyond his cell door. The background prison hubbub gave way to a primeval chanting. He tried to make out what was being shouted. Something about 'fifty-three'. The chant became louder and then, with a chilling realisation, he heard the words, 'fifty-three on the threes.'

His cell.

The chant turned into a call and response. A lone, aggressive voice shouted, 'What do we do with the nonce?'

'*We give him the jug!*'

'Nonce, nonce, nonce.'

'*Jug, jug, jug!*'

Brennan jumped up and went to the cell door, putting his ear to the cold metal.

'What's his name?'

'*Bren-nan. Bren-nan. Bren-nan!*'

'What's his fate?'

'*Jug, jug, jug!*'

His blood froze. The sheer ferocity of the refrain sent shuddering shockwaves through him. Farley must be behind this.

'You hearing this alright?' a low voice rasped from the cell to his left. There was a hollow laugh. 'You sicko.'

'Sicko? What the hell are you talking about?'

'Word is that you're a paedo,' the voice said. 'Shouldn't be on this block. They've got a place for you lot.'

A paedophile? Why would anyone believe that?

'That's crazy. I'm not in for that.'

'That's not what's going around. You better be careful tomorrow. The kitchen boys'll make you a special brew.' The voice dropped menacingly. 'It's their way of getting revenge. They'll get their justice. You're in for a jugging, sicko.'

'What's a jugging?'

The voice laughed. 'Sugar and boiling water. Mixed in a jug. Turns into treacle.'

'Treacle?'

'Hot treacle, mate. Like napalm, that stuff. Carefully applied by pros.'

'Applied? Where?'

Brennan staggered back to the bed. He didn't wait to hear the answer. He crawled under the blanket and tried to block out the raucous din coming from outside. It was getting louder, angrier. They were feeding off each other and working themselves up into a frenzy.

Brennan rammed his fingers in his ears to dampen the cacophony. He pictured himself caught in the showers by a gang of Farleys, their faces like gargoyles, eyes ablaze with fury, holding aloft jugs of boiling treacle.

But then, very deliberately, he visualised them turning away from him and circling another figure. Through the steam, Brennan could see he was wearing a suit. A dripping charcoal suit that was being pulled off him by the prancing gang. The man stared at him and Brennan looked calmly into the eyes of Doug Matterling.

Outside, all hell was raging.

9

HMP Belmarsh
   December

BRENNAN WOKE with a start and stared at the ceiling. He had hardly slept. The hostile chanting had echoed in his head long after it had died down outside. His body was still rigid. As it had been all night. Stiff with premonition.

The ceiling was covered in graffiti, just like the walls. Large square lettering in the centre proclaimed: *It's Only Time*, an aphorism that did nothing to alter Brennan's perspective. He was in Belmarsh Prison, the worst in England. Full of murderous psychopaths. Most of whom had recently been screaming their intent to pour boiling treacle over his genitalia.

He closed his eyes but the reality of what was about to happen would not disappear. He heard the banging of heavy metal doors. The jangling of key chains. Doug Matterling's face came into view, his eyes flashing with satisfaction. Brennan pushed the image away.

Matterling would have to wait. Right now the only thing that mattered was survival.

'Unlock. Everybody Out.'

A key turned in the lock and his door was flung open.

'That includes you, Brennan. Association time.'

One warder hung back while his two colleagues went on to the next cell. He looked at Brennan pityingly. 'You must have had a bad night. I'll give you the choice to stay here, if you want.'

A choice? This was the first time he'd been treated as a sentient being since he'd arrived in this hellhole. So far, he'd just been ordered around like the worthless scum he had become. He swung his legs onto the floor and processed his options.

'If you stay, I'll bang you up again. For your own protection.'

'How long will I be here, do you think? Here in Beirut.' He knew what the answer would be.

'No idea. You'll just have to wait.' It was said matter-of-factly, without emotion.

It was certainly tempting, to just stay in here and not venture out, to avoid Farley and the mob who were baying for blood last night.

'Just stay out of trouble if you do associate,' the warder said. 'Any nonsense and it'll affect your record at the next place. No nice trips into town if you get to a Cat D.'

A Category D? An open prison? That sounded too good to be true right now. He'd deliberately not researched prisons while he waited for sentencing because it seemed like tempting fate. But he was aware that the tabloids depicted open prisons as holiday camps, with their stories of pizza deliveries, luxury accommodation and cable TV.

The warder gave him a long look. 'No matter who causes it. Just keep out of trouble.'

It was pointless advice. Why would he seek out trouble? He didn't want to be on the receiving end of a jugging. The prospect was as nauseating as the stench of the mattress beneath him.

The warder started to close the door.

'Leave it open, officer. I'll be right out.'

Brennan stood up and straightened out his clothing. He was breathing hard. But he would not cower in his cell and let them win. He knew that there was no real choice involved. He still had to live with himself.

He joined the long line of prisoners on the landing and they slowly shuffled along towards the stairs. A man emerged from the cell next to his. The one who'd called him a sicko. He turned to Brennan as they reached the top of the stairs.

'Enjoy your breakfast, mate,' he said cheerfully and turned away before Brennan could reply. 'Don't mind all that palaver last night. It was only the lads letting off a bit of steam. The drugs help with that.'

Brennan nodded as though he had hardly noticed.

Breakfast was a small plastic bag of cornflakes, a packet of long-life milk, a teabag and a stale bread roll with jam. Brennan collected his rations and sat at a long table next to a small group of Chinese men. He devoured the food and stuffed the teabag into his pocket.

One of the men watched him squirrel it away. 'Been here long?' he asked. 'Don't think I've seen you before.'

'First day,' Brennan replied warily.

'But saving already, eh?' The man obviously approved. Brennan smiled; these guys seemed safe enough.

'Let me give you some advice,' the Chinese man continued. 'Trust no one but us. We're the only ones you can trust in here. The rest would sell their own mothers for a burn or some tackle. Trust us, we know.' He grinned a toothless grin. 'We're the ones who sell it to them.'

'Thanks for letting me know. But I don't need anything.'

'You will. Trust me. No one can get through this without some kind of help. They'll grind the life out of you. We can get you anything. And you'll stand a better chance getting through the MDT with the harder stuff. Best quality papers. Coke, meth, heroin. Even suboxone. It only stays in the bloodstream for two or three days. We can get it all.'

Brennan must have looked confused because another in the group chimed in.

'Mandatory Drugs Test. A piss test.'

'Oh, right. How often do they happen?'

'Every three weeks if you're not grassed up. So they'll catch you if you just smoke a joint. That stays in the system for a month.' He looked at Brennan intently. 'Hard to believe but I wouldn't risk it.'

'Okay. That's good to know. I'll know where to come.'

'Ten minutes,' shouted a warder from the bottom of the stairs. 'Exercise time.'

Brennan nodded to his new acquaintances and got up from the table. He followed a line of prisoners filing out to the yard. Outside, he looked up at the high brick walls punctuated by the regular pattern of the barred windows of the cells. The sky was a dark grey and the air was heavy with moisture. Some of the prisoners broke into a jog and started to circle the enclosed space. Brennan followed the main group that was walking and talking.

He thought about the Chinese gang. He hadn't used drugs since his early twenties and even that had been confined to smoking cannabis and the occasional low-dose acid trip. All quite tame compared to the enormous variety of chemical substances available nowadays. He hoped he'd have the strength to resist in the months ahead. With that hope, he crossed himself, something that he hadn't done since he'd been an altar boy so many years ago. Long before he had become an avowed atheist.

He walked briskly. Fast enough to avoid falling into conversation with anyone but not so fast as to attract any attention. Just keeping his head down and maintaining a low profile. That was his intention.

And then, from the corner of his eye, he saw Farley again.

He was hunched against the wall, in conversation with two other prisoners. All with shaved heads. A protective gang with a defiant message to any other prisoners: stay clear. Brennan moved towards the middle of the yard, maintaining his pace, head down, hands deep in his tracksuit pockets.

The door to the kitchen was behind him. If he turned around and headed straight for it, he would be going against the flow. That would cause some disruption and Farley would certainly see him. Best to complete the circuit before making his exit. A couple of guards stood in the middle of the yard and he started to cut inwards, to be closer to them.

He found himself in a tight knot of prisoners and he passed the spot where he'd seen Farley. Then past the guards and onto the last part of the lap. Soon he would be back through the door and up the stairs to the threes. Back to the safety of his cell. His stinking cell.

The backs of two shaved heads were suddenly in his face. The bodies belonging to the heads slowed him down to a shuffle and he was forced to the outside of the swirl of prisoners. He could sense Farley right behind him.

Brennan stopped and swivelled around. He was right. Farley jammed up against him. Their eyes locked. There was a momentary look of surprise in Farley's. The two of them stood there, facing each other as the other prisoners circulated by. Farley's two associates backtracked and took their places on each side of him. Brennan studied the jagged lines of the blue lightning bolt tattoo, from the bridge of Farley's nose up his forehead and back down again.

Farley jabbed his face forward. He was a couple of inches shorter than Brennan and made up for his lack of height with unprovoked aggression.

'Sleep well, Brennan? Didn't keep you up, did we?'

'So what's this all about?' he said. His voice was calm. Surprisingly calm. 'What do you want with me? And what the hell is all this about being a paedo?' Controlled anger was surfacing.

Farley snorted. 'You'll get what's coming to you, fucker. A nut boiling, at least. We'll see to that.'

He started to turn away. Brennan glanced at the two accomplices who looked back at him with contempt. They also started to turn away. Brennan knew that this was his moment. He couldn't leave it like this. He couldn't just let them bounce him around. There had to be redress.

'Why the "we"?' he asked quietly. 'I'm sure you can sort this yourself.'

Farley stopped and turned slowly. He stared at Brennan, nonplussed.

Brennan was feeling pretty nonplussed himself. It would have been easy just to let them drift away, happy with their posturing and their threats. So why was he doing this? Why hadn't fear taken hold as usual?

'You're not exactly the timid type, are you?' Brennan continued, maintaining a controlled tone, the anger gone now from his voice. 'After all, when something needs saying you say it. I can see that.'

'What the fuck are you on about, nonce? You'll be in for more than a jugging if you keep this up.' Farley's face was dark with fury. Brennan noticed that the two prison officers in the centre of the yard were now looking over. He decided to press on with his line of attack. It was worth the risk. If he was right about Farley's tattoo he could put him back in his box. But what if he was wrong?

'I'm talking about that.' Brennan pointed at Farley's forehead. 'Your lightning bolt.'

'What about it?' Farley's jaws were working hard, clenching and unclenching. The line had been crossed.

'Your lightning bolt. A big, bold strike.'

Farley's expression changed from fury to confusion.

'Well spotted, nonce. And nothing to do with you.'

'So who is it to do with?'

'Just me. Now why don't you just piss off back to your cell and wait for your punishment.'

'It's about ownership, isn't it?'

This was it—no going back now. He'd researched body markings once, when a client had objected to the use of a heavily-tattooed male model to promote a new clothing line. Two things led Brennan to conclude that Farley belonged in one particular category. The first was the choice of a lightning bolt.

'Ownership?' Farley's spittle hit Brennan's lips.

'It's about your body. It's you reclaiming your body. Telling the world that it's nobody else's apart from yours.'

Farley's head pulled back as sharply as if he had been punched. He shot questioning looks at his compatriots. They looked bemused.

The second pointer was branding Brennan as a paedophile. Most sex offenders were themselves former victims.

'What the hell . . .' Farley spluttered. Brennan could see he was on the right track. But how far to push it?

'So who needed telling? A family friend? Or someone closer?'

'You're talking shit, Brennan. I don't know what you're on about. You're out of it already.' He turned on his heel and rolled his eyes at the two other shaved heads. 'A fucking drugged-up paedo. A complete waste of fucking time.'

The three of them moved away and Brennan lost sight of them in the crowd. There would be no punishment, no jugging. A wave of relief coursed through him. Relief mixed with a strong dose of resolution. Across the yard, the two warders looked him up and down, as if to check there was no physical damage. They resumed their conversation.

A bell sounded and the officers turned their attention back to the prisoners.

'Lock-up, gentlemen. Association over.'

That was some association, Brennan mused as he headed back inside. He could do without Farley's association altogether. He'd seen him disappear up the stairs and he slowed his pace to increase the distance between them. Farley had looked ready to explode.

10

HMP Belmarsh
December

BRENNAN REACHED the second-floor landing and as he was starting up the final flight of stairs, an all-too-familiar blue flash caught his eye through the gap in the treads. The lightning bolt on the top of Farley's head. The head was nodding up and down. It reminded him of one of those stupid dogs on the back shelf of a car. Farley's body was also moving, pushing down onto a thin young man whom he had pinned into the corner under the return of the stairwell.

They were out of sight of the prison officers who were scanning the stairs and the landings from the ground floor. Brennan stopped to take stock. Farley had his fist raised and was making some kind of threat to the youngster. The kid looked barely eighteen.

Other prisoners shuffled past Brennan back to their cells. Nobody was taking any notice. Brennan stood still, gripping the handrail. A couple of inmates brushed past him. If he got involved with Farley again he might turn on him. Especially now that he was in fighting mode. Any involvement in a fight would affect Brennan's potential transfer out of here. He could be in this hellhole for a long time to come. And he seriously doubted if he'd be a match for Farley in a free-for-all brawl. It would be easier just to walk on by and let the warders deal with it.

The boy's head was mashed against the metal landing and Farley had his hands around his neck. He was hissing into the boy's ear, who had his eyes tightly shut—whatever Farley was saying to him, he didn't want to hear.

Brennan looked around for nearby warders. There were none.

The boy's face was screwed up with pain. He was some mother's son, Brennan grimly thought. For the briefest of moments, he imagined a teenage Cara in this situation. One injustice stacked upon another. Brennan had to do something.

He took a deep breath and turned back down the stairs and onto the landing behind Farley. Up above, the metal stairs creaked as the prisoners clattered their way up to the top landing.

'Let him go.' Brennan's voice was calm. 'Now.'

Farley spun around, his eyes wide with surprise. He jumped forward and thrust his chest into Brennan's. His head jabbed forward and would have crashed against Brennan's chin if Brennan hadn't instinctively twisted his neck to avoid the contact. In the same movement, Brennan reached behind Farley's head and pulled it close to his own to prevent another headbutt.

'That's enough, Farley. Just calm down.'

Brennan's voice sounded controlled, even to his own ears, but his heart felt like it was ready to burst through his ribcage.

Farley's upward momentum had unbalanced him but Brennan managed to walk them both a couple of feet further into the corner, keeping Farley's head held tightly against his. Farley's breath was on his neck and Brennan could feel him swinging his right arm back. He pushed out his left arm to prevent the blow and wrapped it around Farley's waist. They hung together for a few seconds, Farley wriggling to get free and Brennan using all his strength to neuter Farley's efforts. After a few seconds, Farley managed to move his mouth away from Brennan's neck.

'What the fuck are you playing at, nonce?' he spluttered. 'What the fuck has it got to do with you?'

'Leave the kid alone,' Brennan said. 'If you've got a problem it's with me, not him.' Brennan saw that the boy had picked himself up and was propped against the wall, looking shell-shocked. 'It was me you were threatening. Leave him alone.'

'That's right, nonce. My beef's with you.' Farley spat in Brennan's face. 'And we'll get even with you, all right. In our own time.'

Brennan sensed that Farley was no longer going to strike out and he gradually relaxed his grip. As they moved apart. Brennan could feel the slimy spittle sliding slowly down his right cheek. He did not wipe it away but leaned towards Farley. He stared at the jagged line of the lightning bolt and then into Farley's eyes.

'If I see you anywhere near this kid again, Farley, I'll tell your mates what your tattoo artistry is really all about.' He paused to ensure Farley understood what he was saying. 'Is that clear?'

They stared at each other for a few seconds longer as the boy slipped past them and made his way along the landing. Brennan looked away from Farley and his gaze followed the boy. A prison officer was finally coming towards them. His pace quickened once he was sure the altercation had finished.

'Okay, you two,' he barked. 'What's this about?'

'Nothing, sir,' Farley said innocently. 'Nothing going on here.'

The officer was a tall, gangly man with slicked-back hair and a trimmed beard without a moustache. He was out of breath even though he had only trotted a few yards.

'You, I know,' he said to Farley. To Brennan, he said, 'But how about you? Name?'

'Michael Brennan.'

'Right. You should both be back in your cells by now. Get going. Quick.'

Farley shuffled along the landing and Brennan went up the stairs. The prison officer watched him from the bottom of the staircase.

Back in his cell, he found a small envelope on the floor, his name and prison number visible through its plastic window. He flopped onto the bed and held it tightly, his mind still processing the spat with Farley. Thank God it had all been over so quickly. Farley had backed down much quicker than Brennan had expected and the kid had escaped relatively unscathed. It could have been a whole lot worse. But he had done the right thing to get involved.

He turned his attention to the letter. Probably not a welcome letter, but at least it was a communication. He opened it up. It was a Prison Transfer Slip telling him he was to be transferred in the morning, to HMP Ford, a Category D prison in West Sussex.

He slumped on the bed and looked up at the ceiling. The large lettering of *It's Only Time* offered comfort now; yesterday it had been a threat. At least they hadn't forgotten about him. Some clerk in a dingy office somewhere in this gothic hellhole had processed the right bit of paper.

Dealing with Farley had done him a power of good. One small injustice had been rectified. Now he had to find the strength to deal with the big one. To find out why Doug Matterling had done this to him. And to avenge the wrong.

There was only one more night to go. Tomorrow, an escape to the country beckoned.

11

London
December

AS MIKE BRENNAN lay on his bed in HMP Belmarsh, hopeful about his transfer to an open prison, a young man named Ben Parfitt was starting to feel hopeful about his own prospects.

Ben was in a London pub seventy miles north of Ford Prison but occupying a very different world. He was standing with a small group listening to a tall man he'd never met going on about a drink he'd never tasted. But he was concentrating on something far more important—his plan to get off with a girl called Naomi.

So far, the plan looked like it might work. After all, he was already standing next to her.

'There are two you must try,' the tall man—Jorge—said, with a look of genuine wonderment. 'These are not for your aunts at Christmas. They are the king and queen of madeira. They will transport you.'

Boring Jorge had never met his aunts, Ben thought. They'd give him a run for his money any day. Jorge smiled at the two ladies next to him. They were hanging on his every word. Completely in his thrall.

Ben stood opposite Jorge. He felt like an outsider in their group of four. Which was a fair assessment. He was.

They were all squeezed up against an ornate pillar in the Old Bank of England pub in Fleet Street. Jorge had his back to the pillar and the two women were on either side of him, holding onto the shelf that ran around the pillar. One hand for the shelf and one hand for the glass of wine. Ben hovered between them, stepping back protectively when the crowd allowed, moving forwards towards Jorge when bodies pressed against his back. It was early evening and the enormous bar was crammed with City workers letting off steam after the stresses of the day.

Ben had seen the two women here last week when he was with a group from the office. He had tried to start a conversation but it hadn't got very far. Only as far as the briefest of introductions. They had taken one look at his companions and decided against it. He couldn't blame them; the brokers he'd been with were a rowdy bunch when they were released from the trading floor. They would put anybody off.

Tonight though, when he'd seen Naomi and Lucinda enter the pub, he'd deliberately moved away from his workmates and tracked their progress as they wound their way through the dark suits of the weeknight revellers. They had looked as if they were meeting someone. And they were. Ben watched as they closed in on a tall, good-looking man who was waiting at the bar. He was mid-thirties, in a glossy dark blue suit and open-necked shirt. Longish black hair, also glossy. Wide sparkling smile and ostentatious cheek kissing as the women came up to him. Smooth as silk, Ben had thought glumly. What chance would he stand?

He still thought his chances were slim, but at least he'd attached himself to the three of them. Jorge, as he had introduced himself, certainly hadn't seemed to mind when Ben had stopped on his way to the bathroom to say hello to Naomi and Lucinda. On his way back he'd stopped again and this time joined their conversation about some big art exhibition they all seem to be involved with. Some shindig at the Met in New York.

Jorge was something important in the art world and Ben forced a smile as he droned on about the various international collectors he dealt with. Their names meant nothing to Ben, but Naomi and Lucinda seemed to know what he was talking about. They were already planning another rendezvous, a lunch sometime next week at a wine bar. And then Jorge had started on bloody madeira, a subject of absolutely no interest to Ben, especially as he was already on his third pint. The only thing he was interested in was Naomi.

He spotted his opportunity.

'What are we waiting for?' he said confidently. 'Why wait till next week? Let's go to that wine bar now. It's only five minutes by taxi.'

Naomi and Lucinda turned from Jorge to stare at Ben. They looked surprised that he was still there; he'd hardly contributed to the conversation. At least now he was registering with them.

'It's ages since I've been to Gordon's,' he said. They were still staring. 'I'm sure it hasn't changed, though.'

They continued to assess him.

'After all, it hasn't changed since about eighteen-ninety, has it?'

He looked at Naomi. She looked at Lucinda. Neither looked very keen. He wasn't surprised. After all, they had only just met and he was already trying to get them to go on to another destination. He had to get Jorge on board.

'The food is usually pretty good,' he said. 'And the wine list is fantastic.' He smiled at Jorge. 'But first, of course, we'd have to try some of Jorge's madeira. He knows the country's treasures and they have a great selection.'

Jorge beamed in agreement. 'Yes,' he said. 'Let's go now. Why wait?'

And with this seal of approval, they left the pub and twenty minutes later found themselves pushing through another crowded bar, this time the underground vault of Gordon's, which claimed to be the oldest wine bar in London. Ben led the way, trying to find a space big enough for them all to occupy. He felt lucky. Things were going well. He had achieved the first objective—to peel Naomi and her friend away.

Miraculously, a small group were getting up from a corner table just as Ben approached. He moved in and bagged the table, offering the best outward-facing seat to Naomi. She smiled at him and sat down. He pulled out the chair opposite her and offered it to Lucinda. She might have preferred to sit next to her friend, but that would have spoiled Ben's optimum seating plan.

He couldn't help feeling pretty chuffed with himself as they all settled into their seats. Not only had he got Naomi away from the noisy pub, but he was now sitting next to her in the candlelit vault of an intimate wine bar. All without having to talk her into it. Just by grabbing the opportunity when it came along.

To make things even better, Jorge was examining the casks of madeira above the small bar and Lucinda was examining them with him. They were deep in conversation already. Ben couldn't hear what they were saying because they were facing away from him, but that didn't matter. What *did* matter was the way Lucinda was leaning into Jorge to catch every pearl of wisdom falling from his lips. That augured well.

Ben picked up a wine list from the table and leant towards Naomi so they could look at it together.

'Are you interested in Jorge's madeira?'

Naomi gave an amused smile. Ben liked the way her lips became fuller when she smiled.

'Not really. But I'm always happy to try something new.'

That was good, he thought. She was saying that she might be prepared to get to know him better. Nothing too crude, just gentle encouragement. She seemed relaxed and he felt her lean towards him slightly as they looked at the list.

'So, you're giving up an evening with your fellow hooligans to be with the three of us. You're all from BWB aren't you?'

'That's right.' She must have remembered from last week. He felt a little kick of delight in his chest. 'But those guys are traders. I'm one of the geeks. I spend far too much time studying annual reports and trading statements. Reading economic forecasts. That kind of thing.'

'An analyst?'

He nodded. 'Tech stocks mainly.'

'And how's that going for you?'

He looked into her eyes. She seemed genuinely interested.

'Pretty good. Can't complain.' And he really couldn't. *Investors Weekly* was just about to run an interview with him, identifying him as one of the rising stars of the sector. His boss, Julie Grainger, had just offered him a twenty-five per cent pay rise. Plus a dinner in his honour next week at The Ivy. A rare honour at Bavaria Williams Burnett, one of the most prestigious stockbrokers in London. Things were, indeed, pretty good.

'And you, Naomi? I bet you're lighting up the world of Old Masters?'

He hadn't been researching only technology companies this past week. In their previous brief conversation, Lucinda had said that she worked for a firm of art dealers in Bond Street with an Italian-sounding name. He'd only caught the last couple of syllables. Naomi hadn't had the chance to add anything further, but from the quick look the two women had exchanged he'd concluded that they worked together. So he'd searched all the companies likely to have at least two employees of this quality and made the match. A firm that specialised in Old Masters.

She threw back her head and laughed.

Good, he thought. Bang on.

'I think "*lighting up*" is probably an exaggeration. It's a pretty staid world. It doesn't get lit up very easily.'

Perhaps not. But the light in her eyes was certainly promising.

'I enjoy it,' she said, her eyes still wide. 'And how clever of you to know that we work with real art. I don't remember getting that far when we spoke last week.'

Ben looked across at Lucinda and Jorge. They seemed absorbed in their conversation. He looked back at Naomi and smiled. She smiled back, seemingly flattered by his interest. His seating plan was working out perfectly. Life was looking good.

12

HMP Ford
   December

BRENNAN WATCHED drops of his sweat spatter onto the frame of
the exercise bike. He had his head down and he was pedalling hard.
Ten kilometres completed and the same distance to go. This was his
new daily target in the gym at HMP Ford. His second daily target in
two days.

The relief at being sent to a Cat D open prison had quickly
turned to nausea when, after a comfortable first night in the induction wing, he'd been billeted with a gaunt shadow of a man in his
early twenties with a bad case of bromhidrosis. Bizarrely, he called
himself Clint.

Brennan couldn't care less what he was called. All he wanted was
to breathe. As well as the stench of body odour, the room was
suffused with a gag-inducing pall of tobacco smoke. He had made a
complaint and they had promised Brennan a move as soon as possible, to conform with their policy of not putting a non-smoker with a

smoker. He'd been told that the move could come as early as this afternoon. But he had also been told that there were no single cells at Ford for his category, so he would have to share a room in one of the whitewashed wooden blocks that had originally been built as barracks for the RAF.

He noticed that they called the quarters rooms, not cells. But he was still worried about who he would have to share with next.

He looked up at the other prisoner in the gym, who was flailing about on a cross-trainer. A pock-marked ruddy round face atop a wobbling mound of pale flesh. A body that, in a previous life, was probably more used to converting industrial quantities of lager into urine than fat into muscle. This could be his next roommate. Brennan shuddered inwardly and turned back to the small screen on the bike that charted his progress. Nine to go. He needed to get into a new fitness regime as soon as possible and as he pedalled, he thought about the last few days.

The highlight of his stay so far had been the long telephone call with Sarah last night. She was chatty and newsy, as if he'd been calling home from a business trip to New York. She had already done a bit of research on Ford and pretended to be jealous of the amenities he'd be enjoying. Could he hear the seagulls from there? No, he couldn't. How was the room service? It wasn't everything that the tabloids cracked it up to be. Anyway, she would visit as soon as it was allowed.

Sarah had held the phone up to Cara's ear so that she could hear his voice. He had tried to sound cheerful, but whatever he'd said wouldn't have registered anyway. She would not be able to comprehend the situation for a long time to come. Hopefully long enough for him to redeem himself in her eyes.

But the call had lifted him. He'd spent at least half the time since descending those stairs at Southwark thinking about her and Cara. And worrying about *them*.

The sentencing had only been four days ago but it felt like a lifetime. He had lost his business and his liberty in short order and now there was every possibility that he could lose Sarah and Cara. The phone call had been breezy but he could imagine how worried Sarah must be about the future. And she had never explicitly told him that she would stick by him no matter what. There was a lot to talk about on that first visit.

Eight kilometres to go. He was at maximum cadence and flying along. He imagined tarmac blurring beneath him. The smell of fields and forests as he ate up the country miles. Perhaps the Sussex countryside he'd seen as they'd driven him here. On that drive, he had made a vow to himself: he had to be in the best shape of his life when he came out. Physically and mentally. There would be no room for fear. Then he would be ready for Doug Matterling.

Doug had disappeared soon after the creditors' meeting. The police had been able to contact him—to obtain statements for their prosecution—but after that, he'd sunk without trace. All the plans to buy the business from the administrator had gone up in smoke after the Radix Research bombshell.

Brennan had to concede that the planning had been elaborate and detailed. He had never doubted that Matterling was clever. That was why he'd gone into business with him in the first place. But he'd never imagined that brilliance being turned against him.

In the gym, the human blob was trying to get off the cross-trainer. He tried to jump off both footpads at the same time, in an elegant star jump, but neither foot cleared the footpads on the way down and he fell awkwardly against the two revolving crank arms. He looked around quickly to see if anyone had noticed. Brennan kept his head down to avoid even a nano-second of eye contact. The last thing he needed was another Farley.

Seven to go. He set himself an additional target, a far more difficult one than simply pedalling away for twenty kilometres. That target was to only have positive thoughts for the last third of his ride. No simmering ruminations about the business or Matterling. No doubts about Sarah. No calculation of the number of days he had left to serve. No thoughts of the fallout from his sentence. No mental pictures of a psychotic new roommate. Only thoughts of what he could achieve. Thoughts of his abilities. Innate abilities and new skills he was yet to learn.

It was hard but it worked. When he eased himself off the saddle, he felt better than when he'd started. Slightly stronger. Slightly happier. Small incremental steps forward. That was all he asked of himself now. Simply to ensure he was travelling forward and not backward. He did not want to add to the list of losses. He could not add his sanity to that list.

As he showered, he thought of Belmarsh, where he hadn't even dared enter the shower block. Was the Belmarsh system justice? Or retribution? Or was retribution a necessary part of justice? He felt for the unlucky bastards who ended up there for years. Victims of the entrenched belief that society must exact vengeance and punishment. At this moment, Brennan preferred Victor Hugo's argument that vengeance comes from the individual and punishment comes from God. Another happy result of belief maybe, but Hugo was right about the first bit—vengeance must come from the individual. There was no doubt about that now.

After drying off and pulling on his clothes he walked slowly back to his room on P2, savouring the fact that there was no one chained to him and dictating his pace. A prison officer was waiting for him at the door, a gentle-looking man who looked like he should be working at a bank rather than guarding hundreds of convicts.

'You've been relocated,' the officer said. 'Get your things and I'll introduce you to your new roomie. They call him the Taxidermist.'

'The Taxidermist?' Brennan said and his pulse quickened. He sounded like some serial killer from a horror movie. What kind of psycho earned a nickname like the Taxidermist?

'Well he was,' replied the officer, 'until HMRC's finest caught up with him.' He smiled a smug, you-can-never-get-away-with-it, smile. 'You'll see.'

13

HMP Ford
December

THE TAXIDERMIST, Brennan thought as he was led towards the outer accommodation blocks. What kind of nutter was he going to have to share with, now? Perhaps he should have stuck with Clint. Surely living with the stench was better than some crackpot who messed around with dead animals. Or dead humans.

He was led into one of the low buildings and shown into a large corner room at the end of the block. Inside, the walls were painted mint green, but the room was immaculate. Two single beds, two small wardrobes, a long wooden table and two chairs. A few small paintings on the wall depicted colourful seascapes.

A tall, urbane-looking man rose from his chair to greet him. Brennan guessed he was in his mid-fifties, with a neat moustache and slicked-back hair that curled onto his neck. He wore a sharply-ironed white shirt and slim-fitting black chinos, in contrast to Brennan's prison-issue baggy green trousers and grey T-shirt. The handshake was firm but not aggressive.

'Terence Atkins. A pleasure to meet you.'

This guy looked and sounded like he'd just walked off a film set. Nothing like the cons Brennan had met so far.

'Mike Brennan,' he said. 'The pleasure's mine.' He meant it. Nothing could be further from the mental image he'd built up of his next psycho roomie. It was like being introduced to David Niven.

'Please,' Atkins said. 'Take a seat. Let's get to know each other.' A broad, welcoming smile displaying expensive dental work.

The guard closed the door as he left and the two prisoners sat at the long wooden table under an oblong window, which looked out onto the prison's vegetable garden.

'Welcome to the garden suite,' Atkins said. 'I've been in many rooms around the estate, but this suits me best. I like the view from here. I even prefer it to A Block where I had a room to myself for several months. It's all a trade-off. Anyway, why don't you start? I'm fascinated to know how you got here.'

Brennan felt his body stiffen with foreboding. The welcoming smile, the easy charm. Was this the civilised ideal cellmate? Or the big bad wolf? With a penchant for dead things.

'Well, Terence, it's a bit of a—'

'Please, call me Terry.'

'Okay, sure, Terry.' Brennan wondered why he'd introduced himself as Terence. 'It's been a bit of a surreal journey, to be honest. A conviction for false accounting—which was itself totally false.' He checked for a reaction. Atkins kept up the welcome smile, as if he wanted to hear more. 'It was my business partner who—'

Atkins held up his hand. 'Mike, Mike,' he said. 'The prison system is full of innocent men. I can count on one hand the number of detainees I've met who admit honestly to their misdeeds. Let's skip the protestations of innocence. Why don't you just tell me about the business you were in and your family? And where you live. That kind of thing. Then I'm sure we'll get on just fine.'

The broad smile again. But he was setting out the ground rules. And Rule Number One was that he couldn't tell the truth. Funny business, this justice system.

'I understand,' he said. No point in banging on about his innocence. Everyone probably did that here. 'Let me tell you about my family. Wife, one. No previous. Daughter, one. Three years old.' Atkins seemed interested again. 'Never realised how much I'd miss them.'

'That's going to be the worst part for you. I know you've just started your time. Belmarsh and now here.'

'You know that?'

'I am party to the selection process.'

Selection process? Who the hell was this guy? And how dangerous was he?

'No brothers or sisters,' Brennan said. 'Which isn't very Irish, I know. But my mother died young.'

'I'm sorry to hear that.'

'Long time ago,' Brennan said slowly. He had said the same thing hundreds of times before—'not very Irish, I know'—to lighten the statement. But repetition could never soften the underlying reality of that blow. 'How about you?' he said and looked around the room. 'You seem to have things set up well here.'

'I need to. Eight years for conspiracy to cheat the public revenue. That's a long time for a simple accountant.'

'Accountant? So why do they call you the Taxidermist?'

'Because I specialise in tax. More specifically tax avoidance. And the screws say I don't give a stuff.' He paused. 'They're entitled beneficiaries of the public largesse. It's their little joke.'

Brennan smiled weakly and his mood lifted. An accountant would be pretty harmless, surely?

'Not very funny,' Atkins said. 'But the nickname seems to have stuck.'

'Eight years? Must have been quite a conspiracy.'

'Let's just say we over-extended. I promoted film-making partnerships. Partnerships that lost money and enabled the partners to claim much more tax relief than they had originally invested. We had some very high-profile investors. Too high-profile for Her Majesty's Revenue and Customs to ignore, unfortunately.'

'Tax relief? That doesn't sound like the crime of the century.'

'Three million pounds' worth of tax relief. It certainly excited their Enforcement and Compliance people. Especially when the losses were manufactured. I'll explain it all in detail to you some time if you're interested.'

'I am, actually.' He *was* interested. Very interested. This could be an opportunity to plug some gaps in his knowledge. 'So what kind of accountant were you?'

'The worst type in the Revenue's eyes. Too clever and too connected.'

'A lot of people involved, then?'

'Film producers, investment advisers, bankers and a couple of previously very successful film directors. It was complicated enough for no one to know the whole story.'

'Apart from you?'

'Yes, apart from me.' He sighed and looked out of the window. 'It wasn't long ago that the view from my office was the Med. Most days it just sparkled in front of me. I lived on the Avenue Saint-Martin, Monaco.' He said it matter-of-factly, not boastfully. As though it were just part of the job.

They both looked out at the steady drizzle falling onto the neat rows of vegetables. So Atkins had been a tax exile, living in Monaco with all the racing drivers and other stars who paid no tax. It was a world he needed to learn more about.

'What's your project. For your time here?'

'Project?'

'You'll need a project. For your sanity, as well as mine. I can't share with someone moping around with nothing to do.' He grinned. 'You're keen on accounting. With a preference for the false variety, of course.'

Brennan winced. He wasn't going to convince Atkins of his innocence anytime soon.

'I could introduce you to the Syndicate,' Atkins said. 'Plenty of accountants in that lot. Lawyers too. And property developers.'

'The Syndicate?'

'A group of us who get together to discuss future projects. There's more business planning going on in here than in all the Ivy League business schools combined. And there's certainly the capital available when we get out. False accounting will stand you in good stead with the lads.'

It sounded like Brennan was in. Atkins approved of his crime.

'You've got to stay focused in here. I've seen what happens to those who don't. After all, we're all here because of someone else. Someone else made a mistake or someone else didn't stick to the plan. Or someone else got too greedy . . . or got away with it and we didn't. If we let thoughts about that someone else eat us up, we're done for. So, we've got to focus on something else. Something that'll make our lives better when we're on the outside. Something that will keep us from festering.'

'I'll be going to the gym every day,' Brennan said. 'And I'll be studying hard. I'll keep out of your way.'

Studying what, he wasn't quite sure of at the moment. But he could tell that Atkins was not prepared to listen to him protesting his innocence at every opportunity.

'I've shared with someone who had nothing apart from his regret to dwell on,' Atkins said. 'It was hell for me. And for him, in the end.'

Brennan wasn't entirely sure what this meant, but Atkins went on, 'I know you'll be thinking about evening the score when you get out. You'll be hell-bent on making your own justice and that's fine. I just ask that you make it your own business.'

'That won't be a problem with me, Terry. I can assure you of that. I'll be signing up for an MBA.'

Atkins looked impressed. 'That makes sense. A Master of Business Administration. It'll help when you start your next agency.'

'My next agency?'

'Don't look surprised, Mike. I've done my research. I know how far you'd come since winning that copywriting competition. There's no internet access in here generally, but I've got my contacts. You'll have to wait for your rottle before you can get connected.'

'My what?'

'Your ROTL.' He spelt out the letters. 'Release On Temporary License. That's when they start letting you out into the world again. But only for six hours at first. Keep your nose clean otherwise they'll deny it to you. No drugs and no boozing. Their rules. And mine.' The two men looked closely at each other. 'Understand?'

'My rules too, Terry. No drugs, no booze and no regrets. And you? What's your project?'

'To keep this room on an even keel. I'm happy just doing my time. I know where I went wrong and how I'm going to lead my life on the out. It has nothing to do with my previous life, but I know what it's all about.'

That sounded confusing to Brennan, but he let it go. No doubt he would understand more in the months to come if he got to share this room. Atkins obviously had the final say on who became his new roommate. But they seemed to have made a pact that would be the basis for harmonious co-existence.

'Perhaps I could pick your brains from time to time,' Brennan said. 'When I have to learn about non-false accounting.'

Atkins laughed. Definitely onside now, Brennan thought.

'I'll be happy to do more than that. If you stick to your side of the bargain, I'll add some extra modules to your syllabus.'

Although Brennan knew he was the new partner in this potential union, he was relieved to be sharing a room with this intelligent and resourceful criminal. There was more to Atkins than met the eye, clearly, but he could live with that. And as for the Terence/Terry game, well that was just a crude display of permission-granting, to show who was the boss.

'This isn't the way I had my career planned,' Atkins said. 'But

I've had twenty-five years' global experience with some seriously wealthy individuals and corporations. You could come out of here more clued-up than most City professionals.'

'And the extra modules?'

'How about *advanced* tax avoidance? Or money laundering techniques pioneered by a number of noble banking institutions? Or the effective use of offshore bank accounts and nominee shareholdings? All the things they don't teach you at Harvard Business School.'

'An alternative MBA?'

'Sure. I like the title.' He smiled at Brennan, who was reminded of a predator yawning. 'I think we have an understanding, don't you? And when you get to meet the other guys in the Syndicate you'll even get to learn about VAT fraud and identity theft if you're interested. We have quite a few VAT specialists.'

'This could be quite an education,' Brennan said. 'Sounds like there's a lot of expertise here.'

'And now that we're all on the wrong side of the law, it's freely shared. It's a model society here. Quite a contrast to the ugly world outside. You can't hide anything here.'

'I think I've got a lot to learn.' There was a balance to Atkins that Brennan liked. It seemed that the Taxidermist had found his own serenity in this place.

'That's the best attitude to have. You've probably learnt a lot since your conviction. About yourself and the people closest to you. We've all been through it.'

Brennan couldn't help but think about Sarah again and his stomach tightened.

Atkins sat back in his chair and looked out at the drizzle again. 'We've all had to think about justice as well. And none of us believes that the treatment we've received amounts to anything like justice. None of us.' He turned back to Brennan. 'If you're anything like the rest of us, you probably used to believe that the world had its way of dealing with injustice and that wrongs were always righted.'

'True. I did.'

'And now?'

'Not at all.'

'I thought not. That's the first thing that falls by the wayside when you find yourself on the wrong side of the law. It's part of the process.'

What was this? Some kind of jurisprudential psychobabble? But what Atkins said was true. And it was good to hear it from someone else. Someone who'd had longer to think it through. But Brennan had already reached his own conclusion, on the day Doug Matterling had produced that red file and handed it to BM's liquidator. From now on, there was only one way for justice to be done. He had to do it himself.

Atkins gave an inquisitive smile. 'Now you've just got to work out how you're going to adjust to that change.'

'Sounds easy.'

'Not if you're anything like the rest of us. If you've ever been part of that thing we call humanity, it's one of the hardest things you'll do in your lifetime.'

Brennan appreciated the advice, but he had his own ideas. He had the determination to make them happen. After all, hadn't he just secured a double win? The ideal room-mate and some higher education to boot. He felt more optimistic than he had at any time in the last gruelling, desperate week.

The door opened and a prison officer stood in the doorway. It was the same officer who had escorted him to his new quarters. 'You're needed, Brennan. Now.' His voice was harsh. The affability had gone. 'Governor wants to see you. Straight away.' He entered the room and glanced disdainfully at Brennan's two black plastic bags next to the chair. 'You can leave your crap here. Come with me.'

He turned on his heel and walked out of the room.

Brennan rose reluctantly from his chair. 'See you later, Terry. Seems like I've been invited for afternoon tea with the top brass.'

Terry gave him a friendly smile and Brennan followed his guide out of the room.

'That's a lot further off for you now, Brennan,' the officer said over his shoulder. 'Your afternoon tea. No tea and treats on your rottle. Not for a very long time, I wouldn't have thought.'

Brennan came up alongside him as he strode along the narrow corridor towards the outside door. Whatever this about, it sounded serious.

'We've just received a report from Belmarsh concerning a fracas you were involved in the day before your transfer. Intimidating another prisoner. Very regrettable.'

'Intimidating another prisoner? That's nonsense. I was only—'

'No point whinging to me, Brennan. I'm just a stupid screw doing my job. But when you put a few stupid screws together, we become quite a force.'

Brennan's heart sank. Good and evil were getting jumbled up pretty quickly in this new world. And justice was no longer the absolute truth he'd never questioned before.

'The Governor takes a dim view of prisoners threatening other prisoners.' They stepped out into the open air. 'A very dim view.'

Brennan noticed that the drizzle had suddenly turned into heavy rain, but he hardly felt it lash against his cheeks as they hurried towards the Governor's office.

14

HMP Ford
December

THE '*STUPID SCREW*' stood close behind him and Brennan sensed from the man's expectant breathing that he was hoping for some good sport. They both stood in front of the large green metal desk and watched as the Governor read and re-read a single yellow sheet of A4 paper. Eventually, he looked up.

'This isn't good is it, Brennan?' The Governor was not particularly old, probably about the same age as him. Thin, no-nonsense kind of face. No pudgy excess. All fit for purpose. Dark hair receding over a mottled forehead. Designer glasses acquired to signal that an individual was at home.

But he was the one with the desk and the uniform. He was the one surrounded by rugged utilitarian metal furniture. He was the one the officer had bowed his head to when entering. He was the one with Brennan's fate in his hands.

'Clear case of threatening behaviour,' the Governor went on and

Brennan felt the wind being sucked out of him. 'I'm going to have to send you back to Belmarsh, pending reassignment.'

Back to Belmarsh? That couldn't happen, could it? Not after he'd found some vestige of salvation by getting here. He couldn't go back to that hellhole.

'But I was trying to protect someone.' Brennan heard his own voice in the distance. It was hollow and unconvincing.

'This asset is Category D status,' the Governor said calmly. 'Model prisoners only.'

Brennan looked at the name badge on his crisp white shirt. *Governor. J. D. Higginson.* He sounded like he'd just been on a course, Brennan thought. As individual as a can of beans. That run-in with Farley looked like it could cost him dearly after all.

'I was helping a fellow prisoner.' At least this came out with more conviction.

'So you were meting out your own justice, were you?'

'I didn't see it as being that subjective,' he said. Justice was justice, wasn't it? Not that he believed in it anymore.

Higginson looked back down at the incident report and read out a few phrases.

'*Hands around another prisoner's throat . . . aggressive posturing . . . lack of contrition when restrained.*'

Brennan's cold disbelief was starting to dissipate. A heat was rising from the pit of his stomach. Just a few months ago, he had been living in what he'd believed to be an ordered world. Now he could see it for what it was.

'The whole edifice is built on a lie,' Brennan said softly. 'Justice is a word that is used as a tool.'

Higginson looked surprised. 'You have just told me you were threatening another prisoner to protect someone else. So, if that's your idea of justice,' he looked at Brennan carefully, 'you can't say you don't believe in it. You can't have it both ways, Brennan. I think you'll find that it's you who's living the lie.'

This guy doesn't know what I'm talking about, Brennan thought.

But Belmarsh Part Two was out of the question—now that he'd got to Ford, he had to find a way of staying.

'This is the criminal justice system in action,' the Governor continued, 'and you're at the arse-end of it. Justice has already been done. The talking's over. Now you've just got to do your time.' His expression lightened. 'But fortunately for the rest of us, not here.'

Brennan felt a gentle exhalation of triumph from the officer behind him. These were probably the moments that made the job worthwhile.

Brennan's rising anger needed to be controlled. It was pointless railing against the system from such a weak position. He had to adjust and quickly. He looked at Higginson for several long moments and then dropped his head.

'I would like to stay,' he said, quietly and steadily.

'From my point of view that would be too risky. You can't just charge around hitting out senselessly, Brennan. I've seen it too many times before. You'll create hell for everyone around you.'

'I'll be that model prisoner,' he said and met Higginson's dull gaze head-on.

Hell for everyone around me? I've already ticked that box. Ask my family.

'I have never been charged with any sort of violent behaviour,' Brennan went on. 'Belmarsh was an aberration. There were exceptional exonerating circumstances and it will not happen again.'

Higginson glanced at the prison officer who shuffled slightly. Brennan felt the dynamic in the room shift. His calm articulation had sounded authoritative.

Higginson spoke slowly, as if concluding the conversation. 'You're seeking revenge. That's natural. But revenge doesn't lead to justice. Whatever your justice is.'

'I can assure you that you'll have no trouble with me. I've got my goals, and disrupting prison life is not amongst them. I don't touch drugs and I can live without alcohol.' He could continue the fatuous crap about justice some other time; the immediate problem was to avoid being sent back to Belmarsh. 'You can see that I'm a trusty in the making. If you send me back to Belmarsh, my replacement will likely be a whole lot harder to deal with.'

He could see Higginson chewing it over. It was a flimsy argument but he had nothing else to offer.

Or perhaps there was one more thing. He thought back to his conversation with Atkins.

'You won't even get any trouble with me on outside visits,' he said. 'I'll forgo any release on temporary licence. I just won't apply and that'll be one less headache for you further down the line. One less risk.'

Higginson's eyebrows flicked upwards. This was obviously a new one on him. He turned back to the yellow sheet of paper and carefully clipped it back into a buff transfer file. He closed the folder and looked up at Brennan.

'That means no trips to town. No reintegration with society. No internet access for your time here.'

'I appreciate that.'

Brennan had already taken that into account. For most of the inmates, their day release meant not only a meal at a local café but also real interaction with the outside world through the internet. Brennan's pursuit of Matterling would be delayed. His quest for revenge would have to wait. But at least he would be in the right environment to prepare. He needed that for a reset. He might be hazy about the concept of justice, but he was crystal clear about the mental realignment needed to ready himself for Matterling.

'But you will get visits,' Higginson said.

The sacrifice of the rottle seemed to have tipped the balance. J. D. Jobsworth had made his decision.

'Who have you got? To visit you?'

'Wife and three-year-old daughter,' Brennan said. Relief started to pulse through him. He was staying. After what he'd been through, he was almost looking forward to it.

15

Hampshire Coast
    December. Twelve months later. Friday morning

THE BODY WAS TRAPPED. Dead but still moving. The body of a man.

A man in his prime, Brennan thought.

Pushed by the current, the bloated head nudged repeatedly against the weed-green wooden piles. The body was wedged between two of the marina piles and waterborne debris had started to collect against the folds of the sodden black sweater and trousers. The arms were being forced awkwardly beneath the torso as the head bobbed face down against the timber. Dark hair streamed out with the flow of the water as it sunk and matted against the scalp as it rose again.

Brennan watched, mesmerised. He had seen only one dead body before, that of his uncle who had died when working in California a few years ago. Brennan had flown out to Sacramento for the funeral and the Scarshaw Funeral Parlor had laid Uncle Greg out in an open casket. The body had been prepared for viewing, nails cleaned, hair scraped into place, skin plasticised like a doll's. Best suit and tie. Hands crossed carefully over the torso. At peace.

Brennan had turned away after a few seconds, humiliated on behalf of his uncle.

But now he watched at close range as a total stranger succumbed to the relentless rhythm of the sea.

Brennan had spent the last hour watching the comings and goings on E pontoon from a distance. There hadn't been anything to see until he had wandered to the far end of the marina and stumbled across this drama. The security gate on the pontoon opposite the quay was open and he had taken up a position close to the end to get a better view.

He had not been noticed by those involved in the recovery operation. These were the employees of Blue World Marinas who had manoeuvred a small crane along the jetty and were lowering a cradle into the water in an attempt to slide it under the body. There had been an agitated huddle and some debate as to whether they should wait for the police, but the yard foreman had made a phone call and Brennan had heard him shout that the body should be lifted out pronto.

A couple of the men climbed down the side of the jetty into the water and secured the straps of the cradle under the body. The two men in the water had to clamber under the jetty's planking to push the man out into the cradle. A lever was released on the side of the crane and very slowly the cradle started to rise from the water. There were two straps attached to the cradle. One was under the man's pelvis and the other under his armpits. As the corpse rose dripping, gravity took over. The legs and head hung limply from the pivot points of the straps.

Brennan swung the small rucksack off his back and placed it on the pontoon. He pulled out his Canon camera and attached a 135mm lens; the purist in him had still not accepted the undoubted quality of modern zoom lenses. He started to photograph the macabre scene.

'That's disgusting,' a male voice said behind him.

Brennan started. He had thought he was alone on the pontoon.

'Well, they've got to get him out somehow,' another voice said.

'Not that,' the first voice said. '*Him*. Standing there as bold as brass, taking snaps for his weirdo collection, like as not. Pornography I call it. Not photography.' This last observation was stated triumphantly, as if the speaker had been waiting to use it for some time and the opportunity had finally arisen.

Brennan turned and was surprised to see a small group of onlookers at the bottom of the steps leading down to the pontoon. They had ventured through the open security gate but not along the pontoon itself. Just far enough to be part of the excitement but not far enough to risk eviction. Brennan strode towards them and tried to identify the voices.

'Police photographer,' he growled. They huddled closer together for safety. 'And you're all trespassing. Only yacht owners and crew down here. Back behind the gate. Now!'

'Oh, right,' said the first voice with forced affability as they retreated up the steps. 'Sorry about that.'

Brennan hoped they were too busy trying to smooth their ruffled feathers to realise that there were no uniformed officers on the scene yet.

He hurried back to his position and continued shooting. By now, the body had been swung onto the centreline of the jetty and the marina employees surrounded it as it was lowered the last few feet onto the boards.

Unlike Doug Matterling, this man had been recovered, Brennan thought. Matterling had sunk without trace.

Brennan had spent much of this first week since his release from Ford making calls and trawling the internet, in an attempt to find out what Matterling had been doing for the last twelve months. None of their former business contacts had had any dealings with him since

BM had hit the skids. No new companies, no networking links, no news stories. Nothing except one photograph in an obscure online trade journal, which Brennan had found while googling various spellings of Matterling's surname.

Yesterday, he had visited the address in Islington that Matterling used in company documentation, but he had been greeted by some Iranian students who knew nothing about Matterling. They had only dealt with a local property agent and had never met the owner. A search of the land registry showed that the house was owned by a Swiss investment company. Matterling's name was nowhere to be seen.

Today's trip to the coast was as a result of his only lead, that online photograph from an IT awards dinner in San Francisco. A black-tie affair featuring a group of flushed execs hanging onto each other in celebration and raising their glasses for the event photographer. Doug Matterling—or Mattling as the caption read—was in the middle of the group, the only one not grinning ecstatically. He looked like a very reluctant partygoer, but next to him was the beaming subject of today's visit, a businessman by the name of Victor de Souza.

Matterling and de Souza had their arms around each other in the photograph and looked chummy enough for Brennan to try to track down de Souza and find out about their connection. A careful examination of the photograph had also shown Brennan something else. De Souza's hand on Matterling's shoulder was missing its ring finger.

De Souza was the CEO of a listed IT company called Elba Technology and was much more of a social animal than his awards dinner companion. He seemed to pop up in the gossip columns with alarming regularity and it was relatively easy for Brennan to call his office and say he wanted an interview for *Wired* magazine. De Souza's assistant said that he had been out of the office for some time but would arrange the interview for this Saturday. He liked weekend meetings to be on his boat in Hampshire.

Their rendezvous was for tomorrow but Brennan had decided on a reccy even though the meeting was still to be confirmed. Just in case of surprises. Just to check out the lay of the land. And the water. His time inside had made him cautious. He also needed to get out of the house and away from Sarah. Badly.

The men around the body looked up as a police car squealed to a halt at the far end of the hard. They all straightened up, as if in preparation for questioning. Brennan looked for the lags, a new habit. He scrutinised each face carefully, trying to detect the flicker of fear that would betray anybody with form.

There were no giveaways, but he did notice someone who had not been there at the start of the recovery operation. A small man with dyed blond hair, wearing a shiny mid-grey suit. He was crouched over the corpse as the others stood. He seemed to be feeling the body's chest.

Brennan was distracted by the sound of a second police car drawing up. He watched as a posse of uniformed and plainclothes officers jumped from the cars and made their way down the short track to the jetty.

He turned his attention back to the group around the corpse just in time to see the blond man turn the corner at the far end of the jetty, heading away from the advancing police. He skipped up the steps onto the hard and disappeared into the boatyard.

It was time for Brennan to disappear too. He swung the backpack onto his shoulder and headed towards the anonymity of the other onlookers. The last thing he could afford was an entanglement with the Hampshire Constabulary. Now that he was on the wrong side of the law.

He walked towards the small car park at the marina entrance and once he was out of sight he looked at his camera's screen to check the results. The last shot was the best one of the body. He zoomed in on the face. His heart sank.

The face was in profile and he could not be sure of a perfect match with the photograph from the awards dinner. But it was a strong possibility. He moved the zoom across the frame until the body's arm was centred on the screen. The enlarged portion of the image confirmed his fears. The arm and the right hand were clearly visible. There was no ring finger.

Brennan's only lead to Doug Matterling was Victor de Souza. And now he was dead.

16

London
Friday morning

'I'M CONCERNED, Ben. I mean, I am *really* concerned.'

Julie Grainger moved her blanched face closer to Ben Parfitt's. The knots of muscle at each end of her jawbone were standing out against her tight skin. 'This is getting to be a habit with you,' she went on. 'A habit that has got to be broken. One way or another.'

Julie's office had always seemed pretty big to Ben, with tasteful black and white landscapes hanging from the neutral calico walls. As if to show that a human lived here. Someone with a heart and a sensitivity for the natural world around her. How wrong that assumption was, he thought now. There was nothing soft and fluffy here. Her office seemed suddenly tiny and from where he was pinned, he felt he could touch all four walls.

He sank deeper in his chair and tried to look nonchalant. *One way or another?* Was she threatening him with the chop? She stood over him, holding out his report on Trimal Digital as if goading him into trying to deny its authorship. Her pink jacket and skirt were just camouflage—a soft-looking shell covering the cast iron money-making machine inside.

She looked down at the report again, as if she had just pulled it from the toilet. 'Shall I quote you again, Ben? Shall I read out loud that final paragraph? Shall I tell you what advice Bavaria Williams Burnett gave to all our clients just three months ago?'

'Er, no, Julie. I think—'

'Yes, I shall, Ben.' He didn't need this. Not today of all days.

'Just three months ago,' she said. 'Not six months. Not even a year. Just three months ago, our esteemed firm, with over one hundred years of successful investment advice behind it, told our clients,' she straightened slightly and shot Parfitt a look of raw malevolence, 'and I quote: *"The star is now rising again on this sector of the technology industry and one of the soundest plays around is Trimal. It has been restructured to take advantage of the enormous potential in the market, its fundamentals are good, its management exceptional and it has the products in place to make it happen. We are looking for a price of 550p in the short term and target £10 within two years. We view it as a strong Buy. Get on board in the current range of 260p to 290p, sit back and enjoy the ride."'*

She threw the offending item into his lap and turned without moving away. She was still standing close to him. Too close for his liking.

'That was when—'

'Enjoy the ride?' she said and glared at him. 'Enjoy the ride? Yes, Ben, we've all enjoyed the bloody ride. A ride to hell and back. That's what our clients have had this last week.' She stared out of the office window as if in a trance, searching the grey skyline of the City of London for inspiration.

He picked up the report from his lap. He smoothed out the creases, waiting for the next salvo. It had been a bad week—this was the second stock of his to have bombed in the space of a few days. It was currently trading at ninety pence after a profit warning had been issued this morning.

It had been a tumultuous couple of months. Ben had gone from being listed in the top ten Technology Analysts of the Year by *Investors Weekly* to getting a bollocking like an errant schoolboy. How quickly fortunes could change. From a top analyst to just another schmuck worried about hanging on to his job. From living in domestic bliss with the beautiful Naomi to being on his tod again.

He followed Julie's gaze. Out there, at this very moment, the wine bars and pubs of the City were rammed with young, noisy, loaded people enjoying their own unassailability. People just like him. And only last week he had been there with them, just as rowdy, just as full of it. But now he was here, cooped up with this crazy she-monster who had no idea about the short-term fluctuations of the market and was breaking his balls for a couple of recommendations that had gone wrong.

What do you expect, Julie? One hundred per cent certainty? Stick it in gilts if that's what you're after. Don't waste my hundred-and-fifty-grand a year time if you're going to self-destruct at every little upset.

Fortified by this spurt of mental bravado, he got up to leave. 'I hear what you're saying Julie, but the market—'

'Sit down.'

He sat down again.

She turned and stuck her face even closer to his. He noticed where her pink lipstick didn't quite make it to the edges of her lips. On each side of her upper lip, two tiny patches of dark hair poked through the layer of powder. The veins in her neck were standing out like hawsers, throbbing with pent up fury.

'I know you haven't got any answers, Ben. I know you haven't got a crystal ball. I know that. I'm paid a lot of money to know that.' She paused, probably waiting for him to wonder just how much.

Did he have any answers? Perhaps he should remind her of the work he had done on Protheus or Harmona, both of which had doubled in value in just the last six months. And there was Elba of course, his star performer. Perhaps this was the time to remind her of his successes to divert her from bloody Trimal. But that would prolong their conversation. And all he wanted to do was to get out of there. He decided to say nothing.

'And you're paid a lot of money to do research. Research, Ben, is about checking your facts. It's about getting under the skin of every company you're asked to look at. It's about gathering data, assessing information, meeting company directors, drinking with them, flattering them, going through their garbage if necessary.' Ben winced inwardly at her jarring use of the Americanism; she always did that when she was being assertive and it always grated. Her cut-glass accent made it sound worse. 'Generally, you should be absorbing every goddam detail into every fibre of your miserable being.'

He looked down again. *There was no need for personal attacks.* Her taut face was close enough to kiss, but the thought made his stomach turn.

'It is not about believing every piece of bullshit that is thrown your way,' she spat. 'And it is not about sponging second-rate opinions off other second-rate bloody tip-sheet hacks whose companionship I know you value.'

This was going too far. 'They're not all hacks, Julie.' He thought again about countering with his top performers but hesitated.

She leaned back, studying him hard. And then, as if suddenly alighting on a previously undiscovered nugget of worth, she became warm and encouraging. 'Come on, Ben. I know you can do it.'

She smiled, a crooked, forced smile that Ben knew would be hard for her to sustain. Christ, she looked weird. 'Just because you've had a few screw-ups doesn't mean you can't do well in the future. After all, look at Elba Technology. A brilliant recommendation. Price tripling in twelve months? Great stuff. You *can* do it. You know you can.'

She walked back to her desk and signalled him to leave.

He didn't dash out. A man had his dignity.

'Thanks,' he said as he stood. 'Thanks for the, er, feedback.'

He closed her office door behind him and let out a long, low whistle of relief. He made his way quickly back to his own office. As he strode along, mentally dusting himself off, he felt his confidence start to return. He tried to put the conversation with Julie behind him. BWB wasn't the be-all and end-all. Wasn't he now being courted by one of Silicon Valley's most successful investors?

He needed to fully regain his confidence. Naomi's departure at the beginning of the week had been a hammer blow and this bollocking from Julie was just what he didn't need.

But she had finished with praise for the Elba call. *A brilliant recommendation*, had been her exact words, hadn't they? He should have brought up Elba as soon as she had thrown the Trimal report at him. That would have saved a lot of aggravation.

Thank heavens for Elba Technology plc.

17

London
Friday afternoon

'IT'S BEEN OVER A WEEK NOW,' Sarah said and pulled her knees up tighter under her chin. She was sitting barefoot on the red sofa with her legs drawn up against her chest.

Brennan cradled the mug of tea she had made him and slowly swivelled on the piano stool. She had called him down from his office, where he had sequestered himself since returning from the marina. They had both been walking on eggshells since that tense drive back from Ford.

'I thought you'd have some interviews lined up by now.' Her eyes were searching for clues. He couldn't blame her. He had been expecting this.

'I had one set up for tomorrow. But that's not going to happen now.'

'Postponed?'

'Nope. He's dead.'

'Dead?' Her eyes widened.

'I was due to meet someone called Victor de Souza on his yacht tomorrow. But he's had an accident. Drowned.'

He had mentioned the journalism to Sarah several times during her visits over the last year, but it had never really seemed to register with her. As far as she was concerned, he should be looking to get back to work for one of his former competitors as soon as possible. She didn't seem to see how problematic that would be. At every level.

'This was for a job, right?'

'Kind of.'

'Kind of? What does that mean?' She hugged her knees tighter.

'I was going to interview him. For a magazine.' He regarded her steadily. This wasn't a lie. Not really. It was what had been arranged.

Sarah frowned deeply. 'You were going to interview *him*? Not the other way around? What kind of business was he in? And what's a magazine got to do with it?'

'Don't you remember? I said I was going to do some writing when I got out. Profiles of the great and the good in business and the arts. That kind of thing.'

'I remember you talking about it. But I remember you talking about a lot of things. And I remember you listening to me as well. And listening to what I was going through. And what I needed.'

'We both went through a lot. It was difficult.'

Sarah looked quizzical again. As if there was no need to state the obvious.

'So who was this guy you were so interested in? This de Souza?'

'Victor de Souza. A tech entrepreneur.'

'Never heard of him. Why would he have made such a great story? And how did he drown?'

'It was an accident. Fell off his yacht late at night, apparently. In a marina.' Brennan ignored the first part of the question.

'So let me get this straight.' Her voice had risen half an octave. 'You've just spent a year mixing with a bunch of hardened criminals, and within a week of being on the outside you're about to meet someone who just happens to die.' She threw her hands up. 'Did someone put you up to it? He was connected to someone you met in prison, wasn't he?' She shook her head but her eyes never left his. 'What have you got involved in, Mike? Or should I say, what have you got *us* involved in?'

'There's no connection.' He stood up to go to her. 'There's no connection to anyone I met inside.'

She turned her palms towards him and he slowly sat back down.

'I promise you,' he said.

Her features softened and he could see she wanted to take it at face value. He wanted to put his arms around her and tell her that everything was going to be all right, but she was too brittle. He had to reassure her that their lives were not going to spiral into a violent underworld of real crime. He understood that De Souza's drowning had triggered her worst fears. Fears that must have been building the whole time he had been away.

'De Souza had an accident. That's what they told me at the marina. The guy drowned in an accident.'

She pursed her lips. 'Okay. But it's quite a coincidence. You must admit that.' He could tell that she was reluctantly rethinking her conclusions. 'And surely you can see it from my point of view. What it was like when you were inside. How I've had to cope on my own. How I've had to do everything on my own.' Her mouth tightened and her lips started to quiver. 'I don't understand why you can't see what you've got to do.' She rubbed at her eyes. 'I just want our life back. That's all. It's not so much to ask for, is it?'

She looked up and her simple request hung between them like a bridge. A bridge he could walk across if he chose.

There had not been one hour of every day when he had not thought of her and Cara. Every waking hour and, as far as he could remember, every sleeping hour. When he had not been thinking of them, he had been dreaming of them.

'I had to keep telling Cara that you'd be back soon. From your business trips.' She looked down at the floor again and stared at it for a long moment. 'And you're going to have to explain it all to her one day. Probably sooner than you think. She's already asking questions.'

'I know. I will. When the time is right.'

He had rehearsed that speech so many times in the last twelve months and his short chats with Cara on the phone had been the hardest of all. It was going to be difficult to gauge when the time was right, but he would know. He was sure of it. Just not yet. He had even given up the option of being tagged for the last couple of months. He could have spent that time at home but he knew it would have raised too many questions with Cara. He wanted a clean start and he was determined to do right by her. In his own way.

'So why would he have made such a great story?' Sarah asked, suddenly all business-like.

Perhaps if she knew what he knew, she would be more sympathetic about him meeting with de Souza. When they had faced tough times in the past, she had always trusted his judgement. Why not now?

'Let me show you something.' He reached into his pocket and brought out the internet photograph of de Souza and Matterling. He offered it to Sarah. She looked at it and her brow furrowed immediately. She made no attempt to take it from him.

Her mouth opened as if she was about to say something but closed again. She shook her head slowly and stared at him as if he were a ghost.

'That's the connection. That's why I needed to talk to de Souza.' Even as the words were coming out of his mouth he knew that this gambit was in trouble.

'No,' she said. 'Please no.' She was still shaking her head. 'You can't think of going after him. Not now. He's destroyed our lives. We have to accept what's happened, move on and recover.'

Brennan put the photograph back in his pocket. He didn't want to antagonise her further.

'Doug Matterling is history for us now,' she said. 'If we let him back into our lives, we let him win again.' Her blue eyes blazed with conviction. Brennan knew she would have spent too many hours dwelling on Doug Matterling and what he had done to them. 'We have to turn weakness into strength. Think of *jujitsu*. You absorb the blow and use its power to respond. The blow has been your sentence. We have to absorb it and respond by rising above it. By getting our lives back and forgetting all about him. That's the only response that'll see us on top. We're the only ones who can live with dignity in this battle. That will be our victory.'

Brennan closed his eyes. He had almost come to the same conclusion over the last twelve months. Many times. But just as many times he had arrived at a very different destination.

The route always started with his father. Brennan remembered him turning to his mother and in his thick Irish accent telling her, *'I'm not faragoch, Eileen. I'm just getting the balance.'* He remembered the raw fear he and his siblings felt when Dad was on the rampage. All that anger—that *faragoch*—seemed to be directed at them. It was only later that they realised it was nothing to do with them at all. Dad's rage was directed at the world. The world that had sentenced him to spend his life working in a builders' merchants. The world that wouldn't let him out of that prison of a yard. His children were an easy target. But as soon as the young Michael Brennan had recognised the injustice at the root of his father's behaviour he had vowed never to run away from misdirected anger again.

Sarah was right to focus on the victory of leaving Matterling behind them. It was what Brennan had tried to do with his own father. Yet Dad's shadow still fell over him like a net.

'I can't argue with your logic,' he said.

Her face relaxed and she smiled hesitantly. 'I know you must have been stewing about Doug for a long time now. But it's the only way that we can get through this. Otherwise . . .' She looked at him helplessly. It wasn't a threat, he knew that. It was a recognition of what was at stake. Not only their marriage but also their family. She didn't need to verbalise it.

Cara was at the heart of this. He had to do the right thing. He also had to make sure that when she was older, she would see her father in a way he had never been able to.

Sarah relaxed and uncoiled her legs. Her bare feet touched the floor. She took a step towards him. He stood up and they looked at each other in silence. She put her forearms on his shoulders and her head under his chin. Her eyelashes brushed his shirt as she closed her eyes.

'Tell me it's going to be all right, Mike. Just tell me. Please.'

'I'll make it all right. I promise you. I'll do everything I can.'

He let her lean into him and there was another long silence as they held each other in the gathering gloom. He felt her take a deep breath. She was hesitating about saying something. He gave her the time to choose her words.

'I've been speaking to Mary McMahon.' She paused to gauge his reaction. He didn't say anything. The McMahons were old friends who ran a small marketing company in Chiswick. He had helped them get started many years ago and had used them for some run-of-the-mill work. Nice enough folks but dull as dishwater.

'She would be interested in talking to you,' Sarah said. She lifted her head and looked him in the eye. 'They want to expand. Increase their "*below the line*" work. Whatever that means.' She gave him a small, encouraging smile.

'It means crap like mailing campaigns, trade shows and search engine stuff. Not my field at all. And since when did you start touting my CV around? Least of all to the likes of Mr and Mrs McMahon, the king and queen of marketing mediocrity.'

'I haven't given them anything,' she said. 'There's no need to be so dismissive of them. You know they were big fans of yours.'

Exactly, he thought. *Were*.

He pulled her gently towards him again and her head sank back against his chest. His arms tightened around her.

'I'll look after Cara tomorrow,' he said. 'You've got taekwondo, haven't you?'

'Mm,' she responded. She sounded like she was still thinking about the McMahons rather than plans for the weekend.

'I'm out on Sunday for a bit,' he added, without going into detail.

He held her even closer. Better than talking at the moment. He had made his choice. Now it was just a question of making it the right one. After all, he had promised.

18

London
  Friday afternoon

'C'MON, Ben. Let's go and sink a few. Forget it all.' Henry Evans' round pink face contrasted with the darkening afternoon sky outside. He had his coat on and was ready to leave.

Ben glanced at him and went back to the Bloomberg news screen. He shook his head in disbelief as he read and reread that one sentence:

Hampshire police have confirmed that the body recovered from the River Hamble this morning was that of Victor de Souza, chairman and chief executive of Elba Technology plc.

'It can't be all bad,' Henry continued, awkwardly shifting his weight from one foot to the other and then back again. 'He wasn't the only guy in the company, surely? And anyway, sometimes these things can go the other way. You never know, the price might rise on the hope of a take-over . . . '

Henry was trying his best to cheer Ben up. But it wasn't working.

A takeover was a long shot at this stage. Perhaps in a year or two, but not just yet.

He stared at the screen for another few seconds then said, 'A drink would be great.' He stood up. 'Has Julie heard yet, do you know?' He couldn't face being yanked back into her office for another dose of vitriol. Not twice in one day.

'I don't think so. She's been in a meeting since one.'

'Let's go then, before she comes out. I've already had one little tete-a-tete with her today.'

Ben pulled on his coat and smiled gratefully at Henry. Everyone else in the firm seemed to have lost all perspective. Every disaster around the globe was analysed in terms of the effect on share prices. An earthquake in Brazil, floods in India, a famine in Africa were all translated into the financial impact on companies operating in the region. That was all it meant to them. At least Henry's view of the world didn't seem so cynically focused. Perhaps earls didn't have to be so mercenary. Although Ben did not know a lot about Henry, he knew he would inherit an ancestral title in due course. Along with a crumbling pile somewhere in Wiltshire.

They left Ben's small office and walked past the fluorescent-lit trading floor. The traders were still working hard, with another couple of hours to go, tapping furiously on their keyboards, shouting into their telephones, constantly scanning the screens in front of them and occasionally pointing excitedly at a price movement that their colleagues might have missed. Ben loved it all. Most days.

But this Friday afternoon he was happy to leave it behind and squeeze into a corner seat at The Astronomer while Henry brought over the beers. He glanced over his shoulder at the circle of celestial clocks on the wall behind him. Never one for science history, he couldn't help but wonder what the stars held in store for him.

'How bad is it?' Henry squashed in beside him. Mid-afternoon and the place was already packed.

'Pretty bad. Elba was going to save my arse. And now the founder's croaked. He was only in his fifties.'

'Drowned, eh?'

'Apparently. I'll get more details later. But I'm sure there was nothing else going on.'

'Another suicide? Like Maxwell?'

Ben rolled his eyes. 'Don't even think it, Henry. '

Henry's patch was pharmaceuticals which Ben had always considered an easier market to analyse than technology. All the major companies were huge, the products in R&D were easier to track and the sales forecasts were more reliable. Technology was very different, with lots of small companies ready to go into orbit—or just as likely to crash back to Earth at any time.

Ben was grateful that Henry had taken the time to commiserate with him. Not that Henry would resist the temptation to go short on Elba just as soon as he could. That was to be expected. And anyway, it had nothing to do with their budding friendship.

'The market will overreact, I'm sure,' Ben said and gulped his beer. 'It's bloody perfect timing for the Sundays. This'll flatten the share price next week if it hasn't already. I can't bring myself to look, at the moment.'

They both stared blankly at the tabletop. Eventually, Henry broke the silence.

'So, Elba Technology develops virtual reality stuff, yeah?'

'That's right. They licence their tech mainly. But there are a few real breakthroughs on the horizon.'

'Pretty high valuation then?'

'Price earnings just over thirty.'

Henry made a face. Ben knew why. It was a stock with a long way to fall if market sentiment turned against it.

'Market cap?'

'Just over a hundred.' Ben glanced at his watch and wondered whether he dared to check the current share price. The hundred-million-pound company valuation had been accurate this morning but he doubted it was still at that level.

'Tightly held though?'

Ben looked at Henry keenly. 'Yes. On AIM.'

Henry frowned briefly. Ben understood his concern. AIM was the junior market at the London stock exchange, comprised mainly of smaller companies with good growth prospects. There was usually a higher risk associated with these companies and Ben knew that Henry would not be used to dealing with them. He pushed on anyway. 'Big family interest and only a few small institutions. One large overseas investment outfit and one venture capital fund in the States. Over thirty-five per cent held by small investors.'

'Where are the sales? And how about this de Souza?'

'US and Japan. De Souza was British. He brought it to market. The technological impetus was a bloke called Salinger. A professor at Stanford who developed a way for the Defense Department to connect all their different types of computers. That was in the early eighties.'

'That's when the company started, was it?'

Ben knew what Henry was trying to do. He wanted Ben to see that the company had great fundamentals. Get him to see again why he had so enthusiastically recommended them in the first place. But he went along with it. After all, it might just work.

'Kind of. Salinger and his mates were running it as some kind of offshoot from Stanford. But as soon as they got it together to resign their posts and make a real go of it, the defence cutbacks came in and they hit hard times.'

'And that's when de Souza stepped in?'

Ben nodded. 'Picked up the government contracts for a song, raised about five million from this venture capital firm in California and away they went. They developed hubs and routers originally, then into wireless and now virtual reality. Operations in San Jose and Maidenhead.'

'So the technology's still there, isn't it? Even though de Souza isn't.'

Ben smiled weakly. 'That's true. The technology is still there. Salinger's retired now. Lives here in England. Down by the sea somewhere. But de Souza made it all happen. He's been the driving force since they listed in London. And he's going to be missed.'

Should he go back and discuss the whole thing with Julie? She might decide to deal with it head-on, commiserate with him on the unfortunate timing and then calmly contact clients with Elba stock to reassure them about the fundamentals. On the other hand, she could simply go ballistic and start yelling at him again.

He looked at Henry for guidance, but Henry was checking the Elba share price on his iPhone.

'Down to one-one-five. Could be worse.' He grinned.

Ben did a quick calculation. 'That's good. Down less than ten per cent.' It certainly could be worse; he had seen some AIM stocks pulverised on news like this. The smaller-than-expected immediate reaction took the pressure off having to go back and talk to Julie. Ben felt himself smiling. First time in what seemed like ages. 'Same again?' he said and wagged his empty glass at Henry.

'Sure.'

He made his way to the bar. This kind of fall was not precipitous. But it had only been an hour or so since the agencies had distributed the story. The price was almost certain to drop further next week, although with the long-term fundamentals being so good it could recover in the following few weeks.

'Two pints of Pride please.' He pushed the empty glasses towards the dark-haired barmaid, who had a large black plastic ring hanging from her nose and a row of metal spikes through each eyebrow. She gave him a big grin which caught him by surprise—he had expected a grunt at best. It transformed her face. Friendly, after all.

If he was right about the market reaction it would make sense to go short on the shares today and cover the position at the end of next week. He would come out with a decent profit in only a few days. Henry would be thinking along the same lines.

He returned to the table and plonked the glasses down. Henry looked at him innocently and let out a low whistle as if he had just thought of something.

'You know, this might not all be as bad as you think. We could make a little bet.'

Ben smiled to himself. Good old Henry.

'How little?'

'I'd have to check but let's assume the spread bet margin was ten per cent on a stock this size. I could do say twenty-five . . .' He let the figure hang in the air.

Ben quickly did the sums. This was more than he'd expected Henry to come out with but if he did the same, they would be able to go short on half-a-million pounds worth of Elba shares. A further drop of about twelve per cent over the next week would net them fifty grand. There would be the bid/offer spread to factor in, of course, but the sums were still tempting. Twenty-five each. A hundred per cent return on capital within a week.

'That's a tad high for me, Henry.'

'Look at it this way. How often does this kind of opportunity come along? The timing's perfect. This bloke kicks the bucket Friday morning, the news is out at lunchtime and the market is too pissed to notice by then. The financial press will get to it over the weekend and Monday morning the share price will go through the floor.'

'That's always a possibility,' Ben said. Henry had been thinking it through. Along exactly the same lines.

'I've got an account with IG that we could use.'

'You have?'

IG Index was one of the largest spread bet traders in the City. Henry was really up for this. Twenty-five grand each would be a very serious bet. Perhaps too serious.

Then he thought about the other downside. A far bigger downside than losing twenty-five grand. If they took a position this afternoon, they would not have the time to act in accordance with the firm's rules for personal investments and Julie couldn't know that he was betting against his own recommendations. Christ, she would wrench his balls off if that came out.

Henry smiled conspiratorially. 'Well it's not me with the IG account, obviously. A distant relative.'

Ben studied Henry. They had never done anything like this together and he was surprised by Henry's ambition. He had always seemed a bit of a joker, the office buffoon. A First in Classics from Oxford, a bit nerdy. A bit of a pillock, really. And now he was ready to organise a fifty-grand bet on a single news item in a share he knew nothing about. Ben was warming to him.

'A *dead* distant relative.' Henry had his phone up to his ear. 'Shall I make the call?'

Ben found himself nodding his agreement.

'Great. Won't be a mo. Bit noisy in here.'

Henry jumped up and walked out through the heavy grey doors. Ben watched him through the window. Henry was speaking animatedly into his iPhone and holding a bank card in his other hand. He seemed to be reading out the details. Good God, Ben thought, he's actually doing it. He's transferring fifty grand to IG.

He took another large gulp of his London Pride. The beer was starting to take effect. For the first time, he dared to think positively. Perhaps this Friday was going to turn out okay after all.

Henry was back within a couple of minutes.

'All done. Five grand a point. In at one-thirteen. Stop at one-two-three.'

Ben did the calculation again. Just to check he had got the numbers right. They were betting five-thousand pounds on every penny movement in the share price. The bid/offer spread was four pence. If the price dropped by fourteen pence, they would make fifty-thousand pounds. If it rose by six pence, they would lose their fifty thousand. The stop ensured that the loss would not be more than the fifty. Ben stopped himself from thinking about that possibility. But he was certainly impressed by Henry. A fifty-grand margin transfer, just like that. Just with a phone call.

'No problems with that kind of size?'

'None at all. It's small beer for them.'

Henry pulled out a business card from his top pocket and wrote some numbers on the back. He passed the card over the table.

'My account details. For your twenty-five.' He smiled. 'No hurry.'

Ben raised his glass. They grinned broadly at each other and clinked their glasses.

'To comradeship,' Ben said grandly. It was not a word he used very often.

'And to profit,' Henry responded with an exaggerated wink.

Mm, Ben thought. *Still a pillock.*

19

California
   Friday afternoon

CARMEL DE SOUZA lay motionless on the lounger. The afternoon sun was at its hottest and waves of exhaustion gently rippled through her body. Her legs and arms had lost all feeling. She felt the wash of her thoughts as they swirled above her and dissipated in the hot air.

She had arrived two hours ago on an early flight from Heathrow to LAX, landing at midday Pacific Time. Immigration had been surprisingly quick and the E-Z-Ride limo service had sped her north to Santa Barbara. Her hotel was nestled in the hills, overlooking the city and the ocean.

Soon after arriving, she had received the call from a female Family Liaison Officer with Hampshire Police. The officer was illogically apologetic that she was not able to break the news in person and told Carmel how she'd obtained her itinerary from her sister Leah, via the neighbours at home.

The policewoman was well trained. She led up to the news but not too slowly. *An unfortunate accident. First reports indicate that Mr de Souza must have slipped off his boat and been carried by the tide to a nearby jetty. Further enquiries were pending. The DSI would be contacting her very soon. When would she be returning to the UK?*

By the end of the call Carmel felt for the policewoman. She would have imagined a very different Mr and Mrs de Souza. A couple that probably loved each other.

Carmel had immediately Skyped Leah and the boys back in London. Conor and Sean were shocked and saddened but not distraught. They had lost their real father when they were very young but Victor had never taken over that role. Their first loyalty was to her.

She had spent the last hour on the lounger, soaking up the California sun. A vivid melee of magenta and orange bougainvillaea hung to the sides of her balcony and the gentle breeze carried up a sweet clinging aroma from the tropical garden below. She inhaled the scent and squeezed out memories of earlier, happier times with Victor. There had been a few good years together before things unravelled. She had shed some tears. For all his failings, she still felt he had been *a good man*. A good man but a terrible husband.

The high-pitched tone of the telephone forced its way into her consciousness and she slowly realised that she would have to move. She squinted into the sun and rolled her legs off the lounger, kneeling briefly on the warm sienna tiles. She crawled into the dark of the suite and felt for the handset by the sofa.

'Carmel. How are you?'

The voice was deep and clear.

'Ken. It's good to hear your voice again.'

'How are you feeling? I didn't wake you, did I? I tried your cell first but I couldn't get through.'

'No, no. I was just laying out in the sun.'

'How are you now?'

'Pretty exhausted. But generally okay.'

'I've just got into the airport. I've got that meeting later in Montecito and then I can come over.'

'Lovely.' Her voice was even, but a rush of relief flowed through her. 'I can't wait.'

'I'll be over at seven.'

'Seven will be great.'

'And I'll book a table. See you then.'

'Bye.'

She replaced the telephone and crawled onto the sofa. Her eyes had adjusted to the dark. She looked down at her bare legs and thought about which dress to wear later. It would be good to wear cool, thin cottons for a few days before having to return to England and dress for winter again. England was a long way away now.

She studied the framed photograph of her sisters and mother that she had put on the coffee table earlier, along with the picture of her sons, the one where they were still young enough to hold hands. Setting these out was the first thing she had done after arriving. She leant over and kissed the pictures tenderly. The small gold crucifix strung between the two frames dropped onto the table and she replaced it carefully. Instinctively, she touched the identical chain around her neck.

Tears suddenly rolled down her cheeks and she made no attempt to wipe them away. She clenched her fists and as they tightened, the tears stopped. She was regaining control. She dropped to her knees by the sofa and placed her hands together in prayer, her elbows on the thin bedcover. She closed her eyes and silently mouthed her Hail Mary. She paused before the final two lines and finished the prayer aloud. Her voice was steady and clear.

'Pray for us sinners now. And at the hour of our death.'

She opened her eyes and stared at the framed print of a West Coast sunset on the wall. Her voice dropped to a whisper.

'Amen.'

KEN OLSON REMEMBERED the table they had shared on their last visit to the hotel and he had made sure they had the same one tonight. Carmel had been wowed by the view.

It was by the window, next to a narrow terrace that was being used as a storage area for the folding trestles that supported the huge silver serving trays. It was a spectacular view down to the ocean, over the lush vegetation and sienna roofs of Santa Barbara, but it was lost on Ken. He had not taken his eyes off Carmel all through dinner.

She had never looked more beautiful. Her dark eyes shone in the candlelight and her long black hair fell upon the smooth, tight skin of her bare shoulders. She smiled constantly, a wide, girlish smile that sent tremors of excitement through him.

Sometimes he had difficulty believing that she had acceded to his awkward advances. They had first met when he and Victor had been negotiating Olson Associates' investment into Elba. Victor had brought her to dinner one evening and it had been obvious that she and Victor were not together anymore. It was all very civil, but there was no tenderness between them. Ken had needed to bide his time. But it was always going to happen.

Whenever he had visited Europe, he had always admired this kind of woman. Cool, almost aloof. Always beautifully dressed. Dressed for effect rather than comfort. The kind of woman who could freeze you with a glance but say everything with the slightest smile. Reserved, confident and in control. With their quiet voices and their tinkling laughter, they shunned the spotlight but were calmly aware of all the attention they received. Their men seemed weak in comparison—necessary accessories, but not to be taken too seriously. She was so different from the women at home.

He probably came across as pretty different as well. Perhaps that was why she had been attracted to him. For a guy of fifty, Ken thought he looked pretty good. He kept in shape and the California sun kept him lightly tanned. He was careful not to get too dark, as a date had once told him that she would only trust a man with a deep tan if he was very young or very old. His teeth were good and he still had his hair. He had recently taken to tying it in a neat, short ponytail that hung over his collar. Not too wild but something to get their interest. As Carmel talked, he relaxed. He was feeling pretty good about himself. He could see what she saw in him.

He leant towards her, to emphasise his concern. 'You must be tired now. Do you want to go?'

She gave him one of those looks that told him to back off. Don't try to be too assertive. He retreated gracefully. But she smiled again, head angled coyly.

'Don't be too anxious, darling.' She touched his wrist lightly. 'We've got a long time together now.'

He smiled back, relieved. She had given him all the reassurance he needed about her commitment. She had been quiet over dinner, preoccupied with something. Or perhaps it was just jet lag. He didn't push it. He was just grateful that she was here with him.

'That's true,' he said. 'But I don't want to wear you out.'

She laughed and moved her hand to his leg. 'Why not? You've tried before.' Her smile widened. 'I'll freshen up while you get the check.'

As she rose from her chair, Ken could feel the attention of the other men in the room turn towards her. They had played at being disinterested before, but now that she was on the move, they were allowed to look. He felt their eyes follow her as she crossed the room. He smiled to himself and signalled for the waiter, knowing that once she was out of sight they would transfer their assessing gazes to him. Most of these guys wouldn't stand a chance with a woman like Carmel. He couldn't imagine many of them being capable of keeping their mouths shut and just listening. And that, he reckoned, was rule number one.

Rule number two was not to take anything for granted. Their affair had developed slowly and each time they met he felt as if they were starting from square one. So he had booked a separate room for the night, not knowing how things would develop. Or not.

When she returned, they strolled from the restaurant through the garden towards the Spanish colonial-style building housing Carmel's suite. The sky was clear and the air warm. Moths were endlessly circling the small lanterns that hung from the garden walls and trellis arches. Carmel lay her head against his arm. The food had been excellent and the wine had performed well.

They reached the steps to her suite. He had to decide. Whether to assume they would be sleeping together or to be more circumspect.

'I'm thataway,' he said quietly, nodding across the courtyard. 'I'll let you rest.'

He touched her lightly on the hip and leant forward for a good-night kiss. She let him brush his lips against her cheek and then angled her face to kiss him full on the lips. She pulled his head firmly towards hers and kissed him deeply.

Eventually she let him withdraw. 'No you're not,' she breathed.

She led him up the steps by the hand. As they entered the suite she let his arm go and put her palm over the light switch to stop him turning it on. She pointed him towards the bedroom. He threw his jacket onto the sofa and went through. The moon was bright and his eyes quickly became accustomed to the silver half-dark. She followed him into the bedroom and closed the door gently behind her. Ken kicked off his shoes and went over to the bed. He lay back on it, hands behind his head.

Carmel stood by the window. The soft moonlight reflected from her white dress.

'Are you ready, darling?' she said. Her voice was gentle but purposeful. He could tell that she knew the effect she was having on him. He quickly pulled off the rest of his clothes and lay back on the bed again.

'Ready.' His voice seemed distant and weak.

'It's been some time since you saw me, don't forget . . .'

He couldn't forget. Every waking hour had been full of her smile, her hair, her skin, her smell.

She stood still for a moment and then pushed her hair back behind her shoulders. She reached slowly behind her. She paused when she found the catch. Ken held his breath. She gently wriggled and the dress slid down her body to the floor. She was silhouetted against the moonlit window and Ken sighed in appreciation.

She leaned back slightly and let him gaze at her body. He drank her in, from the shadows of her shoulders, down past her soft breasts, to the measured spread of her hips. Her waist was narrow and her stomach flat, the sinews of her groin showing clearly in the silky light.

She turned and moved towards him. She was smiling and her teeth flashed white against her darkened lips. She put one knee next to him and gracefully swung the other leg across the bed to sit astride his stomach. Her head came forward and her breasts swayed inches from his face. He closed his eyes and stroked her thighs. She arched forward and kissed the top of his head. As he felt her small, taut nipples brush against his cheek, he thought vaguely about the times they had made love in England. But now it was different. Now they were on his turf.

She seemed different tonight as well. He had not felt her like this before. She kissed his forehead and then his nose. She pressed her lips hard against his and clasped her hands behind his head, pulling it towards hers as her tongue explored his mouth with a steady intensity. Her breathing became deeper and she pushed her hips hard against him, spreading her legs wider to take him in. As he squeezed her waist, he could feel the tension build in her body. Every muscle tightened and every movement became stronger as she settled into a rhythm on top of him.

In the soft light he could see that her eyes were closed. She was breathing hard through pursed lips, in short bursts. The muscles in her shoulders rolled under her glistening olive skin as she pumped her body against him. He felt detached, as if he were watching complete strangers from a distance.

He closed his own eyes and drifted into a different dimension, becoming only dimly aware of Carmel's urgent tempo against him. He thought about their meetings over the last few years and how careful he had been. How he had rationalised the affair in his mind.

An affair with the wife of an investment client. The kind of thing he would never have thought himself capable of but was now pursuing vigorously. She was his prize and it made him feel complete.

He thought about the detailed planning that had gone into their relationship. The trips to London, which had become more frequent over the past year, often for just a few hours together. A lunch, afternoon tea or sometimes an evening out in the West End. She had been cautious and he had taken his time. But he had always made his intentions clear. He wanted her and he would wait if necessary.

Suddenly her face was next to his and her hot breath was on his lips. The pushing had stopped. He felt moisture fall onto his cheeks. Her body was rigid, completely still and her eyes were screwed up tightly. Tears streamed down her face. He held her as close as he could. There was a tremor deep within her and then her body started to convulse. She gasped for air and her legs trembled. Her whole body shuddered. She wept.

It was as if a lifetime's emotions were pouring out. Her body folded onto him, her taut muscles softening. She buried her face in his chest. Her muffled sobs resonated through him.

Gradually, the shuddering subsided and the sobs grew quieter. He held her, not knowing what to say. He was not sure whether her convulsions were from pleasure or pain. But she had never been closer to him. He gently stroked her back.

After several minutes she raised her head and looked at him. The moonlight reflected in her dark eyes.

'Victor's dead,' she breathed. 'He's dead.'

She slowly laid her head back down on his chest. He felt her silky hair on his skin and he stared up at the wood and brass ceiling fan.

Suddenly, everything had changed.

20

Hampshire Coast
   Sunday morning

THE STIFF COLD wind caught Brennan unawares as he grabbed his jacket and camera bag from the back seat.

This time he had parked away from the marina, near the town quay. Many of the fishing boats were still in the small port, a few crew members busying themselves with maintenance. Looking at the rusty equipment and corroded hulls, Brennan was surprised that some of these boats were still operational.

He imagined this place in the summer and remembered his childhood holidays in Padstow. The evening family stroll down to the quay. Fish being unloaded from grimy boats under the curious gaze of holidaymakers excited at seeing the strange-looking creatures being swung onto the scales and loaded into the backs of decrepit pick-ups. The quayside lights had given it all a wonderful, eternal magic. The fishermen enjoyed the attention and chatted to bystanders about the catch while making loud arrangements to meet each other for a beer later in the evening.

He remembered looking at these men in awe, their yellow oilskins streaked with fish blood, still working hard after days at sea. Wouldn't it have been great if his father had been one of them? Then he could have helped with the haul when the boats came in. After the holidays, when he was at home in his safe, dry bedroom, he often thought about those boys. They didn't spend their evenings struggling with the Tudors and the Stuarts or trying to remember the date of the battle of Naseby. They were jumping on and off the boats, swinging crates on to the quay, handling eels and giant crabs with their bare hands and shouting cheerful insults at each other. Swaggering around under the bright harbour lights just like their dads. Learning to be men.

But Brennan was a long way from that boy now. He had spent Saturday with Cara. Conveniently, Sarah had errands to run and friends who couldn't possibly be without her any longer apparently. Still, it had given them some much-needed space after the soul-searching on Friday. He had made a real effort to see it from her point of view and this morning, on the drive down, he had been debating whether to speak to the McMahons after all. Perhaps he would call them this evening when he got back. Just to test the water. It would certainly help the atmosphere at home.

In the meantime, he would give this de Souza lead one last try. It was all he had to go on. The only link he could find to Doug Matterling. Which had now come to an abrupt dead end. Literally.

Despite the cold, he spent the next hour wandering around the marina. Mooring lines creaked and halyards rattled against aluminium masts. There was little human activity, but the place seemed very much alive. There was a timeless quality about the sway of the pontoons and the constant gurgling of the water as it swirled around the gleaming hulls. Brennan could see why this place would have a strong appeal to an average office-bound weekend sailor like de Souza. Ownership of one of these yachts was presumably a just reward for a life of deal-making, interminable meetings and corporate shenanigans. He wondered if he was contemptuous or just plain jealous.

'Morning, sir.'

The voice came from behind him, friendly but inquisitive.

'Morning' Brennan said and turned. 'A cold one, though.'

The man behind him looked like a young employee of the marina company. He must have just stepped out of his office because he was not dressed for the cold. He wore navy trousers and a matching sweater with official-looking epaulettes and a logo on the breast pocket. The kind of pocket that would sometimes sport a neat row of differently-coloured biros.

The employee rubbed his hands together vigorously and kept transferring his weight from one foot to the other. 'Are you looking for anyone in particular?'

'No. Just looking around.' Brennan needed to get him onside—he might have information on de Souza's death. 'My boat's moored on the East Coast at the moment and I was thinking of keeping it down here.' It occurred to him that perhaps he should have referred to it as 'she', but it was too late now.

'Come up then' the young employee said, clearly relieved at the opportunity to get back to his office so quickly. 'I'll give you some information.'

Brennan followed him up the steps to his office which was situated above the toilet and shower facilities at the edge of the marina. Once inside, the employee began to rummage through the papers on his desk and pulled out leaflets on the marina facilities and information on mooring charges for the coming year. Brennan examined his host. Mid-twenties, thin, medium height, cropped hair and a smudge of a moustache covering a harelip. Under the sweater he wore a cheap white shirt with a collar that had bubbled in the wash. The trousers finished one stop short of his ankles. His name was on a label above the Blue World logo—*Gary Rogers*. The picture ID hanging on a lanyard around his neck confirmed it.

The office was small and untidy—a desk, telephone, filing cabinet and a notice board with what looked like a duty roster pinned to it. A thin green cabinet under the window. Various bags and boxes stacked against the wall. Brennan noticed a long brown fishing rod bag and a blue plastic box of fishing tackle.

'You've certainly got a great set-up here,' Brennan said. He felt obliged to restart the conversation.

'You'll probably find it a little more expensive than the East Coast, sir. But from here you're out onto Southampton Water in five minutes and we have access at all states of the tide. And with the town on our doorstep, you've got everything you need right here.' He handed Brennan a sheaf of papers. Brennan noticed the size of Rogers' hands, which were far too big for the rest of his body. Fingers like sausages.

'This'll tell you everything you need to know.'

'Thanks. Thanks a lot.' Brennan paused and looked into the boy's lifeless brown eyes. 'I guess you'll be pretty quiet here until the spring, won't you?'

'You'd be surprised, sir,' Rogers said. 'We have a lot of people come down during the winter. Fitting out, maintenance, that sort of thing. And on a good weekend you always get some people going out.'

'Of course, of course. And from here you can keep an eye on everything that goes on, I suppose?'

'That's right, sir. Security is very good here. There's someone on duty every day of the year.'

'And every night?'

This put Rogers on the defensive. He stepped back a fraction and wariness flickered across his eyes. 'Well, not exactly twenty-four hours. But we never have any trouble. Not real trouble anyway.'

Brennan turned as if to leave. 'Didn't I read something about an accident here a couple of days ago. A drowning or something?'

'Ah, yes.' Rogers was prepared for this one. 'Most unfortunate. We couldn't have done anything to prevent it. The owner fell overboard one night. Must have been working on his boat during the week and probably had too much to drink. Stupid really, to be alone like that.'

'Must have caused a bit of a stir, locally.'

'Seems he was some kind of tycoon or something. From London.'

'You knew him?'

'Only to say hello to.' Rogers shuffled awkwardly. 'He was down here a lot. Never seemed to sail though. Just liked to spend time on his yacht.' He looked up sheepishly. 'Entertaining.'

'Entertaining?'

'Well, you know . . . *entertaining*.' His cheeks coloured and he started to straighten his papers.

'Business meetings as well, I should imagine.'

Rogers looked at him quizzically.

Brennan followed up. 'You said he was a tycoon,'

'Well, involved in business, yes. He had quite a few visitors. Some looked like City types.'

'So he just fell overboard, did he?'

'That's right. They found him against the hard. Over there.' Brennan followed his pointing finger. 'Just by those crates.'

'Were you here?'

'Not when they pulled him out, no sir. My day off.'

'How did he get over there? If he fell overboard in the marina?'

'Well, his boat is at the end of E pontoon. E53. You can just about see it from here. It's called *Turmoil*.' He paused, waiting for a reaction. Brennan smiled knowingly. 'The tide must have carried him across. It must have happened late the previous night. No one else was around.' He looked down at his papers again. 'Last shift here finishes at ten in the winter, you see.'

'And in the summer?'

'There's usually someone around until midnight or so.'

'Would that someone usually be you?' Brennan laughed, all mates together now. Rogers smiled weakly, the red in his cheeks deepening.

'Sometimes,' he muttered.

'Is the fishing good?' Brennan nodded towards the fishing gear.

'Not bad.' Rogers was clearly uncomfortable discussing his leisure pursuit, but he seemed to be relieved to move off the subject of the dead man.

'What do you catch?'

'Bass mainly. Sea trout sometimes.'

'Sounds good. I guess you can pick the best spots off these pontoons.'

Brennan looked out at the long pontoons stretching out into the water. Each was T-shaped with narrow finger pontoons between each boat. The last pontoon was G. After that was the slipway leading up to Groom's Boatyard and on the other side was the jetty where de Souza's body had been found. The jetty and the hard-standing above were part of a small promontory, which extended out into the river.

'Thanks for the information,' Brennan said and flapped the papers in his hand. He could tell that Rogers had said all he was going to say.

As Brennan glanced down, he noticed a small brown leather case tucked under the desk. He thought he knew what it was but he wanted to check it out. If it was what he thought it was, it was certainly an incongruous bit of kit for a marina.

He looked up at Rogers. 'Would it be okay if I took some pictures before I go. Just of the marina. And the location. So I can remember it all when I get home.'

'No problem.' Rogers was an ambassador for his company again. 'We hope to hear from you soon.'

As he turned to leave, Brennan let a couple of his leaflets fall to the floor. He bent down to pick them up and looked more closely at the leather case under the desk. It was indeed what he had thought it was—the carrying case for an Uher sound recorder. Ancient kit but extremely dependable and with great sound quality. A professional portable reel-to-reel tape recorder, of the type that had gone out of favour when digital took over. Brennan had worked with a sound engineer many years ago at his first agency who had taught him how to edit audio tape with a razor blade and sticky tape. He still had a reel-to-reel player at home.

He nudged the case a couple of inches across the floor as he groped for the leaflets. It was heavy. The recorder was inside.

He grabbed the leaflets and straightened up. 'That's an interesting bit of gear you've got under there. That old Uher. Years since I've seen one of those.'

Rogers face dropped and his cheeks blazed with guilt.

'Oh that. Is that what it's called? I dunno. I just came across it in the recycling one day. Thought I'd see if it still worked.' He looked hard at Brennan for acceptance of his story. 'I like to tinker.'

'It's a reel-to-reel,' Brennan said. 'Straightforward and robust. Easy to get your levels.' He studied Rogers' face for signs of a puzzled reaction to the term but there were none.

As he opened the door to go, Brennan took a good look at the duty roster on the notice board.

'Thanks again for your help.'

He went down the steps and wandered towards the slipway. He kept pausing to take pictures; Rogers would be watching him. It was lucky that Rogers had not been on duty when Brennan had been taking his photographs from G pontoon on Friday morning. Whoever had been on duty then had presumably been too busy dealing with the discovery of the body to have bothered about Brennan.

He walked towards F pontoon—E would be too obvious—opened the gate and let himself in, trusting that his enquiries about the marina facilities would give him the necessary authority to go to the end of the pontoon. When he reached it, he took a few more pictures. There was a large hotel upriver, on the East bank. *THE HOOP* was emblazoned in huge white letters across the roof. The sea was downriver, with the low promontory jutting out across the water. Across the river was flat marshland. He took pictures of it all then took more shots back towards the marina office, which included all the yachts in between. He made sure to include de Souza's boat, a forty-odd-foot modern sloop with a blue mainsail cover and blue guardrail dodgers that carried its name, *Turmoil*.

For the shots of the boat, he switched to a telephoto and made sure he got several close-ups of the washboards at the top of the companionway steps leading from the cockpit down into the saloon. Then he examined the images on the viewing screen and magnified the ones of the washboards. They were shut tight and looked as though they were locked.

He put his camera away and stood for a minute, watching the water flow alongside the end of the pontoon. A lump of polystyrene floated past, about six inches square. He followed its progress as it passed the end of E pontoon, where de Souza's boat was moored, and then headed towards the hard at the other side of the slipway. The hard that de Souza had ended up against last Friday. The polystyrene curved out into the river as the current pushed it away from the land and for a few seconds it headed upstream before being swept past the end of the small headland and down towards the sea.

Would a body follow the same route? If so, how would it get as far as the pilings? Just because it was heavier?

Brennan checked his watch. Just after ten. He made his way back to the pontoon entrance. Before returning to his car he took some more photographs, so Rogers could see that he was simply being thorough in his research.

He made one last stop. At the Spinnaker Chandlery, just opposite the town quay. There, after a short consultation with an assistant, he purchased one of the large nautical almanacs that were stacked against the counter.

As he walked back towards his car, he thought about the Uher tape recorder. A boon to young reporters of the seventies and their *vox pops*. Easy to operate and robust. He thought about Rogers' flipper-like hands. That old technology would suit him. No stabbing at tiny buttons and touch screens. And easy to operate in the dark. Perhaps while fishing? The perfect cover.

I like to tinker.

Just so, but Rogers seemed to know exactly what Brennan meant when he referred to levels. He could tell from his face. 'Tinkering' was one word for it. Brennan had another.

The McMahons came to his mind. *Bugger them,* he thought. *How are they going to get me justice?*

21

London
   Sunday morning

USUALLY, when Ben Parfitt woke up, his world came slowly and pleasurably into focus. One of the many joys in his life was opening his eyes to see that the digital display gave him another half an hour until the alarm went off. It was a warm fuzzy time when he would gradually remember which day it was; whether it was a workday or the weekend, it would more than likely be a day of opportunity and pleasure. He would then be able to turn over and nuzzle into Naomi's bare back.

Sometimes, he would run his hand down the delicious curve of her hip towards her waist. More often than not, she would then turn to him, half smiling, with a sigh that told him to continue his languid exploration. Without that sigh, they would simply stop there and drift back into their respective worlds of semi-consciousness. With the sigh, they would explore each other with increasing ardour, reinforcing their commitment to each other and, for those few gasping moments at least, keep the rest of the world at bay.

But this Sunday morning, Ben woke up with a crushing feeling of dread pumping through his body and swamping his brain.

It was the first night he had slept properly since she had left and he wished that he hadn't succumbed. Surely it would have been better to stay awake. To have made himself endless cups of coffee and suffered through night-time TV until dawn. At least he wouldn't have had to wake with such a gut-wrenching start to the day. His first Sunday without her.

Half an hour of bitter adjustment later, he swung himself onto the sofa with a mug of black coffee, the *Sunday Telegraph*, the *Sunday Times* and the *Mail on Sunday*. He stared blankly at the *Mail*. Should he cancel it now that she was gone? Or had she really gone? If she were to come back, there was no point in cancelling. But she might take the non-cancellation to be another sign of his complacency and leave again. On the other hand, if he *did* cancel and she came back, wouldn't the cancellation be just another petty, vindictive act on his part?

Before opening the papers, he went back into the bedroom and picked up his wallet from the bedside table. He went to the wardrobe and dug into the trouser pocket of the suit he had worn last Friday. He pulled out Henry's card and returned to the sofa. He opened his laptop and with a few taps transferred twenty-five thousand pounds from his bank account to Henry's.

The phone rang just as he finished the transaction.

'Good of you to call, Henry,' he said. 'How're you doing today?'

It was nine-thirty. He wasn't dressed yet. He had last spoken to Henry late Friday night. They had returned to the office briefly before going their separate ways home. Henry to Limehouse and Ben to Maida Vale.

The Friday night call had been short. Henry had seemed a bit flustered and sounded as if he were having second thoughts. But they had resolved to keep their nerve over the following week and stay with their target mid-price of one hundred and one pence per share to bail out, reasoning that there would be resistance at the one hundred level. They would then be buying at one hundred and three pence. At five grand a point, that would net them a fifty-thousand-pound profit. After that, they would look at going long to take more profits as the price bounced back towards the pre-de Souza one-twenty-five mark. Ben had put down the phone reassured that Henry had the bottle to go through with this.

'I'm doing great,' Henry said now. And he sounded it. 'You?'

'Yeah, great,' Ben lied.

'Great, great. Have you seen the papers?'

'Not yet. Anything interesting?'

'Nothing too dramatic. I've seen a couple of pieces about de Souza. He and his wife seemed to do a lot of society stuff. Always being photographed at previews and that kind of thing. Mind you, she's a bit of a stunner. Have you seen pictures of her?'

'No, no, I don't think so . . .' He was unable to muster any interest in how de Souza's wife looked. It was the company's fate he cared about. 'How about Elba? Any dire predictions?'

'Not that I could see.' Henry sounded distracted. 'I've googled her. Seems to have had a bit of a racy past. One time actress.' He seemed more interested in Carmel de Souza than Elba Technology.

'Nothing on the company then? I guess that's not too surprising if it's still a story for the gossip journos at the moment.'

'I agree. We're in no rush. It would be good to get out by the end of next week, but it could be the week after.'

The week after. Ben groaned inwardly. He had almost forgotten. His trip. He would be away at the beginning of that week. In Hong Kong. His stomach lurched. Not only was he playing with fire by going short on one of his own stocks, he was also getting far too close to one of its major shareholders. He had initially thought that the interest from the Californian VC firm who had invested in Elba was just a toe-dipping headhunting enquiry. But the call from them yesterday had been very specific. They wanted him to fly to Hong Kong with their head honcho.

'*Fantastic opportunity for us to get to know each other better,*' they had said. '*But don't treat it as BWB business. Book a few days of vacation. Let's keep it below the radar.*'

Ben returned his attention to Henry. 'Good to hear from you, anyway. We'll catch up tomorrow.'

He placed the phone back into its holder and viciously kicked a cushion that had fallen from the sofa. The connection was perfect and it flew across the room towards a small, delicate-looking vase perched on a low side table. The vase and its contents smashed against the wall.

Parfitt dropped his head into his hands.

'Oh Christ,' he muttered. 'Not her bloody vase.'

22

Hampshire Coast
Sunday afternoon

IT WAS NEARLY four o'clock when Brennan pulled up outside The Anchor, just across the road from the marina office. The roster in the marina office had shown a day shift and an evening shift. After meeting Rogers, Brennan had gone to The Hoop until after three-thirty and had been afforded a good view of the marina from his window seat. Rogers had not left the warmth of his office all afternoon.

As well as keeping an eye on the marina, Brennan had spent the hours studying the almanac. He was fascinated by the amount of information the book contained. Sections on weather, safety at sea, ports and a large section on tides. It gave the times of high and low tides for the whole year for the UK and the rest of Europe. It also gave detailed information on tidal ranges and, more significantly, the speed and direction of tidal currents at different states of the tide.

Just after four-thirty the office door opened and Rogers emerged, zipping up his jacket and carrying a crash helmet. Brennan hunched down in the car seat and pulled his collar up. Rogers locked the office door behind him. No replacement had arrived. He came down the office steps and pulled out his moped from under them. He set off up the hill away from the town.

Brennan pulled away from the pub and followed at a distance. The buildings thinned out as the road climbed along the valley. They passed a number of campsites before Rogers slowed down and turned into Halliday's Caravan Park. Brennan parked in a small lay-by fifty yards further on.

He turned off the engine and listened to the silence. The wind had dropped away completely. He wound down the window. Nothing. Through the trees he could see a few lights. They belonged to a short row of mobile homes lined up on one side of the caravan park. As his eyes adjusted to the dark, he could see the black silhouettes of the caravans that stood at the other side of the spinney.

He got out of the car and closed the door quietly behind him. He swung a small rucksack onto his back and grabbed his camera bag then set off through the trees. Progress was slow. He had to test each step to avoid cracking branches, which covered the ground. He found himself breathing heavily and his arm ached with the weight of the camera bag. At last he reached the path, which led through the woods and round the outside of the caravan park.

Progress was quicker on the path and he was soon behind the row of mobile homes. There were eight altogether, but only four had lights on. He moved back into the trees so that he could observe them. They all had curtains drawn. The sound of early evening TV seeped from a couple of them. He tried to work out which one might be Rogers', but the moped was nowhere to be seen. It must be parked on the other side.

It looked as though Rogers had settled down for the night, but Brennan decided to stay a while. That Uher had piqued his interest. That and Rogers' reaction when talking about de Souza. He was hiding something.

Brennan was cold and uncomfortable. If only Rogers would go out again, to get a takeaway or do whatever else he might do on a Sunday evening. That would give Brennan his chance. He would give it half an hour.

Twenty minutes later, he was rewarded. The door opened on the furthest of the mobile homes and Brennan briefly glimpsed Rogers as he locked the door and disappeared around the side. A few seconds later the moped coughed into life. Rogers accelerated quickly towards the gate and was gone within seconds. Back towards the town.

As the sound of the bike faded, Brennan was aware of the furious pounding of his heart. He was also aware of how natural this all felt to him. Surprising how a prison sentence could turn your life around. In the opposite direction to that intended. But this felt completely justified.

He ran across the thin strip of grass to the shadows at the rear of Rogers' home. Neither of the adjacent homes seemed inhabited.

There was a small window about five feet from the ground. Brennan pulled off the rucksack, reached in and took out a large screwdriver. He dropped the bag and hauled himself up against the sheet metal of the wall by stepping on the edge of one of the breeze-block stacks that supported the mobile home. The window was warped and at one end there was a gap between it and its frame. He rammed the screwdriver into the gap and prised it open. He heaved himself up and squirmed through the window, landing in a heap on the floor of Rogers' dark bedroom.

The room smelled musty, stifling, a combination of the damp, rotting surroundings and human sweat. Brennan's heavy breathing grew even heavier in the stale air. He crawled to the open door and found himself in the main living area. It was also heavy with Rogers' cloying odour.

Brennan stood up, closed the bedroom door behind him and stumbled to the front door. He clawed at the lock and managed to open it enough to let the cold night air rush in. He stood by the doorpost for several seconds, gulping down the fresh air and listening for sounds of movement from any of the neighbours.

There were still no other lights nearby. He went outside and retrieved his rucksack from under the window.

He took one last deep breath, closed the front door reluctantly behind him and checked that the window blinds were shut. He pulled a car rug from the rucksack and pushed it against the gap at the bottom of the front door.

He grabbed his torch from the rucksack and directed the narrow beam quickly round the room. There were a sofa and an armchair, frayed and dusty. A yellowing bookcase was full of magazines and old newspapers. On top was a small fish tank full of dank, green water. He was surprised to see a dull glint of orange appear momentarily in the thick of it. On the other side of the room was a small Formica-topped breakfast table covered with dirty plates and the packaging from what must have been a week's worth of TV dinners.

He swung the beam back towards the armchair. Between the table and the sofa a large reel-to-reel tape recorder sat on its stand. He recognised it immediately as a Studer, a heavy-duty, professional studio machine. Its polished steel chassis glinted in the torchlight. Brennan had not seen one of these for years.

He squatted by a wooden case next to the Studer. Surely Rogers wouldn't be that obvious—the jerk must have some visitors who would be curious. Brennan raised the lid of the case and found what he had only half-expected—rows of slim boxes containing audio tapes. The kind of tapes that could be used in the Uher and played on the Studer. This seemed to be the one area that Rogers kept tidy, for each box was neatly labelled and sorted in reference order. Brennan looked again at the gleaming tape machine. It was as if all the order and cleanliness Rogers was capable of had been channelled into this one pursuit.

He shone the torch into the case and scanned the labels. Neat block lettering, all in black ink and underlined in red. He pulled out a few at random: *B56 'Pug People and Snorter'*; *B78 'Bunter and Silent*

Blonde; D23 'Blackeyes with Screamer'; D23 'Blackeyes with Low moaner'; D69 'Dream Couple'; D69 'Dream Couple - The Sequel'; D69 'Dream Couple - The Climax'. They were all five-inch reels.

So that was it. Just as he had suspected. Rogers combined his fishing with some voyeuristic eavesdropping. He could picture Rogers on a dimly-lit pontoon, waiting patiently for a bite and listening in to the night-time activities on a nearby boat. *Entertaining* was the word he had used for de Souza. Rogers knew how to get his own entertainment. Brennan was surprised at the imaginative titles Rogers had given to his subjects. Hidden talent.

He continued scanning the row of boxes. He froze when he found them. Three boxes: 'E53 'Grunter and Squeaker'; E53 'Grunter and Blue Eyes'; E53 'Grunter and Miss Proper'. De Souza's berth number. Brennan pulled them out.

He looked around for blank tapes. They were stacked neatly on a shelf behind the case. Brennan removed the tapes he had selected from their boxes and replaced them with blanks. He stuffed the originals into a pocket of his rucksack.

He stood and closed the case's lid. He hoped Rogers wasn't in the habit of listening to his entire collection on a regular basis. And even if he was, this was a theft he couldn't report to the police.

Brennan pulled the Canon from its bag. It was fitted with a 28mm wide-angle lens and an electronic flash unit. He stood at one side of the room and took several shots of the other side, panning and shooting rapidly. He crossed the room to repeat the sequence.

As he brought the viewfinder up to his eye, he heard the faint popping of a moped's engine. It became louder. He shoved the camera back into its bag. The bike was getting closer.

He stuffed the rug back into the rucksack and ran into the bedroom where he pushed the dislodged window lock back into the frame. The moped was right outside now and it flashed past the window before coming to a halt behind the mobile home. Brennan ducked back into the living room and scooped up the camera bag and the rucksack. The sound of the engine died. There was silence.

Brennan guessed that Rogers was taking off his helmet and it would take a few seconds for him to dismount. He still had time to get away as long as Rogers came around to the front door the same way he had left.

Brennan eased the front door open and stepped down onto the wet grass. He swung the door back quickly without letting it slam shut. Then he pushed it closed. The latch bolt of the lock clicked quietly back into place.

Rogers was coming around the side of the mobile home. Brennan backed up to the front and sidestepped out of sight.

He held his breath. Eventually, he heard the front door open and Rogers stepped up into his acrid habitat. The door banged shut and Brennan let his breath out. He gulped cold air to cleanse his lungs of the stench of Rogers' life and then made his getaway, arcing rapidly back across the grass towards the trees.

23

London
   Sunday evening

BEN LAY on the sofa and tried to read at least one article all the way through. The stack of ruffled newsprint on the floor grew higher. He grew more restless. He was killing time.

'Enough of this,' he said and stood up.

It was nearly six and already dark. He was thinking about her too much. Nothing new, just going around in circles. That was enough of brooding over the significance of the Sunday papers in their relationship. He was done with self-pity. It was time to get out and stick to his routine.

He showered, put on a clean shirt and went for a walk. Elgin Avenue, Clifton Road and then down to Little Venice. He walked along the well-lit towpath by the canal, past the houseboats and tiny art galleries. Then he crossed the bridge and turned the corner into Warwick Place for a beer at the Warwick Castle.

This was a Sunday ritual for him. It was when the weekend

started to give way to the work week ahead. He would take his iPad and review the weekend's press share tips and corporate news via a subscription service that condensed it all for him. Getting prepared for the Monday crunch.

He sat in the corner of the pub and looked at his fellow-drinkers. There were a few who had obviously been there since lunchtime; one table in particular was occupied by a group of men who were laughing loudly at each other's jokes and clapping one another on the backs and shoulders. Several hours ago, Ben thought, they were probably sitting quietly together trying to make polite small talk. Great what drink could do.

Right now, he was trusting it to help him forget about Naomi. He found it hard to concentrate on his market digest and bought another pint. At a nearby table, a couple were holding hands and lapping each other up without any hint of self-consciousness. Ben watched them and sipped at his beer. He had seen enough. He finished his drink and stood up.

As he left, two men in long black leather jackets left immediately behind him. He hadn't noticed them earlier and as they stepped out onto the pavement they felt uncomfortably close. Ben turned left and hurried on without turning around. The men followed, only a yard or two behind. But they seemed too smartly dressed for muggers. Ben had even smelt aftershave as they had gone through the door together.

He strode towards the station. He felt the two men quicken their pace but they didn't seem intent on passing. The pavement was wide enough. They could easily get past. He moved across, to give them even more room. Still they didn't pass.

His heart started to race and he realised his palms were sweaty. He broke into a trot past the benches that lined the leafy street. He even looked at his watch, as if to signal that he was late for something. But behind him, they matched his speed. It was too late to run. He felt them close in on him, one on each side. The smell of aftershave and leather swamped him.

He was lifted from the ground and carried for a couple of steps then suddenly spun around and shoved onto a bench. His back struck the metal backrest and he yelped. The guy on the right forced Ben's arm behind his back while the other one grabbed his left forearm and twisted it savagely. His head seemed horribly vulnerable with his arms trapped and his whole body began to tremble.

'Don't move, son,' the man on the right hissed. He stuck his face closer. Early thirties, short black hair, a narrow face and thin lips. Bizarrely, Ben noticed that the man wore contact lenses.

'Just sit quietly and listen,' the other said calmly. 'And don't get any stupid ideas.'

Escape seemed remote, so Ben relaxed his arms and waited for the beating. The men's grips loosened slightly and the searing pain in his shoulders diminished. His heart was still pumping furiously. His body felt drained of any strength.

He turned to look at the one who had just spoken. He looked almost identical to his colleague. Same style of black leather jacket, same short dark hair, same aftershave. They could easily be brothers. If not twins. Probably sharing accommodation and cologne.

Brother One spoke again. 'Just listen. We're not going to hurt you.'

Ben considered debating the last point but decided against it.

The man leant even closer. 'Yet.'

They both twisted his arms and the red-hot pain returned. Ben felt faint.

'Now,' he continued. 'We know about your little scam, Mr Parfitt. And we know how much you need the price to drop this week. We know how much you have at stake.'

This was all about the Elba bet? How the hell were these guys involved? And who had told them?

'Your partner in crime brays into his mobile like a bloody donkey,' the man said as if reading Ben's mind. 'He even stood outside the pub to broadcast his trade. Louder than Bow bells.'

They were being tracked as early as Friday?

'And though you might not think it right now, we're all in this together. We want the same as you. We need that price to hit the floor.'

'What's that got to do with me?' Ben was surprised at the strength of his own voice.

The man's eyes narrowed. Slowly, he pushed Ben's right arm even further up his back. Ben cried out and a gloved hand clamped over his face.

'Another stupid question like that, my friend, and I'll pop this bleeder out.' He twisted the arm again. His narrow eyes were just inches from Ben's. 'Just watch me.'

Ben sagged between his tormentors. The streetlight opposite started to spin around. The smell of their coats was like a leather band being wound around his head. Tighter and tighter. The pain was remote. It was all happening to someone else.

And then he felt a sudden rush of air through his head, yanking his senses back from the brink. His eyes opened and the streetlight snapped back into sharp focus. The smell of leather was immediately replaced by that of his first chemistry set. There was a small brown bottle being held under his nose. Smelling salts.

'We know your reputation,' Brother Two said. 'Listed in the top ten and all that. It seems your skills are held in high regard.'

In high regard, he thought. These guys had never met Julie Grainger. And anyway, what kind of thug used language like that?

'Just don't do anything that'll stop the price dropping like a stone,' Brother One said. 'No Buy recommendations for a couple of weeks or anything stupid like that. Hold off and make your excuses.' He smiled. 'And then we won't have to go drinking together again, will we?'

They released Ben's arms, which was pretty academic now as far as he was concerned; they were completely numb.

Although they were obviously hard men, these guys didn't seem like gangsters. And they certainly weren't common yobs. In different circumstances they were probably quite respectable.

'We will be watching you, Mr Parfitt,' said Brother One. 'And if we don't get what we want, not only will we have another little drink together, but everyone will know about your off-piste activities. You'll be unemployable.'

They both smiled and strode off towards the station. Ben stayed on the bench. There was no one else about. No one had seen their conversation.

He hauled himself upright and tried to shake some feeling back into his arms. He grimaced and stumbled towards Elgin Avenue and home. He remembered the smelling salts. Those guys had known what they were doing.

He only wished that he did too. Being an analyst was supposed to be about poring over financial data—company reports, trading statements, that sort of thing, he thought grimly. This was something else entirely.

24

London
Monday morning

BEN'S MONDAY STARTED EARLY. The previous night had been bad. He had hardly slept, his mind trapped in a racing loop of threats from the brothers of darkness. His body was still racked with pain from their less-than-tender ministrations.

He arrived at the office at seven—it seemed to him that the sooner he could get to work, the sooner this nightmare might come to an end. Even the thought of the inevitable lathering from Julie Grainger had not put him off. Work was normal. Normal was safe. Safe was being in an office with other people just like him. With people who smiled hello and asked how your weekend was. People who drank coffee with you and discussed the footie results. Not people who twisted your arms until your shoulder blades came away from the rest of you and hissed threats at you in the dark.

He scanned Bloomberg for news on Elba. The price was still steady. Not a flicker of interest from the Far East. The *FT* had a small piece on de Souza's accident but no comment on the company. An obituary was planned for the following Friday.

He sent a text to Henry, requesting that they meet up later.

His office phone rang and he picked it up slowly. It was the call he had been expecting. Julie had just got in and wanted to see him straight away. Her assistant spoke slowly and clearly. There was no room for pleasantries. Just information that had to be conveyed as efficiently and unambiguously as possible.

FOUR HOURS LATER, Ben left the building and made his way to The Astronomer. He found Henry in the same corner they had occupied last Friday. Henry was staring at his phone. He acknowledged Ben's arrival with a grunt.

'How are you now, Henry? Tell me the worst.' Ben slumped down next to him.

'One-nineteen.'

'Shit.'

'Yeah. Shit.'

There was a long silence as they contemplated their bet. The price was moving against them.

'Don't want to cut our losses, do you?' Ben asked the question half-heartedly. He wasn't sure what he wanted to do, but a paper loss closing in on twenty-five grand in just a few hours seemed to merit some kind of discussion.

'Not really. You?'

'Nah. Not yet.' There was another long silence, both of them staring blankly at the crowded bar. 'Early days, I suppose.'

'Yeah. Early days.'

'Drink?'

Henry had already set up a couple of beers.

'Cheers.'

They drank their beers slowly.

'Food?' Ben offered, eventually.

'No thanks. Not hungry.'

'Nor me.'

Another long silence.

'Henry?'

'Mm.'

'I'm in a bit of trouble over all this.'

Henry suddenly looked even more worried.

'Don't tell me you haven't got the readies.'

'No. It's not that. I made the transfer yesterday.'

'Thanks. Because at this rate, it looks like we're going to need the lot.' He took a grateful slug of his beer. 'So Julie's being Julie, is she? I heard you got a bit of a tongue-lashing this morning. It was all over the office. And it sounded like she was pasting you all over hers.' He smiled in commiseration. Ben didn't smile back. 'But this morning's price recovery will put her in a better mood. I wonder what's behind it?'

'That's not the problem. I knew the bollocking was coming this morning. As if de Souza croaking it was somehow my fault. And I've got to draft a Buy Note by Wednesday morning. I wasn't expecting anything else.'

He peered at Henry. 'But things have got a bit more complicated.' He paused. 'I had an interesting encounter yesterday evening. I was approached by a couple of chaps who also seem quite keen on Elba's price going south.'

Henry smiled. 'A couple of traders, eh?'

'Possibly. But I got the distinct impression that there was more to it than that.'

'Why?'

'Come with me.'

Ben rose and led the way to the men's toilets. Once inside, he slipped off his jacket, undid his tie and unbuttoned his shirt. Henry looked around uncomfortably.

'What is this?' he muttered.

Ben took off his shirt and turned to show Henry his back. 'That's what they did to me last night.'

Henry's eyes widened as he stared at Ben's tightly-muscled upper arms and shoulders. They were black with bruising. Both sides, almost equally. A continuous bruise from deltoids to trapezium.

'Jesus Christ, Ben,' Henry said and took a step back. 'Have you been to hospital yet? That looks pretty serious.'

'Not yet. I think it'll be okay.' He put his shirt back on. 'It looks worse than it is, now. It was agony last night.'

'I can imagine. So where did these guys come from?'

'No idea. Just came out of nowhere. Outside my local. They roughed me up, told me not to talk Elba up and left. No idea who they were.'

'Perhaps they're connected with the company itself.'

'Possibly. I don't know. Anyway, I needed to tell someone. Just in case something else happens . . .' He couldn't believe what he was saying.

'You'll be okay for your trip next week though, won't you? The jolly to Hong Kong you were telling me about?'

'Hopefully, yes.' He stared at Henry. 'There's another thing. Something that came out of the blue.' He glanced around at the empty stalls and urinals. 'These guys also know about our short. They overheard you on the phone to IG on Friday evening.'

He led the way out of the toilets and back to the table. Henry crumpled into his chair. His face was as white as his shirt. Anyone would have thought Henry had been on the wrong end of the consultation with the aftershave brothers.

'If something else happens,' Henry said at last. 'You said, "if something else happens". How do you mean?'

'God knows. All I know is, they're not the kind of blokes you'd willingly get involved with.'

Henry drained his glass and it rattled on the wooden tabletop as he put it down.

Ben straightened his jacket. Henry was more squeamish than he had imagined. Those bruises must have triggered a bad memory. Something had shaken him. Ben should never have shown him.

'Don't worry, Henry. This kind of thing doesn't happen in Big Pharma.'

'I hope not.'

Henry didn't sound convinced. And he didn't sound like he was thinking about the past. It seemed to Ben that Henry's attention was on the future. More specifically, on Henry Evans' future.

25

London
   Monday lunchtime

BRENNAN HAD BOOKED a table at the Bombay Brasserie for lunch. Neutral ground for his meeting with Fiona Wells. She had seemed flattered when he had phoned her just a few hours ago. Of course she would love to meet up again. And anyway, she hadn't been there for ages. The Conservatory? Wonderful.

The name of Elba's PR firm was listed on the Investor Relations page of their website. And if anyone knew about awards ceremonies the company was involved in, surely it would be their PR firm.

Lovell and Yarde were named, as a 'communications agency that utilises creativity and expertise to deliver the highest standard and deliverable results' according to their website. Whatever that meant. He had discovered that the account manager handling Elba was a Fiona Wells. Could it be the same one? A quick search of LinkedIn confirmed that it was. The same Fiona Wells who had done some work for Brennan Matterling several years ago.

As soon as she rushed into the restaurant—half an hour late, long blonde hair flowing behind her, hand on brow, peering around with a show of anxiety—he knew she would dominate proceedings. He was waiting at their table, sipping his Kingfisher, outwardly composed. When she saw him, she stopped and waved, as though relieved he had waited. She flashed her brightest smile and picked her way through the tables to him.

She leant over and air-kissed his cheek. A rush of coconut shampoo and meadow-sweet perfume hit him hard. She quickly sat and positioned her bag on the floor beside her.

The mental adjustment took several long seconds, both of them imagining the other as they had looked some years earlier and now seeing a different picture. It was like a prelude, an orientation to the new reality.

'So good to see you again, Mike. So, so good.' Her smile was set to maximum voltage, like an actress on a chat show nervously readying herself for an interview.

'Great that you could make it. You look fantastic.'

It was true. She did. A million-dollars fantastic—a modern Grace Kelly. Classic, even features, blue eyes, blonde hair, big smile. Tall, narrow-waisted and curvy. Simple white blouse, dark blue suit, pencil skirt, sheer stockings, high heels. The complete power package.

She had changed so much since they had first met. She had been the PA to a friend of his but it was obvious she was going to go far. Even then she had been filling in for her boss at meetings and gave the distinct impression that he was subordinate to her.

After they had ordered their meals, she was soon in full flow, filling him in on what had happened after he had left BM.

'And of course his job was taken by Pete Jarvis,' she said. 'You remember him?' She looked up enquiringly but Brennan could tell that her eyes were asking another question: *Were you really a founder of Brennan Matterling? Were you ever that sharp?*

'Sure, I remember Pete. We worked together on a few things. Worked out very well. What's he up to now?'

'Didn't you hear?' Mock disappointment in those eyes, quickly replaced by a flash of excitement at being in the know.

'He flipped.' She threw her hands up to the ceiling. 'Went doolally tap.' She looked at him enquiringly again, as if to check that he had linked the term to their current location. He had. 'It was all too much for him. Gave away all his shares to the staff and went to join an ashram in Colorado. Left the wife and kids in Woking with his Armani suits and a huge mortgage.'

Her large red lips smiled at him but they seemed to be asking, *Is that what happened to you, Mike Brennan? Couldn't hack it anymore?*

'I'm surprised you hadn't heard,' she said.

He had to play along. Otherwise he'd be dead in the water. The testing had started.

'That's incredible,' he said. 'He always seemed to be so much in control to me.' He paused and looked into her eyes. He lowered his voice. 'Perhaps he still was.' That would give her something to think about.

If it did, she did not let it deflect her. 'It left a gap at the top, of course. So there was a big shake-up.' She smiled her widest smile, those full red lips against large perfect teeth. 'And that's when I moved to Lowell & Yarde. Everything fell into place. Thanks to you.'

'To me?'

'You made a lot of introductions for me when I was doing that work for you. You opened some important doors for me.'

'It was my pleasure. And it looks like you've made the most of the opportunities.'

She was practically purring with satisfaction. She enjoyed the world she moved in. She loved the corporate game. She was young and bright. Everything to go for. Nothing to lose. He felt an undertow of jealousy.

She was giggly and attentive throughout the meal, hanging on his every word. Examining his face, checking his hairline, taking in his choice of suit and shirt.

They continued with the trade gossip. A game of bat and ball. She would throw a name at him, he would knock it back. This lunch was supposed to be an information-gathering exercise for him but he was beginning to feel that it was the other way around.

'So Mike, why the interest in Elba Technology? On the phone you said that you were writing something about them. Is journalism your new career?'

'I'm doing a series of articles for the *FT* on personalities in business. I was just starting a piece on Victor until . . . well, until the unfortunate accident last week. I wasn't going to take it any further but the *FT* called me over the weekend and asked me to complete my research. They may use it in an obituary.' He paused, but she didn't look quite ready to respond. He led her in. 'As the company's PR agency, you seemed to be the best place to start. Perhaps you could give me a bit of background on the company. And the directors.'

Her smile was on full beam again. She was back on centre stage and would get as much fun out of the situation as possible. As if settling down for a long meeting, she put down her fork and slipped off her jacket.

'Victor joined the company about twenty years ago when they were based in San Jose. He moved here when they developed the virtual reality division. Took the company public about eight years ago.'

She seemed to pronounce Victor's name with something more than professional respect.

'Married?'

'Yes,' she replied steadily. 'Carmel.'

'Family?'

'Only hers. Two children from a previous marriage. Husband died in a microlight crash. Novel way to go.'

'She must be devastated. Especially after the previous loss.'

'Must be. I've never had any contact with her.' She said this without regret and quickly moved on. 'Let me tell you about the FD.'

She worked her way through the board of Elba Technology, singing the praises of the other directors. She had already formulated the strong-management-team-that-can-withstand-the-loss-of-the-MD story that she would be putting out in the coming days.

'What about this Charles Salinger?' Brennan asked. 'He's listed as a shareholder with about four per cent of the company. He's the only individual on the list of major shareholders. The rest seem to be institutions.'

He had found an article in the *San Jose Mercury News* archive on Elba raising cash from a venture capital firm. Salinger had been quoted, saying this would enable the company to expand internationally.

'Wasn't he a director as well?' Brennan asked.

'No longer. He retired when they had the restructuring. That was about the time when—' She stopped short, obviously having second thoughts. 'It was about a year ago,' she finished.

'Ah, I see. About the time I went on my little holiday.'

'Oh, Mike, I didn't mean to—'

'It's okay. Public knowledge. Not a problem. It's over now. I served my time. Back into society as a reformed character.'

'It was dreadful,' she said. 'False accounting? No one could believe that you were behind it. And a prison sentence? A real miscarriage of justice. Everyone thought so.' She looked genuinely dismayed. She lightly touched his sleeve.

'Everyone?'

'Well, you know. Everyone who knew you. Everyone who knew you and Doug Matterling. We all knew it didn't ring true.'

'I appreciate that. But it was me who carried the can. Doug made sure of that.' He paused. 'He knew Victor, didn't he?'

'Did he? Not that I was aware of. But I couldn't keep up with everything Victor did. He was a dynamo, an amazing man.'

'Yes, I bet he was. Just a pity I never got to meet him.'

'So, that's what it was all about?'

'I'm not sure I follow you.'

'Your interview with Victor. You said you believed they knew each other. Is that your interest?'

'Not particularly.'

'Good. That wouldn't be a particularly fruitful route to follow.' She looked at him with concern and then broke into a mischievous grin.

'So tell me about chokey. I'm fascinated. What was it like?'

'Like? Pretty grim most of the time. The rest of the time it was *very* grim. Not recommended. Despite what you read in the papers.'

She let her shoulders fall back slightly so that her breasts rose against her blouse. Her lips pursed and she looked straight into his eyes.

'I hope you got your conjugal visits.'

Brennan blinked at her. Where was this coming from? And had that been a warning about Matterling?

She smiled coyly. 'I'd need them twice a day. At least.' She studied him for a reaction. He gave nothing away.

This wasn't seduction, he thought. It was just raw sexual power. She had it and knew how to use it. He remembered that he had nearly made the mistake of confusing the two when he had first met her.

He said, 'You're assuming you'd be the same person then as you are now. That doesn't happen. Ever.'

She sat up straighter. 'Is that a line you've crossed, then?'

'You could say that.' This was not the direction he wanted the conversation to take, but she was trying to establish something about him. And it had nothing to do with sex. It was just a diversionary tactic to knock him off guard. Another probe.

'The wrong side of the law?' she said. 'Is that where you are now?'

'That's a strange question.' It was uncomfortable, but she had hit the nail on the head. 'Back to Salinger,' he made himself say. 'He was one of the founders, wasn't he?'

She acted impressed and shot him that thousand-watt smile again. 'That's right. In the eighties. You have been doing your homework.'

He smiled at the compliment. Good boy. But she had got her answer.

'Why should he leave the company at this stage? How old was he?'

'Over sixty. Old enough to retire, I suppose.'

She finished eating and folded her napkin neatly to dab her lips. Brennan watched her closely, transfixed by the clear white skin of her hands and the perfectly manicured crimson fingernails. A gold bracelet slid down the smooth alabaster of her forearm.

'Did he leave on good terms?'

'Not really. But you'd have to talk to him about it. I can't comment, as I'm sure you understand. Victor would never say anything negative about him. Or anybody, for that matter.'

She broke off and smoothed out the folded napkin on the table-cloth. When she looked up, Brennan knew that he was right—de Souza had been more than a client to her. They both knew she had let him look too long into those large eyes. It was her turn now to be put on the spot. She had revealed too much to him.

'I was there, you know. When they discovered his body. When they pulled him from the water.'

Her chin dropped. She was silent for a long time, her fingers doggedly working the creases from the napkin.

'The police were there as well. Routine, probably. Whenever a body is found in a river.'

Eventually she looked up at him again. Her eyes were brimming with tears. A bumpy red rash had appeared below her collarbone and her left hand instinctively went up to hide it from view.

Could she be the 'Blue Eyes' of Rogers' tapes? Brennan had listened to them briefly last night on his old reel-to-reel machine. Just to confirm the type of recordings they were. The muffled pantings and moanings held no fascination for him.

'Might it have been anything other than an accident?' he said softly. 'Would the police be looking for anyone else?'

'Not that I know.' She gathered her bag and jacket in one movement. 'Excuse me for a minute,' she said and disappeared towards the toilets.

A waiter appeared and cleared the plates. Brennan pulled a piece of paper from the inside pocket of his jacket. When Fiona returned and sat down, he put it on the table in front of her.

'That's a picture of Victor and Doug Matterling together at an awards ceremony,' he said. 'In the States somewhere.'

She looked at it blankly. 'So that *is* what you're after.'

'There's a connection. As well as researching Elba I want to find out what Matterling is up to these days. I'm sure you can understand that.'

'If I were you, I would keep my distance. There's nothing to be gained by going back to it. Doug Matterling's a very different person to you. Just go your own way.'

Another warning. She *must* still know him.

He changed tack. 'We're not so different. We share a determination.'

Fiona closed her eyes and let the tip of her tongue roll gently across her lips. She seemed to be coming to some kind of decision.

'Okay,' she said eventually. 'Let me help you.'

'Help me?'

'You're not the kind of man who cannot ask for help, are you?'

'No,' he said quietly, hoping he was being truthful.

'I'm sure I can find a number for Charles Salinger. That'll provide you with some history for Elba.' She paused and her eyes widened. 'Then let me tell you about Carmel de Souza's current whereabouts. That might help you draw your own conclusions about Victor's death.'

26

California
Monday afternoon

KEN OLSON WAS proud of the fact that Olson Associates' offices had been designed by one of San Francisco's most innovative young architects. Someone who had been at the early stages of her career and had gone on to help create some of the city's most iconic modern buildings. The twelve-thousand square foot space had been carved from the first floor of one of the Presidio buildings at the northern end of the city. Cold concrete columns and ridge skylights had been replaced with warm, wood-panelled corridors and whitewashed meeting rooms. Large doughnut-shaped acoustic panels hung from the ceilings. It was an exemplar of modern office design.

Ken was sitting in one of the meeting rooms, opposite two fresh-faced young executives. They were both dressed in chinos and casual shirts. One shirt was striped and the other checked. Both men looked like they had not long graduated from college. Both were already dollar billionaires.

All three were examining a two-page investment proposal that had taken Ken most of the weekend to prepare. It was headed:

Confidential
Elba Technology plc - Proposal to Take Private.

Ken leant back in his chair. A lacquered, white swivel chair with no seat padding. It was functional rather than comfortable. Which was intentional. This was not an environment that encouraged long meetings.

He looked across the white table at his companions. Although he had founded the firm nearly twenty years ago, he now depended on the next generation of investment professionals to drive the business forward. He resented no longer being the sole arbiter of which investments Olson Associates made but he knew he was lucky that Peter Hands and Jim Milic were still happy to serve as members of the investment committee. They certainly didn't need the money but both owed a debt of gratitude to him for starting them off in their stellar careers. After leaving him, both had gone on to work with Sequoia Capital, where they had made crazy money and now they were running their own funds. Between them, they had been involved to some degree in many of the West Coast blockbusters, either directly or with a tiny percentage through a syndicate.

Both were regulars in the *Forbes* Midas List of top venture capital investors. Jim Milic had been featured on a *Forbes* cover last year, a black and white shot of his head next to his upward-pointing finger. The finger had been painted gold.

Jim and Peter smiled big toothy smiles at him.

'I like the space,' checked shirt—Peter Hands—said. 'VR is certainly compelling. I've done two deals here just in the last month.'

'I agree with Peter,' Milic said, 'and it's good that they seem to have thought through where this could go. I like the whole shopping experience aspect. We'll never have to leave our houses at all when this shit kicks in.' He laughed. 'And I like that.'

'Putting aside this whole problem with Portentao7,' Hands said, 'and assuming we can get a result there, I see two other areas of concern.' He glanced down at the table. 'The first is the one that you broached when you called this meeting. You know, the relationship thing with the widow—er, Mrs de Souza, I mean. And the other, of course, is that the company's British. That can be a problem.'

'You mean with the compensation?' Ken asked.

'You bet. The Brits never want to give anything back. They spend half their working time devising schemes to inflate their salaries and retirement plans. Then they never seem to do anything with it.'

Ken winced. This was one of Peter's bugbears and he had known it would come up sooner or later.

'That's fair comment. Let me deal with both issues. First, Carmel. Yes, we've been involved for some years now. It's just something that happened. Neither of us can do anything about it. It's there. And it's serious. But this deal would be based on tangible investment criteria. I haven't gotten that soft.' He looked up to gauge their reaction. They were both smiling. Ken doubted either of them had ever had a proper relationship with a woman in their lives.

'All the data behind these numbers,' he indicated the sheets in front of them, 'are on the server in the usual place. I've called it Round Three even though it would be an offer for all the shares not held by ourselves or by the de Souza family.' He paused for a moment. 'How about you, Jim? Would my relationship with Carmel be a problem for you?' Put so directly, Ken hoped that it would not.

Milic reddened. 'No. Not at all. I can't see it being a problem as long as the rest of the case stacks up.'

'Great,' Ken said conclusively, as if that ended the matter. 'Now, to come onto the question of compensation, or remuneration as the Brits call it; we have never really had that problem with Elba. I know what you mean Pete, and I think it's a cultural thing. We kind of have the assumption that once a guy has made it then he has some kind of obligation to his community. That just doesn't seem to exist over there. They just seem to work on the basis that as long as they pay their taxes then their government will look after everything.'

Hands raised his eyebrows. 'And they're getting worse. Every year it's getting worse.'

'But what about the Elba board?' Milic said, bringing the conversation back to the matter in hand. 'How greedy are they?'

'They're fine,' Ken said. 'Nothing excessive and they've all got options which will kick in with our offer. I would then propose setting up a new scheme for them with a three-year vesting period. I think they would recommend our offer. And when we trade the company on in a few years, it'll very likely be to a US buyer.'

'Well that sounds okay then,' said Milic. 'Now what about the offer price?' He studied the summary sheet. 'You're looking at a premium of about twenty per cent on the current market cap. Would that be enough?'

'It would be if we can get control over Portentao7. That's the big question and I think we need to bring in Mrs de Souza at this stage to help answer it.'

The two billionaires looked at each other questioningly. They were obviously not expecting anyone else to join the meeting.

'Great,' Hands said. 'That'll help a lot. If we get the right answer on that, we're looking at funding of about eighty-four million UK pounds?'

'That's about it,' Ken said. 'Plus fees, of course. As you can see, the current market capitalisation is about one hundred million. We hold ten per cent and the de Souza family trust holds twenty per cent. If we can get control over Heilong's twenty-nine then we would only need to get acceptances from another thirty-one. We could get the final ten per cent under the compulsory acquisition rule of their Takeover Code.'

'How about leverage?' asked Jim. 'You don't seem to have anything in for borrowing.'

'That's right, I don't. The CEO passed away last week and we need to be decisive if we are going to make the most of this opportunity. This deal has got to be done quickly. I'm proposing that we are the lead investor and get only two or three others involved. I've got meetings scheduled with Granular and Redstone tomorrow—assuming we're all happy to proceed this afternoon. I think our commitment would be about sixty per cent of the eighty-four needed. It would be all equity.'

'And exiting?' Hands asked. 'Is this three- to five-year horizon realistic?'

'Absolutely. The current development cycle will complete in two years and as you can see from the summary, the offering will be pretty exciting. Those projections are very conservative. The upside is mind-blowing.' Ken smiled. 'Literally.'

He rose from his chair and strode to the door. 'Time to meet Carmel de Souza, gentlemen.'

He pushed one side of the wood-panelled door and it revolved open. He put his head outside and smiled at Carmel who was seated in the reception area. He motioned for her to come in.

As she entered the room Ken could see that she was having the effect he had hoped for.

'Carmel, may I introduce you to two of the Bay Area's finest investment minds, Peter Hands and Jim Milic.' He turned to the table. 'Gentlemen, Carmel de Souza.'

The two young men rose awkwardly from their seats and shook hands. They made minimal eye contact. Carmel smiled broadly at them as Ken showed her to a seat at the head of the table.

Her dark hair was scraped back into a long ponytail and her clear olive skin showed no sign of travel fatigue after the flights from London to Santa Barbara and then up to San Francisco. Neither did she look like a grieving widow. She was calm and completely composed.

'Peter and Jim have now had a chance to look at the figures and see whether they can endorse my proposal to take Elba private,' Ken said. 'But before coming to any conclusions we do need to assess the situation regarding Portentao7. It will be key to whether or not an offer can be made.'

He looked at the other two members of the investment committee. 'As you are aware, unfortunately Carmel lost her husband at the end of last week. However, she has been able to discuss her family's interest in Elba Technology over the weekend and she would be fully supportive of such an offer in order to secure the financial future of her family.'

'Please accept our condolences on your loss, Mrs de Souza,' Milic said. 'I trust that it will not be too strenuous for you to have this kind of discussion so soon.'

'Not at all.' She smiled. 'Victor and I had not been very close for some time. Even though his death was a shock, I can deal with all this. It needs to be resolved as quickly as possible. I've got to look after my sons.' She paused for a moment then said, 'Although we were no longer close, Victor was a good man. He provided for his family and made certain arrangements to ensure that we would be looked after. His shares in the company were put into a trust several years ago for our benefit. And when he got involved with this consortium in Hong Kong, he ensured that he had ultimate control over their investment.'

'What was in it for them?' asked Milic. 'Why invest if you give up control?'

'Victor was always concerned that the company not be sold too soon. He knew the technology would be attractive to the large multinationals and that one day it would be taken over. But he wanted to control that. He wanted the investors to do well and get a good return but he didn't want them putting pressure on him to sell quickly. It was all part of the investment terms. All the money came through a broker over there.'

She waited for the next question.

'As I understand it,' Hands said, 'this company, Portentao7, actually owns the majority shareholding in Heilong Partners, the Hong Kong company. And Heilong owns twenty-nine per cent of Elba.'

His question was to Carmel, but Ken responded. 'Correct,' he said. 'And Portentao7 only has one share. A bearer share. The company is registered in Anguilla. And the bearer share is held for Carmel's benefit.'

'In England?' Hands asked.

'No,' Carmel answered. 'In Hong Kong. At a private bank.'

She opened her small red leather handbag and took out an embossed white business card which she placed carefully on the table in front of her.

'There's the address. And my contact there. That's where the bearer share is.'

'So,' Milic said, 'it's just a matter of someone collecting this share certificate and getting it back to you. And then you'd have control over Heilong?'

'Only the Brits could come up with something this devious,' Hands snorted.

Milic ignored his colleague. 'And you would then agree to us buying the Heilong shares?'

'That's right,' Carmel said. 'I trust Ken. The company would be in good hands. Holding onto our shares for another few years will be the best thing for my family. It's what Victor would have wanted.'

They all looked at the business card on the table. There was a long silence.

'Shall I take it?' Ken said eventually. 'I'll go to Hong Kong myself.'

They all stared again at the card. It was a standard-sized business card. Three and a half by two inches. The name and address on it were in English and Cantonese. Its significance was not lost on any of them, least of all Ken. It could be the key to them taking over a hundred-and-twenty-million-pound company.

Ken leant back in his chair. He had done all he could. All the preparations had been made, even so far as booking the flights for him and that Parfitt guy at BWB. He knew his pals at Granular and Redstone would follow him into the deal. They had been co-investors on many others over the years. But he couldn't do anything without the approval of his investment committee.

Carmel glanced at him and gave a small smile.

Milic studied the summary sheet in front of him again. He nodded at Peter Hands. 'I think you should go, Ken. It all looks good to me.' Then a long pause. 'Peter?'

Hands puckered his lips and squeezed them between thumb and forefinger. Eventually, after looking around the table and making eye contact with everyone—including Carmel de Souza—he said, 'Sure. Why not?'

27

London
Tuesday morning

BRENNAN GRABBED his jacket from one of the silver hooks by the front door. He had spent a sleepless night in the spare room, which he had been using as a study since his release. He and Sarah had hardly spoken since he had returned from lunch with Fiona Wells. He felt like he was under observation.

'So, you're off again?'

Sarah was standing at the bottom of the stairs, arms folded across her chest, shoulder against the hall wall.

'I'll be back by Cara's teatime. This guy lives on the coast near Brighton. It shouldn't take me long. He's keen to meet me.'

Brennan thought back to his brief telephone conversation last night with Charles Salinger. He had expected the man to be defensive and evasive. But he was just the opposite. He wanted to meet as soon as possible. Fiona must have primed him.

'Keen to meet you, eh?' An edge crept into Sarah's voice. 'Let's just recap on progress since we spoke on Friday, shall we? Just so I can get things clearer in my mind.'

He fiddled with the zip on his leather jacket. He knew what was coming.

'Saturday, you looked after Cara most of the day.' She spoke deliberately as if reading from a prepared statement. 'That was appreciated.' She gave a measured nod of respect. 'It helps mum, who by the way, has been Cara's sole parent-in-attendance for the past twelve months. Thank you.'

'Sarah, I don't think sarcasm—'

She spoke over him. 'Then on Sunday, you travelled to an unknown destination to meet someone whose identity you have decided not to share with me. You were out for most of the day. Sunday used to be a family day once upon a time. So thank you for that.'

He kept his mouth shut. She was not finished.

'Then yesterday you decided to have lunch with someone you used to work with in the good old days. Someone who I do vaguely remember as an unashamedly self-centred, ambitious bitch who would be as likely to genuinely help another human being as jump naked from Tower Bridge in the middle of winter.'

She was challenging him to respond. Brennan had not dwelt on his lunch meeting with Fiona. He had known how Sarah would react.

'But full marks for effort on that one,' she said. 'At least it was related to your previous career. A scintilla of hope that there might be some kind of connection to gainful employment in the future.' She smiled bitterly for a second and then it was gone. 'And now we have another jaunt. To Brighton, no less. Why not have a trip to the seaside, Mike? It's not as if you have anything more pressing to do. Or worry about.'

It was all very predictable, he thought. He knew she was simmering about the whole job thing. He had been hoping that she wouldn't come to the boil quite so soon. He just needed a few more days. But now, there was only one thing for it. He had to tell her everything. Tell all and hope. Hope that she would see what he could see and get on board.

'I understand. I do. But there's a very good reason why I've got to meet this guy today. He was one of the founders of Elba Technology. He knew Victor de Souza from the early days.'

'You're just not going to let this go, are you?' Sarah said and her voice trembled. The sarcasm had gone. 'This Victor de Souza is not going to lead you to Doug Matterling. And he's not going to get you what you want. That's an impossibility. Doug's dangerous. We both know that. So why not just leave him alone. I'm sure he's not interested in us anymore.'

'But it just doesn't add up. I'm not sure his death was accidental.'

'Go to the police then,' she snapped. 'Tell them to investigate. What business is it of yours? Or *ours*? What's Victor de Souza got to do with *us*?'

Brennan took a step towards her.

'I will go to the police, I promise. If I find something they aren't aware of, then I'll take it to them. But at the moment I don't know any more than them. Or any more than they can easily find out.' He thought about Rogers' tapes and the women de Souza had *entertained* on his boat. 'Victor's widow, for example. Carmel de Souza. I know she left England for California on the day his body was hauled out of the Hamble. Well, the police know that too because they contacted her there.'

'How do you know?'

'Fiona told me.'

Sarah snorted and wrinkled her nose.

'Mrs de Souza was in California with her boyfriend,' Brennan went on. 'Known him a long time, apparently. Runs a venture capital fund that had invested in Elba Technology.'

'So you think this boyfriend was behind Victor's death?'

'I'm not saying that. I'm just saying that the police will already know this stuff. I've got nothing new.'

Sarah pushed away from the wall. She looked as though she was finished with the conversation. 'If you're just padding around behind the police you're probably going to get in their way. Let them sort it out. That's their job.' She let out an exasperated sigh. 'It's like our conversation on Friday never happened. You just don't seem to get it. And as for our new sleeping arrangements . . . I think it's best we make that permanent. Don't you?'

'No, I don't. But it works for now. Until we get through this . . .' He searched for the word. '. . . this difficulty.' Her expression told him he had found the wrong one. But no word would have been right. She was closing down on him. He had to get her on his side.

'You said something interesting,' he said.

She eyed him suspiciously. 'When?'

'Just now.'

Her eyes narrowed.

'When you asked whether I thought Mrs de Souza's boyfriend was behind Victor's death.'

'Was he?'

'Who knows? But it means you can see that it might not have been an accident. That it could have been murder. And I agree with you. I've been looking at the currents in the river when de Souza supposedly fell overboard.'

'The currents?' She stared at him. 'Mike, what are you talking about?'

'That part of the river is still tidal. The tidal stream at the time of his death was pretty much the same as when I was there on Sunday morning. I've checked the tide tables and the tidal atlas.'

'You have?'

'And the current would have taken him out towards the middle of the river. There's no way a body would have been swept from de Souza's yacht up to the jetty where it was found.'

Sarah didn't say anything for a few seconds. Brennan could see that she was churning through the possibilities. He had managed to pique her interest. Now he had to stretch that to an endorsement.

'Victor de Souza was a serial womaniser. There were a lot of husbands with sufficient motive to have him sink to the bottom of the river.'

'Including Doug Matterling? Is that what you're thinking? How do you even know that they knew each other?'

'I've seen a picture of them together. But Doug didn't have a wife or a girlfriend as far as I was aware. Certainly not when we knew him. Unless you knew any different?'

Sarah shook her head slowly. 'No. He never told me about anyone.'

Good, Brennan thought. *She's contributing now.*

He said, 'I just need to find out a bit more about Matterling and Victor. To make sure Matterling wasn't involved. Just a few days. Then I can get on with the job-hunting and leave the police to find whoever wanted de Souza dead.'

Her brow was still creased.

'I know how you must feel,' he said softly. 'All that time alone. Your husband locked away, out of reach. And now he's back with you, he's running around on this fool's errand.' The corners of her mouth turned up a fraction. 'But I'm here for you and Cara. I'm all yours as soon as I know that Matterling is not involved with this death. It won't take me long.'

'And then you'll leave it to the police?'

'Absolutely.'

'You'll let them dig into Victor's affairs?'

'Dead right.'

'And deal with his widow?'

'Of course.'

'And forget about Doug Matterling?'

'Who?'

She smiled a tiny half-smile. Brennan patted his pockets to check he had his keys. He looked at his watch. 'I've got to go. We'll talk more later. I'll be back this afternoon.' He took a couple of steps towards her and kissed her on the forehead. Then he turned and looked up the stairs.

'She's still asleep.' Sarah sounded matter-of-fact now. She was back in charge of the house. 'I'll get her up in a few minutes.'

He walked back down the hall and opened the front door. 'I'll see you later,' he said.

As he closed it behind him he let out a long sigh of relief. He would soon be taking in the sea air. How bracing.

28

Sussex Coast
Tuesday morning

BRENNAN RECKONED it was what they called a 'modern marine residence'. A large whitewashed slab of a house facing the sea on Shoreham Beach, a few miles west of Brighton. It had taken a couple of hours to get here. A couple of hours thinking about Sarah.

The garden comprised a square of shingle, bordered by dark grey paving. A single large cordyline was situated dead centre, like a spiky palm tree. The house's architectural style was square. Large windows and flat roofs. White and grey paint, wooden panels for effect. The same style had been adopted by many of the new builds on the street.

Last night's call with Salinger had given him hope. The man had been courteous and said he would be very pleased to help Brennan with his piece on Elba Technology. It was a great story and he had seemed pleased that it would soon be told.

Brennan parked on the wide street and walked up to the lacquered front door. He pressed the doorbell. No chimes, trumpet fanfares or sirens, just a short, high-pitched buzz. A no-nonsense announcement that told visitors exactly what to expect.

There was an immediate flurry of activity and the door opened almost at once. Salinger had been watching and waiting.

'Mr Salinger?' Brennan said. 'I'm Mike Brennan. Thanks for agreeing to see me.'

They shook hands.

'No problem,' Salinger said but Brennan realised that this was not true. It *was* a problem. A big problem.

Salinger's face was drawn and his dark eyes flickered from side to side. He was tall and rangy with strands of reddish-grey hair combed back over a freckled scalp. A patchy grey, paprika-flecked beard was spread over translucent skin and a double layer of bags hung below his eyes.

'Come in,' Salinger said and led Brennan up the stairs and into the living room. The sea-facing wall had two huge picture windows set either side of quad-fold doors. Light poured in and bounced off the polished pine floor and white walls. It was bright enough to make Brennan squint. The other walls were bare. There were two over-stuffed white armchairs in the middle of the room, facing each other across a coffee table, laid up with a coffee jug, two cups and saucers and a plate of chocolate digestives.

In the far corner of the room was a large Sony TV and another corner was occupied by two huge Apple computer screens on a plain white table with a white Quaker chair. Apart from that, nothing. Not even the sea-scanning telescope that Brennan imagined was oblig-atory for this kind of room. No pictures, no sideboard, no books, no sofa, no knick-knacks. Brennan smiled to himself—this guy would have no comprehension of *knick-knacks*.

'Great view,' he said cheerily. The tide was full and waves rose in sheets from the steeply-angled shoreline. It was like being on the bridge of a ship. He liked it.

Salinger in person was different from Salinger on the phone. This one was nervy, uncomfortable with someone in his home.

'Please, take a seat.' Salinger waved vaguely at the two armchairs. So, he didn't even have a favourite chair, Brennan thought. A lot was going on with this man. Territorial but completely unpossessive. And as taut as a violin string.

Salinger shuffled towards the window and closed the blinds. Bland vertical blinds of the type usually found in offices, not homes.

'Coffee, Mr Brennan?'

'Please.'

Salinger poured the coffee slowly.

'So, Mr Brennan, what's your connection to Elba Technology?'

Straight in, no small talk. Brennan would have been surprised if it had been any other way.

Salinger sat back, leaving the full cups on the table to cool. He touched his hands together in an arch, fingertip to fingertip. He looked hard at Brennan, his eyes finally still, his gaze steady.

'No direct connection,' Brennan said. 'But as I said to you on the phone, I'm a journalist. And I'm writing a story about Victor de Souza.'

He paused, seeing if Salinger would jump in. He didn't, but his head lowered slightly and his lips tightened.

'I want to find out as much as I can about him,' Brennan went on. 'And his company. I know that you knew him well. Before his unfortunate accident last week.'

Salinger's eyes narrowed. He seemed to be deciding whether to trust Brennan or not. There was silence as Salinger made his assessment.

Brennan shifted uncomfortably in his chair. Eventually, he said, 'So you helped found the company back in the eighties?'

'I did. With two American colleagues in Goleta, California.' Salinger was obviously on more comfortable ground now. 'It started with a contract from the US Government. But you probably know all this, if you've already done your research.'

'My research is only just starting. But the company's history seems fascinating. And I'd appreciate hearing about it from you. From the horse's mouth.' He smiled and reached for his coffee.

'Thank you, Mr Brennan.'

'Please, call me Mike.'

'Mike?' Salinger tried it out with obvious distaste. 'No, I don't think so. And please, call me Mr Salinger. I never could stomach any of that fake chumminess. Even after all those years in America.' He took a sip of coffee that seemed barely enough to wet his lips. 'It started as a small contract. To help the Department of Defense come up with a way to connect all the different types of computers that they were using all over the place. To see if we could get them to communicate together. It was a new concept then, of course. Most people didn't see the need.'

He paused, reliving the challenge of it all. 'For example, how could an IBM mainframe connect to a DEC PDP?' He looked at Brennan in a way that indicated he did not expect a reply.

'By creating a new level of language?' Brennan offered. His grasp of network development was shaky but extended to this basic idea. 'One that sat on top of the proprietary operating systems?'

'Exactly, Mr Brennan, exactly. You *have* been doing your home-work.' Salinger's eyes were flickering again. 'And it worked. It was copied and developed by other companies. And the whole huge business of computer networking was born. And then the internet, of course.'

Brennan was impressed. Could this frail, isolated man have been instrumental in creating the internet?

'How did Elba fare?' he prompted. This was going to be a diffi-cult one to square with the development of the internet. After all, it was a relatively small company.

'Yes, yes. I get your point. And you're right. Unfortunately, companies are run by people. People get distracted. They pursue different dreams. And fall out.' He wrinkled his long nose. 'Our company suffered more than its fair share of the consequences of human frailty. But we still managed to carve out a share of the bridge/router market. Even if we did have to hang on to the coattails of the likes of BT and Nortel.'

As they drank their coffee, Salinger gave him a potted history of Elba's pioneering work with computer networks. He seemed very comfortable talking about the technology—data packets, token rings, thin Ethernet, thick Ethernet. Brennan struggled to keep up.

'And what about the capital behind it all?' Brennan said. 'Were there many rounds involved?'

'We seemed to spend half our lives with the venture capital boys,' Salinger said. 'Presentations and interminable due diligence. Berkeley were good to work with, though. They were the lead investor then.'

'And Ken Olson?'

The name seemed to take Salinger by surprise. 'Yes, that's right. Our contact partner there was Ken Olson. How do you know him?'

This was a turn-up, Brennan thought. The very same guy who had lost Brennan Matterling plc three hundred thousand dollars when he had set up his own outfit.

'My research,' Brennan said. 'It turned up that Berkeley were an early-stage investor and I came across Olson's name when he worked for them. Just a guess that he might have been involved.'

Salinger's eyes narrowed again. He was not wholly convinced but Brennan pressed on. 'When did Victor de Souza take the helm?'

'We were hit hard by the defence cut-backs in the nineties. We needed more funds to survive. He dealt with all of that.'

'You were happy with that?'

'I've never been an administrator. That's not what visionaries do. Let me show you what I mean. Your best starting point might be over here. Follow me.'

He put down his cup and levered his long body out of the armchair. He crossed the room to the computer screens and sat on the white chair. Brennan followed. As he approached, he noticed a box under the table. It was full of masks, like snorkelling masks, but bulkier. Different sizes, all with wires attached.

Salinger moved the mouse and the two screens came to life. Both showed Wikipedia pages. The left screen showed the entry for *Charles Salinger*. The right one showed an entry for *Bearer Instruments*.

'I'll just close this,' he said quickly. Brennan saw that the entry was a redirection from *Bearer Shares* before the screen went blank. 'That's not important. *This* is what I wanted to show you.'

Brennan thought otherwise. Bearer shares could be very important. Terry had taught him about them learned during his alternative MBA. They were shares that were not registered to anybody. So, whoever held them owned them. Terry had even produced a twenty-pound note to demonstrate the principle. He had read out the small print on the front — 'I promise to pay the bearer on demand the sum of twenty pounds'—signed by the Chief Cashier of the Bank of England. 'Of course,' he had said, waving the note in the air, 'this is just a promise. A promise to exchange that note for twenty gold sovereigns. An empty promise now, of course. But a bearer share is an entitlement. An entitlement to a share of the company.'

Could bearer shares be connected to Elba Technology?

Salinger sat back to give Brennan a full view of his Wikipedia entry on the left-hand screen. 'That's your starting point. That'll show you what I've been involved with over the years.'

'Impressive,' Brennan said, not sure how boastful Salinger might get but still intrigued that he had been so quick to close the other screen.

'It is. And it's very comprehensive. I've even been working on it this morning.'

Brennan was taken aback. He had never thought about people working on their own Wikipedia entries. But of course that was entirely possible. He had assumed that a third-party endorsement would be involved, but this was a different angle. The platform was probably full of self-important nutters writing about themselves.

'I work on it most days. Accuracy is a commodity that's in increasingly short supply.'

'That's great, thank you.' Brennan leant towards the screen to show his interest but then stepped back towards the armchairs. He did not want to get drawn into studying Salinger's life, line by line. 'I'll look at it in detail when I get back.'

Salinger stayed put for a few seconds, lingering in front of the screen. Then he slowly raised himself and went back to his armchair.

'As you can see,' he waved around the room, 'I have never really taken to people.'

Brennan stayed quiet. They looked at each other for a long time. Brennan was rapidly reassessing. Salinger nodded as if reading Brennan's thoughts.

'There are no pictures of family or children or grandchildren. No art on the walls, no decorative furniture. You may think it is sterile, lifeless.'

Brennan kept his peace.

'I think it is the opposite,' Salinger said. 'This room is full of the future, full of possibilities, full of hope. It doesn't look back. *I* don't look back, Mr Brennan. I touch the present through my two tunnels into the here-and-now.' He pointed at the TV and the computer. 'But then I think of the future. I think of what might be.'

The future? Brennan thought dismissively. *When you spend half your life editing your own Wikipedia entry?*

'I know what you are thinking, Mr Brennan. You are trying to reconcile my focus on the future with my chronicling of history.'

Brennan tried to look innocent and shook his head.

'You would be wrong to look at time so simplistically. After all, the most important dimension is the here and now. That is where we find happiness, is it not?'

Brennan could feel another reassessment coming on.

'We might feel optimistic about the future; we might feel satisfied with the past. But real happiness is only to be found right now, in the present.' He leant forward. 'And do you know why that is?'

'Why?' He had to be indulgent now. He had to let Salinger finish this homily.

'Control, Mr Brennan. Happiness is having control.' He flicked his hand in the air, swatting away all conflicting theories. 'There is no point in brooding on matters over which you have no control. That is the road to mental purgatory. Happiness comes from the stories we tell ourselves. And if we control them, they can become *wonderful* stories. About the world, about ourselves.'

'I see what you mean. I think.'

'It's not just me. Epicurus said the same thing two thousand years ago.' When Brennan did not respond, he said, 'Look him up.'

'That's some more research for me, then. But I've got to work on this article about Elba. Is there anything more you can add?'

Salinger paused for a long time. Eventually, he said, 'Elba have moved reality way beyond the virtual. They are developing software that helps with those stories we tell ourselves. Elba are developing the opposite of *malware*. Some call it *blissware*. It is far more powerful than the echo chamber we can create for ourselves through social media and content choice on our streaming services.' He picked up his coffee, looked at it for a moment then put it down again, untouched. 'Soon, we will each live in our own worlds, worlds that have been created around our simplest likes and choices. Worlds in which there is no blame or punishment. The feeling of being in complete control is pure contentment. We can do no wrong in our world. It's only other people's worlds that are wrong.'

Brennan flashed back to the world of his recent past. *No blame or punishment? he thought. Sign me up.*

'Sounds dangerous,' he murmured. 'For everyone. Inside and outside these worlds.'

Salinger smiled a slow, knowing smile. 'And extremely profitable for those helping to develop those trusting worlds. Profitable in many ways. Think about what you could create with that much power over so many minds.'

'But what about de Souza? Can you tell me something about his contribution to Elba's development over the years?' Brennan could see that the old boy was spinning away into sci-fi fantasies.

Salinger pulled himself out of the chair again, signalling the end of the meeting. Brennan remained seated for a few seconds before rising reluctantly. Pulling the conversation back to de Souza had undermined the rapport.

'I know what you want, Mr Brennan. Better than you do. You are on a fishing trip. And I know where the big fish are. As you can tell, I am not used to visitors. But I agreed to your request for a reason. In any relationship there has got to be a certain amount of *quid pro quo*. So, before you go, I must give you something.' Salinger's hooded eyes were darting from side to side again. His body was tense, his head quivering slightly. 'And, of course, I will expect something in return. A sprat to catch a mackerel, you could say.' He smiled, obviously enjoying his fishing metaphor.

'Sure,' Brennan replied automatically. Salinger had turned from a frail old pensioner with a potential grudge against his old employer, into a self-important egoist, then into a philosopher with a threatening agenda. 'Whatever I can do.'

'Good. She said that you would be pleased to help and that you knew a lot of people in the City.'

She did, did she? He must mean Fiona Wells. But hadn't Salinger just told him that she hadn't said much? She had obviously cleared it with him before passing Brennan the phone number.

Salinger reached into his cardigan pocket and pulled out a plain white card on which was written an address and a telephone number. He gave it to Brennan. It was a London address.

'You may remember that I referred to human frailty a few moments ago. And you probably thought I was referring to other people. I was. But I am also susceptible.'

Brennan held his gaze, determined not to break this fragile trust.

'And now I am paying the price. There is no need to go into details at this stage. Suffice to say that I am being blackmailed. And the pressure is becoming intolerable.'

Brennan kept quiet again. Salinger was volunteering a lot of information.

'That is the number I have been told to call when and if I succumb. But they don't want money. They want my shares. They want my shares in Elba Technology. And they will pay above market price for them.' He moved towards the door. 'Not such a bad deal, you might think. Especially when you consider what they have on me. But I want to know why. I am sure that you, as a journalist, can find out for me.'

Brennan nodded blankly. 'I'll see what I can do.' It was all he could think to say. Fiona must have painted him in a glowing light. A City boy, who could be useful to Charles Salinger. Who, in turn, was very keen to talk about Elba Technology but reluctant to talk about Victor de Souza. There had been some kind of scrap between the two men. But he was being diverted away from that and pointed towards some security firm near Fleet Street.

Salinger was at the front door. He opened it slowly. 'If you can help me in this matter, I will give you all the help you need with your story. I will also tell you all about our friend, the late Mr de Souza.'

Brennan stepped out onto the apron of bland paving. He pocketed the card.

'As I said, Mr Salinger, I will do my best.'

He turned to say goodbye, but the door was already closed.

29

Hong Kong
 Tuesday afternoon

DOUG MATTERLING PEELED himself from the smooth back of the young prostitute. He rolled off her and swung his feet onto the floor. He was breathing hard but recovering quickly. She lay motionless, her face burrowed deep into the overstuffed hotel pillow. Matterling took in the long slender body, splayed out on the white sheet. Jet black hair spread across the pillow. She had told him her name but it had not registered. It did not matter to him. They were all the same. Just serving a purpose. Just letting him look after them. Like he wanted to look after Mama before he was taken away from her.

The girl on the bed shuddered. She was sobbing into the pillow.

You pathetic tart, he thought. You don't deserve me. You don't know how lucky you are to have me protecting you. I wish I'd had a fraction of this at your age.

Outside, the grey Hong Kong afternoon was closing in and

ominous-looking cumulus clouds were building over Tai Po. A clap of distant thunder echoed between the high-rises of Kowloon.

Matterling turned on the bedside lamp.

The girl started to bring her legs together. He heard the movement and pushed them apart again roughly, a tight grip on the back of each knee. His hands were strong and her body tightened, waiting for his next move. She stopped crying and he heard her breathing quicken. Her fingers clutched at the pillowcase.

He paused and released his grip. He had no need for her now. He grabbed his wallet from the bedside table and pulled out two banknotes, which he pushed between her buttocks.

'Two hundred dollars,' he said and paused to sense the panic rippling through her. Two hundred Hong Kong dollars would hardly cover the cost of the red lace underwear that he had pulled off her less than an hour ago.

'U.S. dollars.' He pushed the notes further into her with a sharp prod of his forefinger. 'For the first two times.'

She said nothing but started to sob quietly again.

He plucked another note from the wallet and threw it onto her back. 'And there's another hundred. For what I just did to you.'

And I can do with you whatever I want.

He slapped her right buttock hard. She let out a muffled yelp. He did the same to the left one and she gasped again. He eased himself to his feet and pulled on a hotel robe. He was smiling now.

Mister Bountiful.

He bent over her and picked up the last hundred dollar note with his teeth. He closed his eyes and inhaled, drinking in the mixture of sweet and sour smells on her body. When he reached the two notes poking out of her he paused, letting her think he was going to take them back. Abruptly, he straightened, opened his mouth and let the bill float down onto her back again.

'As if I would,' he whispered. *'After all, I'm the one looking after you, right? I'm the best relationship you're ever going to get. All in the space of an hour. You lucky, lucky girl.'*

He turned away from her and picked up his suit jacket. He pulled out his mobile phone and punched in a single digit. The call took a few seconds to connect and as it did so, he stared absently at the naked human being sprawled across the bed. She had ceased to exist for him.

The tune at the other end of the line was a jangly piano rendition of *My Old Man Said Follow the Van.* A woman's voice eventually answered.

'You know who it is, Hazel. I just need to make sure that every-thing's in hand. Everything that we've discussed.'

He listened to the response and then cut in.

'Okay, give me the details when I see you. I want to know that we're on track. I've got a few things to take care of when I get to London.'

He ended the call, slid the phone into his jacket pocket and picked up the room telephone. He pressed the button for the concierge.

'Taxi to Chep Lap Kok. Ten minutes.'

He crossed to the bathroom still holding his jacket.

At the door he turned to the bed and barked, 'Two minutes to get out. By the time I've showered I want you gone. Understand?'

She pulled herself onto her knees and twisted towards him, a tiny smile flickering at the corners of her mouth. Her mascara was smudged and her tears had flattened on her cheeks.

'Of course, dahling. I hope I make you happy.' Her voice was robotic, her eyes blank.

She didn't need the two minutes. By the time he had hung his jacket and robe behind the bathroom door she was dressed, even applying a defiant slash of red lipstick before slipping out into the corridor of the Eight Dragons Hotel.

30

London
   Tuesday afternoon

IT HAD BEEN A LONG AFTERNOON, but Ben had stuck to his task. It was now after six and just a few people were left in the offices with a few more in the dealing room. London trading had finished over an hour ago, but the evening shift was continuing. A much quieter atmosphere, just a handful of dealers talking to New York, keeping the deal flow going.

Ben reviewed his work. A six-page analysis of Elba Technology plc—post-chairman de Souza. The report was much more than a damage limitation exercise, much more than the knee-jerk, steady-as-she-goes statement the market would be expecting from them. This was a positive Buy recommendation.

He leant back in his chair and swung his feet onto the desk, dislodging a pile of the research papers that were stacked next to the monitor. He read his work again, more appreciatively. He was pleased with the balance he had struck between detached analysis of the facts and figures and a barely-contained enthusiasm for the company's prospects. Anyone reading it would be convinced that, although untimely, de Souza's departure was probably the best thing that could have happened to the company. Not so baldly stated, of course, but it did not need much reading between the lines.

He flung the paper onto the desk and clasped his hands behind his head. He closed his eyes and smiled to himself. Julie would purr when she read it. It was just what she was after. And she would see him for what he was—a master tactician, a market natural, a predator who could turn disaster into opportunity. She loved that. He needed to impress her to have any chance of saving his job. If it had been in jeopardy before, it would be even more precarious after he went AWOL.

He clicked the Elba tab on his London equities window. The price was creeping up. Close to their short being stopped out. He pulled up a list of today's trades. It seemed pretty busy, a steady number of smallish trades but nothing that jumped out at him. His new Warwick Castle friends wouldn't be so happy with what he had just written. But he would be a long way away when they found out.

He thought about tomorrow's timetable. Julie would look at the analysis at eight. Barring any other major developments, she would then give it Alpha status. At eight-thirty it would be emailed to over two thousand brokers, journalists, clients and traders. Hard copies would also be couriered to the one hundred most influential of those recipients. The rest would receive a copy by post. The forty-strong Bavaria trading team would be briefed at eight-thirty and during the day each of them would be expected to make at least ten calls to clients telling them about the recommendation.

The mighty Bavaria Williams Burnett selling machine would get behind the note and over the next twenty-four hours a similar operation would take place in Frankfurt, New York, Tokyo and Singapore. Julie was one of just half-a-dozen BWB executives who could assign Alpha status to a circular and he knew she was anxious about Elba. It was a minor stock but she couldn't just let it bomb, certainly not in these circumstances. After all, she had her reputation to think of.

He would contact Julie again from the airport just before his flight to Hong Kong and concoct some emergency that had arisen. He had managed to get a last-minute economy ticket with BA. The flight was due to leave at six-forty in the evening. He would arrive there five days earlier than planned but at least he would be well away from the aftershave brothers. He would have plenty of time to impress this Ken Olson next week—he would let him know tomorrow that he wouldn't be flying with him on Sunday. Ben would think of a story by then—a family emergency, that kind of thing. Survival was just a day-to-day matter now.

Ben needed a drink. The last five hours had taken it out of him. He had been in solitary confinement but the end of the sentence would be the sight of Julie's face when she read his Elba circular. He could not afford to think about anything else. He had not taken any calls or responded to any messages. He had only been thinking of one thing. Without that, he would have no chance at all.

He stared at his monitor and the envelope icon flashing in the corner of the screen. He knew he had mail—he always did. But he didn't want to open it just yet. He would leave it until tomorrow. It might all just be routine stuff. But as he got up to leave, he felt his stomach churn. Just as it had when the note came this morning. He looked at the flashing envelope again. He knew they would have his email address. It would be the next logical contact.

He turned out the light. It could wait until morning. He had things to do. The first was to get himself drunk. The second was to find a place to stay for the night. Somewhere safe.

31

London
  Tuesday night

BEN FELL THROUGH HENRY EVANS' front door. Henry helped him onto a flat leather sofa which was shaped like a surfboard.

'Need a drink, Ben?'

'That would be great.'

'Brandy okay?'

'Perfect.'

Ben sat up straight and put his head in his hands, elbows on his knees. He had had a skinful already but he suddenly felt in dire need of a nightcap. The more he drank, the more he needed to drink.

'Thanks for the invite,' he said to Henry. 'It came just as I was leaving the office.' He glanced at his watch and realised that had been nearly three hours ago.

'That's okay. After all, what are mates for? I knew you were under a bit of pressure. With that report, that is.'

'Look, I'm sorry about the timing of this. It couldn't be worse for our—'

'No problem. We'll talk about that in a minute. Let me get the drinks first.'

Henry stepped into the kitchen area. Ben had never been here before. Henry was living the City dream. His flat had been created on the top floor of a Limehouse warehouse, which had once been used for storing hemp and rope. There were no rooms, just masses and masses of space. Strategically-placed, ultra-modern furniture served as dividers. The rope motif had been carried on around the walls, with all types of cords and hawsers displayed in chunky silver frames. The walls looked like the original brick but they had been clear-lacquered. Everything was on show.

Henry returned from the far reaches of the kitchen with two large glasses of brandy. Ben noticed the enormous six-burner cooker which even had knee-level levers to control the burners. When had Henry last used that? This flat wasn't Henry at all.

'Great pad, Henry. How long have you been here?'

Henry sat down on what looked like a giant coiled turd. He took a closer look and realised it was another rope. A foot thick, coiled a few times with a cushion on top. Was that the worst thing he had ever seen or was he just pissed? He couldn't tell.

'About a year, now.'

'It's great.' Ben lurched forward as one of his elbows slid from his knee. He forced himself to refocus on Henry. 'And what about the decorations? All this great rope stuff?'

Henry looked flattered. 'Well, I can't take all the credit for that. My sister Zoe got involved. She's studying Interior Design at Goldsmiths.' He looked around as if seeing it all for the first time.

'Yeah. It's great. Looks like she threw herself into it.' Ben paused. The focusing was getting increasingly difficult. 'Thanks for putting me up tonight. It's appreciated.'

'Not a problem. But what took you so long? Were you still working on that report?'

'That took most of the day. And then I had a few at Balls Brothers. I hooked up with Dermot and that lot from Credit Suisse.' He took a gulp of brandy. 'Elba's price isn't looking too good. Not for our enterprise. It hasn't come back yet. I can't understand it at the moment. There haven't been any upgrades that I can see. The only news is negative.'

'So, no major changes to the report? You're still going with Overweight?'

'Absolutely. I'm praising Elba to the skies. New price target of one-three-five. I'm seeing Julie at eight.' He looked at Henry apologetically. 'I'm sorry that she's jumped on this so quickly. I just don't have any choice.'

'As I say, no problem. It's your job. Anyway, things will look better for you in a few days. Julie'll be off your back and you'll be the star analyst again.'

Ben grimaced. 'But we're taking a bath right now. We'll have to bail out first thing tomorrow. Let's hope we're not too late and we don't get stopped out first.'

'That's what I wanted to tell you. I could see what was happening this afternoon and I've closed the trade. We've made a loss but not as bad as it could have been.'

'You have?' Ben tried to focus on Henry again but gave up and took another slug of brandy. He was pleased Henry had taken the initiative but surprised that he had not tried harder to make contact. They had been in the same building all afternoon; Henry could at least have come for a chat.

'I hope that's okay with you,' Henry said. 'I knew you were tied up with this Buy Note. Do you think Julie will give it an Alpha?'

'Pretty sure.' He paused again. 'You know, I was around this afternoon. I was in—'

'Mm. That should do the trick then.' Henry leant back on his coil. 'I'll transfer back the balance from the margin you deposited. Only a few grand, I'm afraid. If that. You win some you lose some.'

'Thanks, Henry. I'll need it. I might take a few days off after I've seen Julie tomorrow.'

The room was starting to swim around him now. He felt drained. Henry hadn't let him finish his question about the lack of consultation today but he decided not to push it. He would bring it up again in the morning. They had cut their losses and he hadn't lost the whole amount of the margin. He should be grateful for that. He should also be grateful to have a safe haven to retreat to.

'Don't blame you, Ben.' Henry grinned and got to his feet. He took Ben's glass.

'I think you need a top-up before settling down on that surfboard.'

32

California
Tuesday afternoon

A TODDLER SAT on the edge of the pool below them and splashed his feet, instantly disturbing the serenity of not only the water but also of the whole gardens. His parents sat either side, smiling proudly as his destructive little feet scissored away.

Ken Olson and Carmel de Souza watched him play. They were sitting in the tearoom of the Japanese Tea Garden in Golden Gate Park. Two cups of Genmaicha green tea were on the table in front of them.

They were leaning into each other and gazing out across the hall and the gardens beyond. Carefully-sculpted shrubs and manicured grassy slopes surrounded by streams and fountains. Every stone had its place and all around was order and precision.

Carmel felt Ken's hand on her thigh. She placed her hand on his. The warmth from his hand reassured her. They had been together now for four days. She felt a solidity between them that she had not felt before. Or had not let herself feel before.

Since she had told him about Victor on Friday, he had been busy getting ready for yesterday's investment committee meeting. He had been at meetings with the co-investors this morning too but this afternoon he was all hers.

She knew he was enjoying showing her his hometown. Most of their time together had been spent in London and they had spent several long weekends together in Santa Barbara where her other sister lived, but they had never spent time together in San Francisco. Carmel analysed her feelings towards Ken now that Victor was dead. It didn't really feel any different. She had never felt guilty about their relationship. It had always felt like a natural process. Ever since they had first met. And anyway, to her Victor had been dead for a long time.

The afternoon was cold but dry and clear. The gardens were quiet, a few knots of tourists and some parents with young children. The toddler by the pool in front of them had temporarily stopped splashing and was trying to manoeuvre an outsize chocolate cookie into his tiny mouth. His parents encouraged him in his efforts, poking their fingers into the gooey mess to help it on its way. They beamed at him and at any visitor who caught their eye.

'Thanks for inviting me to the meeting yesterday,' Carmel said. 'I'm pleased your partners were keen.'

Pleased was an understatement. The enormous sense of relief had been so tangible she had felt she could hold it in both hands.

'You were dynamite. They lapped you up.' He placed his other hand on hers and met her eyes. 'It'll be a great investment from our point of view. And it'll give you and the boys financial security.'

She smiled and turned her gaze back to the toddler and his mouthful of goo. Things were falling into place. At long last. All the pain had been worthwhile. The penance could now lead to absolution. She just had to trust that Ken could pull this off. It would provide the perfect solution. Now that she believed in them as a couple.

But she chewed at her lower lip and felt her stomach start to churn in that familiar way. The feeling that had started after her father's sudden death when she had been only thirteen. And then Steve's accident. And now Victor. Victor's was different, of course.

'Don't worry about us,' Ken said as if reading her mind. 'We'll put a proper shareholders' agreement in place to protect everyone's interests in all eventualities.'

'That'll be good.' The stomach churning slowed. 'I don't have a very good track record, after all. Two husbands dead already . . .'

'I'll take my chances.'

He put his arm around her and pulled her close. She let her head drop onto his shoulder. This was what she needed. And it had to be constant. She needed absolute dependability. Even though it was very difficult for her to give, she needed it to be given to her. Those were the rules. And so far, Ken seemed to understand them.

'You are very beautiful, you know,' he whispered into her ear.

She sighed. 'I don't think so. You don't really know me.'

He squeezed her shoulder to say that he did not agree.

'Come on,' he said. 'Let's go for a walk. There's a lake made of gravel that I'd like you to see. Incredibly peaceful. It's behind the temple.'

They finished their tea and made their way out into the garden. The path to the gravel lake took them over a small stone bridge and they stopped on it to gaze at the Koi carp below, which were nibbling at the moss under the bank. On the other side of the pool, a shabby-looking tourist in a grey tracksuit was taking pictures of the bridge and the carp. Ken led her over the bridge and past the man with the camera.

'Nice light for you, this afternoon,' Ken said cheerily.

The man looked startled and lowered his camera.

'Yeah, right. Cheers.'

When they were out of earshot Carmel turned to Ken. 'That guy nearly jumped out of his skin when you spoke to him.'

'Just being friendly.'

'Did you catch the accent? Sounded like a Londoner to me.'

'There's plenty of Brits here this time of year.'

She turned and looked back towards the man with the camera. He was pointing it straight at them.

33

London
   Wednesday morning

BEN WOKE UP IN A SWEAT. The surfboard had been as uncomfortable as it looked. His head was thumping. He remembered
drifting off last night and wondering how a two-million-quid gaff
couldn't include a spare bed. No one ever comes to stay, Henry had
said. Ben could believe it.

At least he had slept a bit. The three bottles of Rioja and the
brandy chasers had sent him off. But the effect had boomeranged at
three in the morning when he had woken with his heart beating like a
jackhammer and his brain racing. The next few hours had been
purgatory, with images of Julie and the leather-coated brothers
jostling for position as chief executioner. And his legs stuck in treacle
as he was trying to escape.

He swung those heavy legs onto the cold floor and felt for the
pressure point at the back of his head, which he hoped might turn off

the banging behind his eyes. Through the pain he could hear Henry coming towards him.

'Here you go. Looks like you need it.'

Henry held a small tray bearing a glass of orange juice, a packet of Ibuprofen and a glass of fizzy, cloudy water. Next to the water was an empty packet of Dioralyte.

'Orange juice and Dioralyte,' Henry said. 'The perfect hangover cure. It's nearly seven.'

Ben groped for the pills and popped four from their seals. He swallowed them quickly, gulping down all the juice and then the Dioralyte.

'Thanks.' He wiped his mouth with the back of his hand. 'I had a bad night. Visions of Julie twisting my balls while my new friends with the aftershave kicked the crap out of me from behind.'

Henry winced. 'Shit, it's not going to be that bad. You'll feel fine in a few minutes.'

Henry was wearing red and blue striped flannelette pyjamas. The last time Ben had seen anything like them was on his grandfather. Christ, they even had the cord at the waist. This was obviously not an area over which Henry's overzealous sister had any influence.

'After all's said and done,' Henry said, '*we are* living in a civilised country, with a certain amount of law and order. I know you've had a bad experience with—'

'Shut up, Henry. I've got to use the bog.'

Ben struggled upright and headed for the bathroom. He was feeling worse than when he had woken up. He managed to use the toilet and roll back towards the surfboard. Perhaps he should sit down for a few minutes.

Henry had dressed, ready for work. He was tidying away the bottles and glasses from last night.

'If you want anything for breakfast, I'd suggest the Pret on the corner. Turn left outside. It's about thirty yards away.'

Ben sat back on the sofa and felt around for his watch. He eventually realised he was still wearing it. Seven fifteen. Julie would be expecting him at eight. He grabbed the blanket beside him and pulled it up to his chin. It was one of those tartan jobs that people used to put over their knees at football matches. Henry probably still would. A bowling ball was crashing around inside Ben's head. Julie would have to wait. He'd go in later. He was sick.

His head felt heavy again and exhaustion crashed through his body. He wanted to keep his eyes open but they narrowed to slits. He could hardly see. There was a clean smell suddenly, close by. He could just make out Henry's face, a couple of feet away. Henry was pushing him back into the sofa.

'Probably best if you get some more rest, Ben. You can go in later. I'll tell Julie that you're ill. I'm sure she'll understand.'

Henry's tone was different. Not so hesitant. More purposeful. Ben closed his eyes. There was nothing he could do about it. His body shrunk into itself. His brain was still kicking faintly and he felt a final weak tremor of anger. It was aimed at Henry. But there was no fight left.

Sleep swallowed him whole.

34

London
Wednesday morning

IN A MODERN BLOCK on Long Acre in Covent Garden, Brian Kesey showed Brennan into his office.

It was completely different to the last time Brennan had been here, a couple of years ago. Back then, there had been rows of legal textbooks lined up in dark wooden bookcases behind Kesey's antique oval partners' desk. The volumes had covered all aspects of company and commercial law. CCH, Sweet & Maxwell, Butterworths binders, going back years. Clients would sit opposite them and be reassured by all this legal expertise at their disposal. The side tables had been piled high with client files. Further reassurance. This guy had plenty of clients and plenty of experience.

Now it was as if the arch declutterer, Charles Salinger, had paid Kesey a visit. There was a single conference table, all glass and steel tubes, six modern-looking chairs and two computer screens. And a large TV screen on one wall showing Sky News without the sound.

'This is a change, Brian. What happened to all those dusty books that you never read?'

'Progress, Mike. Progress. It's all on there now.' He waved at one of the computer screens.

Kesey looked well, still trim and raring to go. Brennan calculated that he must be about forty-five by now. His hair was more grey than black but he still had plenty of it. The only sign of the passing years was a darkening under the eyes. And the glasses had changed. He had gone for the type of light clear frames favoured by his fictional American counterparts in TV law dramas rather than the heavy Joe Ninety-style he had once favoured.

He gestured Brennan towards the conference table. Brennan smiled to himself. Not for them the traditional lawyer/client positioning either side of a grand desk. No, now they would be sitting side-by-side, bunkering down to plot their next move against a hostile world. This was the lawyer telling his client that they were all in it together. A council of war.

Kesey grinned broadly as they sat down. 'Well, well. It's great to see you again. You're looking good. Her Majesty's hospitality obviously suited you.'

Brennan managed a brief smile. The flattery was second nature. But at least Kesey didn't beat about the bush. He always dealt with things head-on. Brennan had always liked that about him.

'Thanks. The world seems like a different place now, as you can imagine.'

'And Sarah? How is she? She took it all pretty hard, as I remember.' The grin had gone and he was leaning forward with his elbows on the table.

'Let's just say she's also going through a period of readjustment.' Brennan shifted in his chair and moved on. 'And you? Still playing hard to get?'

'Unfortunately not. Just the same old same-old. Work, work, work. But I haven't ruled it out altogether. Just don't want to make the same mistake again.'

Brennan remembered Kesey's messy divorce. It went all the way to the High Court and cost him a fortune. Even lawyers had to pay lawyers sometimes. The poor sod was probably still working to pay for it.

'Keep looking. You never know.'

Kesey gave him a smile that said it just wasn't going to happen.

'Thanks for seeing me at such short notice,' Brennan went on. 'I hope you didn't mind me calling you at home last night. I'm glad I still had your number.'

'No problem. My planned meetings don't usually start until nine-thirty so I've got time first thing. Especially for a long-standing client like you.'

Brian Kesey had been Brennan Matterling's first port of call for any legal problem for many years. Brennan was pleased that still counted for something.

'It was quite a coincidence you calling yesterday, you know. I'd seen Lisa Richards earlier in the day—she's still a client and I look after bits and pieces for her. She was asking after you again.'

Asking after me? Brennan thought. *Probably hoping I'd become destitute and suffered a painful, lingering death.*

'And then you called,' Kesey added. 'She said she wanted to stay in touch.'

The usual image of Lisa flashed across Brennan's brain again. Just as it had so many times over the last year. Lisa at the creditors meeting, coal-black hair curling onto her cheeks, the sequins, the tight jeans, the steady voice. And the look—a look of cold bewilderment. A look that said, *I trusted you, Mike. And you let me down.*

'I know you've got a meeting so I won't keep you long.'

'No problem. Fire away.'

'Have you ever heard of a company called Elba Technology? It's a quoted company. On the AIM market.'

Kesey's forehead furrowed in concentration. 'Didn't the chief exec snuff it recently. Some kind of accident?'

'That's right. Last week. Drowned on the South Coast.'

'Not the time of year for boating, is it?' Kesey said absently, but it was obvious he was putting two and two together. He was out of the traps already.

'I was hoping to meet him last weekend. I'm doing a bit of free-lance writing and I was going to do a piece about him for the *FT*.'

'Oh, right. Not going back into the business, then?'

'Not straight away. Giving this a go first. I did a lot of writing when I was inside. I'm seeing if I can make it pay now.' Brennan pulled a piece of paper from his inside pocket and placed it on the table. 'That's a list of the major shareholders in Elba. I've got as far as I can researching them on the internet and I was hoping you might be able to dig down further.'

'Sure. Let's have a look.' Kesey took the paper and scanned it. 'Presumably this is just from their website. Holders over three per cent.'

'That's right. The only individual listed is C. Salinger with his four per cent. I met him yesterday. An interesting guy. For a paranoid.'

'Paranoid?'

'He seems to think someone's got something on him. They want his Elba shares, apparently.'

'Is that why you're looking at the other shareholders?'

'He piqued my interest. I'm assuming that whoever wants his shares already owns a chunk.'

Kesey went back to the list. 'This seems pretty typical for an AIM company. De Souza's family trust owns twenty per cent, funds and institutions hold most of the rest. Only a relatively small amount with private investors. How much do you know about the others on this list?'

'The second biggest after the de Souza family is that venture capital firm in San Francisco—Tulare LLC. They hold ten per cent. It seems that de Souza's wife is having an affair with someone connected to that company.'

'Really? How do you know?'

'One of de Souza's lady friends told me. In so many words. She just referred to him as Carmel's knockout Californian boyfriend. Sounded like a teenager when she was giving me the gossip.'

Kesey's eyes widened and he grinned. 'Blimey, Mike. You really are getting down to the nitty-gritty with your research. Sounds more like a story for the tabloids than the financials.'

Brennan grinned back. It felt good to be sharing this with Brian Kesey. Since the beginning of his time inside, Brennan had become more and more of a closed book. He had learned to disclose the absolute minimum needed for survival. Even with stalwarts like Terry Atkins. They all had their own agenda. He had to learn how to trust again. It was a risky business.

He said, 'The largest shareholder is Heilong Partners and they're based in Hong Kong. They've got twenty-nine per cent. That's the one where I need some help.'

'You know about the Takeover Code, do you?'

'I know that when a shareholder owns thirty-per cent or more of the voting rights in a company they have to make an offer to the other shareholders to buy their shares.'

'That's right. So, Salinger's buyer is very likely to be this Heilong company. If they can get hold of another four per cent in one swoop then they would be well-positioned to get the rest. Assuming that de Souza is on board, of course.'

'Or *was*. That's what I was thinking. Perhaps he changed his mind.'

'Mm.' Kesey pursed his lips. 'Let's see what we can find out about Heilong.'

Kesey started tapping at the keyboard on the table. 'Means "black dragon" in Chinese,' he said.

'You're already helping, Brian. Thanks.'

'I'll see what I can find. But we use an agent to get the full list. It would take me ages to find all the different registries online. I can, however, do a quick preliminary search using our company secretarial software, which links to the main databases. It covers all the global financial centres, including Hong Kong. Our agent there should be able to get a complete list of shareholders.'

Brennan waited while Kesey tapped and scrolled.

'Right, I've found them,' Kesey said eventually and leant into the screen. 'This'll give me all shareholders in Heilong Partners Ltd owning over three per cent.'

He rolled the button on his mouse then stopped and sat up in surprise. 'There's only one. A company registered in Anguilla. Which owns fifty-one per cent.'

'Anguilla, eh? One of the last places that allows companies to have bearer shares.'

'You're right. But how do you know that?'

'I had a bit of an education when I was at Ford. Hiding identity was a popular topic in my money-laundering classes.'

Kesey looked impressed. 'I can imagine. But most of the offshore tax havens are tightening up on bearers now. Under pressure from the Yanks to toe the line. But they still do exist. Very handy to hold a share certificate that isn't on any register although now they have to be held by a registered custodian. Before, they could be held anywhere.'

He looked back at his screen. 'This company is called Portenta07. The one that controls Heilong.'

'Sounds bland enough.'

'Exactly. An offshore shell with an off-the-shelf name.'

'All part of the camouflage. What else can we find out? This is all just speculation about the bearer shares. But it would fit in with Salinger's investigations. He was checking out the use of bearer shares before I arrived yesterday. He was looking on Wikipedia.'

'Interesting. I should be able to get a complete list of shareholders in Heilong within the next couple of days. As for this Anguillan company, that will be a lot more difficult. That's why they use them. Finding out who controls that will be next to impossible.'

'And how about Tulare LLC? A limited liability company registered in Delaware, which I know is common enough for tax purposes.'

'You're right again. One of Uncle Sam's little tax havens. Funny that they throw their weight around in the Caribbean trying to control the UK's but show a blind eye to their own. A Not Invented Here prejudice, I guess.'

'What can we find out about it?' Brennan was less concerned about the politics of international tax havens than their efficacy.

'Leave it with me. I should have something later today.'

'Great.' Brennan fingered the card in his pocket. The card that Salinger had given him yesterday. Although they might not be able to get much more information on the Anguillan company, he felt that by the end of the day he would know a lot more about Victor de Souza's world. And possibly how Doug Matterling was involved in it.

Then he would be on the road to finding out why the hell Matterling had done what he had done. For the first time since leaving Ford he felt that he was moving forward rather than stagnating. And it felt good.

He and Kesey both stood and shook hands.

'Good to be working with you again,' Kesey said. 'I'll call you, soon as. Give my best to Sarah.'

35

London
> **Wednesday morning**

HENRY EVANS TOOK a seat near the end of the corridor on the top floor of his Limehouse apartment block. The seat faced west and offered a panoramic view of the City of London. The new icons were set amongst the old. The Shard, the Gherkin, the Walkie-Talkie sitting impudently alongside St Paul's and the Tower of London. Symbols of modern financial globalisation against the centuries-old power pillars of land ownership, military might and religion.

Henry was not taking in the view. Nor was he concerned about the symbolism laid out before him. His seat was in a small communal area off the corridor and hidden from the view of anyone leaving his apartment. The corridor wall was painted white, studded with minimalistic stainless-steel squares in a random pattern along its length. These squares were about a foot wide and highly polished. One of them provided a perfect mirror for Henry to see the reflection of his own front door.

His gaze flicked back and forth from his phone to the reflection.

There was a hiss from the lift shaft. He heard the lift doors open and one of his neighbours emerged and walked down the corridor to the apartment next to his. It was the Czech girl who had just moved in. She was short with cropped dark hair and a friendly oval face. On any other day he would have jumped up and engaged her in conversation. But not today. Today he was on lookout.

She hurried into her apartment without looking around and the door slammed behind her. He heard two locks being turned. Even with twenty-four-hour security, the residents here were careful.

He heard the sound of another doorknob turning. His front door. It was hesitant. Made by someone not used to this door. Forward then backward then forward again until the latch bolt retracted fully. The door opened slowly and Ben Parfitt peered around it. His face was puffy and as he emerged, he kept patting his coat pockets as if checking for his keys. He seemed unsteady on his feet and glanced fearfully up and down the corridor.

Henry shrank further into his seat and checked his watch. Twelve o'clock. Bang on his ETD.

After several seconds Ben closed the door behind him and walked to the lift. It was still at the top floor and the doors opened immediately.

Henry waited until the lift doors had closed. He went back to his phone and quickly tapped at the keypad. He stabbed the send button and eased himself up from the chair. He had been there a long time. He took a couple of steps forward and looked down from the window to the street below. A black BMW 5 Series was parked opposite the building on a yellow line. The front doors opened and two men jumped out. They looked like twins. Short black hair, heavy-set but athletic and dressed identically. Shiny black brogues, smart black trousers, black leather donkey jackets. Both of them thrust their hands into their jacket pockets and hurried towards the south of Henry's building and its elegant lobby.

36

London
   Wednesday. Noon.

THE LIFT DOORS closed behind him. Ben reached for the handrail as the car started its descent. His head was still swimming but the phone conversation he had just had with Julie kept replaying.

'*But Julie, that's what I was trying to say. It is ready and I have spoken to Healey in Communications. It's virtually ready to go.*'

'*And what about me, Ben? Why haven't you run it past me? You know I needed to see it first thing. And now it's nearly twelve.*'

'*I'm sorry. But I promise you it's ready to go. I know you will approve. This morning has been difficult because of this nasty virus I've caught . . . but I'm on my way now. I'll be in by two and we can go through it then.*'

'*Two?*'

He could almost see her tight lips and enraged, bulging eyes. But she had agreed on one o'clock and he had hurriedly pulled on his clothes and found his way out of Henry's apartment.

Now he stared at himself in the lift's mirrored walls. Not too bad, he thought, considering last night. He could see the back of his head in the double reflections of the side walls. His wayward black hair was still evenly distributed, no sign of a bald spot yet. He patted his cheeks and pulled at the skin around the bottom of his eyes.

She would like the Buy Note. It was a good analytical piece and he knew it. Thorough, closely reasoned and persuasive. Anyone who read it would be tempted back into Elba shares. It was just what she wanted. And just what he didn't. His thinking zig-zagged between keeping his job and making his escape to Hong Kong this evening. How could he reconcile the two?

And what the hell was Henry up to?

He reached for his phone to check the current Elba price but the lift car had reached the ground floor and the doors opened. He stepped out onto the highly-polished marble floor of the atrium. It was all steel and glass, a lot more impressive than he had realised last night when he had staggered through here in an alcoholic haze.

He hurried out of the large glass swing doors. He sniffed the air. There was that smell again. A minty, spicy smell that he couldn't quite place. He felt the hairs on his neck start to rise. He saw the sign for Limehouse tube station and headed in that direction. His stomach started to clench. Then the smell of aftershave rushed at him from behind and he placed it exactly. Aftershave and leather.

His brain was in a fog—he knew that he wasn't thinking quickly enough. But it was too late. Powerful arms on each side lifted him off the pavement and propelled him forward. Seconds later he found himself sprawled face down across the back seat of a large car.

No-one spoke. It was like a silent movie. A heavy weight hit the small of his back. His head snapped back and his neck went numb. The smell of the leather seat merged with the leathery aftershave and his eyes closed again. Once more he succumbed to the blackness.

37

London
    Wednesday noon

MIKE BRENNAN ASSESSED the unassuming entrance. It was a small doorway, squeezed between a gents' hairdresser and what looked like what had been an old pub, now small offices. He had parked in the car park at Holborn Gate.

The red and white stripes were peeling off the barber's pole and there was a *Closed* sign hanging in the dirty window.

There were three doorbells and an entry phone on the doorpost. The name against the bottom bell was that of Remus Security. It was the same name as on the card that Charles Salinger had given to him yesterday. The Courier typeface on the doorplate looked as though the name had been there for some time. There were no names against the other two doorbells and the only one that looked used was the bottom one. Perhaps Remus had once just had one floor but had now taken over the whole building.

Brennan was about to press the button when his phone rang. He pulled it from his inside pocket.

'Brian, that was quick.'

He listened intently as Brian Kesey spoke.

'Ken Olson, yes of course I remember the name.' He dropped his voice as if he were being overheard. 'We lost a lot of money through him.' He moved his finger away from the buzzer. 'Okay, Brian. Thanks a lot. I'll speak to you later. At the moment, I'm—'

A rasping female voice screeched from the entryphone's speaker.

'This ain't a bleeding phone box,' it said.

Brennan jumped back half a step and looked up at the curved stone ceiling of the small portico above the front door. Two cameras were pointing down at him.

He stepped back into the entrance and spoke into the entryphone.

'I'd like to speak to your Managing Director.'

'You're speaking to her.'

'Good. Then it's you I'd like to speak to.'

'I'm listening.'

'It's about a confidential matter. I'd rather talk inside.'

There was a long pause.

'And you are?' the voice crackled.

He tilted his head closer to the grey metal box. 'My name's Mike Brennan. I'm here on behalf of a client.'

There was silence for a few seconds and then the buzzer sounded. He pushed at the door and just managed to nudge it open before the buzzer stopped.

'Nice to meet you, too,' he muttered, but at least she had let him in when he had told her his name. As though she had been expecting him.

The entrance hall was dark, with brown walls and ceiling. He stopped for a moment to let his eyes adjust. There was a staircase to the left which led to the upper floors. He took a few paces down the hall and stopped at the top of a steep set of stairs leading down.

'Down here!' the woman's voice yelled from below.

He descended carefully in the gloom, only looking up when his feet reached the basement's floor.

'In your own time, son.' Her came from a room halfway along the hall.

Brennan stepped slowly towards it and opened the door. As he entered, he caught a strong blast of aftershave from behind him. The door slammed shut and a man brushed past his back to step across the doorway. Brennan turned to face him. Young, well-built, slicked down black hair and a donkey jacket. Brennan instinctively dropped his shoulder.

'Take a seat, won't you?' the woman said from behind a wooden desk.

Brennan paused and turned to her, keeping the young man in his peripheral vision for as long as possible. He sat down opposite her on a wooden chair with a dirty yellow plastic cushion.

She was stocky, with a round white face and dyed jet-black curly hair. Probably late forties, he thought. Smartly dressed in a black business suit and white blouse. An expensive-looking gold necklace with a matching bracelet on her right wrist. Her stubby fingers were smothered with rings, although there was nothing on her marriage finger. Her gold earrings contained what looked like emeralds. They matched her dark green eyes which were now fixed steadily on him. She wasn't smiling but she was looking at him expectantly. The smell of aftershave hung heavily in the air.

Brennan leaned back in his chair and crossed his legs. 'Thank you for seeing me,' he said. 'I'm sorry not to have called to make an appointment but I happened to be in the area.'

She looked at him hard, her small mouth crimped shut. She didn't seem to be interested in small talk. He held her stare. She looked freshly made-up. This surprised him, considering her less-than-welcoming demeanour.

'I've been asked to contact you by a Mr Salinger.' He let the name hang, for effect.

Her small mouth opened. 'He's got our number. Why can't he

pick up the phone?' The accent was London, estuary rather than cockney.

'He is reluctant to deal with you personally. For obvious reasons.' Brennan continued to stare at her. Her eyes narrowed.

'*Obvious* reasons?'

'As you know, he is quite old. And rather frail. These kinds of things make him anxious.'

The green eyes narrowed again. 'What kinds of things, Mr Brennan?'

'Coercion. Threats. *Those* kinds of things.'

She said nothing for a few seconds and then burst out laughing. Aftershave joined in. This was obviously his area.

Brennan looked around the room while they went through the theatrics. Her office was organised, with bookshelves running the length of the wall behind her chair. It seemed to be a library on City affairs—Stock Exchange rule books, directories, company law reports, plus the whole range of *Who's Who*. Along the wall to his left were half-a-dozen cream and brown heavy-duty Bisley filing cabinets. To his right a computer sat on a black metal table under a small window. There was a pile of photographs next to it. They seemed to be of a couple standing in a garden.

'Now that, Mr Brennan, is funny.' She was quietening down now.

'I'm glad you think so, Mrs, er . . .'

'Just call me Hazel, Mr Brennan. That'll do for the time being.'

'Okay, Hazel. Who is it that wants my client's shares?'

Hazel looked over Brennan's head. Her face softened.

'Let me introduce you to our little firm. And give you an idea of what we do. The gentleman who showed you in is my son.' She smiled up at him fondly. 'You can call him Joe if you like. And Joe has two brothers. They all work for me in our little family business. We also employ several other, er, consultants, who we bring in for specialist work.'

'Specialist work being what?'

'We are security specialists, Mr Brennan. We help people protect their assets. We make sure that our clients keep what's theirs. And we help them get what they want.' She pushed herself back into her chair. 'Our clients can be very demanding. They are not the type of people who will take no for an answer. They have plenty of money and they are prepared to spend it.' She paused, making sure he was taking it all in. 'We act for some very aggressive companies. And when they set their sights on something, they will employ any means to get it. *Any means.*'

'So Elba Technology is a target for one of your clients?'

Her brow furrowed and she looked at him with mock sympathy.

'You know that's none of your business. All I can do is reiterate what you already know.' She leaned forward. 'Just tell Salinger that we have instructions to complete the purchase of his shares at a negotiated premium to the current market price. And we will do that, using whatever means we have available. He will know exactly what I am talking about.'

She nodded at Joe who took a couple of paces forward and placed his hands firmly on Brennan's shoulders. Brennan tensed and tried to stand. But Joe's grip was too strong and Brennan felt himself immobilised, unable even to raise his arms in defence.

'Tell him not to be greedy. And tell him to talk to us directly next time.' She smiled. 'Get my drift?'

Brennan nodded. He was in no position to argue. 'I'll pass on the message.'

'Our proposition is fair, don't you think?'

'I'm sure it is.' He maintained steady eye contact.

'And you believe in fairness, don't you? You wouldn't be here otherwise, would you?' Her green eyes seemed to be getting darker. 'Helping out poor Mr Salinger appeals to your sense of equilibrium.'

'I'm not so sure I have that anymore.' He wondered where she was going with this, but he needed to think about making an exit. She wasn't going to tell him more than he already knew. But she seemed to know more about him than he was comfortable with. She had been

expecting him. And there were only two people who could have
tipped her off.

'Part of our job, you see, is identifying weakness. Corporate weakness, group weakness, individual weakness. Personal weakness is at the root of it all.' Hazel's estuary accent was receding along with the gentility of her subject matter. 'And after identifying it, we exploit it.' She paused and spread out the fingers of both hands on the wooden desktop.

Brennan looked again at the heavy rings. Now they looked more like armour than decoration.

'The Latin for *root*, Mr Brennan, is *radix*.' Her eyebrows rose, awaiting his reaction. He tensed. 'We exploit weakness hard.'

There was much more than met the eye to this small family business. Especially this MD and her predilection for Latin. Did she know about Radix Research and the whole set-up?

Her thin lips curved into a smile. 'Mr Salinger is starting to become aware of that. Now it seems to be your turn. No matter what it might mean for your family.'

'Family?' he said and a pulse of panic beat through his chest. What was she threatening?

She cocked her head. 'Ah, good. Bullseye.'

She lifted her hands from the table.

'It's all part of what we do here. Just helping people see what they don't necessarily want to see.'

'Their own flaws, you mean?'

'Thank you for dropping in to see us. Joe will see you out,' she said abruptly.

Joe pushed Brennan up and then twisted his arm sharply behind his back to spin him around to face the door. Brennan felt a flash of pain shoot up into his shoulder and he gasped.

'This way, *sir*,' Joe grunted and propelled Brennan into the hallway.

Brennan's head was angled backwards as Joe pushed him towards the stairs, but from the corner of his eye he saw a figure at the far end of the hall. A small blond man was going into another office. The man looked around and for the briefest of moments their eyes met. Through the sharp pain in his back and shoulders, he felt a jolt of shock. Him again. Last week at the marina and now here.

Joe frog-marched him to the stairs and then relaxed his grip so Brennan could stumble up the steep staircase. At the top, Joe pushed his arm further up his back and bundled him out of the front door. He gave Brennan's arm one final twist before letting go.

Joe smiled grimly. 'Thanks for popping by, Mr Brennan. We'll be in touch when we need to.'

Brennan didn't turn around but started to walk back towards Fleet Street. He used his right hand to smooth down his shirt and jacket. His left arm was numb.

Before turning the corner into Fetter Lane, he turned to see if Joe had gone back inside. He hadn't. There seemed to be something going on outside the Remus offices. Joe was on the pavement and had opened the door of a black BMW. Brennan stepped into the shadow of a nearby building and watched.

Joe was peering into the back of the car and there was some scuffling as some other men jumped out. Brennan started to retrace his steps, still clinging to the shadow of the office block's high grey wall. He could see two of the men clearly now. They were both wearing the same kind of clothes as Joe and they both looked like him. The other two brothers. What a family. As bad as the bloody Krays, probably.

As they moved across the pavement to the Remus entrance, Brennan saw another man. He was squeezed between the two brothers. Skinny, tall, short spiky hair, narrow oblong face, sharp black overcoat. He looked dazed. As the three Joes escorted him inside, Brennan could see why. His two companions had one of his arms each and were exercising the trademark family armlock on him. Brennan winced in sympathy as they closed the door behind them. He rubbed his left arm. What kind of an education must those boys have had?

38

California
Wednesday morning

CARMEL GAVE the two framed photographs a final tender stroke with her forefinger and then placed them onto the folded clothes in her suitcase. She covered them with another layer of clothes for protection. She straightened up and looked out of the hotel window onto the busy San Francisco streets below.

It had been a good trip and her instincts were being proved right. Ken was doing and saying the right things and any nagging doubts she may have had about his commitment to her were now fading far into the background.

Tomorrow morning she would be back in London with her boys again. Leah had said they had been wonderful and Carmel could believe it. No-one had ever had finer sons.

The bedside telephone buzzed and she picked it up.

'Hi darling,' Ken said. 'How's the packing going?'

'Just finished. Only took five minutes.'

'You'll have plenty of time at the airport then.'

She looked at her watch. 'The taxi should be here in half an hour. How's the office.'

'Duller without you. But it's busy on the Elba front. I've had written commitments this morning from Granular and Redstone so everything is in place with the finance. My conversations with the Elba board have all been good. I'm meeting them at the weekend but every indication is that they will recommend the bid.'

'That's wonderful, Ken. Thank you so much.' She closed her eyes with relief.

'I just thought I'd let you know and wish you *bon voyage*. I'll keep track of your progress.'

'I can't wait to see you in London at the weekend.'

'I've booked in at the Athenaeum, as usual. Hopefully you'll be able to spend more time with me there now. But I also want to speak to the boys and see how they are about us.'

She stared out of the window again. 'They'll be fine, Ken. We just have to give it time. But I know that everything will work out. I know it.'

'Me too. Have a good flight and think of me.'

'I will.'

'Bye, darling.'

'Bye, Ken. Until the weekend.'

She put the telephone back into its cradle and thought about the past few days and the closeness they had shared. She knew everything would work out fine. Just as she had told him. She had acted just in time. For Ken and her as well as for her boys. She had found the strength and acted upon her conviction.

It had been more than intuition. It had been necessity.

39

London
    Wednesday evening

THERE WERE no parking spaces by the time Brennan got home from the City. After his short meeting at Remus he had walked over to the City Business Library and spent some time reading up on tax havens and Hong Kong company law. The traffic had been bad coming back. As for parking, any time after four and you could forget it. The narrow Queen's Park streets around his home were already full. The place resembled a Bavarian car park. Brand new BMWs, Audis and VWs as far as the eye could see.

He and Sarah had felt like pioneers when they'd moved here all those years ago. It had been the start of the gentrification process, as some would say—although at the time, it had been more about the fact that a working couple like them could afford a house here without relying on a family inheritance. It had been quite a rough area then, or so he would tell his dinner party friends. None of your media types, thank God, he would say self-deprecatingly. There were no gyms, sushi bars or psychotherapists. The Brennans had struck out into unexplored territory.

For the third time he turned left into his street. He had been doing his usual circuit, searching for a parking space. But with nothing close to home, he turned right up the hill. There was usually space by the industrial units. Although it had once been a residential street, during the fifties and sixties many of the tiny houses here had been converted into car workshops and light engineering factories. He found a gap between a crashed Audi and a burnt-out Focus.

He parked and leant over to get his coat from the back seat. He checked the windows and door locks and got out of the car. There were no streetlights, but a security light had come on above the double doors of a garage on the other side of the road. The smell of engine oil hung in the cold air. He locked the car and buttoned up his coat. It was a couple of hundred yards to his house.

He hurried down the hill towards home. The security light went out behind him, leaving the street in darkness. He followed the line of cars. His footsteps echoed against the closed garage doors and empty vehicles. The only other sound was an idling engine in the distance. It sounded like a motorbike.

The conversation with Hazel swirled around in his mind. She had been expecting him, there was no doubt about that. Salinger could have let her know he was on his way but what would have been the point in that? No, it must have been Fiona. She had led him to Salinger knowing that the old man would lead him to Remus. Fiona must have contacted Hazel. They were in it together. But why use him? Just to get a warning from Hazel to pass back to Salinger?

Hazel also knew about Radix Research and she had wanted him to know it. She was telling him to mind his own business and keep his nose out of their affairs.

He turned the corner into his street. Cara would probably be in bed by now. Sarah would be watching TV. He wondered what kind of mood she was in.

Fiona had been keen to tell him about Carmel's affair with this guy in California. She wanted him to conclude that Carmel was behind her husband's death. Did she want him to take that information to the police? If so, why not do it herself? And wouldn't he have needed the name of California Man? She had withheld that because she must have known about him and Brennan Matterling. What was it she had called him in that giggly teen way? *A knockout boyfriend.*

Suddenly he got it. Brian Kesey's call earlier today had thrown up the name. *Ken Olson. KO. Knockout.* Of course. It had seemed such a strange way to describe him. She had been teasing him with a clue. Fiona would know Ken Olson because Elba's PR agency would have plenty of contact with its main investors.

Brennan glanced up and down the street and stepped off the kerb to cross. So, Fiona Wells was pulling the strings. She was the one who had wanted him to find his way to Remus Security.

Interesting.

A movement to his left made him look up. The piercing white light was as blinding as it was sudden. He raised his arm to shield his eyes just as the scream of a powerful motorbike engine filled the air. He didn't feel the impact but he was aware of his face scraping across tarmac as his body sprawled somewhere behind him. The rider's hard leather boot had smashed into his chest, knocking his breath out of him. His head seemed to bounce gently off the tyre of a parked car. He was in his body, but he felt nothing. His systems switched off.

The numbness enveloped him and he sank into the watery warmth of unconsciousness.

40

London
Thursday morning

WHEN BEN CAME TO, he was lying on his back. There was something rough around his throat and when he probed it with his fingers, he found it was the edge of a coarse blanket. He pulled it away from his neck.

He was in total darkness. The air was damp and sour with the smell of hops. His head was swimming. He felt for his phone inside his jacket. Gone. He brought his left wrist up to his face and pressed the button on his watch that illuminated the dial.

Green numbers hovered against the black background: *7.50.*

He tried to push himself up on his elbows but he did not have the strength. Instead, he rolled onto his side and after a couple of heaves managed to sit up. He was on a thin, lumpy mattress. He reached over the side and touched the floor, about a foot below. A bed. In some kind of cave.

There was no light. No windows or door. He swung his feet onto the floor and grabbed the bed's cold metal frame for balance.

All night, he realised as he sat there. *I've been here all night.*

The last thing he remembered was being face-down on the back seat of a large car with the same two characters that had attacked him last Sunday. They hadn't stopped to chat this time. Straight from the street to this place.

He rolled his shoulders and stretched out his legs. His body was starting to work again now. He patted himself down. All dry, no blood. His wallet was still in his jacket. Just the phone was gone. A powerful feeling of relief flooded through him. He was still alive. And physically intact. Even if he couldn't see a thing.

Suddenly there was a sound. Scratching. Quite close. And getting closer. A rat? He stamped a foot and the scratching turned into a scamper as it ran off. *How many more were there?* He stamped both feet on the ground, just to let them all know that there was a bigger beast around.

He stood gingerly but was able to keep his balance.

He heard a clunk and a squeak. The sound of a door opening. High above. He sat down again as if that would help him hear better.

The muffled sound of quick footsteps came down stone steps. Then silence. A giant square of white light appeared as a door opened and a light flicked on overhead. Ben screwed up his eyes. One of his captors stepped in and the door closed behind him. He swivelled around and slid a large black bolt into place. Ben rose slowly, expecting another confrontation.

That ionising blast of aftershave again. The same guy who had nearly dislocated his shoulder on Sunday evening. And thrown him into the car yesterday. He was dressed the same, black trousers and black jacket. But not the same menace this time. He was holding a bottle of water and a packaged sandwich.

'Breakfast,' he announced and tossed the meal onto the bed.

Ben quickly took in his surroundings. He was in a cellar, stone flagged floor and vaulted brick ceiling. He felt the cold seeping into his bones.

'Who are you? And why am I here?

'Just following instructions, Mr Parfitt.'

'Whose?'

His captor laughed. 'We'll keep you fed and watered, don't worry about that. No beer left now, though.' He nodded towards the far wall where the curve of the bricked ceiling met the floor. There were a few metal beer barrels stacked up, gathering dust. 'It seems you haven't been following orders.'

'I'm doing what I can to keep that price low,' Ben said. 'You've just got to give it more time. Once the market realises how important de Souza was, I can assure you the price will drop.' This was rational talk, but was this a rational listener? This guy was just the muscle—Ben needed to go higher up the food chain.

'You're not fooling anyone, son. Except yourself. Didn't your mother ever tell you that honesty is the best policy? The stuff you were writing on Tuesday was not designed to keep the price low. Who the hell do you think you're kidding?'

Tuesday? How does he know what I wrote? And when?

'So you'd better just stay out of the way for the time being.' He waved around the cellar as if '*time being*' might mean 'for a long time to come'.

'It's for your own good.' The menace had returned.

He turned and unbolted the door. He was out in a second and Ben heard the key turn in the lock then footsteps taking several stairs at a time.

'Shit,' he said to himself and slumped back on the narrow bed. He looked at the sandwich. Marks & Spencer. Salmon and cucumber. A bit classy, that. He would have expected something more basic. But the stakes had been raised and he wasn't hungry. It wasn't just his job that he was trying to protect now. It was his life.

41

London
Thursday morning

THE NIGHT HAD BEEN a rolling cacophony of moans and groans, punctuated with cries of pain. Brennan had drifted in and out of sleep. He had sensed people moving around him. The pungent smell of urine hung in the air. Then one loud yelp of pain woke him with a start. As his eyes opened, he realised that the yelp had come from him. His ribs throbbed. He felt an enormous weight pressing against him. He could hardly breathe.

It was light now. He was propped up at an angle on a large bed. He slowly focussed and saw an old man lying on a bed opposite him. The man was semi-conscious and his blue hospital gown had ridden up around his waist. His legs were wide apart and his genitals hung between them like withered fruit. Brennan closed his eyes again.

Further away, a bedpan clattered across the floor and released a fresh tang of urine. Brennan turned and saw he was surrounded by small old men on large mechanical beds. Many were asleep or in a fragile state of consciousness, mouths hanging open, eyes glazed. Some were trying to move, changing position on their beds or even attempting to get up. One of them must have sent the bedpan flying.

A rotund nurse moved slowly between them, straightening blankets, plumping up pillows, mopping up spillages. She dealt with the errant bedpan and pulled down the old man's gown.

She saw that Brennan was awake.

'So, how are we this morning, my darling? We had a bit of a bump last night, didn't we?' She spoke with a Welsh accent. Black hair fringed a round face, a circle atop the bigger circle of her body, like a cartoon of a nurse. But she was real. She held his hand. Her touch instantly made him feel safer.

'You were involved in an accident near your home. We found out where you lived. Your wife said she'd be in again later on.' She looked around at her charges and smiled at him. 'Sorry they had to put you in here with the golden oldies. It was the only bed they could find. But don't worry, you should only be here for a day or so. Doctors want to keep an eye on you for twenty-four hours. Because of the concussion. We've given you painkillers, so you'll be quite drowsy for a while.'

'Oh, right.' Brennan had never heard his voice sound so weak. 'Thank you.'

That was all he could think of to say although his mind was a fog of questions.

'You just get some rest now.' She squeezed his hand. 'Doctor will be round in an hour to have another look at you.'

She squared the soft red blanket over him. He realised he was wearing the same kind of gown as the others, a wrap-around affair that creased up awkwardly underneath him. She sensed his discomfort and slipped her hand expertly beneath him to pull out the folds. She patted his leg as she moved on to the next bed.

He closed his eyes again and slid towards sleep. He could be in Bedlam. But at least he was safe.

42

London
   Thursday afternoon

THE BUTTERFLIES DISAPPEARED AS SOON as he saw her come through the door of Witherow Ward. The butterflies that had started fluttering mid-morning, when he had received the message that she had called and was intending to visit this afternoon. He had certainly been apprehensive but now she was here, the nerves were steadying. She spotted him through the glass of the swing doors and gave him a wide, welcoming smile as she entered the ward and crossed to his bed.

Lisa Richards looked just the same as Brennan remembered. Short, dark hair curving onto her neck, large brown eyes, impish smile. She leant over and kissed him on both cheeks before pulling the privacy curtains and sitting on the chair next to the bed. A proper kiss, he thought. Not one of those token air kiss jobbies.

'Great to see you, Lisa. Quite a surprise.'

It was. The last time had been at the creditors' meeting. He had

thought about her a lot during his incarceration and he was determined to repay the money she had lost as soon as he could. Even if
she never wanted to see him again, which seemed likely.

'Well, the nurse said you needed a bit of cheering up.' She said it
matter-of-factly, with no hint of conceit.

'But how did you know?'

'Brian. Brian Kesey. After you called him this morning he got on
to me. He thought I'd like to know. He told me that you saw him
yesterday, the first time since you got out.'

Brennan had been unsure what to expect from this visit. Had she
been waiting for his release just to vent her anger or was she
genuinely concerned about him? They had been friends after all.
Until BM had hit the buffers. 'How have you been?' he said
eventually.

'No big changes since I last saw you. But none sought. I'm simply
happy being happy. Between jobs at the moment. Still teaching. But
never mind me, what happened to you? Anything broken?'

She seemed friendly enough. Perhaps he had been worrying
unnecessarily. 'Not as far as they are aware. Just some bruising.' He
rubbed his chest. 'And concussion. That's why I'm still here.'

'What happened?' Her voice was soft, earnest.

'He came out of nowhere. I just heard the roar of a massive
motorbike. He swerved towards me and rammed his boot into my
ribs. And then he was gone. It all happened in a flash. That was the
last I knew. I went flying and must have cracked my head against
something.'

'And how did you get here?'

'Apparently someone in the flats near where I parked called the
ambulance. I was out for the count.'

'Who the hell would have done that to you?' She huffed in disbelief. 'You make it sound deliberate. No one would want you dead.
Would they?'

'Not dead perhaps. But warned.' He thought about Joe's last
words to him. *We'll be in touch when we need to.*

'Warned?'

He looked into her eyes. He needed to share these latest developments with someone. She was looking at him expectantly.

'No, I didn't mean that. You're right. The guy must have just lost his balance and I ended up in the way. He was just going too fast.'

He could tell she was not convinced. She knew he was backtracking. He had to change the subject fast. He also had to say something he had been rehearsing for the last twelve months.

'Look, Lisa, I am so sorry about what happened with the company. I know how much your family lost by investing in us. They backed us to the hilt and it was appreciated.' He paused to gauge her reaction. She gave nothing away but kept looking at him questioningly. 'Regardless of how things have gone for me, I can only offer my sincerest apology for what happened. After the first five years of crazy growth, I genuinely thought we were going to continue to do well and that one day Martin Sorrell was going to come along and buy us out and all the shareholders were going to make a bomb. A lot of things went wrong at the same time.'

There was a long silence.

'You will get that money back,' he said. 'I promise. As soon as I am in a position to repay you and your family, I will. I promise.'

Another long silence.

'So no ramming of boots?' she said.

He was momentarily non-plussed. She was picking up from where he had left off talking about the accident. It was though he had not even started with the apology.

'Perhaps that was a bit fanciful,' he said.

'I don't think so. You wouldn't have said it if you didn't mean it. You've had all day to remember what happened and go over all the details. You don't think it was an accident and you think that I'm too stupid to realise that.'

This was another dimension, he thought. She sounded aggrieved.

'No, no Lise.' He realised that he had used her familiar name from habit. 'You know I don't think that. It's just that it all happened so fast. I can't be sure of anything.' As he said it he knew that he did not believe it. He knew exactly what had happened. He *had* been rammed. Deliberately.

'Too stupid to realise that you're changing your tune. And stupid enough to have invested in your sodding company in the first place.'

'No Lise, I—'

'I came here with the simplest of intentions. To visit an old friend in hospital. Now I'm thinking it wasn't such a good idea.' She started to get up.

'No, please don't go. You've only just got here. I've been looking forward to seeing you. Ever since your message this morning.'

She studied him. 'Well, that sounded genuine at least.' Her back was up and he had to stop her leaving so soon. He suddenly realised how much he needed to talk it all through with someone. The events of the last few days had been spinning around in his head ever since he had woken up.

She sat back down and put her hand on the side of the bed. Not on his arm, probably because she did not want to hurt him, but close enough to restore the bond between them.

'And you're too stupid to realise that I'm here to help if you could only ask. Why don't you start by telling me who might be warning you? And why. You must have some idea.'

Thank God, he thought. She had calmed down. She was giving him another chance. He looked deep into her eyes. She was ready if he was. They had always been straight with each other and it was not as if she had any connection with Elba Technology or any of its directors or shareholders. She was a primary school teacher with no business experience who had simply had some family money to invest. They were from China and wanted to park some money in Europe. Brian Kesey had introduced her to Brennan and Matterling.

She looked worried. He decided to tell her about Remus Security and why they were the ones that had in all likelihood been behind his accident.

But before that he needed to give her a bit of background. In for a penny, in for a pound.

Over the course of the next ten minutes he told her almost everything, starting

with de Souza being fished out of the Hamble and his theory that the tide would not carry a body from his moored boat to the jetty where he had washed up. Furthermore, he had found out that a drowned body would sink to the bottom and stay there until its intestinal bacteria produced enough gas for it to float again. Which could take a few weeks in cold water. So, de Souza had probably gone in close to the jetty. Either accidentally or on purpose.

He concluded by telling her that Elba Technology was a takeover target for an unidentified buyer and that a less-than-conventional security firm was being deployed to help move matters along. He mentioned the young man being bundled into their offices yesterday under duress.

'That's how they seem to operate,' he said ruefully.

She listened to his story quietly. He was relieved to articulate all the facts and suppositions that had been whirring around in his head these last few days. It helped him restore order.

'But why this Victor de Souza? Why did you want to interview him so badly?'

Brennan pointed to his clothes which were hanging off a hook on the wall. 'Could you hand me my jacket, please.'

She unhooked it and laid it across the bed for him. He reached inside and pulled out the folded photocopy. He handed it to her and she opened it up.

She smiled. 'You *are* trying to track down Doug Matterling. I did wonder. And this other guy must be Victor de Souza.' He nodded. She folded the picture and slipped it back into his jacket pocket. 'Is that all you've got to go on? Just a picture of him at a fancy dinner with de Souza.'

'That's it. He's disappeared off the face of the Earth. I don't suppose you've heard anything of him, have you?'

She shook her head.

There was silence again as they processed their own thoughts. Brennan could see that she was going through what he had just told her. He realised he needed a new plan. He had been led to Salinger and then to Remus. It was time to get onto the front foot.

'What are you going to do now, Mike? It seems that someone wanted you to end up here. And the most likely candidate is this Fiona Wells. She must have known what would happen to you after you met that creep Salinger.'

Brennan smiled to himself. Lisa was on his side now, lining up against any potential enemies. It was if they had jumped back in time. They had leapt over the hundred grand she had lost with Brennan Matterling.

'I agree. Fiona was keen for me to meet him and she also made sure that I knew all about Carmel, the merry widow.'

'So that you would go to the police?'

'She knew that wouldn't happen. Firstly, I don't have any information that they couldn't find out for themselves at this stage. And secondly . . .'

'Secondly?' she prompted.

'Let's just say that my belief in British justice has been sorely tested of late. I am not inclined to put it to the test again. Not just yet. Fiona worked that one out pretty quickly.'

'I can understand that.' She put her hand on his and gave it a gentle squeeze. 'We were all shocked at what happened. None of us ever imagined you'd end up in jail. It was a travesty. I believed you at the time, that the Radix fraud was a set-up.' She leant towards him. 'I believed you then and I believe you now.'

Brennan looked down at her hand. 'It will balance out, Lise. Don't worry about that. I'll get my . . .'

She waited a few seconds. 'Revenge?' she asked eventually.

It was a difficult word for him to say when he did not know what form it would take. But yes, he needed revenge. To restore his faith in justice.

'So you're going to pursue it?' she said. 'Find out who's behind this takeover?'

'That'll come to light pretty quickly.'

'And how's Sarah? It must have been terrible for her.'

This was a sudden change in direction. Or did Lisa realise how inextricably linked the two were?

'She's fine,' he lied. 'She was here earlier. You just missed her.' He felt like he was apologising for her. It had been an awkward visit and he had been pleased that he could blame the sedatives for drifting off when her scrutiny of him became too accusing. He had not talked with her like he could talk with Lisa. Her scepticism was an impenetrable barrier.

'Pleased to have you home?'

'Kind of.'

'And your daughter? She must be thrilled.'

'Yes, she is.'

'Do *they* know you've got a family?'

'They do. That's the kind of thing they find out pretty quick. They also knew about Radix Research. And they're connected to de Souza's death somehow.'

'Connected? That's diplomatic,' she said slowly. The unspoken threat hung heavily over them.

'I'll be careful, Lise. Don't worry about that. I'll do the right thing by Cara. *And* Sarah. I've thought it all through. I can't *not* pursue it.'

'Let me know if I can help. I'm no expert in company takeovers but I do know what is right and what is wrong. I also know that you've got to think carefully about what you want and what you need. You're aware of one, but I'm not sure about the other.' She smiled at him and patted his arm. 'One thing you do need is to get some rest.' She reached into her small handbag and pulled out a notebook and a pen. She wrote down a telephone number, ripped out the page and gave it to him. 'Call me tomorrow to let me know how you are. She gave him a mock-stern look. 'If I don't hear from you, I'll come looking.'

She stood up. He would not have minded if she had wanted to stay. His ribs weren't hurting as much now.

She leant over to kiss him goodbye and her freshness filled his nostrils again. A few seconds later she was pushing through the swing doors. He watched her disappear into the corridor.

Her visit had helped resuscitate him. He was glad to have talked it all through with her and he vowed to himself that if he was ever in a position to repay her failed investment, then he would pay back every penny.

But he also thought about the bit that he had left out of his story— the identity of Carmel's lover. He had a question that needed answering before he could let her in on that.

43

London
Friday morning

IT HAD BEEN another bad night in the Witherow Ward. They had promised to move him to another ward but that had never happened. So Brennan had to stick with the geriatrics and the noises and smells of old age. He had tried to make conversation with a couple of the other patients, but they were beyond it. He did not belong there, just like he had not belonged at HMP Belmarsh and HMP Ford. An outsider inside.

All the discharge papers had been signed early this morning. As early as he could, just to make sure there wasn't any delay. He was anxious to leave St Mary's and meet with Brian Kesey again.

He had no trouble getting a black cab in Praed Street. It was not far to Covent Garden but every bump in the road sent a scorching dagger of pain into his ribs. He hung onto a strap over the door for support. He found that the pain was not as bad if he lifted himself slightly from the seat and rode above the undulations. He smiled to himself. He was adapting.

The cab dropped him at Long Acre. A smartly-dressed receptionist showed him into Brian Kesey's office. Kesey was tapping away at a computer. He jumped up when Brennan entered.

'Blimey, how are you, buddy? I didn't think you'd be out so soon.'

'All intact, just about.' He rubbed at his ribs. 'The coward hit me pretty hard.'

'Coward?'

'Yeah, he was wearing a crash helmet. I couldn't hit him back.'

They both laughed. But this laughter was more nervous than before. They took the same seats at the conference table that they had occupied last time.

'So, Brian, what have you come up with?'

Kesey looked at him doubtfully. 'I've got some info back from my guy in Hong Kong.' He paused. 'But are you sure you want to pursue this? After what you've just been through I'd have thought you might want to walk away. You could be getting involved with some real hooligans. From what you told me over the phone, it didn't sound like an accident. Aren't you scared?'

'Sure. But not of them.'

'Who, then?'

Brennan shrugged dismissively. 'Just someone I used to be.'

They looked at each other for a few seconds.

'Is that the list there?' Brennan looked down at the table.

Kesey picked up two sheets of paper. 'Our agent has obtained a list of shareholders in Heilong Partners.' He handed Brennan one of the sheets.

Brennan cast his eyes down the list. There were a lot of Chinese names, meaningless names that did not give a clue about what they did. Brennan looked up at Kesey blankly.

'I know what you mean,' Kesey said. 'It doesn't tell us much. Apart from the fact that none of the individuals on the list have a big percentage. The only major shareholder is that Anguilla company, Portenta07. With fifty-one per cent.'

Brennan studied the sheet again. 'The addresses are interesting. Mainly Hong Kong. No mainland addresses or nominee companies registered in the BVI or somewhere similar. Isn't that what you would expect from a regular investment company in Hong Kong?'

'Guess so. But perhaps it was just a local network that got involved.'

'Very local. Look at the number of times this one address comes up.' He pointed to the sheet. 'That's worth checking out.'

Kesey frowned. 'Lockhart Road. It's one of the main roads in Central. Let me see.' He tapped on his keyboard for a few seconds. 'No, nothing. Just seems to be office suites for sale at that address. Seems familiar, though. Perhaps a client of mine had an accommodation address similar.'

'I've been thinking about Elba and the possible takeover,' Brennan said. 'With the de Souza family's twenty per cent, Heilong's twenty-nine per cent and Salinger's four per cent you'd have well over half the company. Plus whatever shares you might hold through a nominee mopping up small numbers in the market without creating too much of a splash.'

'"You"?'

'Whoever is lining up Elba as a target. Over fifty per cent would give you control over the board and the board would recommend a takeover offer. But they would have to have the de Souza family on board.'

'With just a few holdings. That's the problem with these AIM companies.'

'Problem? Seems perfect for a predator. And a good result for the Heilong shareholders who are keen to launder some cash.'

'Money laundering?' Kesey raised his eyebrows.

'You know as well as I do that Chinese investors and money-laundering are not complete strangers to one another. Quite an overlap on a Venn diagram.'

Kesey pursed his lips. 'It's as though Heilong were set up for it. Loads of small investors and a large one that holds control.'

'Probably an SPV for this one investment. In Elba Technology.'

'Special Purpose Vehicle? Since when did you get involved in such things, Mike?'

Brennan smiled. 'I told you about my prison studies. Some fascinating electives. As I said, money-laundering was one of the most popular. I bet most of these Heilong investors just want to turn their Hong Kong cash into clean hard currency.' He turned back to his list. 'At the moment, for example, Mr Tau from Kwai Tsing holds shares in Heilong. He would probably have subscribed for those shares with cash, Hong Kong dollars. The only market for those shares is in Hong Kong. So even if they rise in value, he would only get back Hong Kong dollars. But if Heilong invests in a UK company like Elba, and Elba gets taken over by a US company, then Heilong would receive shares in whichever American tech giant buys them. Those shares could then be distributed to Heilong shareholders as a dividend in specie.'

'Quite an elective you chose there.' Kesey seemed impressed. 'I'm not sure that I've dealt with a lot of divis in specie.'

'It's just a dividend that isn't a cash payment. Mr Tau would receive shares in a publicly-listed US company, which he could then hold in the States or sell for US dollars. He could be part of the American dream.'

'Nice.'

'But if Elba's growth prospects are good, then a more fruitful strategy for a shareholder like Heilong would be to launch its own takeover of Elba, buy out the other shareholders and then sell the company for a fat profit a few years further down the line. Even if the de Souza family didn't want to sell, Heilong could still get control.'

Kesey was studying his list again. 'The average shareholding is certainly quite small. Probably just small businessmen finding somewhere to park some family money.' He waved at Brennan's crumpled jacket. 'Maybe the tailor who used to make those smart suits for you when you travelled there. They probably all know each other in some way, part of the same networks. When someone finds an opportunity, they share it. The more that pile in the better. If it works out, they're owed a favour. If it goes wrong, they're all to blame and they'll just move on. It's a way to squirrel away some cash and get it out of the country.'

'And they're probably layering the dodgy money with the legit stuff.' Brennan looked out of the window and rubbed his ribs. He thought back again to his alternative MBA at Ford under Atkins' tutelage. There was nothing academic about that degree; it was all expertise born out of real-world practice.

Then he thought about another angle. 'Hopefully you're right and these guys are on the safe side of psychotic. Hong Kong can produce some pretty nasty characters. I only went there a couple of times. Mainly to get those suits you saw. It was much more Doug Matterling's project. He spent a lot of time there.'

'I remember setting up the company there for you. Never took off though, did it?'

'Just a name on the list of subsidiaries that we included in the accounts. Never came to anything. Despite Doug's best efforts.' Brennan couldn't hide the sarcasm in the last sentence.

'You were looking to buy another agency there, weren't you?'

'That's what he was doing. Nothing materialised, though. Just another dead end. Just like our investment in Olson. Thanks for finding out that Tulare is one of his funds. He effectively controls ten per cent of Elba.'

'Quite a coincidence. I remembered the name coming up when you were drafting your bit for the statement of affairs. It was an investment into one of his high-tech funds, wasn't it? About three hundred grand, US.'

'That's right. We had to write off the lot. But we didn't go into a fund. We went into just two start-ups. The direct investment route. For their so-called *sophisticated investors*. I still need to find out what happened.' Brennan paused. 'But Olson's been carrying on with Victor de Souza's wife. She's in California with him now.'

'Doesn't sound very ethical.'

'Been going on for some time it seems.'

'Still doesn't make it ethical. But it makes him a suspect if de Souza's death wasn't an accident, doesn't it?'

'That's one of the reasons I've got to find out more about him. I want to make contact with him.'

Kesey rocked back in his chair and looked at Brennan as though studying him for the first time.

'Make contact? Suppose he's behind de Souza's death and possibly connected with these Hong Kong investors. Could be dangerous.'

'I'll just have to take my chances, won't I?' Brennan spoke with a quiet determination, which was how he felt. Elba Technology was still his only tangible connection to Matterling. He had to find out as much as he could. 'By the way,' he said, moving the conversation into a different direction. 'I saw Lisa yesterday. She said she'd spoken to you.'

'Yes. She phoned again and I told her about your accident.'

This was a slightly different version of events to Lisa's, but Brennan let it go. He had been so drugged up he was surprised he could remember anything from yesterday.

'It was good to see her. She seems pretty sanguine about the money she and her family lost in BM.'

'She's been in regular contact since the liquidation. Always asking whether you were out yet.'

'Funny she never tried to get hold of me.'

'Probably thought it would be a bit awkward. While you were inside, that is.'

The subject of imprisonment created a pause in their conversation. Kesey was the first to break it.

'I guess you do a lot of thinking, don't you? When you're inside.'

'Only about eighteen hours a day.'

'So what keeps you sane? How do you stop stewing about the past and recycling the same old thoughts?'

'That's the difficult part.'

'I'm sure that it would send me doolally.'

'Doolally?'

'Stir crazy. Nuts.'

'Mm. I know what it means. Not doolally *tap*?'

'Tap? What do you mean?'

'Where the expression came from. Deolali was a transit camp in India. The British soldiers often spent a long time there awaiting their next posting. They went a bit barmy. I think *tap* is the Hindi word for 'fever'. I knew someone who used to say it a lot.'

Kesey looked perplexed. 'Okay. Etymology isn't my thing.' He turned to his keyboard and started typing. 'Let's have another go at that address. The Hong Kong one.'

Doolally tap, Brennan thought. That was what Fiona had said at their lunch. Most people would just say *doolally*, as Kesey had. The only other person he knew who used the full expression was Doug Matterling. He had said his father was in the military and that's where he had got it from—but where had Fiona got it from?

While Kesey stared at his screen, Brennan thought again about his lunch with Fiona. She had been keen to unburden, to tell him about Carmel and Olson. But only after she had established that he had no intention of going to the police. Would she have been so forthcoming otherwise?

Kesey's desk telephone rang with a shrill buzz. It reminded him of the screeching entryphone at the offices of Remus Security.

'That'll be my meeting,' Kesey said, twisting away from his keyboard to pick it up. 'Sorry, Mike.'

'No problem.' Brennan shifted in his chair and started to get up. A sharp pain shot through his left side and the acrid smell of exhaust from that motorbike suddenly filled his nostrils. The heavy force of the biker's thick boot crunched into his body again. Joe's grip tightened on his shoulder. And now there was a Hong Kong connection.

He thought briefly about the Triads and all those Jackie Chan films. The Remus boys would fit in well there.

Suddenly it all seemed a long way from those friendly, civilised fittings at the Zen Tailor Shop in the Central District of Hong Kong, with the fresh smell and soft touch of rolls of worsted cotton.

'Thanks,' Kesey said into the phone. 'I'll be right out.' He replaced the handset in its cradle. He extended his hand. 'Good to see you again, Mike. In worse shape than yesterday but still in one piece. I just hope you manage to keep it that way. In spite of yourself.'

Brennan gave him a reassuring smile and a two-handed hand-shake. 'You've been a great help, Brian. Send me your bill.'

'No charge, buddy. Least I can do. And anyway, I don't think the case is over yet.'

It certainly wasn't. As well as navigating past Remus Security to get to the bottom of the de Souza/Matterling link, there was now also this crook Olson to deal with. All while trying to prevent Sarah from giving up on him.

He felt like he was about to be launched into space.

44

London
Friday afternoon

HENRY EVANS HAD TAKEN the box of Fortnum and Mason chocolates and put it in his briefcase. Aquamarine packaging, milk and dark selection. That had been ten minutes ago, when the two of them had met at the top of the ramp leading down to the entrance of Tate Modern.

Now, they were both standing in front of Paul Klee's *Classification*. Henry was peering at the segmented heads. His companion was dressed in a sharp dark suit and stood out from the shabby mass of art lovers shuffling through the enormous exhibition.

Henry shuffled as well, transferring his weight from one foot to the other as they stared at the canvas.

'*Making Visible*, Henry.'

'Eh?' Henry looked sideways at Doug Matterling and shifted uncomfortably.

'The name of the exhibition. *Making Visible*. They've set it out chronologically. You can see Klee's developing vision. Look at the eyes. The number of eyes in this.'

Henry looked. The eyes looked back. Neither party was any the wiser.

'When you see a man's work set out like this,' Matterling said and swept his arm around the gallery, 'it makes you think, doesn't it?'

'S'pose so.'

'It makes you realise how you have to have a plan. You can't just react when things happen to you. A plan gives you the right to direct events. A plan gives you the opportunity to put things right. When you've been wronged.'

Henry clutched the handle of his briefcase tighter and checked the clasp. Shut tight. He rolled the numbers in the combination lock again. Checking again, like a wife or husband nervously touching their wedding ring and twisting it around for security. This briefcase was his security now.

'Take a look at this one. You'll see what I mean.'

Matterling strode into an adjoining room and Henry dutifully followed. They stopped in front of a wooden-framed painting, which consisted of small squares of colour. The squares were set out in lines, not precisely but as a grid which was uniform on the left side but more haphazard as the pattern progressed to the right.

'Is there a plan there? What do you think?' Matterling touched Henry on the elbow, squaring him up to the painting.

Henry gazed at the blobs of orange, red, brown and blue.

'It looks pretty random to me,' he offered hesitantly. 'Just experimenting with colour. Like a kid.'

Matterling smiled. 'No, not random. Look closely.' He held his hands up to frame the image and moved them around as if to focus. 'It fits into big planes. And look at the blues. The small blue squares. Extend the blue squares. Can you see how that creates the whole structure of the composition?'

Henry screwed his eyes up and moved his head back and forward. Matterling stepped closer to him.

'You see, everyone needs a plan. Klee had a plan. He had control. And I have a plan.' He nodded at the briefcase and they both looked down at it briefly. Matterling's voice hardened. 'The problem is that part of my plan isn't working at the moment. Is it, Henry?'

Henry sucked in air. His eyes darted between Matterling's narrow gaze and the squares of colour in Klee's *Number 8o*.

'Something isn't going to plan with Elba's share price this week,' Matterling said. 'It's on the wrong trajectory.'

'I've done everything I can, I swear. I've kept close to Ben Parfitt. Really close. I've even had him stay at my place. The price has been out of my control. But at least the Buy Note hasn't gone out. Without him around for follow-up, they've decided to postpone the release.'

'Well done,' Matterling said without conviction. 'Things will change. They have to.' He reached down and touched the briefcase with his index finger.

Henry's grip tightened as he spoke. 'I did what you asked. With that Remus outfit. They've got him now. And he won't be able to make that trip this Sunday.'

A bench became available behind them and Matterling indicated for them to sit down. They sat in silence for a minute, absorbing in their own ways the sombre functionality of Bauhaus.

'What's next for me?' Henry said eventually.

'I was waiting for you to ask that. It's time to get you closer to the truth. The true you.'

Henry chewed at his lip.

'We must act out of self-interest at all times, Henry. Anything else is hypocrisy. So it's time to go up to the next level.' Matterling's tone was cold, mechanical.

'The next level?'

'You've got to show me that you trust in me completely.'

'You know I do. You've been good to me, Mr Matterling.' He glanced at the briefcase.

'You want the payments to keep coming, don't you?'

'Of course.'

'There could be a big bonus soon. But I've got to know that I can trust you as well. I've got to know that you will be able to go through with whatever I ask of you. You know what else is at stake, of course.'

He knew exactly what Matterling was talking about. Henry's sister, Zoe. It was how Matterling had first made contact. When he was looking for a trusty lieutenant at Bavaria Williams Burnett, to keep tabs on Ben Parfitt. As well as making generous payments to Henry, Matterling had also made generous payments to his sister's then-boyfriend to make intimate videos of themselves. He had made it crystal clear to Henry that if necessary, he would have no compunction in uploading the material to a revenge porn website. And then let her Facebook friends—and everyone in the highly-respectable Evans family—know where they could view it.

Henry was determined not to let that happen. He would protect Zoe no matter what. It was a question of honour.

'A bonus,' Henry said with a steady determination. 'Of course I'll do it.'

'Whatever I ask?'

'Whatever you ask.'

'Stay here. I'll be back in two minutes. I need to collect something from the cloakroom.'

Matterling disappeared towards the entrance. When he was out of sight, Henry put his briefcase on his lap, rolled the numbers on the locks and released the clasps. He looked around to check that no-one was watching him and then opened the case. He lifted the lid of the Fortnum and Mason box. There were no chocolates. It was packed with fifty-pound notes.

He closed the briefcase and set it back down by his side. Matterling reappeared, this time carrying a bag of his own. It was a small leather holdall. Black, with blue and orange stripes.

'Follow me, Henry.'

Matterling led the way out of the Klee exhibition and into the giant Turbine Hall, which had once housed the generators of Bankside power station. The ground floor was packed with visitors and a large contingent of Japanese students had just arrived, led by a middle-aged man with a wispy beard. He was holding a red pennant aloft for his group to follow.

Henry and Matterling took a lift to the top floor and Matterling led the way to a viewing platform that looked out onto the vast exhibition floor below. A stream of people filed along the platform, making their way to the smaller exhibitions set off the main space. There were glass panels along the edge of the platform, underneath a brushed-steel handrail. Matterling found a space next to the edge and leant on the rail, looking down on the throng five storeys below. Henry took his place next to him. The people behind jostled their way past.

'In a minute I am going to give you something.' Matterling's gaze was fixed on the crowd below. 'I want you to hold it in front of you.' He held his hands over the handrail as if holding a football. 'And then I want you to let it go.'

He moved his hands apart and the imaginary football fell sixty feet onto the unsuspecting crowd. Henry followed its descent.

'By the time it lands you will be at the top of those stairs.' He nodded towards the stairs next to the lift door. 'You will then leave the building and go home. Then I want you to get ready for a trip. You will be going to Hong Kong. Sunday night, I'll text you flight details. Bring along your contract of employment and security pass for Bavaria Williams Burnett.' He turned and stared at Henry. 'Understand?'

Henry met his gaze. 'Absolutely.'

Matterling smiled. 'Don't take aim. There is no target. A target would imply intent. And intent would imply a response. A response such as revenge. We are executing a justice much purer than that.'

Matterling unzipped the leather holdall and took out what looked like a present. A gift-wrapped silver block. There was a red ribbon tied around it with a neat bow on top. He shielded it from the view of the people behind him as he passed it to Henry, who took it with both hands.

'A Class A engineering brick. Fired in Staffordshire. Weighs seven and a quarter pounds. Nothing special.'

He zipped the holdall shut.

Henry held the package close to him and squared himself against the rail. He looked at the silver block and then down onto the herd of humanity congregating on the concourse below. 'I like the wrapping. Nice touch, Mr Matterling.'

'A silver lining. Every cloud has one.'

DOUG MATTERLING TURNED AWAY from Henry and melted into the flow of visitors pushing along the corridor. He made his way down the five flights of stairs and onto the ground floor of the massive Turbine Hall.

He was approaching the exit when he heard the scream from behind him. A piercing wail that echoed around the massive space. The hubbub of the crowd ceased abruptly and everyone turned towards the source of the scream. Matterling turned with them. The orderly lines of the Japanese students disintegrated as they crouched around something on the floor. He caught a glimpse of the object of their attention. It was a body. The body of a girl. She lay face down, motionless. A crimson pool of blood was starting to spill over a scrap of silver paper that lay on the concrete floor next to her head.

There was a collective gasp followed by a chilling silence as people looked around anxiously. Then the whole group started screaming. Security guards rushed towards the melee. Matterling turned back to the exit. He smiled to himself as he left the building. He didn't care whether the girl was dead or alive. That had nothing to do with it.

45

London
Friday afternoon

KEN OLSON FELT his phone vibrate on the mattress next to him. He had switched it to silent when he had lain down to get some rest after the flight from San Francisco. He picked it up and swung his legs off the bed.

'Fiona,' he said as he walked through to the suite's living area. 'Good to hear from you.'

'How was your flight?'

'Good thanks. Very good.' He looked out from the top floor of the Athenaeum onto Green Park and watched the pedestrians and joggers flowing along the pathways.

'Ken, I know your schedule is pretty tight but I need to update you about something.'

'Go ahead.'

Fiona Wells had always been a useful contact for him when dealing with the directors of Elba Technology. She took her role in investor relations very seriously and he liked her enthusiasm for arranging presentations and keeping the dialogue going between both sides.

'It's a bit delicate, I'm afraid.'

Olson smiled to himself. Such an English thing—they were always saying how afraid they were. But he was glad to be back, all the same. London had a solidity about it that he always enjoyed. And if all went to plan with Carmel and the takeover, he could spend a lot more time here in the future.

'How do you mean, delicate?'

'It's about your relationship with Carmel.' Fiona's voice was compassionate as if she had bad news to pass on.

'Carmel? What's happened? Is she okay?'

He realised as he asked that if anything had happened to Carmel, Fiona Wells would not be the one telling him about it. But the mention of Carmel made him anxious.

'She's fine. It's not about her. It's about you.'

'Me?'

'Not just you. You and Carmel. It's about your relationship.'

'Our relationship? What the hell has that got to do with anyone?'

'I agree, I agree.' Fiona's tone was soft now, clearly trying to keep him calm. 'But the tabloids have got hold of the story. They're about to run with it.'

'The story? What story?' What had they found out? That Olson Associates was about to launch a bid to take Elba private?

'They've got pictures of you and Carmel together in California. They know that she went there to see you.'

'Okay,' he said slowly. 'But why's that such a big deal? Man meets woman. Woman meets man. Not exactly Pulitzer material, is it?'

'No, but what seems to intrigue them is that she flew out the same day that her husband's body was discovered. In what may or may not have been an accident.'

'May or may not? What are you saying? Victor drowned by accident. Fact.' He paused. 'And where are you getting all this baloney from, anyway?'

'I know a lot of people in the press. It's my job. And this kind of merry widow story gets them excited. Especially when the widow and the lover look the part.'

'The part? We're real people, Fiona. This is a complete non-story. I think there's been a miscommunication. Someone's taken you for a ride.'

'Ken, this is serious. This is real.' She sounded more urgent now and Olson felt that he had to take notice. Familiar though England was, there was plenty here he didn't understand.

'An agency has got hold of this and they'll sell it as a package. They'll have commissioned a freelancer to make it as salacious as possible. They'll describe the husband as a brilliant entrepreneur who died in suspicious circumstances and never reached his potential. The widow will be a ruthless femme fatale whose first husband also died in an unconventional manner. Both she and her new lover are, whether you like it or not, very photogenic. Straight out of central casting.'

She paused. He didn't respond immediately. He was concentrating on the picture she had painted.

'The photographer would have trailed around after them,' she said, 'looking for pictures that will be used out of context.'

He closed his eyes and remembered the photographer in the Japanese Tea Gardens.

'I understand they've got some shots of you hand in hand in a park somewhere.'

Shit. So that's what the jerk was after.

'Does Carmel still wear her wedding ring?' Fiona asked.

'Wedding ring? No. Not last week anyway. I remember that.'

It was the first thing he had checked for when they had met in Santa Barbara, on the day she had been told of Victor's death. He had been pleasantly surprised. He had taken it as a sign.

'That won't go unnoticed,' Fiona said. 'In fact, I bet that portion of the shot will be blown up and shown as a bubble. With a big arrow pointing to her bare ring finger.'

He could see the photo spread now. He was starting to feel queasy.

'Can you remember being in a park with her? Last week?'

'Yes.' he said quietly, then mentally gave himself a good shake. Why the hell was he starting to feel guilty? 'I can see what you're saying. But aren't there laws against that kind of misrepresentation?'

'Can you remember what she was wearing?'

He could. The same bright red suit that she had worn for the meeting with Peter and Jim.

'Sure. A red suit. She was the best-dressed person in the park that day.'

'They'll make that a very vivid red, I can assure you.'

'Sheesh,' he said and sighed. 'So aren't there laws?'

Fiona didn't reply. He knew the answer.

The last thing he wanted was to be splashed all over the tabloids, depicted as some kind of sleazy lothario preying on vulnerable widows. He had spent his career avoiding the spotlight. He was the guy in the background. The guy behind the entrepreneurs. He enjoyed being known within the VC community but that was as far as it went. That got him the best opportunities and the best deals. What if this agency sold the story to the US tabloids as well?

'What can we do?' he said, to stop the train of thought. 'You seem to know a lot about how these slimeballs operate. How can we beat them?'

'The first step is to hire our own publicist.'

Fiona sounded like she knew what she was doing, but he didn't like the sound of what she was saying.

'Hire someone?'

'They can pressurise the relevant editors to publish corrections for factual inaccuracies. There are bound to be some. And then get your side of the story out there—you being an old friend of the de

Souza family. Shoulder to cry on. Support at a time of personal tragedy. That kind of thing.'

'Suppose we do nothing and let the whole thing blow over? I can't see the public being that interested.'

'That's a strategy. But it would be high risk.'

Maybe so, he thought. But the old 'friend of the family' line also seemed pretty high risk. It could easily blow up in his face if the truth about their affair came out.

'These stories can easily build their own momentum,' Fiona said. 'It just needs a few angry comments and a couple of sanctimonious columnists with their own cooked-up moral take on it and pretty soon you've got yourself quite a media storm.'

The consequences of what she was saying started to sink in. He closed his eyes. He was still standing by the window overlooking Green Park, but he didn't see the people below. He was looking at himself. He could become a national hate figure in next to no time.

'I'm sorry, Ken. It's going to be a rough few days.'

'Who the hell could be behind this?' The phone was trembling in his hand. His love affair with this country and its super-polite citizens was careering towards the buffers. 'I mean, it's not as if we're national celebrities.'

'Not yet,' Fiona responded, 'but you've got to nip this in the bud. You must *not* do nothing. Or be seen running away from it.'

Olson's gut tightened. 'This is really bad timing. I'm flying to Hong Kong on Sunday.'

'Oh.'

She didn't have to say any more; he knew what she was thinking. Running away as soon as these stories hit the newsstands was not a good look. And leaving Carmel to face the press by herself. What a heel.

'Is that trip essential?'

'Sure is. I need to collect some documentation for a deal I'm involved in. We're sunk without it.'

'Some documentation? Why can't you FedEx it?'

'It's not that simple. I need to go in person.'

'Couldn't someone go in your stead?'

She had a point. He was only going himself to demonstrate to Carmel how important this acquisition—and their future together—was to him. Handling this tabloid story properly now seemed just as critical. But getting one of the guys from the office over here now would be difficult. It was the weekend and they would all have plans. They would have to come through London so that he and Carmel could set them up with the ID paperwork for the bank.

He looked at his watch. Even if he could find a volunteer, time was running out.

'It's going to be difficult at such short notice,' he said.

'What if I could find someone?' Fiona said. 'Someone completely trustworthy and highly motivated.'

'Are you volunteering?' Olson felt relief flow through him. He had worked with Fiona for many years and she had always impressed him.

'No,' she said and his heart sank. 'You need me here. You need my help to find the right publicist. And then we need to coordinate your campaign.'

She was right, of course. This was uncharted territory for him. He had to work with professionals who knew how these British tabloid bastards worked. If Fiona was right, he was going to have a real fight on his hands.

'I do have an alternative,' she said. 'Someone I have known for a long time and trust implicitly. I know he's keen to meet you because he was scheduled to interview Victor.' There was a respectful pause and Olson thought he detected a slight crack in her voice when she continued. 'That never happened unfortunately.'

'Interview?'

'He was writing a piece about Victor for the *Financial Times*.'

'A journalist?'

'Nothing like the characters who write for the tabloids,' she said quickly. 'This one is very different.'

She sounded confident. She had known this guy for a long time and Olson took comfort from that.

'Let me set up a meeting tomorrow,' she said. 'We could do it before your other meetings. I won't mention any of this to him. As far as he's aware, it'll be an opportunity to find out more about Elba Technology from a major investor. If you approve, just give me the nod and I'll make the suggestion. I'll leave it to you to come up with the fee proposal.'

'How do you know he'll accept?'

'Just tell him that he'll be helping to stop Doug Matterling getting his hands on Elba Technology.'

Olson jerked the phone away from his ear in surprise. 'How do you know about that?'

He could hear the smile in her voice. 'It's my job, Ken.'

46

London
   Friday afternoon

MIKE BRENNAN ROCKED BACK in the creaky captain's chair and tapped his fingers on the small desk. In the last thirty minutes he had received two offers of help. From two different women.

The call from Fiona Wells he had been expecting. What she had had to say, he had not. He had expected her to follow up on his meeting with Charles Salinger but she never mentioned it. She wanted him to meet someone else who could help with background on Elba Technology and Victor de Souza. One of the largest investors in Elba. An American called Ken Olson who was apparently in town and on his way to meet the Elba directors. He could squeeze in a meeting tomorrow, as a favour to Fiona.

When he had heard Olson's name, Brennan had feigned ignorance. He didn't say anything about BM's previous dealings with Olson Associates. He accepted the invitation graciously. His gratitude was genuine—he would relish the opportunity to meet the man who had lost Brennan Matterling plc so much money.

The other call had been from Lisa Richards, who was full of concern after her hospital visit yesterday and wanted to help in any way she could. Brennan had accepted her offer too. She could come with him tomorrow—he wanted to check out Rogers, the security guard at the marina, again. He had a question to ask him. Lisa would be the perfect Mrs Brennan, accompanying her husband on his search for a new berth for their yacht. He didn't tell her about her new role but it would be good to have an ally.

He rocked forward in the chair and the pain in his ribs caught him unaware. He gripped the edge of the desk with both hands to hold his upper body still. He could feel the thud of that biker's boot crashing into him again. It could not have been a coincidence, coming just a few hours after meeting Hazel and her Rottweiler sons. Just who was trying to get hold of Salinger's shares? And why not just raise their offer rather than resorting to force?

Hopefully, Kesey would come up with more on this Heilong company and who was behind it. That would be key.

Fiona's involvement was also interesting. Sarah's character assessment of her had been entirely accurate. So why was she so keen to help him with his piece on de Souza? A piece that was now an obit. Did she believe he was now a journalist?

As the pain ebbed away his resolve grew stronger. In hospital, he had decided on what he needed to do to protect Sarah and Cara. There was only one course of action he could take.

It took him several minutes to get from his desk to the bottom of the stairs and when Sarah saw him clutching the newel in the hallway she reached out with both arms.

'Christ, Mike. Why aren't you lying down? Isn't that what they told you at the hospital?'

He shrugged off her efforts to help him back up the stairs. 'It's nothing. I'm okay. Just the occasional aftershock now.' He grimaced. 'Anyway, I'll lie down in a minute. Right now, I need to talk to you.'

His expression must have been more sombre than he had intended because a shadow of concern passed across her face.

'Sure,' she said. 'Let's sit down.'

She put an arm around him and helped him into the lounge. They sat on the red sofa and she kept her arm around his shoulder.

He straightened his back and looked directly at her.

'I'm sure it was just an accident,' he said. 'It could have happened to anyone.'

She shook her head slowly. 'You don't believe that. I can tell.'

'Where's Cara?'

'Don't worry. She's painting in the playroom.'

There was a long silence. He turned slightly on the seat and winced.

'They tried to kill you,' Sarah said robotically, as though unable to believe it.

Brennan snorted. 'You can't say that for certain. It was either an accident or, at worst, a warning. A clumsy one at that.'

'Okay, so it was a warning. Let's take that as our premise. It still means you were a target.'

She was deadly earnest. Her arm was still around him and for the first time in a long time he felt that they were on the same side. She was a reluctant participant but he knew she was there for him. She had said '*our premise*', hadn't she?

'So what now? What do we do?' Her eyes were still on him.

'I've got to pay another visit to the marina. I've got one more question that needs an answer.'

Her arm tensed around him. It wasn't the response she wanted but he was being completely straight with her now. She looked lost in thought for a moment. Then she said, 'I don't want to know why. I know you want to tell me. But I've got to prioritise now. I've got to protect us.'

'Us?'

'Cara and me.'

There was a long silence.

'So?' she said eventually. 'What do we do?'

'If they try anything else, I don't want you involved.'

Her arm dropped away and she moved a couple of inches along the sofa. She was in survival mode and she would not pretend otherwise.

'I've packed a bag,' he said. 'I'm moving out.'

She was perfectly still, except for her eyelids, which blinked rapidly.

'Keep everything bolted,' he said. 'If I find any evidence that definitively points to de Souza being murdered, I'll take it straight to the police. Believe me.'

'Where will you go?' she said quietly.

'I'll find somewhere. A cheap hotel in the suburbs. Somewhere anonymous.'

Her fists were clenched. She saw him looking and unclenched them. She laid her hands flat on the sofa and her shoulders sagged as though she was already resigned to him going.

'I won't be gone for long. Just until I know what happened.'

He searched her face for a clue as to how she felt about him leaving. Whether she felt the same as him, that this was just a temporary precaution. Or whether deep down she was hoping it was a more permanent arrangement. The words she had used on Tuesday morning.

She was staring through the conservatory at the back garden. She placed her hand on his and turned towards him again. He felt her softening.

'I'll let you know when we can see each other again,' he said. 'I'll go and say goodnight to Cara. I won't make a big deal out of it. She's used to not having me here. If she asks tomorrow, please just tell her that I'll be taking her swimming very soon. I don't want her to think that I've run off again.'

'I don't know what's going to happen. But I do know one thing. I know that you're not running away.'

She smiled a small, affectionate smile. It was all he needed.

He slid his arm around her waist and pulled her closer, ignoring the pain building again in his ribs. Although she didn't respond, she didn't resist.

She was right—he wasn't taking flight. Just the opposite.

47

London
  Friday afternoon

HAZEL HAD MADE sure that all her sons were present for the meeting. None of them had dealt with him directly before. It had all been done through her. But they were lined up now. In a row behind her. She was sitting down, they were standing. Opposite her sat Doug Matterling.

If he was affected by the powerful aroma of aftershave, it didn't show. He was making small talk.

'Excellent exhibition, Hazel. I'd recommend it. Especially if you're interested in Bauhaus.' He scanned the faces of the three sons. There was no flicker of interest. They looked at him with hostility, but that's how they looked at everyone. Even their biggest client.

'I'm not,' she replied blankly. 'My only interest is in having a happy client. I think we're doing everything necessary. Do you agree?'

Matterling leant back in his chair, completely relaxed even in the

cramped offices of Remus Security. He looked around at the paraphernalia of City information and his gaze settled on a painting of the
busy London docks.

'To a degree,' he said eventually. 'To a degree. You've got this kid
Parfitt. That's good. I need him out of the way until next week. Pity
you couldn't have used him better when he was at work. Elba's share
price should have dropped by now.'

He snapped his attention back to her and looked her straight in
the eyes. She flinched. She had not expected direct criticism. Her
sons tensed.

'And as you told me this morning, Brennan's still nosing around.
You didn't hit him hard enough.'

He looked up at her sons. Their faces tightened. No-one had ever
told them they didn't hit hard enough.

'Do you want a different solution?' she said. 'Just say the word.'

'No need for that. I want to see him dangling first. I'm
arranging for him to be in Hong Kong with us next week. He's still
got a job to do. And so have you.' He pointed at the boys. 'Which
of you are coming?' The two brothers at the ends of the row
stepped forward a half step. 'Good. You'll get your instructions
there.' He turned to Hazel again. 'And how's the Carmel campaign
going?'

'It's started already. The teasers are out there. The pressure will
be on tomorrow. I've got stories running in all the tabloids.' She
smiled grimly. 'With pictures.'

'The good old British press. Consistently gullible. What would
we do without them?'

'So it's a definite, is it? No last-minute change of heart, like last
time?' Hazel raised her eyebrows in an exaggerated show of defiance.

'It wasn't a change of heart. It was all part of a negotiation. I
needed that IP story pulled when the deal went my way. There's no
need for sarcasm. You got another very lucrative job out of it. As you
very well remember.' He stared at her for several long seconds. 'What
kind of pictures?'

'Shots of them walking hand in hand. Some park in San Francisco. All lovey-dovey.'

'No kissing?'

She shifted in her chair. 'It's clear what they're up to.'

'Not good enough. Osculation would have been optimal.'

Her three sons all stepped forward together.

'Easy boys, easy,' Matterling said sharply, his chin jutting towards them. 'That's not criticism. Think of it as customer feedback. I'm sure you can make amends next week.'

He reached into the holdall on the floor and pulled out a large Fortnum and Mason chocolate box. He placed it on the desk and got up to go.

'For you, Hazel. To share with the family.' He grinned, his teeth bright against his tanned face. 'More next week. When I recover what's rightly mine.'

He left the room and closed the door behind him. Hazel looked appreciatively at the box. Her three sons stared at the door. All three leant forward but their feet stayed rooted to the floor. Three attack dogs on a single leash. They let out a collective snarl. Hazel smiled proudly.

48

London
Saturday morning

BEN HAD BEEN HERE for two days now. Sleep came and went. A spluttering kind of sleep. There was no routine to it. He paced around the cellar for a bit, sat for a bit, half-slept for a bit. Then he paced again and tried to find a weak spot in the walls or ceiling. There were none. Only two points of access. The door into the cellar from the steps leading up to the ground floor and the double trap-doors, which he presumed opened up to the street.

The only routine was the mealtimes. Three times a day. One of the brothers would appear, instruct him to sit on the narrow iron bed opposite the door, then put a plate and a bottle of water on the floor. Breakfast was a sandwich; lunch was a plastic bowl of salad; dinner was a microwaved ready-meal. All from Marks and Sparks. Then they would back out, turn the key and slide the bolt behind them.

After the first morning they hadn't said anything, other than telling him to sit down. They refused to answer his questions. They just looked at him as though they were longing to take a pop at him but were under strict instructions not to harm the prisoner. It didn't make for a great atmosphere.

Ben had tried to climb up to the trapdoors without success. He had stacked the empty barrels to get some height but the doors were too high above. There were a couple of wooden wheels next to the doors which he assumed helped open them when they were unlocked. At one time there had been a ramp positioned under the doors, so that beer barrels could be rolled down into the cellar. But only part of it now remained. The rest had been cut away and removed. A dungeon had been created.

There was a squeak from the top of the stairs. The top door was opening. Ben checked his watch—nearly eight.

He had been running his hands around the door to check for any weakness. He hurried back to the bed and took his position.

The sound of quick footsteps. The key turning. The bolt sliding.

'On the bed,' a voice commanded and the door swung open.

The musty, beery air was suddenly permeated with a blast of aftershave and Ben felt a pang of gratitude for the change. This time he had decided not to try and start a conversation. The tallest brother entered, slightly thinner than the others. He kept his eyes on Ben as he placed the tray on the floor. He was in the uniform. Black shoes, black trousers and black polo neck sweater. He stood up slowly and kept looking. He was obviously thinking hard. Ben kept quiet.

'This time next week,' he said at last.

'What about next week?' Ben said.

'It'll all be over for you. By this time next week.' He looked uncomfortable, perhaps because he was speaking. 'Thought you'd like to know.'

'It's Saturday, right?' Ben had been trying to keep track of time but now he wasn't so sure that he hadn't missed a day. Time and consciousness were starting to play tricks on him.

'Right.'

'I've got a flight to catch. Tomorrow. If I'm not there, they'll come looking for me.' Even as he said it, Ben realised it was no threat. No-one knew where he was. Except for one person: Henry Evans. He was the only one who could have told the gang of Ben's whereabouts before he was captured. And Henry had kept him at his hideous rope-themed flat long enough for them to pick him up in broad daylight.

His captor gave a short contemptuous snort. 'Don't think so, chum. And don't worry about your seat to Hong Kong. It's gone.'

With that *he* was gone, locking and bolting the door and running up the stairs.

Gone? So, these guys knew all about his travel arrangements. And if he was not going to Hong Kong with Olson, then who was? He hadn't had time to tell Julie about the family emergency that would have let him get there on Wednesday. It had to be an employee of BWB to meet the conditions for the pick-up, he knew that much. Perhaps it would be Henry. Christ, the pillock couldn't be that desperate for a trip to the Orient, could he?

Ben lay back on the bed and let out a long breath. At least the end was in sight. They would let him out and he could get his life back. Presumably something would happen with Elba and they wouldn't need him out of the way anymore. He could return to work, have Julie be all sympathetic to him after all he had been through and everything would get back to normal. That was what the taller brother had been saying, wasn't it?

By this time next week.

He got up from the bed and went to pick up the tray. But after a couple of steps, he froze. Perhaps that wasn't it at all. Perhaps he was saying something completely different.

It'll be all over for you.

That was what he had said.

It'll be all over for you.

The wave of relief receded quickly as Ben reinterpreted this one sentence. Then the tsunami hit. His whole body shuddered. He stepped back unsteadily and collapsed onto the bed.

49

Hampshire Coast
   Saturday morning

'WE'RE JUST HOPING this security guy's going to be here, right?'
Lisa said.

Brennan had enjoyed having her with him for the drive down
from London. After he had left his room at the Premier Inn on
Hangar Lane he had driven south to Barnes to pick her up.

'Ideally, yes. He was the one I spoke to last weekend. But anyone
might be able to let us know if there has been any further activity.'

He sounded indifferent but this morning's excursion was predicated on Gary Rogers being at work today. He should be, according
to the roster Brennan had seen on his previous visit. He had told Lisa
that they were on a fishing trip. Just a nose around.

They pulled up in the car park behind the marina. The morning
was sharp but bright. It wasn't even nine o'clock.

He had picked her up from her tiny pink terraced house just
before seven and they had made good time before the Saturday

morning traffic started to build. On the drive down they had talked about Elba Technology and Victor de Souza, going over again what he had told her in hospital. She had been interested in what he and Kesey had found out about the Heilong share structure. Her family were from Hong Kong and she had laughed knowingly when he had told her about his money-laundering theory.

He had not told her about his new domestic arrangements. Nor had he told her about his upcoming meeting with Ken Olson. Best not to mention Olson to her at the moment.

'The marina office is just behind those yachts,' he said, pointing at the jumble of masts to their left. 'Our boat's currently on the east coast, don't forget. Place called Woolverstone, if he asks. And we're just making enquiries at this stage.'

Lisa grinned. 'The happy yachties, eh? Matching Guernseys, I hope. How sweet.'

Brennan smiled back. She was enjoying the role. Right now he could think of worse things. Plenty of worse things. He had an ally.

They picked their way through the melee of haul-outs filling the hardstanding between the car park and the marina, each boat set upon its own arrangement of struts and wedges to keep it secure through the winter. The steps up to the marina office were still damp with dew. Brennan pushed open the glass door, which was misty with condensation. He ushered Lisa in.

Rogers was on duty, as per the roster. He was sitting behind the wooden desk. Brennan glanced at the floor underneath it but there was no recording equipment now. Brennan scanned the rest of the office. It looked much like last time.

Rogers was poring over an article in *The Sun*, his fat index finger pushing along a line of print as he read. He looked up guiltily. 'Er, morning, morning. Can I help you?'

Brennan stepped up to the desk. 'I hope so, Gary. I was here just over a week ago. We're thinking of moving our Beneteau here.' He glanced sideways at Lisa. 'You gave me some information. Do you remember?'

'Er, yes. Of course, sir.' He started rising from his chair, looking relieved that he was not being presented with a new challenge. 'On the east coast at the moment, isn't it?'

'That's right. I just thought my wife should see the marina facilities before we make a decision.' Brennan could feel Lisa straighten with surprise that they were now married. He turned to her. 'She would need to, wouldn't she?'

'She certainly would,' Lisa replied with an amused glint in her eye.

Brennan glanced down at the article which Rogers had been reading.

TYCOON WIDOW LOSES HEART IN SAN FRAN

A large colour picture showed an elegant lady wearing a bright red suit, arm in arm with an equally elegant middle-aged man. They were on a small bridge over a pond, replete with waterlily pads. Brennan recognised her immediately from his internet research on Elba Technology. It was Carmel De Souza.

He also recognised the man from his googling—Ken Olson of Olson Associates.

'One of your clients, eh?' Brennan pointed at the newspaper. 'What's she been up to?'

Rogers' face turned bright red. 'Dunno. Haven't started reading it yet.'

'Do you mind?' Brennan turned the newspaper around on the desk. He scanned the article. 'They're making out that she's already carrying on with someone else before she's even buried her husband.' He looked at Rogers inquisitively. 'Romance at the Japanese Tea Gardens for the merry widow. Well, Gary, what do you think?'

'Me? No idea. Never met her.'

'You met her husband quite a few times, didn't you? That's what you told me last week.'

'Did I? Well, he is—I mean, he was—an owner here.' Rogers put a meaty hand on his newspaper.

'Surprising that the tabloids have got hold of this story though, isn't it? Did you realise that de Souza's private life would make the papers?'

Rogers looked defensive and alarmed at the same time. 'No, no. Not me. I mean, I wouldn't have thought that.'

Brennan smiled to himself. He knew that bringing up de Souza's private life would make Rogers squirm and it was serendipitous that this tabloid story could get him onto the subject straight away. But the fact that de Souza's life was now a matter of public interest might create some complications.

'Anyway, sir,' Rogers said and turned the newspaper back around. 'What other questions about the marina do you have?'

Lisa had adopted an expression of mild disinterest and seemed keen to stay in the background. She had asked Brennan's reason for visiting the marina again but he had kept it vague, just saying that he wanted to look again at the currents around where de Souza's body had been recovered and pay a quick visit to the marina office while he was there.

'Let me show you another newspaper photograph.' Brennan reached into his pocket and pulled out the photograph of Victor de Souza with Doug Matterling. He placed it on top of the newspaper and watched Rogers carefully. The young man's face dropped.

'Well?' Brennan said.

'Not sure what you're after, sir. But that does seem to look like our late client. Any other questions should be directed to our PR department. I can't discuss our clients' affairs. I've got the number here.' He pulled a drawer open and reached inside.

He had gone into corporate mode. Just following instructions.

'How about that one?' Brennan said steadily. 'That's the guy I'm asking about now.' He pointed at Matterling in the photograph. 'Have you ever seen him here before?'

Brennan leant over the desk as he spoke. The casual conversation had become urgent. Rogers' hand froze in the drawer. His eyes darted down to the photograph and back up to Brennan. He looked hesitant.

'I'm . . . I'm not sure what you're asking about. It's nothing to do with me.'

Brennan had seen the flicker of recognition in Rogers' eyes when he had looked at the photo. Behind him, he felt Lisa shift her weight from one foot to the other.

'Your company,' Brennan said. 'Blue World Marinas. I would imagine it prides itself on being an ethical company, doesn't it?'

Rogers looked confused. 'Yes. Yes, of course. It's one of the largest—'

'I'm sure it is,' Brennan cut in. 'And it expects certain standards from its employees. Am I right?'

'Absolutely, sir.' Rogers started to fold his newspaper. 'What is the length of your Beneteau?'

Brennan ignored him. 'It would certainly expect all employees to demonstrate a duty of care to its customers, wouldn't it?'

'We cannot be held responsible for an owner falling into the water, if that's what you're referring to.'

'I'm referring to an employee taking more than a professional interest in the affairs of its customers. Way beyond a duty of care.' Brennan held Rogers' gaze. 'And when I say affairs, I mean *affairs*.'

'I have no idea what you're talking about, sir.'

Brennan smiled. 'I think you do. But let's talk about that drowning. I'd like you to tell me everything you know about it.'

'I told you last week. I don't know anything about it. Just that he must have slipped and fallen off his boat late at night. That's what I told you and that's what I told the police. They seemed happy enough so why are you still asking questions?' Rogers paused. 'What's going on here? What do you want?'

'Let's just say I'm looking for another dead body.'

Rogers looked at him blankly.

'Never mind,' Brennan said. It would be too confusing to bring the concept of justice into their conversation. Better stick to the questions. 'You told me last week that you weren't there when they pulled him out. But it sounded like you were there at some point.' He pointed out at the jetty. 'Over there. By the crates. When were you there? And why?'

'I have to patrol all parts of the marina. That's part of my job. I can't remember the last time I was there.' His gaze dropped to the photograph on his desk. 'That's all I can tell you. I don't have to answer your questions anymore. I've told you enough.'

'That jetty is not part of the marina. There is absolutely no reason why you should ever have gone there as part of your job. Not part of your job at Blue World Marinas, at any rate.'

Rogers looked up from the photograph and quickly glanced at the wall below the window. Brennan followed the tell-tale glance. A few cardboard boxes and the large blue fishing tackle box that Brennan remembered from last week. Rogers was agitated. And holding something back.

'What's in the blue box, Gary?'

Rogers looked suddenly alarmed. 'Only fishing gear. Nothing to do with you. If you've got no further questions about the marina, I'm going to have to ask you to leave.' He shot Lisa an apologetic glance. 'Or I'll have to call my supervisor.'

Brennan moved around the desk and stood next to Rogers. 'I don't think you want to do that, do you? I don't think your supervisor wants to hear about your little hobby, does he? I'm not talking about fishing. I'm talking about your collection of recordings.'

Rogers' eyes widened and his cheeks blazed.

'My what?'

'Now, just tell me when you were last over by the jetty and why.'

Brennan maintained the stare. Fear was dancing in Rogers' eyes. But what was he so afraid of? Not just of being found out as an eavesdropper. There seemed to be more at stake.

'You're just guessing,' Rogers said. 'There is no collection. I don't know what you're talking about.' His voice was quiet, almost a whisper. He rose from his chair and glanced at Lisa in embarrassment. She remained expressionless.

'It's a simple enough question.' Brennan spoke slowly, with controlled exasperation. 'The sooner you tell me, the sooner I'll be out of your hair.'

Rogers held Brennan's look and then his face hardened. He shook his head slowly. 'There's nothing to tell.'

Brennan had reached the end of the road as far as politeness was concerned. There was nothing else for it. In one swift movement he grabbed Rogers' tie, twisted it quickly around his hand and yanked it towards him. Rogers jerked forwards. Lisa gasped

Brennan released the tie and forced his fingers between Rogers' collar and neck. His knuckle pressed into Rogers' larynx..

'For the last time, Gary. Just tell me.'

Rogers gurgled and his eyes bulged. He scrabbled at his collar but Brennan's grip was too strong. There was no space for him to insert his thick fingers. He nodded frantically and Brennan released his grip just enough for the gurgling to stop but not enough for Rogers to get any purchase.

'It was a few weeks ago,' Rogers gasped. 'I'll tell you.' He gulped for air. 'Just let go. Please.'

Brennan released his grip and Rogers slumped back into his chair. He rubbed at his throat and looked up at Brennan in shock.

'I was there a few weeks ago. I found the key. In the water. I'll show you.'

He pulled himself up and went to the plastic fishing tackle box under the window. He opened the lid and several drawers concertinaed out. He rummaged around at the bottom of the box and pulled out a cork ball about the size of a golf ball. It had some writing on the side. A single key hung from it. He held it up for Brennan to see.

'The key for *Turmoil*,' he said. 'It was floating by the piles, caught up in some netting. It hadn't been taken by the tide.'

'How long ago?' Brennan asked softly. Rogers was ready to talk now and Brennan didn't want him clamming up. But the photos that he had taken last Sunday indicated that *Turmoil* was locked up. So, de Souza would have had the key with him when he went into the water.

'Three weeks, I would say. Perhaps a bit more. Can't remember exactly when I was told.'

'You were told to look for it?'

Rogers glanced furtively at the photograph on the desk as he resumed his seat, still clutching the boat key.

'By that man?' Brennan pointed at Matterling's face. Rogers nodded meekly.

'How come?'

'We had an arrangement.'

'What kind of arrangement?'

'I would keep an eye out for him. Let him know what was happening. He would come by every now and then when he was visiting Mr de Souza . . . The pay here's not too great, you see.'

'I do see. And presumably your brief was to keep an eye specifically on Mr de Souza.'

Rogers nodded again and then his gaze drifted out of the window and towards the pontoon where *Turmoil* was moored.

'I would just let him know when Mr de Souza came and went. That was all he seemed to want to know.'

'So had de Souza been working on his boat the day before he was found? As you told me last week?'

Rogers bit his lip. 'I hadn't seen him since I found the key. I thought he must have gone home for a bit. But he left his car here for some reason. It's still in the car park.'

'And you didn't think to report that to anyone?'

'None of my business. That's what he told me. For my bonus.'

He seemed defeated but relieved to have told Brennan about the arrangement with Matterling. Brennan felt that he had gone as far as he could.

'It was good of you to tell me. You've done the right thing. It won't go any further and I've got no intention of talking to your boss. Or anyone else at Blue World. We'll leave you alone, now.'

Rogers' face relaxed with relief.

'Can I just have another quick look at that article?' Brennan nodded towards the newspaper. Rogers pushed it towards him. Brennan looked at the top of the article and ran his finger under the name of its author. 'Thanks, Gary. Have a good day.'

Brennan and Lisa stepped out into the chill and looked across towards the jetty to where Victor de Souza had been craned out. They were both silent for several seconds.

Lisa eventually said, 'Christ. Since when did you start roughing people up like that?' Her voice was interested, not judgemental.

'Since I realised there's no such thing as natural justice. Just because I was in a Cat Four, that doesn't mean it was stuffed full of Gentleman Jims, you know. I had to take care of myself. In whatever way was necessary.' He smiled at her. 'Anyway, let's get you back to Barnes. And after that I've got a call to make. To a real low-life.'

She raised her eyebrows. He turned towards the car park as he answered her unspoken question.

'The scum of the scum. A tabloid journalist.'

50

London
    Saturday morning

FIONA WELLS HURRIED to the end of Halkin Street and turned left at Belgrave Square. She stopped about ten yards short of the armed policeman standing guard at the covered entrance of the Turkish Embassy.

She tightened the belt of her fawn Barbour coat and checked her watch. Right on time. She noticed the policeman checking her out quickly. She was used to that lightning-fast top-to-toe look, although she knew that his scrutiny had a different focus. Looking for concealed weapons and explosives rather than assessing her physique.

She looked back towards Halkin Street. The traffic was coming from that direction. A couple of cars slowed down for their drivers to take a closer look at her. She avoided any eye contact.

A large black Mercedes with tinted windows crawled around the corner. The nearside lane was kept clear for drop-offs and pick-ups at the embassies and consulates that lined the square. The Mercedes stopped at the kerb when it reached her. The policeman kept up his calm surveillance. Another black Mercedes in a land of black Mercedes.

This time she looked in. Two solid-looking young men sat in the front, both wearing black polo necks. Both had dark hair and both just stared ahead, giving nothing away.

The rear door opened. She peered in and smiled at the passenger in the rear seat. She slipped in next to him, her long legs folding smoothly into place. The door closed behind her and she leant across to offer her cheek. The man inside kissed it lightly and put his hand on her knee. She placed her own on top of his, her crimson nails extending onto his thigh.

His free hand pulled a holdall out of the footwell. It was black leather with an orange stripe down the middle. He placed it on his lap, unzipped it slowly and pulled out a turquoise Fortnum and Mason chocolate box. He pulled his left hand away from hers and used both hands to set the box down carefully on her lap.

She lifted the gift as if to gauge its weight. She placed it back on her lap. Then she slid closer to him across the seat. She moved her head towards his. Her red lips parted slightly as they reached his. Slowly, she extended her tongue. She moved its tip along the length of his top lip then down and across his bottom lip. She pressed herself against him and her hands stayed on the box as her lips touched his. He reached for her waist.

She slowly retracted her tongue and moved away. She smiled and took his hand. She extended his fingers and slipped his hand under her coat. She held it there for several seconds. Then she withdrew it and placed it back onto the handle of the holdall, which was still on his lap.

The door opened and her legs unfolded. In one graceful move-ment she had swung off the seat and was standing on the pavement. She removed a green Harrods plastic bag from her pocket and put the chocolate box into it. She gently closed the car door and bent over to look through the window. She mouthed an exaggerated '*Thank You*' into the glass then pulled herself up and walked away quickly, back in the direction she had come from.

The Embassy policeman watched her disappear around the corner. The Mercedes glided off towards Victoria. The policeman shifted his weight from one foot to the other and returned to gazing out over the garden square. Just another slow shift in Belgravia.

51

London
Saturday noon

BRENNAN MANAGED to find a metered parking bay in Halkin Street. Just opposite the Caledonian Club where he was shortly due to meet Fiona Wells and Ken Olson. As he turned off the car engine his phone rang.

'Good morning, Mr Brennan. I trust you are well.'

Brennan instantly recognised the self-important tones of Charles Salinger. He felt a spurt of anger. He had been debating whether to phone Salinger ever since he had left St Mary's. After all, it was Salinger who had led him to Remus Security in the first place. With his bloody sprat.

'Not as well as I might be, Mr Salinger.'

'That's a shame. I just wondered how you were getting on with your enquiries.'

'Slowly. I've been *hors de combat* for a couple of days. As you are doubtless aware.'

'Aware? Aware of what?' He sounded genuinely surprised. 'Out of action? How?'

'An errant motorbike ploughed into me a few nights ago. Not long after I'd visited the offices of Remus Security on your behalf.'

'Oh.' Salinger's voice was flat.

Brennan waited for more but there was a telling silence. Although Salinger did not sound as if he knew about the hit, he didn't sound like he was too surprised either.

'Is that it? Nothing more to say?'

'I regret that you have had an accident. And that you are connecting it with your visit to my contact. I can assure you that I had nothing to do with it.'

'I have a question about my visit to your house. You knew that I was going to call you, didn't you?'

'I wish you a speedy recovery, Mr Brennan. Goodbye.'

Brennan took the phone from his ear and stared at it. Salinger didn't want to know. But if he knew about the hit-and-run then why call? Which pointed to Fiona being behind it.

The phone rang again. Brian Kesey's name flashed up.

'Hi, Brian. What's up?'

'A couple of things, buddy. You okay?'

'Better, thanks. Just got back from the coast. I'll tell you about it in a minute. You first.'

'Right,' Kesey said doubtfully. 'Firstly, I've been looking at the recent share trades in Elba Technology. The price has been holding up well over the last week. Although there have been a few big sells, there has been a constant pattern of buying. The order quantities are often sixty-six thousand and eighty-eight thousand. These quantities keep coming up. I'm no expert in these things but it looks like it could be a broker working an order for someone. A broker who has been instructed to buy in these quantities.'

'Thanks for looking. Sounds like stake-building.'

'Someone superstitious.'

'Sixes and eights. I agree. Chinese lucky numbers. Could be buying before a takeover offer. How far back have you looked?'

'A couple of weeks so far.'

'Mm. I'm just about to meet Ken Olson, that American venture capital guy.'

'Really?' Kesey sounded impressed. 'How did you manage that?'

'Through a lady called Fiona Wells. She does Elba's PR and she knew I'd be keen to meet him. She phoned me yesterday to set it up.'

'That'll give you a chance to find out what happened to your investment.'

'Exactly.'

'Be careful, Mike. Don't lose your rag or you'll find yourself on the wrong end of a lawsuit. You know what the Americans are like.'

'It's not just that. My trip to the coast this morning was about Victor de Souza. His boat was locked and his body was discovered in a place that isn't consistent with him falling off his boat accidentally.'

'Olson?'

'He would have the most to gain, wouldn't he? Now that he's hooked up with the widow.'

'I saw that story as well this morning. Do you think it's true?'

'Never had you down as a *Sun* reader, Brian. But yes, I had been told by someone else.' He did not mention Fiona's name again but she did seem to be figuring prominently now.

'Let me get on to the second thing. It's this list of shareholders for Heilong. You know there seemed to be a few addresses that kept appearing? Well, I've been looking at it again. Do you remember when we set up the Hong Kong company for Brennan Matterling? I don't think you ever used the company, but I remember using a lawyer there called David Yin to set it up. His firm's offices are on Lockhart Road in Wan Chai. I double-checked the address and that same address kept coming up in our list.'

'That wouldn't be surprising if it's a big law firm, would it?' Brennan said. 'I'd imagine quite a lot of shareholders give their lawyer's address rather than their private address.'

'I agree. But I just thought I'd check. So I gave David a call earlier. I guessed that he'd still be in his office on a Saturday—they're eight hours ahead but they work all hours anyway.'

'Go on,' Brennan said tentatively. Kesey was leading up to something.

'We had quite a long chat. He was pleased to hear from me and I said that I might have some other work for him.'

'Which you might.'

'Anyway, he was pretty talkative. He seemed to think we were kind of colleagues. He told me he acted for a number of the shareholders and they had all made their investments in Heilong through an outfit called Rozario Capital.'

'Based in Hong Kong?'

'That's right. Also registered at David's address. Also a client of his. So I checked out this firm Rozario.' Kesey paused, stretching it out. 'It only has one shareholder and one director.'

Brennan's stomach started to sink.

'You'll never guess who it is.'

'Tell me.'

'Doug Matterling.'

'Oh, Christ.'

The mental picture of Matterling flicked up again. Yesterday Brennan had been able to look beyond him. Today, he was bigger, looming over everything. His involvement with de Souza's demise was unquestionable. Taking over Elba Technology would open the way to laundering a big chunk of cash out of Hong Kong. Possibly in cahoots with that shyster Ken Olson.

'You've been a big help,' Brennan said.

'No problem, buddy. Speak soon.'

Brennan stared at the Caledonian Club entrance through the car window. Were Matterling and Olson in it together?

There was only one way to find out.

52

London
   Saturday afternoon

BRENNAN FINISHED FEEDING the parking meter and turned to cross the road to the Caledonian Club. Fiona Wells had appeared and was standing under the Saltire hanging over the neo-classical entrance. She looked quintessentially Belgravia in her waisted Barbour and high heels. She looked as good as when Brennan had seen her earlier in the week. But he was seeing her in a different light now.

She flicked a wave of blonde hair away from her face and rose slightly on her toes to kiss him on the cheek, although there was no need, as her heels made her about the same height as Brennan.

'Mike. How great to see you again. Twice in one week. What a lucky girl.' Her red lips spread tighter against her megawatt white smile. 'Come in, come in. Ken's already here.' She pushed open the carved wooden door, letting him hold it for her. 'I'm sure you'll love it here. I'll quickly sign you in and then we can go through to the bar.'

She leant over the extravagant visitor book on a table in the lobby. To Brennan's left was the reception desk. The receptionist smiled warmly at him as she got up from her chair and came towards them. She was dressed in a blue tartan suit.

'Sign here, Mike,' Fiona said. She had written his address as simply *London, England.*

Fiona led the way. A wide, sweeping staircase with ornate iron-work balustrades flowed down into the hall. Sombre portraits of Scottish lairds and dignitaries lined the walls leading to the floor above. The far corner of the hall showcased a tall longcase clock and statuettes stood in the other corners of the grand space.

As he took in his surroundings, Brennan thought about how Matterling might be connected to Ken Olson. De Souza's death would certainly be convenient for Olson if he wanted to be with Carmel. And if Heilong were building a stake in Elba technology, then de Souza's death could open up the company to a takeover from them. All very neat. Matterling gets the company, Olson gets the girl. So why would Olson want this meeting? What use could Mike Brennan be to them?

'We're through here,' Fiona said over her shoulder.

They turned left into the bar area. At a corner table, an athletic-looking man was looking expectantly towards the doorway. Brennan recognised him from this morning's newspaper. Tanned skin, healthy good looks, like he had just come from the country club after a day of tennis and swimming. Very Silicon Valley. Tortoiseshell glasses, preppy Brooks Bros blazer and khaki pants, as he would call them. He jumped up and stepped towards Brennan with a big grin and an outward stretched hand. Brennan took it.

'Ken, this is Mike Brennan. Mike, Ken Olson.'

Olson pumped Brennan's hand vigorously. A real bone-crusher. 'Mike, great to meet you,' he thundered, as if this were the highlight of his life so far.

'Likewise,' Brennan said, thinking just the opposite. After all, this was the guy who had lost BM three hundred thousand dollars. Olson hadn't made the connection. That wasn't surprising; he had only dealt with Matterling. Brennan was just a name on the corporate account. But this was also the guy who might be behind de Souza's murder. And carrying on with his victim's wife. Brennan had to admire his front.

Fiona gestured at them to sit down while she remained standing. 'Ken's drinking bitter, an Eighty Shilling. What can I get you, Mike?'

'Great ale,' Olson said, smacking his lips.

'That sounds good,' Brennan said and smiled.

Fiona turned and went to the bar. She moved assuredly, with measured steps. Olson's eyes followed her. Brennan studied Olson while his attention was still on Fiona. A flattish nose, wide mouth, almond eyes, marked crow's feet spreading towards his temples. Dark hair streaked with grey. And a stupid, stubby ponytail. Handsome, all the same, Brennan conceded grudgingly.

Olson's gaze finally left Fiona. 'Quite a bar, don't you think?'

'Yes, very comfortable.'

The barman was smartly-dressed in a tie and tartan trousers. Behind him, shelves full of whiskies stretched along the length of the wall. The facing wall featured crests from what Brennan assumed to be Scottish regiments and there was a large shield with crossed swords over the door. The carpet was a vivid blue tartan, the same as that sported by the receptionist and barman. It had a warm, homely feel. Home from home for Scots in London.

They had the bar to themselves apart from a thin, gangling man with red hair who was perched on a stool at the far end of the bar reading The Scotsman. Brennan heard Fiona asking for a pint of Eighty Shilling and a Gin and Tonic. The barman responded in an East European accent.

She brought over a glass of frothy, tawny-coloured beer and set it on the table in front of Brennan. Then she leant over and placed a hand on each of the men's shoulders. She looked at them in turn and squeezed. Her raw sexuality coursed through her touch. It was as if she was using it to glue them together.

Brennan smiled a neutral smile at her. She was some operator.

She squeezed tighter, her perfectly manicured nails digging into the cloth of their jackets. 'A couple of club rules in here, by the way. No business papers and no mobiles.' She smiled at Olson. 'Cells, I mean.'

Olson was acting like he didn't have a care in the world. But it wasn't for Brennan to broach the subject of the San Francisco liaison featured in the tabloids. The purpose of the meeting was to talk about Elba. Once he had a better understanding of the early days of the company then he would tackle Olson on the failed BM investment.

Fiona took a seat and the barman brought over her drink. There was a certain hierarchy here, Brennan thought. And for some reason, he was at the top.

'Thank you so much for sparing Mike some time,' Fiona said to Olson. 'With everything that's going on.' She turned to Brennan. 'Ken has an irritating PR matter to deal with as a matter of some urgency. It's all a bit tedious, to be honest with you.'

'I know,' Brennan said. 'I've seen the papers this morning.' Olson started to look uncomfortable.

'I can't believe people can publish that kind of thing,' Olson sighed. 'But if I could get hold of the little bitch that wrote it, I'd wring her goddam neck.'

'You can see how the papers blow something innocuous out of all proportion,' Fiona added calmly. 'But we'll respond robustly. It'll all be over in a few days. A storm in a teacup.' She looked at Olson. 'How's Carmel?'

He bit his lip. 'Pretty cut up about it, as you can imagine.'

She leant back in her chair and took a sip of her drink. 'So, as I explained, Mike is doing a piece on Victor de Souza for the *FT*. An obituary now, unfortunately.' Her head bowed a fraction. 'And I thought it might be useful for him to get your perspective. You knew Victor a long time, didn't you?'

Ken nodded and waited for her to continue.

'So fire away, Mike. I'm sure you've got some beady questions.'

That was the tabloid story dealt with, then. She had hit it as the first item on the agenda and swiftly moved on. Olson now looked preoccupied and was staring at the row of whiskies with what seemed like more than academic interest. Brennan decided not to mention what the 'little bitch' had told him that morning. At least for now.

'What attracted you to Elba all those years ago?' he asked.

'Our criteria are quite simple,' Olson replied. 'Solid IP that will shape the market, high barriers to entry and exceptional management. Elba had all three.'

'And now that Victor's no longer there?'

'A great loss, there's no denying that. But he built a good team around him. Plenty of talent coming through. We're still committed.' Olson seemed unperturbed by de Souza's demise.

'And the technology?'

'Cutting edge. They focus two cycles ahead. Pipeline is exciting. Elba has proved a great investment for us but there's plenty more to come from them.'

Olson's enthusiasm for Elba was to be expected. Now Brennan had to take him in another direction.

'The people whose money you invest. What kind of people are they?'

'A mixture. Quite a few other private equity funds spreading the risk. Individuals, family offices, some pension funds.'

'Spreading the risk? How about direct investment?'

'Direct investment?' Olson frowned. 'I'm not sure what you mean by that.'

Brennan's stomach tightened. 'Direct investment. Where an investor puts his money directly into one or two companies. A couple of start-ups, say.' He gulped down a large mouthful of beer.

'Oh, I see. No, no, we don't do it that way. All investors go into a fund—we have quite a few for different types of investment, different industries or different stages of business development. You know, start-ups, early-stage, expansion, that kind of thing. But our funds make the investments. We don't just take a single investor's money and put it straight into one company. Especially not a start-up.' He laughed. 'We wouldn't have much of a reputation if we did that kind of thing. There are bound to be a few failures but we have to spread the risk and then the real winners easily outweigh the few losers.'

Brennan's stomach tightened even more and he could feel the colour rising in his face.

'And has this been your policy over the last few years?'

'Sure. Since we started over twenty years ago.'

Brennan hadn't intended to get onto the subject quite so quickly but Olson's flat denial that clients could invest directly into start-ups had side-swiped him.

'Do you remember a client called Brennan Matterling?'

Olson's expression hardened. His professional guard went up. 'I cannot comment on individual clients. You must know that.'

'But you can talk to them.'

'Of course.'

'Well, go ahead. I'm the Brennan of Brennan Matterling.'

Olson smiled. 'Really? Well, that's a coincidence. So, you would have come across my name even if I haven't come across yours. Apologies, I had no idea. I remember Doug, of course. He always said you were far too busy creating magic for your clients to get involved in the boring detail of corporate investments. I'm sorry you didn't stay with us longer.'

Stay with us longer? What the hell was Olson on about?

'It wasn't as if we had a choice, was it?' Brennan was just about managing to keep his voice under control. He had to be prepared to let the BM matter go. It was just one of those things. Win some, lose some. Now that he had Olson in front of him he needed to concentrate on Olson's relationship with Matterling. To see what they were up to.

Olson looked apologetic. 'I was sorry to hear about your cash flow problems. It was a pity about the timing. The fact that you had to withdraw your money from us to put back into your own company. I told Doug at the time that the funds you went into were really going to perform.'

Brennan stared at him. The apologetic look had turned into one of commiseration.

'I was right.' Olson hesitated. 'An average of over thirty per cent increase in value. In the last twelve months.'

Fiona was rapidly switching between them for a clue as to what they were talking about. 'Do you two already know each other?'

Brennan needed to get this out of the way as quickly as possible so he could get the meeting back on track. 'Brennan Matterling plc invested in Ken's VC fund some years ago. Sorry that I didn't mention it yesterday, Fiona, but I didn't think it would be relevant. It was just one of those things. A bet that didn't pay off. Let's get back to Elba.' He grimaced at Olson who had his chin on his fist, looking straight at Brennan.

'You're talking like you lost money,' Olson said. 'You know that wasn't the case.'

'Of course we lost money. We went into two start-ups and both of them failed. Look, let's just move on, shall we? No need to go over old ground.' Brennan did not want to move on but this would give Olson the opportunity to show his hand. If he did want to change the subject then he was lying about the direct investment route.

'No. Let's not move on. Your company got back every cent of your investment with us. Plus a small profit. I handled the matter personally.' Olson spoke slowly and deliberately, his voice rising. The barman looked up from arranging his glasses and the member at the end of the bar put down his paper.

'Not according to the auditor's certificate.' Brennan spoke softly, trying to lower the temperature.

'What auditor's certificate?' Olson rose an inch from his chair, his palms on the chair's arms, ready to defend his reputation. Brennan tensed. This was not going as planned.

'A certificate of loss was presented to our meeting of creditors,'

Brennan said. 'August last year. I was also told about a class action against you.'

'Our auditors do not issue reports relating to individual investments and there are no class actions against us.' Olson spoke steadily, defiantly.

As the words settled, Brennan knew. He could tell from the blaze in his eyes. Olson was not lying.

'The transfer was made in June last year,' Olson said, closing his eyes as if mentally flicking back through the Brennan Matterling file. 'Some three hundred thousand dollars US. To the account the money had originally come from. Through your Hong Kong subsidiary. Where your treasury function for Asia and the US was based, I remember Doug saying.'

'Treasury? We did have a Hong Kong subsidiary but it was never used. Dormant . . .'

Olson opened his eyes and the two men looked at each other for several seconds. The bar was quiet again, apart from the glasses clinking as the barman went back to arranging them on the shelves. The newspaper at the end of the bar rustled in witness to the concentration being applied by its reader.

Fiona took a sip of her gin and Brennan took a deep breath to help him digest this new information. He could see from Olson's reaction that he was on the level. If not, why agree to this meeting?

Fiona placed her glass on the table. 'Excuse me, gentlemen,' she said quietly. 'It looks like you need a minute and I've got a call to make.'

She left the room and Brennan stared after her absently. This BM angle was news to her but there was another reason for this meeting that was yet to become clear.

What *was* clear was that the auditor's report must have been a forgery. Matterling was behind it and there was evidently no collusion between him and Olson. Three hundred thousand dollars had been siphoned out of BM by Doug Matterling, routing the cash through a bank account in Hong Kong that Brennan thought had never been used.

That was a matter for the police and Brennan resolved to take it up with them as soon as practicable. But now there were complications. After all, a business colleague of Matterling's had just been murdered and Elba Technology was suddenly in play. And it looked like Matterling was trying to get his hands on it.

Brennan let his breath out slowly as he started to contemplate the consequences.

What had Salinger said about Elba?

Think what you could create with that power over so many minds?

The stakes had suddenly got a whole lot higher.

53

London
   Saturday afternoon

IN THE WAREHOUSE FLAT, one corner had been designed as the sleeping area. The corner walls were exposed brick and the other two edges comprised flat shoji screens suspended by wires from ceiling rafters. The gap between the screens provided access. There was a modular oak and steel wardrobe unit along one of the brick walls. The bed was circular, like a giant elevated pancake.

Henry had put his suitcase on the bed and started packing. It was half full of clothes. He stood on a kick step, reaching into the back of one of the storage cupboards at the top level of the modular unit. He found what he was looking for and stepped down onto the floor. He returned to the bed with a bundle of polythene-coated brown packing paper.

He placed it next to the suitcase and carefully unwrapped it. Inside was a black leather sheath. He held it up and withdrew a fifteen-inch Bowie hunting knife. The tang of the blade extended the whole length of the hardwood handle. The handguard was made of brass. He ran the tip of his thumb along the edge of the blade and smiled.

'Thank you, Mummy,' he said softly and slid the knife back into its sheath before laying it gently on the clothes in the suitcase.

54

London
    Saturday afternoon

KEN OLSON LOOKED GENUINELY CONCERNED. The fact that his firm had been unwittingly involved in the embezzlement of over three hundred thousand dollars was a serious matter.

'It'll be by the end of the week,' he said to Brennan. 'I should be back in the office by Friday. We'll get all the ID formalities dealt with and I'll send you the transfer details so you can see that we were following the mandate. Happy to answer any questions your fraud boys may have for me.'

'Thanks,' Brennan said, though he wondered whether the police could be persuaded to launch a fraud investigation now that BM had been liquidated. But he had to pursue every angle. He would try to get hold of that Hong Kong lawyer Matterling had used. He might have been involved in setting up the bank account.

Fiona appeared at the doorway, paused for a second to assess the state of play, and then joined them.

'Matter resolved?' she said as she took her seat.

'For the time being,' Olson said.

Brennan nodded. There was not much more they could do about it now. But it made Hong Kong even more important. Now that Matterling was based there.

'Good,' she said. 'Well, you two seem to be on the same side now.' She looked at Olson searchingly but he avoided her eyes. 'I just spoke to someone I know at one of the big agencies. Seems that the Sundays want to run that damn story as well. They think there may be more to come but there's a bidding war going on for the next instalment. They didn't know who was behind it.' She studied Olson again. 'It could be a bigger deal than we first thought.'

This time he did meet her gaze. The relaxed veneer had disappeared.

She turned to Brennan. 'Any more questions on Elba?' she asked smoothly.

'Just a couple. The first one is about Elba's real value. My understanding is that what the company is doing will blow the new big data norms sky high. It could make Google and Amazon look like fumbling street researchers with clipboards. Incredibly powerful software.'

Olson nodded. 'They're out to disrupt the disrupters.'

'And dangerous in the wrong hands.'

'That's why the company will only distribute to selected developers, for them to include as an additional dimension to their established offerings.'

Olson sounded like a corporate schlepper, resorting to the preformulated company line. However, Brennan could see Elba's software being exploited in a far more sinister direction. It just needed a change in strategy. Which could easily be effected by a new owner.

'My second question goes back to Victor. I hear what you say about the management team, but the fact that Victor is no longer at the helm would create some takeover interest, surely?'

'It would,' Olson said. 'Save for one important detail—that de

Souza's family have a substantial interest in Elba and even though it's a quoted company, no one could take it over without agreement from them.'

'But they could still get control, couldn't they? That substantial interest is only a minority interest.'

Olson's eyes narrowed but he said nothing.

'Which would account for the stake-building.'

'Stake-building?'

Brennan noticed a vein pulsing in Olson's left temple. 'It looks like a buyer in China.'

Olson stared blankly at him.

'Suppose that buyer already had a deal with the de Souza family,' Brennan went on.

Olson continued with the vacant look. He looked suddenly preoccupied with other matters. Probably wondering what the tabloids could come up with next.

Brennan pushed further. 'Possibly not the best deal for Tulare, though. I'm not sure you'd be getting full value if you were to sell just at the moment. Not when things are just getting interesting at Elba . . .'

'You must know that I cannot discuss our exit strategy.' Olson shot a glance at Fiona. Suddenly he didn't look so sure of himself. 'Especially not with journalists. It's market sensitive.'

'I think you can,' Brennan said. 'You discuss your investments all the time. With management, with analysts, with trade buyers, with new investors. And especially with journalists. It's your job, isn't it?'

Olson's frown deepened. He was paler now. Thin white lines were visible through the tan. He didn't answer.

'Okay,' Brennan said. 'Let's just talk about the share structure. You said the de Souza family owns a substantial stake in Elba, right? That's public information. Nothing market sensitive there.'

Another glance towards Fiona from Olson. She was studying the fingernails of her right hand. Not helping Olson out, Brennan thought. The conversation must be going in the direction she wanted.

'Right,' Olson said. A pause. No elaboration.

'It would seem that there is one vital piece of information that is not public, though.'

'What's that?' Olson focused back on their conversation.

'The identity of whoever is holding the bearer share?'

Olson nearly dropped his glass. 'The bearer share?'

'The only share in Portentao7. The company that controls Heilong. Registered in Anguilla. Correct?'

Olson nodded slowly. 'Where did you get all this from?'

'Anguilla is a British protectorate,' Brennan went on, ignoring the question. 'Population fifteen thousand, area about thirty-five square miles. Tiny. Beautiful white beaches, creole cooking. Currency is the East Caribbean dollar. The national flag has the Union Jack in one corner and their coat of arms on a blue background: three circling fishes. They look like sharks to me . . .' He trailed off, giving Olson the opportunity to opine on the fish. He didn't.

'Sounds idyllic.'

'It is certainly very attractive to investors who want to keep a low profile. One of the few jurisdictions that still allow bearer shares.'

Olson was being civil enough but Brennan could sense that any further discussion of offshore tax havens would be fruitless. Time to change tack. 'One thing I don't understand though is why Matterling doesn't control Heilong. He seems to have driven all the investment into it using this Rozario company as a brokerage. So why give away ultimate control?'

'More drinks?' Fiona broke in. To give Olson some thinking time, Brennan thought. She was looking at Olson. There was another question in the air and it wasn't about drinks.

'Sure. Thanks.'

'Yes, thanks,' Brennan echoed.

Both men made to get up but she waved them down. She turned to the barman and pointed at the table. He grinned and nodded.

There was a long silence. Brennan felt Olson studying him closely.

'That was part of the deal,' Olson said eventually. 'De Souza needed to keep control. He was happy for the investors over there to make a profit and get their money out of the country but that was it. He wanted to keep control.'

'Who came up with the idea for Portentao7 and the bearer share?'

'That was Doug Matterling. It was part of the deal on his commissions. He had okayed everything with the lawyers to keep on the right side of your Takeover Code and Victor accepted the terms.

'You knew Doug well?' Brennan still needed to make sure that there was no collusion between Matterling and Olson.

'No. I was involved with Elba a long time before Matterling came on the scene. I've only recently found out about this bearer share—from Carmel. I first met Matterling a couple of years ago, when Heilong started investing in Elba. That was when he asked whether your BM company could invest into my California funds. Completely separate from Tulare's investment in Elba.'

That made sense. Matterling must have been operating Rozario while he was working at BM. That's what he had been doing all that time in Hong Kong. Not BM business at all. The BM investment into Olson had come about after Matterling had come into contact with Olson. When Matterling saw an opportunity to divert funds out of BM, he had jumped at it.

'Anguilla has a custody scheme now, doesn't it?'

A flicker of concern passed across Olson's tightening lips.

Brennan needed to get onto Olson's plans. Now that de Souza was out of the way he could pursue Carmel. But Elba would be part of their future. Surely they must have worked out what they were going to do with the company.

'A custody scheme prevents their bearer shares floating around the world,' Brennan continued, checking Olson's reaction. 'After all, possession isn't just nine-tenths of the law, is it? For those things, it's ten-tenths.'

'Quite right.'

Olson sounded irritated. A touchy subject. Perhaps the bearer share was not safely under lock and key with a licensed custodian in Anguilla. But if not, where was it?

The barman brought over a tray and set out the new round of drinks. He took away the empties.

Fiona waited until he was gone then put a hand on Olson's fore-arm. 'We can use a meeting room later. I've got some ideas for our response. A few visuals as well. I need to show them to you.'

That was the second time, Brennan noted. The second time she had turned the conversation back to the tabloid stories. Each time Olson had looked more concerned. He was hiding it well but it was hurting. And for some reason, Fiona didn't want to defer the pain until after this meeting. She was pushing Olson. And using the tabloid story to crank up the pressure.

Perhaps he should help her out. One good turn and all that. Time to toss in a grenade.

'I happened to meet Sophie Loretta earlier today,' he said.

Fiona snapped her hand back from Olson. 'What?'

'Who?' Olson asked hoarsely.

'The 'little bitch' that's giving you grief at the moment,' Fiona said quietly, but she was staring at Brennan. 'Why would you be meeting with her? She's a very different kind of journalist to you, isn't she?' There was a hint of menace in her voice. It sounded like she was questioning his whole journalism schtick. He had hit a nerve.

'Unfortunately, Ken,' he said, 'there *is* more to come.'

His tone was sympathetic and it was genuine. He had suffered the same treatment when BM had gone down. It was limited to the trades and a couple of London papers, but it hurt all the same. The self-serving moral prurience, meted out to those that had fallen or were about to fall, had sickened him. Never kick a man when he's down, the adage goes. Unless you've got the weight of a tabloid newspaper behind you.

'She told me they're going to drip feed the story over a few days.'

'The story?' Something switched in Olson and he suddenly

clenched his fist and banged it on the table. 'What fucking story? There is no story.'

The paper at the end of the bar was laid down again and the barman turned from polishing his glasses. Olson was still staring at Brennan. Fiona managed a half-smile towards the bar to gloss over her guest's outburst.

Before leaving the marina, Brennan had sent a brief email to Loretta's address which was given under her merry widow story. By the time he had dropped Lisa off, he had received a reply. With a phone number. He had called and she had been eager to hear what other information he could give her on Mr and Mrs de Souza.

They had met at a coffee shop on Hammersmith Broadway and she had been just as grasping as he'd expected. He hadn't told her much—nothing more than that he was due to interview Victor de Souza but had witnessed him being fished out of the river instead. She had been disappointed not to hear any salacious details about the de Souza's marriage.

'They do have more,' Brennan said. 'A maid's interview at some Santa Barbara hotel, some mobile phone footage of you guys in the lobby of the Athenaeum, even a statement from a police officer who broke the news of Victor's death to Carmel. They seem to have quite a lot.'

'The Athenaeum?' Olson shook his head vigorously. 'That must have been yesterday. And a police officer? What about professional confidentiality? We should get that officer busted out of the force.'

'"Public interest" they call it,' Brennan said. 'The new way of saying "private interest".'

Olson's shoulders slumped and he continued shaking his head.

'Why did she tell you this?' Fiona said coolly. 'And why did you ask her?'

'I asked her because I couldn't believe that a newspaper would send a photographer out to California to pursue a couple who are not exactly A-list. If you see what I mean.'

'And what did she say to that?' If Olson was offended by the non-A-list categorisation he didn't show it.

'She just said that the story came from an agency in London. Small provider. She chose the bits she needed and added her by-line. As you know, various versions ran in several tabloids.'

'But why did she talk to you?' Fiona would know there had to be some kind of trade.

'I told her that I was doing a piece on Victor for the *FT*. She thought she could be onto some other dirt.'

'And was she?' Fiona's tone had gone from cool to ice-cold.

'No,' Brennan said firmly. 'Absolutely not. That's not me. But she did tell me something else of interest.'

He waited for them to acknowledge that they believed him before he offered more. Fiona exchanged glances with Olson.

'Go on,' she said sweetly.

'As well as telling me the agency is going to drip feed this story, she also told me that they were peddling another story some time ago. They were publicising a rumour that Elba had a serious intellectual property issue and was facing imminent legal action. It would have torpedoed the share price.'

'Did you know about this, Fiona?' Olson turned to face her.

'It's a new one on me. We would have denied it strenuously.'

'So what happened to the story?' His attention was back on Brennan.

'It was pulled. At the last minute. The agency said they had been misinformed and the source was unreliable.'

'So someone changed their mind and decided not to sink the share price?'

'That was my conclusion,' Brennan said. 'Loretta would sell her own mother to get published. Easy meat for an unscrupulous news agency. Loads of them like her out there.'

'So we can expect more over the next couple of days,' Fiona said, gently bringing the conversation back to the current problem. She was studying a tartan coaster on the table. She ran a scarlet fingernail along the lines of the pattern. 'Not great timing is it?' she said to Olson. 'Having to leave Carmel alone to deal with the press mongrels over the next few days.' She let the thought hang for a few seconds. 'What if there was an alternative?'

Olson rocked back in his seat and stared at the ceiling.

Brennan kept his silence. He could feel that they were leading up to something. Olson knew what she was talking about and he was mulling it over. Brennan was being assessed. There was something important that they were holding back. And where was Olson off to?

Olson eventually rocked forward and placed both hands flat on the table. 'An alternative? Go ahead, Fiona. Let's have your idea.'

Fiona turned to Brennan. 'Ken is due to make a short trip to Hong Kong. Leaving tomorrow night. He has to pick up that bearer share you were talking about. It's at a bank there but it needs to be collected in person.'

So his intuition had been right. It was not safely with a custodian in Anguilla.

'It's a straightforward pick-up,' Fiona said. 'In and out in three days. First-class flights, top hotel. Like a minibreak.'

The smile was on full beam again. Then it dawned on him. They were going to ask *him* to go.

'The tickets are fully transferable,' she continued. 'You would be helping Ken enormously. He needs to be here to deal with this tabloid story and I need to stay and help him. Otherwise I'd love to go.'

'Sounds like you've already discussed it.'

Fiona kept smiling.

'What's the urgency?' Brennan said. 'Why now?'

Olson leant towards him. 'What I'm about to say is strictly confidential. Is that understood?'

'Sure.'

'Because of Elba's long-term potential it makes perfect sense for the de Souza family to take the company private. With my firm's help, they can achieve that. We are planning to launch our bid next week. Hence the urgency. This bearer share being in Hong Kong is a loose end, which we need to tie up.'

Brennan gave himself a moment. Assuming Olson wasn't the superstitious type and buying in sixes and eights, then there were two bids for Elba about to break.

He had also been right about the bearer share being key to any successful takeover. And now he was being presented with the opportunity to help Olson and the de Souza family make the successful bid. Which would stop Matterling dead in his tracks.

'But why me?' he said. 'How can you trust me? We've only just met.'

'Two reasons,' Olson said. 'We know about the stake-building. Of course we do. We know who's behind it as well. Our old friend Doug Matterling. Fiona told me that you would be motivated to stop him from getting his hands on Elba. I understand now why she told me that.'

'And the second?'

'There will be a fee involved. A substantial fee, payable on delivery. I propose one third of the Lehman scale. Based on yesterday's market value of Elba Technology. That's my insurance policy.'

So this was it. This was the real reason for the meeting. Fiona gave him a congratulatory smile.

Brennan had come across the Lehman scale during one of his sessions at Ford. With one of Terry's mates, an investment banker who thought the only Chinese wall he needed to know about was over ten thousand miles long and could be seen from space. Not the type that investment banks put in place to stop confidential information being disclosed to colleagues in other departments who could make a killing from it.

The scale was often used to calculate brokerage fees in company sales and acquisitions. Brennan did a quick calculation. It was one hell of a fee for a courier job.

If Olson was planning to go himself then how dangerous could it be? And what better opportunity to help foil Doug Matterling?

Fiona and Ken were looking at him expectantly. Half an hour ago, Brennan had walked into this room believing that Olson was a rogue financier and possibly a murderer. Now he was considering travelling halfway around the world to help him take control of the murder victim's company.

'You'd be going out tomorrow night and flying back on Wednesday,' Olson said. 'The bank in Hong Kong will only release the share if the person collecting it is accompanied by an employee of Bavaria Williams Burnett. They are Elba's stockbrokers and when Victor deposited the share he gave the bank those instructions. The family was close to a director there and they wanted to be ultra-careful.'

'I can understand that. This bearer share is critical to any takeover.'

'So you'll have some company for the trip.'

Somehow, Brennan had managed to gain Olson's trust. Thanks to Fiona Wells.

He thought about his short meeting with Sophie Loretta this morning and felt for Carmel de Souza. Brennan knew that Carmel's life meant nothing to Ms Loretta. Just another piece of collateral damage in her grim climb to the top.

It made sense for Olson to stay and duke it out with Loretta and her cronies.

'I could do with getting away for a few days,' he heard himself saying.

'Lovely time to go to Hong Kong,' Fiona said breezily. 'The weather will be perfect.'

Olson offered his hand over the glasses. 'This pick-up is vital for us. And it'll keep us on course to launch our bid on Thursday.'

Brennan shook his hand and then picked up his beer and took a swig. Fiona looked very pleased with herself. Job done. But whatever he might be walking into, he knew he had no other choice. This was the only way that he could get to Doug Matterling. He would happily cross the globe for that.

Olson was rummaging around inside his jacket. He pulled out a small notebook and found a page in it. 'You would have been travelling with a guy called Ben Parfitt but I got a call from his colleague this morning saying he had to be with his mother who's just had a stroke. I've known Ben for quite a while because he covers Elba for Bavaria Williams Burnett and we compare notes from time to time.'

'Sounds cosy.'

Olson gave him a sharp look but continued unruffled. 'This colleague of his has offered to go in his place. As I said, the bank will only release the share to you if you are accompanied by an employee of BWB. This guy is another young analyst there. He's got an old girl-friend in Kowloon he wants to look up apparently. Entertaining her at the Mandarin Oriental at someone else's expense seemed to appeal.' He smiled reassuringly, 'I'm sure you'll get on fine with him.'

Brennan nodded. It would be good to have a younger bloke along-side, just in case there was any trouble.

Olson transcribed some details onto a blank page in his notebook. He tore it out and handed it across the table.

'Here's his name and number. Sounds like a stand-up guy. Name of Henry Evans.'

55

Towards Hong Kong
    Sunday night/Monday morning

THE HERRINGBONE LAYOUT of the Virgin upper-class deck ensured that all passengers were afforded complete privacy. Brennan's pod was on the right-hand side of the Dreamliner and Henry Evans' was across the aisle from him. As Brennan cradled his glass of Chilean Carmenere, he reflected upon the short time he had spent so far with his travelling companion.

Henry seemed like an amiable sort, always ready to laugh and unstintingly polite. He had shown Brennan respect and seemed eager to help in every way. There was even a hint of deference towards him, which Brennan was surprised at but enjoyed all the same. They had enjoyed gin and tonics together in the Virgin Clubhouse and had filled the waiting time with the usual small talk about sport, families and London property prices.

The flight attendants were now gliding efficiently around the cabin, making up beds and distributing black sleepsuits. The subtle lighting had changed from a soft fuchsia to a warm orange and the atmosphere was calm and soothing. Plenty of food had been served, the drinks had flowed and the impeccably-dressed flight attendants were ensuring that every need was catered for.

The whole experience was other-worldly, Brennan thought. He was suspended in a magical bubble, cocooned from the elements outside—and from his problems and distractions.

Yesterday was a blur. So much had happened that he had not processed the separation from Sarah yet. He had now spent two nights away from her. In completely different surroundings from Ford and a completely different kind of separation. This time, it was voluntary.

What are we going to do? She had kept asking him the same question. Her fear must have started to build when she realised that looking for a salary was not going to be his first priority. A fear that was compounded after he had been run over. But she had accepted his decision to leave as the only thing that made sense at the moment.

He had slipped into the house to pick up a bag and some clothes earlier today. He had known that Sarah would be out at her Sunday taekwondo session and Cara would be on a playdate. He had not told Sarah about this Hong Kong trip; it would have been pouring petrol onto the flames. But if he was successful, he had a fighting chance of freeing her from fear and winning her back. Their relationship was the real prize.

'Some more wine, sir? Or perhaps something else to drink?' The flight attendant smiled at him. Brennan landed gently back in the here and now. The young woman was focused on him and him alone.

'I'll have a Bailey's, please.' He returned her smile. 'A large one.' He finished the last of his wine and handed it to her. 'And how's the flight going for you?'

'Fantastic, sir. Thank you for asking. With ice?'

'Please.'

She backed away and turned towards Henry's seat. Brennan saw her lean in and speak to him before disappearing towards the bar area.

Brennan closed his eyes and Cara's beaming face came into focus. How could he possibly know what was going on in a mind so young? A mind that was absorbing data exponentially each day. But also a mind that would one day assess her father's actions against the morality he espoused. That would be his real judgement day.

The flight attendant returned with two large glasses of the creamy liqueur, one for Henry and one for him. A reassuring coincidence. She handed Henry his nightcap first and then turned to give Brennan his.

Another big smile. 'I hope you and your colleague sleep well. Please let me know when you want your bed made up. I won't be far away.' She melted away into the orange glow.

Brennan closed his eyes and tried to order his thoughts. Yesterday's meeting with Olson had capped a crazy week. A week dominated by a company he had never heard of before and that had seen his marriage teetering on the edge. Salinger's expression floated into his mind—*blissware*. He could do with some of that. It sounded like Elba was creating a perfect world.

He took a sip of the soothing whisky. Its warmth seeped through him, holding at bay all the swirling concerns about Sarah, Cara, Doug Matterling and the trip ahead.

AS MIKE BRENNAN was finishing his last drink of the evening, so was Doug Matterling. His last and only.

They were separated by five hundred miles. Brennan was to the east of Matterling. Both were at forty thousand feet and both were cruising towards Hong Kong International airport.

Matterling gave his empty champagne glass back to the Chinese flight attendant and ordered her to bring him more water. 'I'll be sleeping soon,' he told her. 'Leave me alone for the rest of the flight. I cannot be disturbed.'

Then he took a walk along the aisle. He left his suite in First Class and passed through Business and Premium Economy before reaching the Economy cabin. He stood next to the curtain separating the two areas and looked out at the densely-populated rows of seats.

He spotted his target and strode towards the two employees of Remus Security. They looked up at him impassively, unsmiling. Both were drinking water and neither seemed to be engaged in any of the usual airplane activities like reading or dozing or staring at screens.

Matterling produced two white D5-size envelopes from his jacket pocket. He handed one to each of the brothers.

'These are your instructions,' he said. 'As I told your mother, there are directions to your hotel inside as well as phones. Have a good flight.'

He turned on his heel and left for the refuge of First Class. When he returned to his suite, the flight attendant was waiting for him.

'Are you sure that I cannot get you anything to eat, Mr Matterling?' she asked. She was holding the menu and the wine list. 'I just wondered whether you might have changed your mind?'

'I never eat airline food,' Matterling snapped. 'You should know that by now.'

'Of course, Mr Matterling,' she replied. 'But anything more to drink?'

Two bottles of water had been set on the mahogany table curving out from under the windows, one still and one sparkling. He glanced pointedly at her name badge.

'Look, *Kim*,' he said. 'I'm not sure how often I have to fly with this airline for you guys to understand that I'm not interested in your amuse-bloody-bouche or your blinis or your Calvisius caviar. One glass of Krug is fine and then I just want to be left alone to get some sleep. How often do I have to tell you?'

Her eyes fell and she glanced towards the entrance area, where the inflight manager would be listening out for any frisson of discontent amongst the passengers.

'I'll be sure to let everyone know,' she said quietly, 'and if there is anything, please do not hesitate to use the call button.' She bowed and backed away.

56

Hong Kong
   Monday evening

BRENNAN SLUMPED on the bed and absorbed his surroundings. He was on the twentieth floor. The window had sweeping views of Victoria harbour below and Kowloon in the distance. Boats criss-crossed the water in the evening gloom. The room was sumptuously furnished. There were no plain surfaces. Everything had a pattern. The patterns were all subtle and closely repeated. Curved leaves on the bedspread, squares on the ceiling, flowers on the pillows, petals on the curtains. The colours worked well together; golds, browns and greys. The three apples in the glass bowl on a side table were rosy red. The room lights brightened imperceptibly as the day became darker. Exactly the right levels of light and shade. A steady balance between day and night.

The TV was showing a looped video of the hotel's facilities. The soundtrack was an anodyne piano and strings piece that Brennan reckoned was supposed to convey a feeling of calm, affluence and coddling. Refuge at last for the weary but discerning traveller. At the Mandarin Oriental.

He picked up the remote and flicked through the channels. All the usual international news and some Hong Kong channels were available. He was drowsy after the flight but he did not want to give way to sleep. He had agreed with Henry that they would meet for dinner in a couple of hours.

A news channel was showing a clip of a New Year's firework display in Victoria Harbour. The massive IFC tower was the centre-piece and fireworks seemed to burst out of every window, a constant barrage of noise and colour. Then the other buildings joined in and the whole skyline was ablaze with enormous exploding balls of fire. Back to the studio and a man was being interviewed next to a table covered in drawings. They were speaking English so Brennan stopped flicking. The interviewee was explaining that these were the plans for the next display, coming up soon on New Year's Eve.

'Over six thousand kilograms of fireworks will be used in this year's display,' the man was saying. 'The main shipment came into Kwai Chung last week from Hunan. We bring them into the harbour by barges for safety reasons.'

The interview cut to footage of a string of wide barges sailing into the harbour with green tarpaulins covering their cargo.

'We are not allowed to transport them by road and all the chemicals used in their manufacture have been approved by the government. We're not just a bunch of cowboys.' He grinned into the camera reassuringly. 'There are, of course, environmental effects associated with setting off over twenty-five thousand tiny bombs in a ten-minute time period. But unlike Beijing or Shanghai—where they get trapped—the wind here dissipates the chemicals fast—'

Brennan switched the TV off and his thoughts turned to the business in hand.

Henry Evans seemed okay. A bit wet but nice enough to travel with. He was due to hook up with an old girlfriend here so he probably wouldn't be around much after tonight. Just needed at the bank tomorrow as a representative of his firm so they could collect the share certificate. And then Brennan's job was done.

He lay back on the bed and put his hands behind his head. He allowed himself a few moments of contentment as he contemplated the next couple of days. If all went to plan with the pick-up in the morning, he would deposit the case in the hotel safe and lie low until the flight back to London. Then it was over to Olson to complete the Elba takeover and Matterling's plan would be dead. That would flush him out into the open.

LESS THAN FOUR HOURS LATER, Brennan was feeling far from content. He was concerned, very concerned.

Dinner with Henry Evans had been an amiable affair. They had eaten at the French restaurant in the hotel. *The perfect fusion of Paris passion and Hong Kong chic*, the display screen had proclaimed. Pretentious twaddle, Brennan had thought as he surveyed enormous white plates featuring tiny but elaborate food stacks at the centres. They had ordered wine and the evening had passed pleasantly enough. Henry had told him about his work analysing pharmaceutical companies and had explained in great detail the long approval process needed to bring new drugs to market. Brennan had been tired and let it all wash over him. They had made arrangements to meet in the morning and had gone to their rooms. As soon as he had returned to his, Brennan had looked up the *Investors Weekly* website where Henry had told him he had featured in an article on Big Pharma. Just to find out a bit more about his travelling companion.

Before he got to Henry's story he noticed a black and white photo of another investment analyst and this was the reason for his concern. The profile was of a young man with a thin, sensitive face, wide mouth, thick eyebrows and a bristling wave of dark hair.

Brennan recognised him immediately. The portrait showed him looking much better than when Brennan had seen him in the flesh. In the picture, he looked alert, inquisitive and *compos mentis*. In the flesh, he had looked groggy and anything but *compos mentis*. That had been last week. Wednesday. When Brennan had seen him being hustled into the offices of Remus Security by the three brothers.

He had been listed in the magazine's Top Ten Technology Analysts and his name was Ben Parfitt. The same Ben Parfitt who had been due to accompany him to Hong Kong to collect the bearer share.

Brennan's phone rang. It was Lisa. He checked his watch. Early afternoon in London.

'Lisa, how are you doing? This is a surprise.' The last time they had spoken was on Saturday when he had dropped her at her home in Barnes.

'How are you, Mike? Ribs okay now?'

'Good as new.'

'I didn't recognise the dial tone. Where are you?'

'Hong Kong. The Oriental.'

'And how's the weather?'

The weather? Why was she asking about the weather, of all things? He might have expected her to apologise for potentially waking him up. And why not just hang up when she heard the foreign dial tone?

'Good thanks,' he said. 'All good.' He didn't want to offer any more details about his reason for being in Hong Kong. It was too complicated for a single sentence. 'I was just about to get some sleep. Perhaps I could call you back tomorrow.'

'I just wanted to check that you're on the mend and see if there is anything I can do to help you.'

'Help? Can't think of anything, Lise. But thanks for the offer. And thanks for coming down to the marina with me on Saturday. You were the perfect yachtie wife.'

He was expecting a little laugh, at least. But she sounded insistent. 'I have family there. In Hong Kong. Anything you need, they'll be able to help.'

'That's good to know. Thanks.'

He was still staring at Parfitt's face on the screen, wondering how he had fared at the hands of Remus Security. They must have wanted him in connection with Elba Technology. Perhaps to find out more about the company on behalf of their client. Whatever the reason, it certainly didn't look like it was in accordance with City rules.

'Or here in London,' Lisa said. 'Anything I can do to help.'

Perhaps she could help, he thought. The way Parfitt had been forced into that office certainly looked like some kind of abduction. He had been the one scheduled to make this trip on behalf of BWB but had cancelled. He had called Henry on Saturday morning, hadn't he? Or so Olson had been told.

'I wouldn't want to put you in any kind of danger,' he said.

Was Parfitt's mother's stroke genuine? But was it right to involve Lisa any further? It was enough that he'd taken her to the marina.

'Don't worry about me. I can look after myself. I know you're trying to find out more about Victor de Souza. And I know you're trying to trace Doug Matterling. I can understand that and I would like to help.'

The offer couldn't be clearer. She knew what he was trying to do and she knew what she might be getting herself into. She had also lost money through BM so she was already involved. He took his eyes off the screen and gazed out at the black of the harbour and the lights dancing in every direction. He was alone in Hong Kong with a side-kick who might not be as trustworthy as he had thought. Tomorrow he was stepping into unknown territory. He was a long way from home. He needed every bit of help he could get.

'You remember De Souza ran a company called Elba Technology?' he said.

'I remember.' She sounded resolute.

'Well, the company stockbroker is a firm called Bavaria Williams Burnett. Quite well known in the City. There is an analyst who works for them called Ben Parfitt. I think he may have gone missing.'

'You want me to talk to this firm?'

'Perhaps. But first I just need a reccy done. Of some offices near Fleet Street belonging to a firm called Remus Security. I saw Parfitt being taken there on Wednesday. He wasn't in great shape and he was being frogmarched in. I want to see if there are any clues as to what might have happened to him.'

'I'll go there now.'

She was certainly keen. He knew he had made the right decision. She could prove invaluable.

He checked his watch. 'Great. People will be packing up for the day by the time you get there. You might get to chat to a cleaner going in or something like that.'

'No problem.'

'I don't want you to go in. Just see how things look from the outside. Check out what kind of activity there is.'

'And the address?'

'I'll message you.'

What a trooper, Brennan thought. He just hoped she would be careful. It wouldn't do to get on the wrong side of those hooligans.

57

London
  Monday afternoon

LISA RICHARDS STOOD across the street from the scruffy front door with its black peeling paint. It was four in the afternoon and freezing cold. This was the address Mike Brennan had sent her earlier. She thrust her hands into her jacket pockets and shivered.

She walked fifty yards up the street, crossed the road and made her way back down again, past the front door of Remus Security. The vertical window blinds in the offices were all drawn shut. There were no lights on. The tarmac outside glistened with the light sheen of earlier rain. Streetlights punctuated the developing mist with yellow orbs.

The Remus offices were next to a corner building that looked like it at once been a pub but had now been converted into small offices. Lisa saw that the window blinds were the same as Remus'. Their offices seemed to extend into the next building.

She walked up the side street leading past the corner building and retraced her tracks back to the corner. All was quiet. She pulled out her phone and held it to her ear while she stood at the corner. A few office workers bustled past but there was no movement around the offices of Remus Security.

She mouthed into her phone just in case anyone was watching. She glanced down and noticed that she was standing on a pair of wooden trapdoors set into the pavement. She assumed they opened into what would have been a cellar underneath the pub. The doors looked normal enough but there was a shiny padlock fastened to the rusty bolt across them.

As she continued to mouth silently into her phone, she flicked the padlock up with the toe of her boot. It clunked back onto the metal plate supporting the rusty bolt. The padlock looked brand new, unlike the rest of the fittings on the doors.

There was a sudden sharp noise from beneath the doors. It sounded like a stone hitting the timber. Then again, slightly louder. And again. Lisa stepped off the doors quickly, as if they might suddenly open up. There was a definite tapping against their underside.

A few yards away, there was a rubbish bin, which had been placed outside an office door. Lisa hurried over to it and opened the lid. Among the usual office detritus, there was a discarded stapler. She pulled it out and went back to the cellar doors. Crouching, she dropped her handbag onto the door and rummaged around in it with one hand while with the other, she lightly struck the stapler against the door three times.

She was answered with three taps, each louder and with more urgency.

She tapped back twice. The noise would only draw attention to her and possibly to whoever was below. Perhaps it was Ben Parfitt. But she had to be circumspect. She had to find a different means of communication.

She pulled a notebook from her purse. She scribbled a short message and tore the page out. She looked around to make sure that no one was watching and slipped the page between the two doors.

She glanced around and strode away from the cellar doors. She pulled out her phone again and started googling.

———

HALF AN HOUR LATER, Lisa stepped out of a black cab and paid the driver. It had been a short trip back from the HSS hire shop at Tower Bridge. She was back where she had started. This time she carried a pair of bolt cutters and a coil of rope.

The area was still relatively quiet. Quiet enough for a petite lady with three-foot-long bolt cutters to break into a beer cellar without attracting too much attention. She hoped.

Before returning to the trapdoors, she circled the block and checked out the front of the Remus offices. There was no sign of movement within.

She tracked back and rounded the corner to the cellar doors. As well as googling the location of the nearest tool hire shop, she had looked for the best way to cut through a padlock. The idea was not to try and cut through the shackle—which was made of hardened steel— but simply to cut open the body vertically. It looked simple enough in the video.

A couple of office workers were entering the door closest to the cellar and Lisa waited for them to close it behind them. There was no one else around.

She tied the end of the rope to a nearby lamppost and then uncoiled it quickly. She tied several single loop knots along its length and then coiled it again and set it down next to the cellar doors.

She crouched and lined up the bolt cutters with the body of the padlock. The mechanism was about two and a half inches long and the cutting edges of the cutter extended halfway along the body. She closed her eyes and squeezed the cutter's arms together.

When she opened her eyes, the blades had closed together effortlessly and cut through half of the body casing. Another quick cut and the padlock came apart. Now for the difficult bit. The rusty bolt.

This had to be tackled from a standing position, so she straightened up and with a single decisive swipe of the bolt cutters she dislodged the bolt, which slid out just enough to release the doors. She was going to need some leverage to pull the heavy doors open.

There was a loud creak and Lisa took an involuntary step back. The doors started to lift of their own accord. They lifted slowly, pushed by two wooden struts that were being forced upwards by a toothed wooden wheel. Lisa leant over and peered into the gloom. The turning wheel was attached to a drive wheel, which was being powered from below by a belt. The belt had been fashioned from a strip of sheet looped around an old barrel and secured on a stand. As her eyes became accustomed to the dark, she saw a thin young man with spiky black hair, hauling down on the sheet as if his life depended on it.

There were two clunks from the lower sides of the doors and Lisa could see that two wooden stops had swung into place to prevent them from slamming shut.

'Far enough,' she shouted down. 'They're wedged open.'

'Thank you!' he shouted back. 'Whoever you are, thank you so much.'

Lisa smiled to herself. What a polite young man. She pulled one of the doors fully open so that it swung flat onto the pavement and threw the rope into the cellar.

After a few seconds of grunting the polite young man managed to haul himself out. He stood up in front of her and grinned awkwardly for a moment. Then he extended his hand. 'Ben Parfitt. *Really* pleased to meet you.'

She shook his hand. 'Lisa Richards. Likewise. Now, let's not hang around.'

She untied the rope from the base of the lamppost and let it fall to the cellar floor. They took one door each and swung them back into their closed position. Lisa scooped up the remnants of the shattered lock and threw them into the bin, along with the bolt cutters. Then they half-walked, half-ran away from Remus, Lisa in the lead, looking out for a taxi. She flagged one down and they jumped in. They both sank back into the welcoming black leather of the rear seat. She gave the driver her address and he nodded.

'Where are we going?' Ben said. 'And who are you? How did you know I was there?'

'We're going to my place.' She wrinkled her nose and moved a few inches along the seat. 'You need a shower. And on the way you're going to tell me everything you know about Remus Security. After that I'll deal with your questions.'

'Is that their name? The gang who were holding me?'

'Every detail. I want to know every detail.'

'I'll try.'

'And you'll need to be quick in the shower because I've got to get to the airport.'

'Where are you going?'

'Hong Kong.'

Ben was clenching his fists. 'Me too,' he said. 'Let's share this taxi if that's okay with you. I'll shower at the airport.'

She stared at Ben for a moment, then said to the driver, 'Change of plan. Heathrow Airport please.'

He nodded and glanced into his side mirror. The cab slowed sharply before performing one of the favourite manoeuvres of the London cabbie—a tight U-turn into speeding oncoming traffic

58

Tuesday afternoon
   Hong Kong

THE BANK MANAGER'S manicured forefinger slowly ran down each of the letters of authority, which Mike Brennan had handed him a few minutes ago. He was studying each paragraph carefully.

Brennan and Henry were sitting with the manager in a side office at the Central branch of the Singapore Merchant Bank. Brennan watched the manager's face closely. Henry gazed at the glossy photographs on the wall, all of the high-rise office blocks that constituted Hong Kong's skyline.

Eventually, the manager looked up and smiled. 'That all seems to be in order, Mr Brennan. Could I see your passports please?'

Brennan and Henry handed over their passports and the manager continued his laborious scrutiny, carefully checking them against the photographs in the passports.

Brennan's stomach tightened as the seconds ticked by. If there was a problem with the paperwork, the long journey here would have been in vain. Henry seemed to be quite relaxed and enjoying his trip to the Far East. Perhaps Brennan was being overly paranoid about Henry's presence here. Perhaps the stock analyst pictured on the *Investors Weekly* website was not the same man he had seen being bundled into the offices of Remus Security. After all, there were lots of gawky-looking young men like him in London nowadays.

If that was the case, Lisa's reccy would have been a waste of time.

'Thank you, gentlemen,' the bank manager said and passed back the passports. 'Follow me and I will take you to your box.'

He led the way out of the office and passed through several reinforced steel doors, each with an elaborate access procedure using keypads and iris recognition systems. Brennan was reminded of the doors at Belmarsh and of the warders who swaggered around with enormous bunches of keys swinging from their belts. The contrast was stark. At Belmarsh, the system was designed to prevent escape. Here at the bank, the system was designed to prevent access.

They entered a small, airless room with a wall of security boxes. The manager opened one of them and stepped back.

'That's the one,' he said. 'Go ahead.'

Brennan turned the handle and pulled out a sliding steel drawer. He looked inside and saw a small leather attaché case. He took it out of the drawer and noticed that the bank manager had not moved out of sight from the box. He had dropped his gaze to the floor but he was still discreetly monitoring what was being held in his bank's vaults.

There was no combination lock on the attaché case, just two simple brass clasps. Brennan put the case on a small table across the room and opened it. There it was. A thick, cream-coloured sheet of parchment paper with ornate green decoration and a red company seal. The certificate was headed *Bearer Share Warrant* and *Portentao7 Limited* was printed in a large serif font below it. Below that was more flowery print, a couple of convoluted signatures and a number of official stamps.

Brennan closed the case. He did not have time to study it in detail. Right now, he needed to transfer it to the hotel safe as quickly as possible.

But seeing the physical certificate gave him a lift. The trip was going to plan and he was a step nearer to destroying Matterling's takeover attempt. Revenge was starting to taste good.

He nodded to the bank manager who closed and locked the drawer. He led Brennan and Henry out of the room. They passed back through all the doors to the side office. The manager had a release form for the two of them to sign and then he escorted them out to the bank's glass foyer.

'Goodbye, gentlemen,' he said. 'It was a pleasure doing business with you.' He gave a modest reverential bow and they all shook hands.

As they left, Brennan started to feel vulnerable. They had left the security of the bank. They were out in the open. He held the case tightly and wondered whether he should have brought a chain, to handcuff it to his wrist like they did in movies. But then they—whoever *they* might be—could cheerfully chop his arm off to steal the case.

'You okay, Henry?'

'Yeah, great. That all seemed to go pretty smoothly, didn't it?'

They headed back along Lockhart Road towards the Wan Chai MTR. The pavements became busier as they neared the station and Brennan found himself leading with his shoulder as he pushed through the crowd. Pedestrians had to share the pavement with piles of empty boxes, put out by the bars and clubs much earlier that morning. Some of these bars were opening up and a couple of the clubs already had girls sitting outside, getting ready for the evening's trade.

Brennan and Henry passed the Old China Hand bar and the Queen Victoria pub. Henry probably had nothing to do with Ben Parfitt's involvement with Remus Security. If it *was* Parfitt.

They were in sight of the station entrance when Brennan felt someone keeping stride with him. Someone shorter than Henry. Before he could look around, he felt someone on his other flank.

When he stepped to the left, to avoid someone coming the other way, it seemed like two other pairs of legs did the same. He glanced around. A stocky westerner with short, dark hair looked straight ahead, hands shoved deep into his coat pockets. On his right, another one who looked exactly the same. Brennan recognised the look. They were like the two he had seen escorting the young man into Remus Security.

Christ. Was it them?

He swerved to give way to an oncoming pedestrian and took a quick step across the pavement towards the road. A row of red and white taxis was lined up on the other side.

'Come on, Henry,' he shouted over his shoulder. 'Let's get a cab.'

He turned. No Henry.

His two new companions had also changed direction. No time to wait for Henry. He strode across the road towards the taxis, narrowly avoiding a couple of passing cars. He checked again when he reached the other pavement. *Yes, it was them.* The two guys from Remus. They must be working for Matterling. There was no other explanation.

They stared at him. Or, more specifically, they stared at the attaché case in his right hand. Henry had disappeared.

So much for back-up, Brennan thought and pulled open the nearest taxi door. There was no driver inside. Brennan slammed the door shut. He didn't have time for this. The two Remus brothers were halfway across the road, standing at a gap in the line of sparse foliage which divided the traffic. Time to run.

He headed for the bridge ahead. If he could get on a train he might be safe. But the oncoming pedestrians made it hard to build up any pace. He had to keep slowing and swerving. Another look behind. They were definitely gaining.

He approached the bridge. Suddenly the train seemed like a bad idea. What were the chances of jumping straight onto a train and having the doors shut immediately behind him, leaving the brothers stranded on the platform as he accelerated away to safety? Something else that only happened in movies. He would likely have to wait at a platform. And then they would get him.

He was at a cross street. It looked clear to his left. He had to chance it. There weren't as many pedestrians and he was able to run more freely. He was breathing hard but he was moving well. He felt strong. The prison work-outs were paying off. A quick backwards glance showed he was pulling ahead. His red-faced pursuers were labouring. Probably more used to short, sharp bursts of energy rather than endurance events. Short, sharp bursts of energy. Like punching someone's lights out.

Next junction coming up. He just needed to keep going. Busy street ahead. Couldn't afford to get held up by traffic. But he was suddenly in a throng of people crossing the wide road. He stayed with them. At least they were moving. Another look back. No sign of pursuit. Keep going.

The throng dispersed and Brennan carried on in the same direction. He was slowing. He couldn't keep this up for much longer. There was another busy cross street ahead. With trams. It looked like there were a lot of them.

He came out onto the wide street and saw the tram-stop straight ahead. Large painted advertising panels in the middle of the street. People waiting each side. He half-staggered to the far side of the panels and leant against one of the columns supporting the shelter's roof. He peered around the panel. The brothers were side by side on the far side of the street, hands on hips, scanning the road. Breathing deeply. They had lost him but it wouldn't be long until they came across to the tram-stop and looked behind the panels.

There was the sound of a ringing bell and a high, white tram pulled up to the stop. The waiting group swarmed around him and moved to the rear door, funnelling Brennan towards the tram. He crouched as much as possible so that his head wasn't visible above the crowd. They shuffled forward slowly. Too slowly. It was taking an age to get on board. Then, as if sucked into a vacuum, he was in. And being propelled towards the front of the carriage. The rear door closed. There was no sign of the brothers on board. Brennan peered through a window to his left. A head shot up beside the tram and glared in at him. One of the brothers.

They stared at each other and the tram started moving away. Brennan still had a chance. He pushed past a couple of squat ladies clutching black bin liners full of clothes. He needed to get to the window. The tram curved away to the right and his view of the road behind receded.

He could just see the two brothers standing by the side of the road, waving. They were flagging down a taxi.

He tried to get his bearings. The passing cityscape gave him no clues. Just a high-rise metropolis covered in Chinese signs. Now and then a street sign in English—Arsenal Street, Queensway, Justice Drive. Sweet irony, that.

The tram rumbled on, stopping frequently at traffic lights or tram stops. He worked his way towards the front door. As each stop neared, he looked fearfully at the rear door, expecting the brothers to appear. No sign of them yet. After three scheduled stops, he guessed they had decided to play the waiting game. They would be following closely, waiting for him to make his move. The trouble was, he had no idea where he was heading nor how long the tram trip would last. He would have to seize his chance when it came.

The buildings seemed to be getting denser. And higher. He must be in the middle of the city. The tram pulled up again and Brennan tensed. People flooded on. In front, people flooded off. No sign of the goons.

The chances of losing them here were remote. Traffic was flowing past the tram line on the inside and they would have plenty of opportunities to pass and board the tram further up the line. But he might jump off earlier if they made that commitment. So, they would play the waiting game. Waiting for him to bolt.

Brennan saw a sign for the Macau Ferry. Pointing ahead, in the direction the tram was going. He knew that Macau was to the west of Hong Kong Island, so he was heading west or north-west. The high-rises were older, tattier. Black electrical cables dangled across the facades like loose rigging. It was still heavily built-up but more apartment blocks were appearing. He was going to have to make a run for it. For all he knew, he could be heading for open terrain where he would find it much more difficult to hide.

The next stop. He made up his mind. This would be it. He fumbled the correct change for the fare out of his pocket. His legs were heavy. All the other stops had been slow, really slow. Far too slow, giving too much opportunity for an assailant to jump on board. This one seemed to come up lightning fast.

One second he was bunched up with the crowd in the tram, the next he was spewed out onto the pavement. His fellow passengers fanned out, speeding off in all directions. Suddenly he was alone, momentarily petrified on the pavement. He spun around to assess the options.

The narrowest street. That was what he was looking for. Narrow meant less visibility.

He set off left, across a lane of cars and into the street opposite the stop. He ran past shops and mini-markets, swerving around men with trolleys. Christ, every other person seemed to be wheeling boxes around. Every corner was a market. There were stalls selling piles of seafood, all colours.

He was making good progress. Hong Kongers seemed to sense when someone wanted to escape. Despite their sheer numbers, they melted away before him. His breathing was regular now. The searing fire in his chest was gone and his legs were moving freely. A bright yellow grocery truck pulled across in front of him. He slowed and took the opportunity to look over his shoulder. No sign of them. He sidestepped around the rear of the truck.

Keep left. Keep left. It was working. Another corner. Another stall of dried squid. Another one of scallops. Then seaweed. No one seemed interested as he pelted by. He ran towards a mountain of dried prawns. His balance was good; he was avoiding all the obstacles. He felt like he was flying.

And then he was.

Something collided with him from behind and he was launched into the air. He crashed headfirst into the prawn mountain and his legs were thrown high above him. The table collapsed under him and the startled stall-holder leapt up in fright. Brennan couldn't see a thing. All he could feel was a heavy weight across his back. His legs were still in the air. The salty smell filled his head and in one slow, groaning motion the table crunched to the ground. With it came the rest of Brennan's body and the weight on his back. The smell of the prawns was overpowered by the stench of aftershave.

Brennan felt the attaché case being torn away from him and both his arms were twisted up behind his back. He knew exactly who it was. He had seen them say hello like this before.

They got off him, still twisting his arms. He said nothing. They'd caught him and they had what they wanted. He was yanked to his feet. He snorted a couple of prawns from his nostrils. His attackers brushed themselves down one-handed.

One of them pulled out a wallet and extracted a handful of notes from it. The notes were offered to the stallholder who grabbed the money and grinned. He picked up a red string sack from below his chair and started to shovel the prawns into it. It seemed for all the world as if this were just an occupational hazard, all part of a day's work. Having a body flung across your stall by a couple of psychos.

'Let's get him back,' one of the psychos said.

'Someone wants to meet you,' said the other. 'Someone who can't understand why you don't just stay out of the way. That's all you had to do.'

That someone could only be one person. Matterling was here in Hong Kong.

'Let's hope you get the message this time,' the first one grunted in a tone suggesting he didn't care one way or the other.

They marched him back the way they had come. One of them was getting directions from his phone and they walked at speed. Brennan struggled to keep pace with them, and when he could not, they dragged him painfully along for a couple of steps. They crossed the street carrying the trams and were soon at a ferry terminal. Brennan saw the name *Central Pier*. Ancient-looking green and white ferries were moored up either side and torrents of people were pouring in and out of the terminal building.

'Bet you wish you were on a day trip to Kowloon now, don't you?' one of his captors said.

'Two piers along,' the other said grimly. 'Just past the museum.'

They continued through the throngs to a concrete-covered structure stretching out into the harbour. They pushed their way along its length, the chaos of the crowds offering perfect camouflage to the three of them, bundled tightly together. Brennan felt like he was being held in a vice. There was no hope of escape.

They steered him abruptly towards a wide set of concrete steps on the right, which led down to the water. They stopped at the top and the three of them looked down at a grey motorboat moored below. Brennan recognised it as a RIB, the anacronym for a reinforced inflatable boat. A RIB of this size would be strong and light, capable of high speeds and very manoeuvrable. Two crew were standing on the bottom step, holding bow and stern lines turned around the pier's bollards and ready to go.

Brennan was guided down the steps. He didn't know where they were taking him but he knew who was waiting to meet him. Despite everything, he was calm. He was ready for Doug Matterling.

59

Tuesday evening
Hong Kong

THE SLEEK GREY lines of the superyacht took shape as the RIB rounded the headland of Kellett Island. *Kamakura* was anchored about two hundred yards off the rocky shoreline. Brennan looked across at the imposing viewing deck of the building that dominated this corner of the bay. He recognised the whitewashed exterior from his previous visits. It was the clubhouse of the Royal Hong Kong Yachting Club, one of the territory's most illustrious social hubs from the British colonial days.

They headed towards the enormous yacht. Brennan reckoned *Kamakura* was at least a couple of hundred feet long. It was breeze-block grey, like a battleship, with black-tinted windows along its sides. The rows of deck lights highlighted its sheer lines as the gloom of the evening descended. The bow was set at a sharp angle to the water, forceful and purposeful. The colour was no accident—this thing had been designed to threaten. It was a statement, an ugly, predatory declaration of intent.

It was Matterling's new home. Very appropriate.

When they came alongside the landing platform at the yacht's stern, two crew members were waiting to take lines. Brennan was bundled onto the platform by his two minders. They held him tightly by each arm as they took the steps up to the afterdeck. Across the harbour, Brennan could see the myriad lights of Kowloon reflecting from the water.

A sharp pain in his shoulders forced its way through the anaesthetising adrenalin that was coursing through him. He was pushed up the steps towards large glass doors. The doors opened.

Doug Matterling stood in the doorway with his feet apart and his hands behind his back. There was an enormous silver mirror behind him. The saloon's dim lighting was a mixture of low-level blue and a golden glow above. Matterling looked smaller than Brennan remembered.

To his surprise, the spinning ball of fury within him started to slow. He had been sure that on seeing Matterling he would have had just one urge. The feeling of Matterling's throat in his grip had sustained Brennan through many painful nights in his prison bed. But now that he was here, there was no such desire. Instead, he felt unexpectedly calm. Calm and curious. What was driving Doug Matterling?

The calm was disturbed as Matterling stepped forward. The golden light from the ceiling caught his thin cheeks and gave them the same burnished appearance as the yacht's sleek hull.

'What the hell were you doing, Mike? This was none of your business.' Behind the rough tone, Brennan could detect real bewilderment. He didn't understand why Brennan was pursuing him.

'Certainly not the way I would have expected you to show your appreciation.'

'Appreciation?' What was this about?

'For everything I've done for you. Over the years.'

"Everything?'

'With BM. And before.'

Before? Not that again? That stupid incident when they had first started working together. Before they had even started thinking about forming their own agency. Matterling just couldn't let it go. 'Payback time' he used to say. It would come up on a regular basis when they were running BM. Whenever either of them had to acquiesce to the other Matterling would start to mutter darkly about 'payback time'.

'It was nothing, Doug. You just covered for me in a small way over one minor incident. OK, I screwed up. I admit it. I should never have lost my temper with the powers that be and I should never have threatened to quit so publicly. But it was nothing. A storm in a teacup. It was forgotten about as soon as it had happened.'

'And who was it that persuaded them not to accept your resignation?'

'You were there, Doug. Yes, I accept that. But it was their decision. Which I then went along with and I withdrew the letter. I can't believe that you have built it up into such a big debt that I owe you.'

'You just said it. I was there. I was there for you. You needed me and I was there.' Matterling slowly shook his head as though dealing with an imbecile. Then he snapped back into interrogating his subject.

'You've been using Brian Kesey to dig for you. Why?'

'I'm chasing justice. For everything that I've lost because of you.'

So Matterling knew about his meetings with Kesey. He had been followed. It must have been Remus Security. But for how long?

'You can't talk about justice,' Matterling said. 'Not from where you're standing. On the wrong side of the law. And I only took what I was owed.'

Brennan looked into Matterling's eyes. There was no hint of obfuscation. He seemed clear in his mind that everything he had done was right and justified. According to his morality, he was entitled to what he had taken.

'Give me the case,' Matterling said brusquely and one of Brennan's escorts handed it over. Matterling put it on the chart table and opened it. He checked the contents.

'Why did you let de Souza have this bearer share in the first place,' Brennan asked. 'Why didn't you just keep control of Heilong?'

Matterling turned and smiled a tiny smile. 'I always had control. You shouldn't confuse control and ownership. Just like our partnership.'

The morality of his entitlement was all-powerful. Brennan could see that Matterling regarded the bearer share as his to take. It had always been his, as far as he was concerned. There was no argument to be had.

A look of boredom fanned across his face. 'Anyway, let's decide what to do with you. We've got two choices. The Salinger option or the Macau option.'

'The Salinger option?'

'Someone else who wouldn't take a warning. Even though we knew all about his predilection for young boys.'

Brennan caught his breath.

'Electricity,' Matterling said. 'Something we all take for granted but it's intrinsically lethal. He must have got his wires crossed messing around with all those virtual reality masks. They found him with a ring of burns around his neck. Terrible way to die.'

Brennan forced his voice to remain calm. 'The police? Did they find him?'

Matterling's smile widened. 'Eventually.'

The threat was obvious. Brennan suddenly felt a long way from safety. If Salinger had not been safe in his fortress, what chance did Brennan stand in the wild undergrowth of Hong Kong?

'So what about his shares in Elba?'

'Being transferred today. Some sleepy solicitor in Sussex has never had to move so fast to liquidate an estate. Lucky that we knew of the deceased's wishes ahead of time. I'm glad to donate so generously to the local Dogs Trust. The sole beneficiary.'

The Dogs Trust? Salinger must have thought long and hard about that one. There was an irony there somewhere but Brennan didn't have the time to explore that at the moment.

'Or there's the Macau option,' Matterling said slowly. 'A trip to the mainland will keep you out of the way for a few weeks. Then you can come back. You'll be a bit thinner and much sorer, but it'll make you stronger, I'm sure.' Matterling smiled knowingly. 'My friends in Macau should be able to keep you alive. They don't lose many. Then we can have some more fun when you get back.'

'When your takeover of Elba is complete?'

'Precisely.'

Matterling looked very pleased with himself. Genuinely looking forward to toying with his catch at his leisure. That answered one question that had been on Brennan's mind since getting hit by the motorbike: why he had not been disposed of just like Salinger. Matterling enjoyed the torture.

'Suppose Carmel de Souza fights you for it.'

'She won't. Not now.'

'Now she's busy dealing with the tabloid press, you mean?'

'That's one factor. There are others. She won't deceive me again.'

'Deceive you?'

Matterling shook his head in irritation.

Brennan remembered Fiona telling him some details of Carmel's trip to California. Then, when they were in the Caledonian Club with Olson, Fiona had kept coming back to the tabloid story. She had been convincing him to stay in London to deal with it. It wasn't an obvious story for the tabloids. Someone had spent real money getting those pictures. Fiona was perfectly placed to set it up. Matterling must have been behind the whole thing. To pressurise Carmel and lure Brennan to Hong Kong.

He thought about the picture of Carmel and Ken in the Japanese garden. He had seen something similar recently, in the pile of photographs in Hazel's office at Remus Security. He was sure they were the same images.

Matterling looked irrational as well as irritated. The mention of

Carmel had triggered something. Something ugly. Brennan wanted to keep Matterling talking. At least at the moment he was being offered a chance of survival. Even if the Macau Matterling had planned was different from the Macau in the tourist brochures.

'I underestimated you,' Matterling said. 'I thought your stint at Her Majesty's pleasure would be the end of you. Your family needs you now. Sarah has stood by you. Unbelievably. And Cara is doing so well now. Cannon Park nursery seems like a good choice for her. But she was never really abandoned, was she? You loved her even when you were locked away.'

Brennan felt like he had been kicked in the stomach. Had Matterling been spying on his family?

'You know you can't go back now, don't you?' Matterling said. 'You've stupidly sunk yourself into shit that'll never wash off.' He switched his attention to the men still holding Brennan's arms. 'Get him below. You know where to put him.'

The two men started moving him towards the back of the saloon but Brennan held firm. He dug his heels into the polished teak floor.

'Just one more question. Before I go.' He returned Matterling's gaze. 'Who was abandoned, Doug?'

He was still playing for time. *But* he had heard Matterling use the word 'abandoned' before. It had been in the BM gym. That early morning when they had talked about the Kinross presentation. The boy with his grandfather. They had touched on Matterling's childhood. His dispatch to a freezing England at the age of seven from the balmy warmth of Singapore. Being sent away by his father and separated from his mother. Papa and Mama he had called them. *Where's the wonder in being abandoned?* he had said. And then, something about not being able *to 'look after her anymore.'*

Perhaps that's why he had made such a big deal about 'being there' for Brennan in that stupid resignation incident. In a way that he had not 'been there' for his mother.

'Take him away,' Matterling ordered and turned back to close the attaché case.

'Don't ever use my family again,' Brennan said. 'They're nothing to do with this. Deal with your father in whatever way you want, but don't bring my family into it. Ever.' His tone was hard and signalled that they had moved into a different world order now. One where the usual rules of fear and retribution didn't apply.

Matterling stiffened and turned slowly around. 'My father? He's got nothing to do with it.'

'Sure,' Brennan said, without a trace of conviction.

Before he had a chance to probe further another door opened in the saloon. A young man stepped into the golden light. It was Henry Evans, hair sticking up like a hedgehog, looking like he had spent the day in bed after accompanying Brennan to the bank. He started, obviously surprised that Matterling had company.

'Oh, Mike. Didn't realise you were coming over.'

Henry's entry into the saloon had changed the dynamic. They had all turned to look at him. The Remus brothers had released their grip slightly and Brennan could feel a breeze from the harbour on his neck. The door was still open and if he was quick he could probably make it. A minute earlier and he would have had no hesitation. But the mention of Cara had turned everything on its head. Should he just go along with Matterling, stay out of the way in Macau for a few weeks, and hopefully return to England in one piece? Or should he risk it all and make a run for it?

He looked at Matterling and in that instant realised that there was no decision to be made. He was dealing with a psychopath. Matterling's logic was not the same as his own. He wasn't simply a jealous rival who would trample on anyone and anything to get what he wanted. He was on a different plane of behaviour.

There was no guarantee he would get out of Macau alive. Salinger's death had been no accident. And that was just so Matterling could get hold of another four per cent of Elba. God knows what he would do if he was threatened.

Brennan flung both fists out and caught the two Remus boys in their stomachs. They were not strong blows but they were enough to stop them grabbing him again for a split second. That was all he needed to duck and twist around. By the time they regained their balance, Brennan was through the door. He leapt down onto the stern landing deck. He could hear the brothers coming down the steps behind him.

The yacht's underwater lights illuminated the water around the hull for a couple of metres. After that, it was just an uninviting blackness. He looked up at the shore and the white curves of the Yacht Club. Away to his left was the mainland. That had to be his destination. The rocky shore of Kellet Island wouldn't give him any shelter—he would easily be picked out by *Kamakura's* powerful searchlights. He took a deep, shuddering breath.

Then he dived into the forbidding inky water of the harbour.

60

Tuesday evening
Hong Kong

AS BRENNAN SURFACED, he twisted around to see if the Remus brothers had followed him in. They were untying the tender. They were going to go after him by boat.

He had to cover as much distance as possible before they gave chase. He turned towards the lights of the mainland and started to swim. His jacket tightened around his shoulders and he was barely able to move his arms. The sodden jacket was like a lead weight across his back. He trod water and transferred his wallet and phone to his trouser pockets. Behind him, the RIB's engine coughed into life. He tried to slip out of the jacket but it clung to his shirt.

A pool of light hit the water beside him. They had turned on the RIB's searchlight. In the glare, he saw Matterling on the *Kamakura's* bridge, a radio in his hand. The RIB pushed away from the landing deck. Brennan saw the silhouettes of the two brothers on board.

He wrestled again with his jacket and after a furious few seconds of wrenching at the sleeves, he managed to free himself from it. It drifted down into the murk. The RIB was heading in his direction and it was crisscrossing the water methodically, its searchlight making circles on the surface.

He forced his head down, tasting the saltiness on his lips and struck out towards the lights of the mainland. If he kept stopping and looking for the RIB, he would be caught. He had to concentrate on swimming and forget his pursuers.

He was a strong swimmer but those lights looked a long way away. He slowed his stroke to reduce the splash. If he switched to breaststroke he would be able to get his bearings but the crawl was faster.

He felt that he was making good headway. He surged through the water and fell into a steady rhythm. He would count two hundred strokes before stopping. Distance was the priority.

Eventually, he neared his stroke target. Although he kept his eyes open, he could see nothing. The water below him was pitch black and the height of the waves meant there was nothing to see even when he lifted his head to breathe.

Two hundred strokes completed. He stopped swimming and trod water. He had expected to see the shore lights ahead, much closer. But they weren't there. He twisted around to look for *Kamakura*. She had disappeared. There was nothing to see at all. But as he peered into the darkness, he finally saw the rocky shoreline of Kellett Island. It was much further away than he had expected. And the row of deck lights in the distance to his right must belong to *Kamakura*.

The current had pushed him out into the bay. The waves were double the size they had been when he had entered the water.

But at least there was no sign of the RIB. He had given them the slip.

All he could do now was carry on swimming, even though his arms and legs were dead with fatigue and the shock of being carried so far from shore had made his heart race even faster. He took a few huge, gasping breaths to slow the numbing sensation that was creeping through his body. No time to panic.

He plunged forward, switching to breaststroke. It was slower but he could see where he was going. He swam at an angle to the current this time and after a couple of minutes, he realised that this was pushing him towards the shore. The lights were getting closer. He felt his strength returning and he lengthened his stroke.

The waves were smaller now and he could see some moored junks ahead. He was approaching shallower water. The boats had lanterns swinging from their rigging and these spread a dim light around them.

As he focussed on the junks he saw a small dark shape. It looked like a tennis ball that had floated out to sea. On his next stroke he noticed that the ball was moving. Then he saw a V-shaped ripple behind it.

It was coming towards him.

He stopped swimming and pushed up in the water for a better view. The ball now looked like a head. Behind it, he could see a long body curling through the sea. White bands were visible along its length.

It was a sea snake and it was coming right at him.

Brennan's knowledge of sea snakes was pretty hazy. But he did remember someone telling him once that non-venomous snakes swam with only their heads visible, whereas venomous snakes swam with their lungs inflated and their whole body on top of the water.

This was no time to test the theory and Brennan turned sharply to his left and swam with the current. He reverted to the crawl and after a dozen furious strokes he turned to see where the snake was. He sank back into the water and let out a long breath as he saw its tail scything away from him.

Then he heard the sound of an engine starting. It was louder than before but it was the same engine. The RIB. They must have decided to stop combing the search area and just sit and wait for their prey to make himself known. Which he had just done with his burst of splashing.

The sound of the engine was coming from further out, towards the open harbour. The moored junks were still between him and the shore. They offered a hiding place. Somewhere he could rest and avoid the penetrating glare of the searchlight.

He took a deep breath and struck out at an angle to the current again. He continued with the crawl, knowing that the RIB's powerful outboard would drown out his splashing. He had to get over to those junks before the searchlight caught up with him.

His arms were getting heavier with each stroke but he managed to keep up the pace. He had to force his legs to kick as hard as possible. By concentrating on his stroke he was able to put the thought of the Remus brothers to the back of his mind.

His right arm crashed into something solid and he was brought to a painful halt. He kicked hard and raised his body in the water. He felt the obstruction with both hands. It was a couple of feet foot wide and circular with a wire mesh attached to one side in some kind of pattern. He felt around the rim. It was an old dartboard.

He pushed it away. Ahead of him, the closest junk was less than ten strokes away. Behind, the searchlight was gaining, scanning the water with long slow arcs. It would be upon him soon.

The final few strokes towards the dark hull of the junk were laboured but he kept going until he could feel its smooth surface with both hands. The beam of the searchlight scoured the water behind him and the roar of the RIB's engine echoed louder around the harbour.

He pulled himself along the side of the junk towards its bow. As the searchlight scanned the moored boats, he managed to drag himself around the stem of the hull. The fierce light passed the bow and he clung on.

The light continued its search and the RIB slowed as it entered the cluster of boats. The engine faded, grew stronger, then faded again. The RIB was circling around, checking each junk.

It was only a matter of time before the light hit his side of the hull but it was too high to climb and there were no visible handholds. But he spotted the anchor rope, which led from the harbour bottom up to a hole about two thirds the way up the hull. If he could climb the rope up to that hole he might be able to use it to heave himself onto the deck.

The RIB's engine was getting louder again. It was coming in his direction.

He pushed away from the hull and grabbed the taut rope with both hands. He wrapped his legs around it and squeezed it between his feet. He pushed up and moved his hands further up the rope. He repeated the movement and started to climb.

His body came out of the water and he looked up. He was about halfway there.

Then the sound of the motor suddenly became much louder. The RIB hove into view, heading towards him. The searchlight's arc would pick him out within seconds. There was no time for more climbing. He had to get out of sight. Fast.

He released his grip and slid down the rope into the water. He took a deep breath and pulled himself further down towards the anchor. He kicked with his legs and submerged fully. Then he swung his legs below him and they gripped the rope. His head was about a foot below the surface.

He held his breath.

Above him, the searchlight settled on the junk and the water lit up. Brennan could see the decorative pattern along the top of the hull. He hoped that his dark clothes and the murky water would conceal him.

The light moved along the hull. Before darkness descended again, Brennan saw several pale blobs in the water between him and the junk. They looked like some of the plastic bags which littered the harbour. They drifted closer. As they made their slow approach he realised that they were not plastic bags. They had long tentacles trailing below them.

Jellyfish. And lots of them.

His breath was jammed in his throat and a few bubbles escaped from his mouth and raced to the surface. The searchlight had stopped moving. Brennan could not surface yet. The jellyfish drifted closer on the current.

The light remained steady. The closest jellyfish was inches from his face. He pulled his head back as far as he could without letting go of the rope and closed his eyes. If he tried to push it away with his hand, he would be stung.

The soft, gelatinous body brushed against his cheek and he jerked his head involuntarily. He felt it react to his movement and then its body pressed against his face again. He felt it pulsating steadily against his skin and he tensed as he forced his breath deeper into his lungs. Then, very slowly, it started to move away. As it drifted away from him he felt its tentacles drape over his arm and shoulder. He braced himself for the pain. The tentacles explored the material of his shirt and then started to reluctantly pull away. His teeth clenched tighter together. Several seconds passed. The pain didn't come.

He opened his eyes. The jellyfish were drifting off to his left.

No movement from the searchlight. They must be examining something.

His chest was aching badly. He couldn't hold on for much longer.

The light started moving again. It swung towards the stern of the junk. Brennan started to let out his breath. In small, evenly-spaced bubbles. The light disappeared.

He let himself float slowly to the surface. He pulled himself up with the anchor rope and watched the RIB as it headed towards Kellett Island. Its searchlight was still working the area ahead of it. It was a long way off. He gulped several deep lungfuls of air.

Then he heard a gentle chugging coming from the other side of the junk. A small, low sampan rounded the bow. It looked like some kind of fishing boat. There were two men aboard. It was the best sight Brennan had witnessed all evening.

He took another deep breath and launched himself towards it.

61

Tuesday evening
Hong Kong

THE TWO FISHERMEN nosed their boat towards one of the construction sites lining the Hung Hing Road where the new waterfront was being built. They came alongside a flight of concrete steps. One of the fishermen was at the bow and he grabbed a wooden pole on the bottom step. The other held onto a rope hanging horizontally along the length of the steps. The sampan came to a halt.

Mike Brennan stepped off unsteadily.

'Thank you, gentlemen,' he said as he looked back across the water toward the curved white facade of the yacht club in the distance. 'This kindness will bring you luck.'

There was no sign of the Remus boys and their searchlight. They must have directed their search further round the headland where the boulders made a more obvious landing spot for an escaping swimmer.

He wobbled onto the bottom step and pulled his wallet from his trouser pocket. He gave both fishermen a sodden five-hundred Hong Kong Dollar note and they smiled broadly, their weathered faces breaking into creases. The bow man pointed up to a gap in the fencing above and once Brennan had nodded his understanding of where he needed to go, they pushed the boat back into the darkness. He waved his thanks to them as they reversed out into the bay and set off again in search of squid.

The gap in the fence opened into an alley formed from long strips of hoarding, which served as the border between two construction sites. He squelched along between the boards and came out onto the Hung Hing Road. He looked at the traffic nervously—it wouldn't be long before the brothers gave up searching the water and headed for his hotel. He weaved across two lanes of traffic to a gap in the central reservation and squinted at the vehicles coming out of the Cross-Harbour Tunnel. A minute later he saw an empty taxi. He waved it into the gap and as it slowed, he jumped into the back.

The taxi driver stared into his rear-view mirror, aghast.

'Mandarin Oriental. Quickly,' Brennan said.

The driver was still staring so Brennan pulled out another damp five-hundred-dollar note and offered it forward. Eventually, the driver reached across and took it.

'That's just for cleaning,' Brennan said. 'I'll pay the fare on top. But we need to be quick. Mandarin Oriental. Connaught Road. Central.'

Ten minutes later, he was standing in the doorway of Van Cleef & Arpels, pretending to look at necklaces but in reality watching the Mandarin Oriental entrance across the street. He was still soaking wet but no one was paying him any attention. He could have been caught in one of the afternoon's showers. There was no sign of the Remus boys. Yet. But he was sure they were not far away. Henry would have told them where he was staying and they would surely give up their search of the harbour soon to come straight here.

A dark blue BMW squealed to a halt outside the hotel entrance. Brennan pulled back into the doorway.

Both rear doors of the BMW were flung open and the two brothers jumped out. He was right. They had already cut their losses at the harbour. Pragmatists to the last.

They ran into the hotel. Brennan gave them twenty seconds to get in a lift or take the stairs, then he hurried around the corner into Icehouse Street. The high-rises all around provided a warren for him to escape into.

He strode southwards, desperately seeking invisibility. All he wanted to do was merge into the stone and glass surrounding him. He was alone and at rock bottom. He fingered his phone in his inside pocket. He was sure they had got to it. Otherwise, how had they tracked him so easily this morning? Henry Evans could easily have installed one of those hidden tracker apps on it. Brennan just needed to test it.

He stopped at the end of an alleyway and pulled out the phone. The dunking in the harbour didn't seem to have caused a problem; when he turned it on, it was working fine. He looked back up the street from where he had come. He didn't have to wait long. Within a minute of turning the phone on, the blue BMW turned into the alley and headed towards him. He turned off the phone, slipped it back into his pocket and trotted away.

HALF AN HOUR LATER, his mood had lifted. He was sitting in a noodle bar, hidden away in a narrow street half a mile from the Mandarin Oriental. His clothes were starting to dry out and he had a bowl of Yunnan noodles on the table before him. He poked the end of a chopstick into the fried egg on top and watched the yellow yoke run into the white vermicelli.

The temperature was dropping sharply and the windows of the

small restaurant were steamed up. The place was busy with office workers and excited students who shuffled around in their seats as their groups got larger. Everyone seemed to have rucksacks, which were constantly being moved from table to seat to floor. The noise levels were rising as the number of customers increased. Brennan juggled with the noodles on his chopsticks.

At least he had some cash. He might be alone, he might be on the run, but at least he had some cash in his pocket and some food in front of him. He could find some anonymous hotel for the night where he couldn't be found, where he could buy some time and work out his next move.

For the moment, he was safe. This little corner of Hong Kong even smelt safe. Hot, steamy, aromatic and safe. He thought of Sarah and Cara and wondered what they were doing now. He pushed Matterling's comments about Cara to the back of his mind.

He was physically exhausted. He had run and swam and had nothing to show for it. He had lost the attaché case and Matterling had beaten him again. He shivered—Matterling's mention of Cannon Park nursery crept back into his thoughts.

The noodles kept slipping from his chopsticks but some managed to find his mouth. He paused in the struggle and pulled out his phone. He laid it on the table next to the noodles. It would be the most natural thing in the world to turn it on and make a call. To Lisa's sister perhaps? He had to get some help. But that would be too dangerous. They would be onto him like wolves.

He went back to the noodles. Eating was helping him think. There was only one way to get the bearer share certificate back. He had to return to Matterling's yacht and somehow get past the Remus security barrier. There must be a way.

'Are they good?'

He started. The voice came from a long way away. A telephone voice. A friendly female voice. He looked up as a woman in a black slimline coat slid into the seat opposite him. It was as if she had emerged from the steam and the chatter. She put her hand on his forearm and smiled.

Brennan froze. Noodles slipped off his chopstick. He felt a crashing mixture of shock and gratitude.

'What the hell are you doing here, Lisa?'

62

Tuesday evening
Hong Kong

'SO WE'RE STILL in Central, are we?' Brennan heard himself asking.

'That's right. My sister's been in this apartment for years.'

Lisa and her sister Gina sat opposite him on a black and white checked sofa. They were drinking tea like it was a Sunday afternoon family gathering. Brennan was drinking a fruity Malbec. Lots of it.

'Must be worth a fortune,' he said softly.

The sisters glanced at each other and smiled. 'A family inheritance,' Gina said.

They looked like twins. Brennan couldn't decide who was the older. Both wore their black hair in half-moon curves. Both were wearing black jeans and pale blouses. Gina had thick, black glasses that camouflaged her brown eyes.

'Tell me again how you found me,' he asked. 'The car ride was a bit of a blur.'

Gina had driven them all back from the noodle place at break-neck speed and he had not been able to hear their replies to the questions he had been hurling from the back seat. At the apartment, they had insisted he change out of his damp clothes and now here he was in an outsized bathrobe being plied with wine.

'Lucky break,' Lisa said. 'I was coming to your hotel and I saw you disappear around a corner. I looked in all the likely places and eventually found you.'

'You were coming to my hotel?'

'Yes. You told me where you were when I phoned the other night. I was coming to tell you about my visit to Remus Security.'

'And?'

'You were right. They were holding Ben Parfitt.'

'They were?' Brennan suddenly felt very sober. 'How did you find out? And why did you say *were*? Is he still there?'

'No. I released him.' She looked concerned. 'That was the right thing to do, wasn't it?'

'Of course. Why was he being held? What did he say?'

'Nothing. He ran off as soon as I opened up a door into an old beer cellar. Just shot off into the night without even a thank you.'

'You opened a cellar door? From outside? From the road?'

'Yes. It was easy. There wasn't even a lock on it. Just a couple of bolts. I was standing on it, waiting for something to happen inside the offices. Then I heard someone calling for help and when I pulled the door up, he was there on the steps. Ready to make a run for it.'

'Ungrateful little tyke.'

'That's what I thought.'

'Anyway, well done. Thank you.'

Brennan was impressed. Lisa had sounded determined on the phone and she had certainly come up trumps by getting Parfitt out so quickly. It was a pity he had scarpered though. He had to have some relevance to de Souza and it would have been good to find out what.

'No problem,' she said. 'That's what friends are for.' She smiled warmly.

'So how come you're here in Hong Kong all of a sudden? I'm sure you didn't come all this way to tell me that. I didn't know you were planning to be here.'

Lisa laughed. 'Come on, Mike.' There was an edge to her voice. 'You know nothing about my life. I come here a lot to visit family.' She cocked her head. 'And what's with all the questions? I thought you'd be pleased I got Parfitt out. I also thought you might be grateful to be rescued from what looked like the worst noodles in Hong Kong.'

Brennan laughed. The exertions of the day had probably made him tetchy. There was no reason to be suspicious of Lisa. She was bending over backwards to help.

'And note that we're not giving you the third-degree about using Victoria Harbour as a swimming pool,' Lisa said. 'Nor about being press-ganged into service on some billionaire's yacht.'

'What?' he said sharply.

'One of Gina's colleagues at the Yacht Club saw you. They keep a good look-out there.'

'And they reported back to you?' he said to Gina.

'We keep each other informed,' she said deliberately. 'And safe.'

'Well, he's not a billionaire,' Brennan said. 'And I'm doing everything I can to prevent him from getting anywhere near it.'

It sounded harsher than he had intended and the two sisters simply sat in silence, looking at him calmly. He took another slug of wine. It had been a long day and it had not gone according to plan. His companion had been a plant and this whole Hong Kong farrago had been a trap. He had walked into it with his eyes open but so far he had nothing to show for it. Fiona Wells and Henry Evans had turned out to be Matterling's monkeys and God knew who else might be working for him. Perhaps even Olson and Carmel were part of his plan.

Lisa and Gina smiled at him. No, he thought, that was unfair. He couldn't tar everybody with the same brush. He owed them a better explanation. He picked up his glass again.

'I'll explain a bit more in a minute,' he said after another swallow.

'But please. Tell me about your family. You're obviously close. And I remember you telling me how you had acquired your current surname.' Lisa had told him about a brief marriage but she had not wanted to go into details. He had assumed it was some kind of arrangement, made by her family.

'You know the Jingsheng family,' Lisa said. 'We made an investment in your company. A good investment.'

'Of course. I wasn't forgetting that. I was just wondering about your immediate family.' He had not forgotten about the money they had lost with Brennan Matterling. Far from it. But how could she call it a good investment when they got nothing back?

'Our whole family is immediate family,' Gina said. 'When you deal with one, you deal with us all. And when one helps you, then we all help you.'

'And that is very much appreciated.' Brennan wished he had not started down this track. But he had one more question. 'Why did you say that your family had made a "good investment", Lisa? You know how devastated I was when you lost it all. And I'm sorry for that. Very sorry.'

'The money was only part of the investment,' Lisa said. 'It was one part of the relationship. It was a good relationship. It should have continued.'

He had been hoping for the same. At the time, he remembered dealing only with Lisa but he knew that she was acting on behalf of her family. It was a long time ago. There was nothing to be gained now by dredging through that period.

'Let me tell you more about why I'm here,' he said. 'It's the least I can do.'

Lisa leant over and topped up his glass. She seemed different here than in London, he thought. More constrained. More Chinese, as if he really knew what that meant.

'As you know,' he said, 'I was writing an article about a British businessman who headed a company called Elba Technology. Unfortunately, he accidentally fell off his yacht and drowned. But now it seems it was no accident. The story led me to a shareholder in Elba and I am helping him out by collecting some paperwork here in Hong Kong.'

'Which you have collected?' Gina asked.

'I had,' Brennan said ruefully. 'And then I lost it. Or rather it was taken from me.'

'By Douglas Matterling,' Lisa said.

'That's correct. But how do you know?'

'That grey yacht belongs to him. *Kamakura*. It is well known here. And one of the guys accompanying you was holding a small briefcase. Presumably that was the paperwork you referred to.'

'Well, yes. You're right. Your man at the yacht club is very observant.'

'And why is this paperwork so important?' Lisa asked.

It was the obvious question. But should he tell her? After all, this was confidential. On the other hand, if he stood any chance of getting hold of the bearer share again, he needed help. And at the moment, Lisa and Gina were his only option.

'Can I tell you in confidence? To go no further than the three of us?'

They both nodded.

'Inside that small briefcase is a piece of paper called a bearer share. And whoever holds that share is going to control a large share-holding in Elba Technology.'

Lisa leaned forward as if waiting for more information. Brennan didn't elaborate.

'So there's some kind of takeover fight going on?'

He couldn't help but be impressed. Again. But there was no point in coming over all coy. Not now.

'That's right.'

'And Matterling is involved as well?'

'Correct.'

'That's why Ben Parfitt was a party of interest.'

'Yes. Pity you didn't get a chance to ask him a few questions.'

Lisa's face dropped. He didn't want her to think he was criticising. 'Not that you could do anything about it, of course. You did great.'

'What's your next step?'

Brennan took another sip from his glass. 'I've got to get that brief-case back. Somehow I've got to get on board *Kamakura*, get hold of it and get out of Hong Kong by tomorrow night.'

Now that he had articulated what he had to do Brennan could see how impossible it seemed. Especially as he had to get past Remus Security to get anywhere near the case.

'Sounds like we need a plan,' Lisa said quietly. She looked at her sister.

'We?' Brennan said.

'Yes. We. We'll help you.'

'Help?' He appreciated Lisa's help in England and also this evening's rescue. But now they were up against Matterling and his attack dogs.

'If you let us.' Gina bowed politely.

'You are a good man, Mike,' Lisa said. 'We have always thought so. And you have conviction. We don't need to know any more. We trust you.'

Conviction. It sounded like he had been assessed. But it was good to hear it from another source—it was the same assessment as his own. Sitting in wet clothes at the noodle bar, staring defeat in the face, he had come to the same conclusion. He had put everything on the line in coming to Hong Kong to pursue Doug Matterling. He had to find justice now.

'To set a trap, we need some bait,' he said heavily. 'And I guess that would be me.' He could think of nothing else that would draw Matterling out. Matterling's raw hatred of him had to be the motivator.

But how could the sisters help? And could he trust them? Their alliance seemed very convenient, perhaps too convenient. Less than twenty-four hours ago he had been speaking to Lisa on the telephone and now here she was in person, apparently willing to risk her safety, as well as her sister's, to aid his quest.

On the other hand, they were all he had here. Lisa had put herself out by going to the Remus offices and releasing Parfitt. Everyone else was lined up with Matterling. Could Matterling have got to Lisa as well? He looked into her dark eyes. Somehow, he doubted it. After all, she had lost money to him. But he had to be careful.

He took a deep breath. Despite the volume of Malbec he had consumed, he was thinking clearly. A plan was formulating.

'We need an anchorage with a mobile phone signal onshore. An anchorage suitable for *Kamakura*.' He pulled his phone from his inside pocket and set it down on the table. 'If I were to turn that on, we would have Matterling's goons at the front door in an instant. They're tracking it. But we can use it as a lure.'

'Are you sure?' Lisa asked. 'That's quite an assumption.'

'I turned it on this evening and they appeared within minutes.'

'Could have been coincidence. Was it near the hotel?'

'Well, yes.'

'So, they knew where you were staying, didn't they? If they were that interested in you, that would have been the easy part.'

Brennan had to concede to her logic. Lisa was helping him remove the variables.

'We could have a look.' She pointed at the phone. 'If your plan is predicated on that phone being tracked, then we'd better make sure.'

'You mean look for the tracker app?'

She nodded.

'That would mean turning it on.'

She nodded again.

To prevent the phone from emitting a signal when he turned it on he would need to either disable it quickly or place it in a protective environment. He could flick it into airplane mode as soon as it was turned on, but it would be risky. There could be a brief transmission before any signal was quashed.

'Where's the bathroom?' he said.

She pointed towards the hallway. 'Opposite the bedroom you changed in.'

Brennan went into the hallway. He opened the bathroom door and looked around the tiny space. Perfect. He turned around and found Lisa right behind him. She was holding a large roll of aluminium foil in one hand and a roll of clear sticky tape in the other.

'Doctor Faraday, I presume,' she said, smiling. She had anticipated his request for the foil.

'You presume correctly,' he said, acting surprised. But he wasn't at all surprised—she was as sharp as a tack.

The bathroom was as small as a functioning bathroom could be, with no windows and just the one door. The wall and ceiling could easily be covered with foil, providing an electromagnetic shield that would block any signals being received or transmitted from his phone.

'Let me,' Lisa said, stepping past him. 'You drink your wine. It won't take me long to fix this up. The microwave's no good because you'd have to get your hands in to turn the phone on.' She started to unwrap the foil. 'The gap would let the radio waves out. But I bet you thought of it.'

He went back to the lounge and finished his wine. The rustling of foil and the zip of tape filled the room for the next ten minutes. It wasn't foolproof but he had to take the chance.

'Ready,' Lisa called. 'Come on in.'

Brennan picked up the phone from the table and went to the bathroom. Gina sipped her tea and watched them.

He slipped in next to Lisa. She held out her hand for the phone and he closed the door behind him. She had transformed the cubicle and he scanned the aluminium-covered interior for gaps. There were none. She had even made a foil trim around the door which could be pushed down once they were in. He ran his finger around it and made the seal.

Lisa raised her eyebrows, asking the question.

'Go ahead,' he said. 'But if this doesn't work I'm going to have to scram.'

She turned the phone on and they both watched anxiously as it powered up. Nothing. No signal at all. They waited for ten seconds. Still nothing. Lisa smiled at him.

'Great job, Lise. We've disconnected ourselves.'

She tapped expertly on the screen a few times and then turned the phone towards him.

'There it is,' she said. 'There's your tracker app. Hidden in plain sight.'

They stared at the bright yellow logo, a human footprint in a triangle, no brand name but a code number below it.

'Henry,' Brennan said quietly. He thought back to their dinner, when he had left his jacket on the back of his chair while he went to the bathroom. Henry must have got hold of his phone then. He wasn't as stupid as he seemed.

Lisa had her own phone in her other hand.

'Watch that bit of seal,' she warned, looking behind Brennan at a strip of foil that was coming away from the doorframe. He turned around and stuck it down.

'I've retraced my steps through your settings,' she said, handing him back his phone, 'and switched it off. You were right. They'll be waiting for that phone to turn on again. Then they'll be onto you like a missile.' Her smile had gone. 'You'd better tell us your plan. We'll give you all the help we can.'

Brennan opened the small door and they went back to join Gina.

'So,' Lisa said as they sat back down. 'You need an anchorage with a mobile signal.'

'Yes. Somewhere not too far from Causeway Bay. Somewhere Matterling could get to on his yacht and somewhere where we can get our own launch. A small RIB or something like that. I need to put the dogs on a false trail.' He raised his phone. 'And get one-to-one with Matterling. Any ideas for that kind of location?'

The sisters looked at each other and then came up with the same answer.

'Middle Island,' they said together and gave Brennan a triumphant smile.

'It's just the place,' Gina said. 'The yacht club has another club-house there that they use for dinghy racing. We can use one of the Club's RIBs if that's what you need.'

'Perfect,' Lisa said.

Perfect. Brennan hoped he would be thinking the same by the end of tomorrow.

63

Wednesday afternoon
   Hong Kong

BRENNAN WALKED to the promontory on the west side of Middle Island. He placed his phone on a large rock jutting out from the precipitous, wooded hillside. He turned it on and checked the signal. Four bars. He left it there and quickly retraced his steps along the beach, past the Tin Hau temple and back to the clubhouse.

He entered the large storage area on the ground floor and found the room where the sails were stored. He pulled Gina's key from his pocket and tested the lock. Satisfied, he left the room unlocked and climbed the five flights of steep red steps up to the terrace overlooking the bay.

He took a seat at a table next to the low parapet overlooking the water. Pre-race drinks were on offer in the bar below and there was no one else on the terrace. He was watching and waiting. Waiting for Matterling's predatory yacht to come into view.

There was a purposeful buzz about the clubhouse. Wednesday

afternoon racing was getting underway out on the water. A dozen two-man Laser dinghies were criss-crossing each other behind the start line. A signal cannon was fired from the balcony in front of the race office and Brennan watched the Blue Peter flag being hoisted. The dinghies kept manoeuvring around each other, waiting for the starting gun.

His mouth was dry, his body tight. His knuckles were white where he gripped the arms of the chair. He was getting ready for his own test. He was positive that Matterling would come after him. Matterling's expression on the yacht yesterday had told him as much. Brennan had gone from irritant to threat in an instant. Gina had estimated that it would take an hour or so for Matterling's yacht to make the passage south from where it was anchored at Kellett Island.

Earlier, Gina had parked her Mini in the Deep Water Bay BBQ area. She, Lisa and Brennan had come down the steps to the Seaview Promenade and then walked to the small ferry pier. A club sampan had quickly appeared and ferried them over to the island clubhouse. While Brennan had been planting his phone, Gina and Lisa had readied one of the orange safety boats. The club operated two safety boats for every race and they had volunteered to operate one of them. They would be ready to peel away from the race as soon as Brennan needed them.

He could see the ferry pier from where he was sitting. It was not more than a hundred yards away but it felt like a hundred miles. He was a world away from safety. He felt like a rabbit tethered to a stake. Bait for a killer wolf.

Lisa looked up from the orange RIB and waved. They were standing by now, close to the start line. Brennan gave her a thumbs-up. She had made it clear that if he wanted to change his mind they could pick him up from the pontoon and whisk him away. She had been checking back with him every ten minutes. A wave up to the terrace. And his response had always been the same—a thumbs-up. He knew what he had to do.

He looked at his watch again. It had been an hour and a quarter since he had turned the phone on. If Matterling was coming, it would be any minute now. The yacht would round the headland to his left, coming from the south. Behind him, the near-vertical hillside was thick with impenetrable foliage. No escape in that direction. The clubhouse had been built on one of the few viable sites on this inhospitable island.

He had to trust his plan and his ability to cope with whatever Matterling might throw at him. Neutralising Matterling's bid for Elba was just the start. Disclosing details of his true commission arrangements to Heilong's investors would finish the job. When that came out Olson had laughed that it would be 'a matter of hours before you could buy him by the pound, strung up at Causeway Bay market.' That sounded just fine to Brennan.

He continued to watch the ocean beyond the headland. A patch of water that lightened as a cloud drifted overhead and then darkened again.

Suddenly the grey water was full of grey steel. The bow cut through the waves in a gushing spume of foam. Brennan could see Doug Matterling at the wheel on the flybridge. Yesterday he had counted three crew members and he could see them again now, one at the bow and two at the stern.

The yacht came to a halt in front of the clubhouse, the foam subsiding in a circle as the hull levelled off and sat down in the water. There was a loud rattling as an anchor was dropped and then a low hum as the yacht reversed to dig it in. In less than a minute a tender was lowered from its davits and a shore party was on its way to the clubhouse.

Brennan saw four men step off when the tender was tied up against the pontoon. One of them was Doug Matterling. He stood for a moment, looking up at the clubhouse. He had his hands on his hips, defying anyone to challenge his right to be there. Another was Henry Evans who stood sheepishly behind Matterling. The other two were the Remus employees and they were studying their phones. They both looked up at the beach and after exchanging a few words with Matterling they strode off towards the promontory.

Brennan looked out towards *Kamakura* and saw Gina bringing the safety boat to within twenty yards of the pontoon. As well as Lisa, a boatman from the club was aboard. Gina was at the wheel, standing ready.

There was a sudden bang from the balcony in front of the race office. Out on the water, sails were flattened, hulls were angled and the fleet of dinghies headed off in the direction of Deep Water Bay.

Matterling was still glaring up at the clubhouse and his gaze swung round to the terrace. Brennan glanced towards the beach. The Remus boys had disappeared, chasing down his phone. He stood up and leant on the flat top of the parapet. He stared down at Matterling. The stare was returned. A strange calmness overcame him. The plan was working.

But Matterling was too fast. Something seemed to detonate inside him as soon as their eyes met. He raced along the pontoon and up the steps to the terrace, taking them three at a time. Brennan backed up along the terrace with a table between him and the top of the steps.

He couldn't see Matterling as he reached the last flight up to the terrace, but he heard a man's voice calling out, 'You can't anchor there, sir. There's a race—'

The voice was cut off as Brennan heard the crack of bone hitting bone. Then Matterling was suddenly in front of him, his chest heaving, the hard muscles of his upper body bulging under the tight polo shirt. He stood with his legs apart and his fists clenched. There was blood on the knuckles of his right hand. His eyes were narrow slits.

'Thank you, Mike,' he hissed. 'You've confirmed my decision. A trip to Macau is no longer an option for you. It's got to be the Salinger solution.'

Brennan slowly backed up. There was no one else around up here. He had to get Matterling talking, to slow things down.

'That wouldn't be any good to you,' he said. 'Not after all this time. Anyway, it's your father you really want, isn't it?' He saw Matterling's eyebrows knit together. Brennan only needed enough time to plan his next move. 'I'm just an irritant,' he went on. 'I'm not the one behind your pain.'

Henry Evans staggered onto the terrace, red-faced and out of breath.

'Well done, Henry' Matterling said. 'You made it at last. The other two will be here in a minute. We'll hold him until then.'

Matterling started to move around the table and signalled for Henry to take the other side. Brennan continued backing up. He was moving in the wrong direction. He had to move the fight downstairs; he was isolated up here on the terrace. He could hear voices from below but no one else had come up.

'You're more than an irritant now. You're an enemy.' Matterling shook his head. 'Never a good idea. But entirely your choice.'

Henry looked flustered as he advanced around the table. Brennan knew he was the weak point and if he could get past him, he could get to the steps. For now, he stepped slowly sideways.

'It was pointless you trying to hang on to that share,' Matterling said. 'Elba has always been mine. It was just a question of when I decided to take it. I can do whatever the hell I want with it.'

'Would that include some changes in the way you were to book profits from those long-term licensing contracts?'

Matterling smiled. 'Quite the forensic accountant now, eh? A bit late in the day.'

The eighty-odd pages of Elba's last financial statements had been interesting reading on the flight over. Brennan had read the accounts in light of all the profit manipulation techniques Terry Atkinson had taught him. He realised that there were several ways in which Elba's profits could quite easily be inflated by a new owner. Especially an unscrupulous one like Matterling.

Brennan turned towards Henry and stopped moving. He squared his shoulders and waited for Henry to come to him. Brennan drew back his right arm—a fast punch to the solar plexus would stop Henry in his tracks and give Brennan the chance he needed.

But Henry suddenly produced a large hunting knife, which he held up like an Olympic torch. He pointed it at Brennan and charged. Brennan swivelled and managed to grab Henry's wrist, pulling the knife harmlessly by. They tumbled to the ground together and as they fell, Henry pulled his arm free. Brennan's head hit the tiles hard and the world spun momentarily.

He felt a weight on his shoulders. He also felt the knife flat against the side of his throat. Matterling's knees were pinning him to the ground. Henry was still holding the knife, grinning.

'Don't move a muscle,' Matterling hissed into Brennan's face. 'Henry here is capable of anything.'

Henry drew back slightly to give himself more leverage. Brennan felt the knife lift from his throat and he tensed, readying himself for a last attempt to wriggle free. He forced his right hand up between their bodies and grabbed Henry's wrist again. He twisted as hard as he could. Henry's grip loosened and the knife clattered onto the floor.

There was a howl from behind Henry. 'Bastard!'

Brennan twisted towards the top of the steps.

Christ, he thought. *Ben Parfitt*. What the hell was he doing here?

Ben launched himself at Henry. Brennan rolled away as Ben landed on Henry's back and the two of them crunched onto the terracotta tiles.

Brennan staggered to his feet and Matterling sprang up to face him. They both looked down at the knife. Brennan instinctively kicked it away before either of them could bend down to pick it up. It rattled across the floor into the far corner of the terrace.

Matterling was a yard closer to the knife and he started after it. Brennan turned away and headed for the steps. Ben and Henry rolled towards the parapet, both trying to throw punches but holding each other too close to deliver a decisive blow. They struggled to their feet, still clutching each other.

Brennan stopped at the top of the steps and turned around.

Matterling had already scooped up the knife and was back with Henry.

'This one's yours, Matterling said. He offered Henry the knife. 'I'll deal with the bloody accountant.'

Brennan couldn't just leave Ben to it. He didn't stand a chance.

But he was wrong. Ben aimed a perfect kick at the knife and caught the handle just as Henry was about to take it from Matterling. It flew into the air and spun several times before coming back down between Ben and Henry. Ben was half-a-foot taller and he managed to jump and catch it, twisting into Henry as he landed. Matterling had also jumped for it but he had been too far away. He lost his balance as he landed and the three of them crashed into the parapet together.

Ben pulled himself up against Henry, fighting for breath. He looked shocked to be the one holding the knife. Henry was folded over the parapet, winded. An easy target, Brennan thought. Ready for Ben to take his revenge.

Matterling was pulling himself up from the floor and Brennan saw the opportunity to hit him. But he held back. He couldn't afford to get into a fist-fight right now. That wasn't the plan. Instead, he waited for Ben to strike.

But nothing happened. Ben still looked shocked. He was staring at the knife in his hand.

Matterling got to his feet and wrenched the knife from Ben's frozen grip. Henry rolled over and Matterling placed the knife firmly into his hand. He closed his fingers around it.

'It's your time now,' Matterling said quietly. 'Just like at the Tate. Your time has come.'

He turned and without warning hurled himself at Brennan. They both toppled over and fell across the concrete nosing of the top step. Matterling twisted Brennan's right arm up behind his back.

So much for not getting into a fist-fight.

His face was squashed against the tiled tread of the top step and he glimpsed Henry holding the knife to Ben's throat, who was spreadeagled along the top of the parapet.

'Please, Henry,' Ben was pleading. 'Please.'

Henry's face was expressionless. 'One more thing,' he said. 'Before you go. There was no bet. There was no phone call to IG. There was only the twenty-five grand you transferred into my account.'

'But those Remus blokes. They confirmed it,' Ben gasped. His arms were wrapped around Henry and he was trying to pull him closer, to reduce his room for manoeuvre. Henry's weight was pushing them both closer to the edge.

Henry shook his head slowly. 'They were only repeating what they'd been told. There was no phone call.'

He lifted the blade from Ben's throat and Brennan lost sight of it behind Henry's body. A look of relief flooded momentarily across Ben's face and then it contorted in pain. His eyes rolled up. As Henry struggled away, Brennan could see only the knife's handle. The rest was buried in Ben's chest.

Matterling's full weight was on Brennan's back. 'See,' he said into Brennan's ear. 'He who hesitates and all that. You've got to take your revenge when it's offered to you. Otherwise . . .' He breathed into Brennan's neck. '. . . how are you ever going to get your justice?'

'You gave him the knife. You're just as much the killer.'

'It's the consequence, Mike.'

Brennan bucked and twisted violently, kicking out at the same time. Matterling was thrown against the wall beside the steps. Brennan sprang up and as he did so, he saw Ben start to topple over the parapet. Henry was flailing about but he was sliding over with Ben.

Brennan started down the steps. He heard Matterling pulling himself up.

At the bottom flight he turned to gauge Matterling's progress. He was about twenty steps away and gaining.

Brennan had taken only a few steps towards the storage area

when he heard two enormous crashes. He turned as he ran and saw Ben and Henry sprawled over the wreckage of two parked dinghies. The force of the fall had crunched the hulls into the concrete and the standing rigging vibrated against the aluminium masts. There was no movement from either body.

Matterling was only yards away. Brennan darted into the storage area. He rushed past a few young sailors who were taking off their lifejackets and headed for the sail room. The door was open. He could feel Matterling behind him and could hear his determined breathing as he chased down his prey.

As he reached the doorway, Brennan dropped to his knees and curled into a protective ball, his back braced and his head tucked into his arms. Matterling was too close behind to stop in time and his legs smashed into Brennan's back. He nose-dived into the storage room and landed in a heap against the back wall.

Brennan was on his feet and closing the door before Matterling was able to coordinate his limbs. He extracted the key from his pocket and locked the door.

He ran back out to the front of the clubhouse. The sailors were congregating around the bodies and the Remus brothers were jogging dutifully back along the beach. Gina had brought the orange RIB up to the pontoon and the two sisters were looking anxiously at him.

He rushed onto the pontoon and scrambled into the motorboat. Gina reversed away then spun it around and opened the throttle. The Remus brothers were just a couple of minutes away from their tender and the huddle around Ben and Henry had grown bigger.

'Christ,' Brennan said, trying to get his breath back. 'Where did that skinny stockbroker bloke come from? Ben Parfitt? I thought he was in London.' Another deep breath. 'They've both copped it.' He looked at Gina and Lisa in turn. 'For what?'

The sisters stared ahead and neither of them replied. The RIB was headed straight towards the bow of Matterling's yacht. A small Chinese man, decked out in the RHKYC uniform, stood between

Lisa and Gina. If he knew that he was part of the plan, he didn't show it. He simply stood by to take orders.

'Part One complete,' Brennan said. 'Now for Part Two.'

Gina slowed the RIB when they were about thirty feet east of *Kamakura's* anchor chain. Brennan reached down into the plastic box of distress flares that Gina had loaded onto the boat when they had launched it. He took out a buoyant smoke flare, pulled the start ring and threw it into the water. He did the same with a second flare and stuffed a couple of hand flares into his jacket pockets in case he needed to create some fizz when he got aboard.

The easterly breeze started to blow the thick orange smoke towards the grey hull and soon it was billowing up beneath the bow.

Gina steered the RIB into open water and started to circle slowly back. They watched *Kamakura* and waited for their moment. Behind them, the yacht's tender had left the pontoon and was heading in their direction. The Remus brothers were in pursuit.

Kamakura's crew of three appeared at the bow carrying fire extinguishers. Gina headed towards the yacht's stern and came alongside the landing deck. Brennan leapt onto the deck and Lisa jumped aboard after him. They ran up the steps and into the saloon. He had seen Matterling place the attaché case in the chart desk yesterday and he was banking on it still being there. He only had a limited time before the crew realised that the flares were just a distraction.

He opened the desktop and let out a low whistle of relief. The case was still there. He opened it and saw the share certificate. He closed it again and Lisa pointed to the open door. He led the way back down the steps and they jumped onto the RIB. Gina opened the throttle at once and they headed back out to sea.

The fleet of racing dinghies had rounded the mark out in Deep Water Bay and was on a run back to a buoy west of the clubhouse. Their sails were let fully out and they were goose-winging this leg. Brennan could see the helmsmen craning forward to get a better view of the course ahead—a two-hundred-foot obstruction anchored in the middle of the course wasn't helping them. Nor was a large orange cloud of smoke, obscuring the obstruction.

Once in clear water, Gina changed course and they headed for the ferry steps. There was a lot of shouting as the racing dinghies tried to steer through the smoke and avoid the giant yacht, as well as each other. There was the splintering sound of a significant collision. Brennan peered into the smoke but could only see a tangle of sails and masts. The dinghy crews shouted at each other, at *Kamakura* and at *Kamakura's* tender, which had ploughed into the melee.

As the RIB reached the small landing stage, the three of them jumped out and the Chinese man took over at the wheel of the safety boat. He roared away towards the action and Brennan took a final look behind him.

One of the dinghies had been forced free of the commotion. It was moving sideways and listing at a forty-five-degree angle. As the smoke cleared, the reason for the listing became visible. The hull had been skewered by *Kamakura's* tender and the indignant crews of both boats were grappling with each other over the upturned gunwale of the dinghy. The dinghy's crew were soon dispatched into the water and the Remus brothers gazed helplessly towards the ferry pier.

'Part Two complete,' Brennan said, putting his arms around the shoulders of his companions. They hurried back along the path towards the parked Mini and he added, 'Now for the getaway.'

64

Wednesday morning
   London

THE KNOCK on the front door was firm. Four heavy strikes. A caller who sounded like they didn't care if they woke any occupants who might still be sleeping.

Sarah had just sat down at the kitchen table with a cup of Gold Blend. Cara had just gone down for a morning nap. The kitchen floor had been swept. Breakfast plates put away. The dishwasher was on, gurgling away quietly. Ten minutes of peace.

Until the knocking.

Who the hell was this? They'd better have a good reason for disturbing the quiet of the house. A bloody good reason. Hopefully, Cara was already asleep. If so, then even this would not wake her. She could sleep the sleep of the righteous when she was tired enough.

And boy, she ought to be tired. They'd been up since four this morning. Establishing sleep patterns had been difficult for both of them since Mike had left last Friday. All Sarah wanted was for this whole nightmare with Doug Matterling to be over. The last week had been nearly as bad as the trial.

She slipped off the high stool and stomped down the hall. She didn't want to give the caller time to repeat the intrusive volley. A glance up the stairs as she passed. Not a peep from Cara. Thank God for that.

'Coming,' she said loudly as she reached the door, hoping that the irritation in her voice would transmit to the caller. Plus the rest of the sentiment: *Why knock so loudly you idiot? We can hear.*

She slid out the two bolts but kept the chain secured—since Mike had gone, she had kept it attached diligently. *Keep everything locked,* he had said. Which was what she did.

She twisted the deadbolt knob and opened the door a few inches. She peered through the gap to see the moron responsible for the interruption.

A fluorescent yellow high-vis jacket stood out against the gloom of the winter morning. It was worn by a young policeman. He gave her a broad smile. A nice smile, she thought grudgingly.

'Good morning, madam,' he said cheerfully. 'I hope I'm not disturbing you.'

She took in the rest of him. Black trousers and shoes, a belt bristling with equipment, black epaulettes with silver numbers, a yellow device that looked like a pager clipped to his right breast pocket. He doffed his cap as he spoke, a black, flat cap with a chequered band around it.

He sounded like a typical policeman with his clipped, efficient monotone. But Sarah remained sceptical. Her nerves were in shreds and she trusted no one. If those people could run Mike over with a motorbike, they could do anything.

'We're following up on some reports.'

She wondered whether to ask him for ID. Even if he had nothing to do with whatever Mike was mixed up in, there were plenty of scammers about. But asking a policeman for ID? Was that being paranoid?

He held out a small plastic wallet showing his ID. No need to ask. She looked at the picture quickly and followed the hat as he put it back on his head. There was a badge on the front of it —*Metropolitan Police* circling a grand *ER*. It looked genuine.

'From a couple of your neighbours.'

He folded the wallet back into an inside pocket.

'Neighbours? What are you talking about?'

Had there been complaints about something? Perhaps Cara had been making too much noise in the garden. Or maybe the broken fence had been banging in the wind. But surely that wasn't a police matter.

'It seems someone was seen on top of the wall that runs along the back of your house and the adjoining properties. Looked like he was running away.'

'Good God. When was this?'

'About half an hour ago. There was an escape from the Scrubs last night. It could be connected. We're checking all the gardens along here.'

'I see.'

Wormwood Scrubs prison. It was only a couple of miles away. Sarah immediately pictured an escaped convict hiding under that canvas awning at the bottom of the garden. She had been meaning to get rid of it for ages but it was so wet and heavy that it needed two people to lift it. She had been waiting for Mike to help.

'We need to check sheds and outhouses,' the policeman said. 'That kind of thing.'

The shed. The decrepit old shed they never locked. Shit.

'Of course,' she said.

A violent criminal holed up in their shed. Laying low until the dust settled. Crouched next to the garden spades and forks that were hardly ever used. Like a cornered rat. She shuddered.

'It would be a great help if we could have a quick look round. I can go down the side if the gate is open.' It was an end-of-terrace house and there was a concrete path down the side to the garden. 'I'm sure there's nothing to worry about.'

His radio crackled and Sarah could hear some indistinct orders being given and acknowledged. He reached up to the handset and turned the volume down. He smiled at her and glanced at his watch.

'It shouldn't take a moment, madam. Just a quick look around in the garden then I can leave you in peace. I don't need to come into the house. Keep everything locked until I've left.'

He was saying the same as Mike. *Keep everything locked.* She certainly would. As soon as he'd gone.

'I'll go and open the side gate,' she said and realised that she would have to go out into the garden to go around and take the latch off the gate. Christ, a convict on the loose. He could be dangerous, some kind of maniac. 'No,' she said decisively. 'Come through the house. It'll be quicker.'

She unlatched the security chain and opened the door fully. 'Come through.'

He smiled and stepped past her carefully, politely ensuring that he did not make any physical contact. As he passed, she noticed a strong clean smell. He seemed capable and confident. He could deal with any miscreant who might be taking refuge in the back garden. He could radio for back-up if necessary.

She closed the front door. He was standing still now, head slightly bowed, waiting respectfully for her to lead the way down the hall.

The chain on the front door clanked against the frame as it settled. She headed for the kitchen. This must be quite a manhunt. How many gardens were they searching? She had not noticed any other policemen in the street when they had been talking at the door. Nor many police cars if it came to that. Didn't they normally flood the place with a million pounds worth of vehicles when there was an incident?

Where were the others? A shiver of alarm shot through her and she started to turn back to him. But that strong sweet smell seemed suddenly overpowering. It surged into her brain. It became sickly, like too much aftershave.

Her head was suddenly yanked back and a firm hand clamped around her mouth, pressing cold cotton against her face. The stench of chemicals replaced the aftershave and her body disappeared beneath her.

65

Wednesday afternoon
  Hong Kong

GINA PROVED to be as adept at driving a Mini as an RIB and it took only a couple of minutes to get onto Route 1 at Ocean Park. But as they headed north towards the city the traffic started getting heavier. By the time they were within sight of the large signs above the Cross-Harbour Tunnel, they were crawling along. As they approached the tunnel entrance, they came to a complete stop.

Brennan looked at his watch. Time enough to get to the airport and catch the flight back to London. Lisa was planning to go back to Central with Gina. The airport would be the obvious destination for Matterling as well. If they could have a clear run through to Lantau Island, then Brennan could get through check-in to safety.

That clear run was not happening at the moment.

Matterling had two options when he got back to his yacht. He could either motor back around Hong Kong island to the north and pick up a car; or he could go west and out to the airport by sea. Either way, he would be at least half an hour behind.

Brennan looked out at the bay. This was where he had emerged from his enforced swim. Where he had found a taxi and its reluctant driver. He couldn't believe it had only been yesterday.

The traffic was still stationary. He looked at his watch again.

Gina turned to him and smiled. 'It's always busy here,' she said. 'Especially at this time of day. Don't worry, we'll be at the airport before you know it.'

The traffic started moving again, very slowly. Then it stopped again. They were in the tunnel now. Committed. It was darker than he had expected with just a single strip of lights above the road..

It was stop-start for the next mile as they crawled along underneath Victoria Harbour. By the time they reached the toll booths at the Kowloon exit, Brennan's stomach was in knots. They'd spent an eternity in that damn tunnel. Their margin was in jeopardy.

Gina picked up speed as they crossed Kowloon. It was not long before they were on the West Kowloon Highway and making good progress again. She was weaving between lanes, in and out of the taxis and decrepit trucks that were rumbling westwards. She drove with a quiet determination that gave Brennan confidence. They must be extending their lead again.

He started to relax and his thoughts turned to Sarah and Cara. The fee from Olson would help them get everything back onto an even keel. At least in the short term. He thought of Cara and her innocent, gap-toothed grin. Big blue eyes like her mother. He gripped the attaché case even tighter.

The picture of Henry's and Ben's motionless bodies on top of the wrecked dinghies spun into his mind. It was accompanied by Matterling's voice: *You've got to take your revenge when it's offered.* The sentence repeated as the minutes dragged on.

In the back seat, Lisa's eyes were closed and she was in her own world. Brennan turned back to the highway. It was busy but the traffic was still moving. He glanced in the wing mirror. Nothing untoward. He closed his eyes for a few seconds then took another look. A blue BMW had appeared. It was right behind them.

'Oh shit,' he said softly. 'Looks like we've got company.'

Gina checked in her mirror. 'How do you know it's them?'

'Last night. I'm sure it's their car. The two Neanderthals that we sent chasing my phone on Middle Island.'

Lisa opened her eyes and Brennan saw her exchange a glance with Gina in the rear-view mirror.

'They must have taken the eastern route,' he said. 'But how did they know where we were exactly?'

'This is the main road to the airport,' Lisa said. 'I guess they just took a chance.'

He turned around and looked through the rear window. It was them alright. The two Remus brothers stared grim-faced at him. He couldn't see anyone else in the car. Perhaps Matterling had decided to leave them to it. They were probably champing at the bit after being sidelined on Middle Island

'We'll just have to give them the slip,' Brennan said. They were in the middle lane of the three lanes going west, heading towards a layer cake of blue and green high rises. Trucks lined the inside lane and the Mini was coming up fast on a large white truck. 'For that, we need a slip road . . .' He peered ahead and tried to decipher the road signs. 'There should be one coming up. Shall we give it a go, Gina?'

'Worth a shot,' she replied.

'How about leaving the turn to the last second? Let them get close and then shoot left.'

Gina didn't look convinced. 'Maybe . . .' She gauged the distance to the turn-off and checked the outside lanes ahead. 'Or,' she said slowly, 'we could do something like this.'

She stamped on the accelerator and swung into the outside lane, past the white truck.

A quick look in the mirror. 'They're still with us. So now we can do this.'

She swerved into a gap barely long enough for the Mini then jumped further left into the beginning of the slip lane.

The tyres squealed and so did Brennan.

'Yes,' he breathed. 'That works too.'

He twisted around and looked behind. No sign of the BMW. It must have been boxed in by the trucks. Lisa had closed her eyes again. She seemed to be smiling.

The slip road branched off from the highway and further ahead it narrowed to a single lane with walls on each side. As Brennan focussed on the road ahead there was a loud thud from the off-side and the Mini was rammed up against the concrete wall at the side of the ramp. There was a scraping crunch and Gina wrestled with the steering wheel to keep the car from grinding to a halt. The BMW was pushed up hard against Gina's door.

'Where the hell did he come from?' Brennan yelled.

The BMW eased to the right and this gave the Mini enough space to keep going. Gina put her foot down again and they spurted ahead. The BMW accelerated smoothly to keep up. Gina slammed on the brakes in an attempt to force the BMW ahead, but its driver anticipated the move and braked even harder. As the road narrowed, the BMW moved in behind the Mini. It was jammed up tight behind them.

'Brake again!' Brennan shouted above the squealing tyres.

'I'm trying!' Gina shouted back but the smaller car kept going at the same speed—the BMW was forcing the Mini along. The sharp smell of overheating brake pads seeped into the car.

There was a fork in the road ahead, with the slip road continuing down to the right and a narrower, darker road to the left.

Brennan reckoned that the right-hand route looked safer and he pointed in that direction. Gina tried to steer the car towards the slip road but the BMW was pushing them left. They were past the junction in seconds and being shunted down a steep service road. Gina tried to accelerate but the BMW stayed with them, glued to their rear bumper.

A sharp right turn loomed at the bottom of the slope and Gina was forced to brake again. Ahead was water. She made the turn and the BMW turned with them. As they skidded along the water's edge, the BMW accelerated hard against the Mini's rear left-hand side and then came to a sudden halt. The Mini spun in a complete circle and also came to a stop, just yards away, face to face with their pursuers.

There was a long pause and then as if on cue, everyone reached for their doors. But the Remus boys had a few seconds head start and they were onto the Mini in an instant.

Brennan felt the air being sucked from the car as the doors were wrenched open. He was pulled out and shoved up against a metal container at the side of the road. The attaché case was ripped from his grasp and flung into the BMW. Lisa and Gina were bundled up next to him. The Remus brothers stood in front of them, surveying their catch.

Gina and Lisa stood tall, heads held high. Both looked calm.

Brennan looked around quickly. They were at a scruffy dockside, hidden away from the massive cranes of the large container ports. It was well lit with two rows of streetlights. Fenced yards full of containers, cranes, vans and other haulage paraphernalia lined the side of the street facing the docks. The docks were full of small piers and small freighters, lighters and a few fishing boats with nets and pots in small piles on the jetties. There was a neat row of red barges covered with green tarpaulins. The barges looked familiar but he wasn't sure why.

'Just stay perfectly still and no harm will come to you,' the stockier of the brothers said.

'Well, not yet,' the other said and grinned. He walked over to the BMW, opened the boot and pulled out several coils of rope, which he threw onto the ground in front of them.

He tied Brennan's hands behind his back at the wrists and used the other end of the rope to tie him at the ankles. He gathered up the slack in the middle of the rope and ran it behind a vertical bar on the end of the container. He pulled the loop sharply and Brennan's back slammed against the hard metal. He tied the loop around a bracket holding the bar in place, part of the door locking mechanism. Brennan was unable to move.

They tied up Lisa and Gina next. If there was such a thing as being tied up in a gentlemanly fashion, then this was how it was done. They were careful about how and where they touched their captives and although the bonds were secure, there was no unnecessary force used. Even the last stage, when the slack rope was pulled taut to hold the women flat against the metal door, was executed with a certain elegance.

It all seemed strangely civilised to Brennan. The five of them there on a deserted industrial dockside thousands of miles from home, but still playing by the rules. Three captives pinned to a steel container, two captors looking over them. There was an order involved, even though fate had determined that they were on opposite sides.

The stockier brother stepped away and made a phone call. They all watched him as he read out some numbers from his phone screen.

'He'll be here in fifteen,' he announced.

Another element was going to be introduced, Brennan realised abruptly. An element that would change the order completely.

66

Wednesday afternoon
Hong Kong

FOR THE SECOND time that day, Brennan watched *Kamakura* drop anchor. And for the second time that day, he saw Doug Matterling coming towards him in the grey tender. Coming to get him. But this time there was no chance of escape. This time, he really was tethered.

The three of them were. Lined up against the end of the brown container and tied to the door locking bars. They watched as the tender approached.

The motorboat came alongside the dock next to one of the red barges and Matterling climbed the landing ladder up to the road. He strode across to the three captives and stood there, hands on hips. The two brothers moved back respectfully. Matterling stepped up to Brennan and stopped barely a foot away.

Brennan felt strangely calm. He remembered the way he had felt at the creditors' meeting over a year ago. The calmness then had come from knowing that there was nothing left. But that was just financial. Now everything was at stake. Cara, Sarah, his very being. This time, the calmness stemmed from the enormity of it all. There was no time for any more conjecture. Matterling had him and would kill him. He had no other option. He would dispose of Lisa and Gina at the same time. The three of them would end up in the bottom of the harbour. There was no escape now. It would all be over within the hour. He accepted what was about to happen. That calm acceptance took him by surprise.

Matterling frowned deeply. He stared at Brennan in bewilderment. 'You must be enjoying yourself,' he said. 'Now you've got me chasing around after you. That's the game isn't it? Nothing to do with the bearer share. After all, what the hell is Elba to you? No amount of money would entice you into the shithole you've jumped into. It's just the game of cat and mouse.' Matterling stepped closer. Their chests were touching. 'And for some fucked-up reason, you insist on being the mouse.'

Brennan strained against the ropes, determined not to let himself be pushed backwards. He knew his fate but he would be defiant to the end. Matterling grabbed the ropes where they crossed. He pulled them away from Brennan's chest and twisted them hard. A stab of pain shot through Brennan's shoulders as the ropes tightened.

He winced and Matterling smiled. 'The enjoyment is mutual. Now that you've triggered the trap. Nothing better than seeing you trussed up with nowhere to go.' Matterling released his grip. 'I admire you, Mike. So bloody dependable. Indulging me by falling into every little trap I set you. You've been so good for me.'

He turned around as if to go back to the tender, but then spun quickly and delivered a powerful single punch to Brennan's solar plexus. Brennan's body tried to fold but the ropes held him against the side of the container. He managed to slide down far enough for his knees to touch the ground. His lungs screamed for air.

As he slumped against the container door, he fought to separate his thoughts. One part of his brain was processing the physical pain, giving the necessary instructions to his body to ensure survival. The other part was concentrating on Matterling's intentions. Was he just playing cat and mouse before the inevitable conclusion? But what about Gina and Lisa? Could Matterling really have them killed as well? They were the innocents in all this. And would Matterling get the same kind of satisfaction if the three of them were to go the same way? Wouldn't that devalue Brennan's death in Matterling's eyes?

Those eyes flashed and Brennan thought he was going to get kicked. But Matterling's feet were planted wide apart. He pulled out a phone and searched for something on it.

'Let them go,' Brennan gasped. 'It's nothing to do with them. It's only me you need.'

Matterling looked at the two women disinterestedly, as if he had just noticed their presence.

'Creativity, Courage and Conviction,' Brennan said, slowly getting his breath back. 'Do you remember our creed from the early days? That's how we were able to build something that was worthwhile.'

Matterling lifted his eyes up from his phone.

'Getting nostalgic, are we?'

'The confidence to think it, the balls to get it out there and the guts to stay with it. That's what we shared, Doug. That's how we lived back then.' Brennan searched Matterling's face for a reaction but he had resumed tapping on his phone.

'If you have any of that left you would let them go.' He looked towards Lisa and Gina. 'They can't harm you, they've got nothing to do with us.'

'Have *you* got any of that left, you mean?' Matterling stopped with the phone and stared at Brennan.

'Conviction came easy to you, as I remember. As long as I was around to pick up the pieces. You should look at yourself to answer that one.'

Pick up the pieces? Did he really believe that?

'I have looked at myself. I've had plenty of time. And I realise that I did lack conviction.' He drew himself up a couple of inches. 'I should never have let you get as far as you did. I should have called you out as soon as I had suspicions. I should have backed my own judgement about you. I had no problem in backing my judgement when it came to the clients. It was with you that I failed.'

'So why are you here?'

'To make amends.'

"Revenge?'

'I guess you could call it that.'

'You've no idea, have you?' Matterling's tone was harsh. 'You've got no fucking idea why you are here just getting in my way. All that bullshit about your judgement. That's all it is.' He looked down at this phone again. 'Ah, good. Showtime. We'll deal with your bullshit later.'

He had located what he was looking for on his phone and he turned the screen towards Brennan. The image was bright against the gloom of the late afternoon and Brennan tried to focus on what Matterling was showing him. He focused on controlling his breathing and saw a video of a staircase.

'Real-time, Mike. This is happening right now.' Matterling's voice had raised a notch. He was getting excited.

The staircase looked familiar. The person holding the camera was climbing the stairs slowly. The camera levelled and the doors leading off the landing became visible.

Brennan's breathing stopped. He felt like he had been punched again. It was his landing. It was his home and someone was in there at this very moment with a camera, feeding pictures back to Matterling.

'What the hell is this?'

'Questions, questions,' Matterling said. 'I just thought I'd show you how things are at home. You've travelled a long way to interfere with my life. I thought the least I could do is return the favour.'

Brennan looked back at the screen again. The camera was moving along the landing. It stopped outside the first door. The cameraman slowly opened it.

It was the bathroom. Brennan recognised the towels on the floor and the collection of Cara's bath toys on the shelf just above the taps. It was daytime there but the camera must have had its own light because Brennan saw a reflection flash in the big mirror behind the shelf. The reflection disappeared as the angle of vision changed but he could not see any figure reflected in the glass.

'Who the fuck is in my house?' His chest was tight and it was an effort to get the words out.

'A man called Joe. Related to these two.' Matterling waved towards the Remus brothers.

Brennan strained at the ropes. Where was Sarah? And Cara? Surely they weren't there?

'Sarah's taking a nap.' Matterling sighed. He looked at Brennan with mock alarm. 'But don't fret. Joe made sure she was tucked up tight.'

Brennan struggled to keep control. The mention of Cara on the yacht yesterday had set off a tremor. Matterling had been keeping tabs on his family but the question was, for how long? Since Brennan had started to find out about Elba Technology? Or long before that?

This was the logical next step in Matterling's game of torment. To threaten Cara in front of him.

The second door along the landing was Cara's playroom. And then her bedroom. It would be mid-morning there, he thought. Cara would probably be in her playroom while Sarah cleared up downstairs. Or sometimes she had a short nap before they went out. Wherever she was in the house, she would be scared half to death when she saw the intruder.

'Whatever you want, Doug. I'll give you whatever you want. You can take me out there,' he nodded towards the blackness of the harbour, 'tie me to a concrete block and drop me over the side. Anything you want. You can chop me up into little pieces first if that will give you pleasure. You can do anything you want to me. Just get that fucker out of my house. Now.'

Matterling looked relaxed and happy. This was not just about torture. The man certainly enjoyed the control and the pain, but the choice of torture was significant. He had chosen to target Cara. Not just because it was the most painful for Brennan. There was more to it than that.

The two Remus brothers here probably had no idea what their brother was up to in London or what Brennan was witnessing on this live feed. It was just day-to-day work for them. They were standing a few yards back, watching their client amuse himself and keeping an eye on their latest captives.

Lisa and Gina were standing firm, watching Brennan's reaction to what he was seeing.

'Let's just see what's through the next door shall we?' Matterling said. 'Just for fun.'

Brennan closed his eyes and took a deep breath. He had to brace himself for what might happen in the next few seconds. Cara would look up from her toys and see a stranger. She would scream for her mother. A scream that would not be heard. What were Matterling's instructions?

'My daughter's in the house. Does he know that?' Brennan's voice was strained. He could feel the rope cutting deep into his flesh as he struggled against it.

'*Round and round the garden, like a teddy bear. One step, two step.* Let's just see, shall we?' Matterling's eyes were glazed and he spoke in a childish, sing-song voice.

The camera moved along the landing to the next door. It waited for several long seconds before the door was pushed open. A trail of toys and baby clothes lay across the floor and the camera panned around the brightly-painted playroom. The walls were covered with cartoon characters and decorations. Mobiles hung from the ceiling. But there was no sign of Cara. Brennan sagged with relief.

'Oh no,' Matterling said. 'No one's at home.' He bowed his head in mock disappointment. 'We'll have to go further down the garden. Down towards the lake. Through the big leaves.'

Something was happening in Matterling's twisted mind. But

feeling was returning to Brennan's legs. He pushed up against the container door to help his breathing. As his hands moved up the metal, he felt a handle beneath his right palm. He tugged at it. It was loose.

Matterling moved around slightly, to get a better view of the phone's screen. He was enjoying the show, moving closer to Brennan so that they could share the spectacle.

The camera retreated through the doorway. It swung around to point along the landing and moved to the next door. It stopped again for several agonising seconds and Brennan recognised Cara's bedroom door. She must be in there. If she was, he hoped she was asleep.

The door slowly opened. A box of children's books came into shot and then a giant cuddly panda. Then a small bedside table. The camera moved closer to the table and showed a small jewellery cushion under the bedside lamp. In the middle of the cushion was a gold charm bracelet. With a gold piano charm attached. The bracelet Brennan had given her all those months ago. She had placed it pride of place next to her bed. Her *No Harm Charm*.

Brennan struggled to breathe as the camera continued its exploration but Matterling's breath quickened next to him. He continued to work at the loose handle on the container door. He could feel rusty flakes fluttering down to the ground.

The camera swung around and Brennan saw a lump of bedclothes. He recognised the cloud and seagull pattern. There was nothing under the bedclothes but as the angle of view opened up, he saw Cara lying next to them. She was on her back in a pink T-shirt and pink leggings. Her arms and legs were spread out, like a starfish. She was facing away from the camera. She was fast asleep.

'Time to wake up and see your daddy, little girl,' Matterling said. 'You'll like that, won't you, Mike? A chance to say goodbye perhaps.'

Goodbye? What was Matterling going to do? Surely not . . .

'These days it doesn't matter that you're so far away,' Matterling said in that sing-song voice. 'But I never got to see Mama again after I was sent away. Never again. Although I knew what was happening. I knew what was happening every night with father. I felt it, every time that strap came down on her.'

'Look at me, Doug.' Brennan's voice was hard; he was not going to repeat himself. Matterling was deranged, capable of anything. But Cara's safety was all Brennan cared about right now. Matterling's way of ordering the world was secondary. 'Let me tell you one thing— and I have never meant anything as much as I mean this.' Matterling looked up from the screen and turned the sides of his mouth down in a clown's sad face. 'If you harm a single hair on her head, I will kill you. I won't involve the police or anyone else. I will kill you with my own hands. I promise.'

'You're not really in a position to issue threats. And as for all that revenge shit—well, it's just talk. You've always been good at that though, haven't you? Talk.'

Brennan strained harder against the rope and he felt the handle on the container door loosen under his grip.

Suddenly he froze. A high-pitched scream cut through the air. A piercing female scream that echoed around their dark corner of the harbour.

It was coming from Matterling's phone.

67

Wednesday afternoon
Hong Kong

BRENNAN AND MATTERLING craned closer to the screen. As the scream subsided the camera swung around to the doorway. Sarah was standing beyond it, on the far side of the landing. She was wearing blue jeans and a blue T-shirt. Her feet were bare and her face was white with fear. Her mouth was still open from the scream. She was staring helplessly at the camera.

Brennan looked up at Matterling. He seemed amused.

'This is a bonus, Mike. Two birds with one stone.'

Brennan ignored him and concentrated on the screen. He strained at the ropes and pulled harder at the handle. His wife and daughter were being threatened six thousand miles away but he could do nothing to save them. Nothing.

The angle of view changed. It was fixed now. The camera had been placed on the dressing table next to Cara's bed. It pointed at Sarah and the space in front of her.

'Think you're going to enjoy this, Mr Matterling, sir.' Brennan recognised the voice from his brief meeting with Hazel and her sons. Joe sounded bored. Just another day of intimidation and terror.

Then Joe's back came into view as he stepped away from the camera. He seemed to be wearing a policeman's uniform.

So that's how he managed to get in.

Matterling turned to check the whereabouts of the two Remus brothers. They were standing by the car, patiently awaiting further orders. While Matterling was distracted, Brennan gave the handle a yank. It came away from the metal door. He glanced at it. It was about a foot long with a large rusty screw attached to a small flange plate at the base. The screw was firmly rusted into its hole. If he could somehow use it to loosen one of the knots, he might have a chance.

There was something else that was starting to challenge the inevitability of his imminent demise. This live feed from London. Matterling had gone to great lengths to set this up. If he had just wanted to get rid of him quickly, then why put him through this torture first? No, Matterling wanted to draw it out for as long as possible. That was the kick for him. That meant that Brennan had time. Perhaps enough time to somehow overcome the odds.

Matterling turned back and held his phone up again for Brennan to see. On the screen, Joe was moving towards Sarah, slowly and purposefully. There was another scream. It sounded like the scream of a young girl waking from a nightmare. It was Cara screaming, but she was waking into one.

Joe looked behind him towards Cara and Sarah rushed towards her daughter. He must have seen Sarah from the corner of his eye because he turned and held out an arm to stop her. Sarah grabbed it with both hands and swung underneath to pull him off balance. She swivelled at the hips and pushed him towards the bedroom window.

Their positions were switched. Sarah now stood between Joe and Cara. Brennan watched as she squared up to Joe. His heart thudded in his chest. Thank God for those taekwondo lessons, he thought. And for a mother's primordial ferocity in defending her child.

Brennan slowly started to jiggle the handle against a knot pressing into his calf, which secured the two ends of the rope. He moved his leg outwards a few inches to clear the knot from his flesh. He pushed the screw into the middle of the knot and started to work the handle.

The glimmer of hope that had come from realising that time was on his side was also now starting to illuminate what life could be like in the future. If he were to live, he would be the best damn father the world had ever seen.

'Cara's a lucky girl,' Matterling said. 'But Sarah's mad to stand up to Joe. You'll see.'

Joe had recovered his poise and moved slowly towards Sarah. He looked annoyed and impatient to get the job done.

Brennan's efforts were starting to yield results. The knot had opened up slightly and the screw was forcing it apart. To undo it, he had to pull at both parts simultaneously. The only protuberance anywhere near the knot was the lower hinge, which was half-a-foot away. He was tied so tightly it was impossible to reach.

Joe continued to approach Sarah. Cara was crying in the background but Sarah did not turn to comfort her. She was not backing away. Instead, she moved towards Joe. Brennan braced himself. She had no chance against that animal. But she still moved forward. As brave as any human being could be. And as for him, all he had to do was shift six inches to the right.

He took a deep breath and tensed every muscle in his body simultaneously. Then he relaxed and pushed the last ounce of air from his lungs. He forced every part of his body a fraction of an inch closer to the door's hinge.

Sarah had stopped moving and the two faced each other, just a few feet apart. Joe lunged forward. There was a blur above his head and a sharp crack as Sarah's bare foot scythed down onto his left collarbone. He stopped dead and his mouth dropped open. He clutched the point of impact but his left arm hung uselessly at his side. He crumpled slowly to his knees and looked up at Sarah in bewilderment.

Brennan was also bewildered. He could not believe that Sarah was capable of such a blow.

'Joe,' Matterling shouted. 'What the hell's happening? Get up. Follow your instructions. Get up!'

Joe did get up. He rose unsteadily and stepped backwards. His right arm was holding his left arm tightly into his side. His left shoulder had collapsed. She must have snapped his collarbone.

'Get out of my house now,' Sarah hissed.

Joe lurched to the door and Matterling pulled the phone away. Brennan continued to tense and relax his muscles. He could see the hinge coming closer.

There was no sound from the phone and Matterling started shaking it as though that would elicit the response he wanted.

The rope felt as though it had cut through to the bone but Brennan kept tensing, relaxing and pushing. Tensing, relaxing and pushing.

There was less light on the hinge now that Matterling had moved his phone away. But Brennan could see enough from the light of the streetlamps. The knot was hanging next to the hinge.

He pushed down a couple of inches and the lower loop of the knot was level with the bottom edge of the hinge. He manoeuvred the handle towards the knot and slowly used the screw to push it around so that the loop caught on the hinge. As soon as he felt it catch he pushed up, so it would hold. He brought the end of the handle around to the other side of the knot and gently pushed the tip of the screw under the top loop. He pushed harder. It dug into the side of the rope.

It was ready. Matterling was still busy with his phone and the two Remus brothers were still standing by the car. They were watching their captives but they were not close enough to see what

Brennan was doing. He glanced at Lisa and Gina. They were looking along the dockside back towards Kowloon.

He took a deep breath. He slid his body slowly up the side of the container and pulled up on the handle. The upward pressure from his body started to open the lower loop, which was hooked fast onto the edge of the hinge. The upper loop was also opening as he pulled. A couple more inches and the two loops of the knot came apart. As the short end of the rope fell to the ground he let himself breathe again. He was almost free.

He wriggled out of the rope and saw that Matterling was giving up on the stricken Joe. He turned towards Brennan. Their eyes met and Mattering looked down at the loose rope on the ground.

Brennan launched himself at Matterling.

They crashed to the ground with Brennan on top. As Matterling's head hit the concrete, Brennan shoved the metal handle across his neck. He bore down with all his weight.

The pressure that had built up over all those months in prison was focused on this one point. The metal dug into Matterling's neck and his eyes widened. Brennan could feel his strong body writhing beneath him, but he had to hold on to him.

Matterling was still holding his phone and Brennan briefly saw Sarah on its screen, holding Cara. They appeared unharmed. Joe must have staggered off.

'You'll never do anything like that again,' Brennan said. 'Never.'

Matterling's eyes bulged and he gurgled deep within his throat.

From the corner of his eye, Brennan saw the Remus brothers running towards him. He had just a few seconds and he knew that they would hit him hard. He met Matterling's eyes and saw confidence as well as fear. Matterling had numbers on his side.

Suddenly there were flying bodies all around him in the dark. He had been expecting the Remus brothers to jump him but there seemed to be too many of them. There was shouting and scuffling. The shouting seemed to be Chinese.

The crunching of body against body filled the air and he sank lower against Matterling. Their eyes were only inches apart. Matter-ling's confidence was turning to confusion.

Brennan was confused as well. The sounds of blows being exchanged went on interminably. But none of the crunching had involved him so far. He sucked in a lungful of air and waited.

68

Wednesday evening
Hong Kong

BRENNAN FELT himself being pulled off Matterling by two men, one on each side. But there was no searing stench of aftershave. As he regained his balance he saw that the two men were not the Remus brothers. They were dressed the same, all in black, but these two were Chinese. Like the Remus boys, they were both expressionless. Just doing their job.

A lot had happened while he had been getting acquainted with Matterling's throat. The Remus brothers had each been attached to a side door of the BMW by means of thick bamboo poles, which had been passed through the open windows. They had their backs to the car. Their arms were stretched out along the poles, secured by string tied around their thumbs. They were twisting and bending but to no avail. Ingenious, Brennan thought. Just poles and string. But they were unable to escape.

There was also something going on at the waterside. Two men, similar to the two that were now pushing him back to the side of the container, were clambering over one of the red barges. They were rigging up some kind of bamboo frame on top of the green tarpaulin.

Further along the road he saw the three crew members of *Kamakura* running away. Not the fighting types, obviously.

One of Brennan's captors released him and pulled Matterling up from the ground. The other one wrenched the handle away from Brennan and flung it away as he forced Brennan's left arm high behind his back. Matterling was bundled up next to him against the container. Lisa and Gina had disappeared.

Brennan heard a woman's voice shouting orders in Chinese. It sounded like Lisa. More orders, then he and Matterling were spun around to face their new captors.

Lisa and Gina stood there, feet apart and hands behind their backs. Lisa looked relaxed, in complete control. Gina looked nonplussed.

'Thank you,' Lisa said. 'We have the briefcase now.'

Brennan stared at her. Was this just opportunism? The chance to snatch something that others wanted? If so, what was she going to do with the share? Sell it to the highest bidder?

Or was this the culmination of a longer game? Hadn't Kesey told him that she had been asking after him regularly when he was in prison? She had been waiting for his release. But why exactly? She was certainly cool, he had to give her that.

'How the hell did you know about it?' Matterling spat. His question was addressed to Lisa but he was looking hard at Brennan.

'I have a long-standing relationship with Brian Kesey in London,' she said. 'I just needed to get the two of you together to seek our retribution.'

'The two of us?' Brennan said, trying to recall their conversations since she had visited him in hospital. 'Why?'

'I told you last night. I told you that we believe in relationships. Relationships are more important than transactions. My family's investment in your company was only one aspect of our relationship.

We were very surprised that you made no further contact after your company went under. But we understand your circumstances.' She gave him a small smile. 'But as for you, Doug, we had to put it down to a lack of manners. For which there is no excuse.'

'It was a commercial investment,' Matterling said flatly. 'Win some, lose some. That's the end of it,'

'You are so wrong.' Lisa watched the activity on the barge for a moment. 'My family are helping me to help you, gentlemen. Now that we have received your gift, we are going to send you on a tour of our magnificent harbour. That will give you both time to think. Time to see beyond money. Time for you to contemplate integrity.'

The two men on the barge had constructed an A-frame out of bamboo poles which spanned the width of the boat. They had lashed *Kamakura's* tender to its port quarter. The engine was running and the wheel was tied in position. Brennan could see that this would provide the necessary propulsion. It wouldn't be fast, but it would be enough to send the barge chugging out into the harbour.

'My cousins have made a viewing platform for you,' Lisa said. 'You will be tied to the bamboo so you can enjoy the sights.'

'Please have a good look around,' she continued. 'Force yourself to see more than your brain wants you to see. We are all flawed in the same way but we can overcome that human fallibility.'

She looked at Brennan keenly as she said this. She must be refer-ring to his partnership with Matterling. That he had chosen not to see the signs. Had he been that absorbed with his own role?

He stared into the deep blackness of the harbour. Evening had descended and the lights of Hong Kong island blazed in the distance. He did not fancy another swim in that water. Even if he got the chance.

What did Lisa want to do with them?

'I'm not sure what your understanding of integrity is,' Brennan said. 'But this seems to be over-compensating. Why didn't you take me at my word? I told you I would repay your family's investment. If you let me take that share back to London, I will have the means to do so.'

'I know exactly what you were expecting to get,' Lisa said, frowning. 'I should thank you for getting involved. A lack of integrity must have consequences. Either retribution or revenge. Out here the only real form of revenge is death.'

As he tried to process Lisa's words, Brennan suddenly remembered where he had seen the barges before. They had been on the TV news report when he had arrived at the hotel. The upcoming pyrotechnics. These barges were carrying fireworks for the New Year's display. Each was packed full of explosives. And Lisa was about to send him out into the harbour on one. Did she know what was under those tarpaulins?

Was it revenge they were after rather than retribution?

Lisa said a few words to the two guards and they marched Brennan and Matterling down to the road and towards the barge and the A-frame. Lisa hung back and Gina stayed by her side. The time for conversation seemed to be over.

How could Lisa know what he was due to be paid for delivering that share? *I know exactly what you were expecting to get,* she had said. There was only one answer: Olson must have put her up to it. Now, she would receive the fee. This was difficult to swallow. He could not see Olson switching horses just like that—Lisa and her family had to be providing something that Brennan could not.

The place was deserted, no other people or traffic. Brennan saw a couple of cars with the markings of a security firm on them but there was no one around. Any guards had bunked off. Or had been dealt with by the Jingshengs.

Lisa had planned this well, he thought. She must have had him followed as soon as she knew he was at the Mandarin Oriental and she must have planted some kind of tracking transmitter on *Kamakura* when they boarded it earlier. The family would have known just when to strike. This was no random location—Gina had driven them here deliberately.

As for the Remus boys hunting them down, that was no lucky guess. Lisa had encouraged him to double-check his phone at Gina's apartment. She would have identified the tracking software when they checked it in the toilet. She must then have set up her phone to be followed in the same way. That whole rigmarole with the Faraday cage was simply so she could set herself up to be tracked by Remus Security, just like him. Plus, she would have had another tracker so that her family knew where she was.

Two separate tracking systems pointing to her location. One for her tribe and one for her enemy. Clever.

But the pressing question now was, did Lisa and her cousins know what was on the barge?

There was only one way to find out but he had to pick the right moment.

They were taken across the road and the two men on the barge jumped ashore to help get Brennan and Matterling onboard. Lisa stood by the Mini with her sister. From the look on Gina's face it seemed unlikely that she had been party to Lisa's plot beforehand. Probably just given the driving instructions.

Lisa nodded towards Matterling and three of the men took him up onto a wooden step then escorted him across a board and onto the bamboo frame. They tied his hands and feet to the frame so that his legs and arms were spread apart. He was facing the shore. He offered no resistance but kept looking impatiently towards the BMW as if expecting the Remus brothers to finish a tea-break and come to rescue him.

Brennan was next. The engine on the tender had been put into forward gear. The two aft lines from the stern were pulling on the bollards. As the three men came off the barge, Brennan felt the remaining captor's grip relax slightly, ready to hand him over. This was his moment.

He spun and jabbed his elbow into his captor's stomach. He released Brennan's left arm, who swung around and pulled the man towards him and then threw him into his three cousins. They were all momentarily thrown off balance and Brennan pulled one of the hand flares he had been carrying since Middle Island out of his inside pocket.

He tore off the cap and pulled the tab. The flare fizzed into life and orange smoke poured out. He pointed the flare at the barge and lifted the edge of the tarpaulin. He moved the flare towards the gap. The four cousins jumped back with shocked expressions on their faces. So, they did know what was under the tarp. They had not been planning a sightseeing trip for him and Matterling.

Brennan swivelled again and charged straight at them, swiping the flare from side to side. The cousins stumbled back in confusion and Brennan was able to shove the two nearest to him backwards. They crashed into the other two who were each holding homemade petrol bombs. To be thrown onto the barge once it started moving, Brennan realised. They had been intending to blow up the barge with Matterling and him on board. Bastards.

He threw the flare at them. They all lost their balance and tumbled into the water. They dropped their bottles, which rolled harmlessly into the harbour. Brennan watched as the men thrashed around in the cold water. None of them looked like they were able to swim. He didn't feel a great deal of sympathy.

He ran at Lisa and Gina. They tried to get into the car but he grabbed each of them around the waist and hauled them towards the brown container.

'Don't struggle,' he barked. 'I'll throw them a line. Time permitting.'

The sisters glanced at each other and raised their arms. Brennan bundled them up against the container and tied them to the door with the ropes they had just escaped from.

'Good decision,' Brennan said to Lisa. 'I get the disappointment about your loss in BM. And I can understand why you were tempted by the fee. But why not tell me about that kid, Ben Parfitt? You must have known he was going to come here. If I'd known he was going to chase his colleague down, I could have done something to keep him out of it. I could have saved one life, at least.'

'War is about numbers, Mike.' She closed her eyes to indicate it was all she had to say.

'In other words, he was expedient. Just another foot soldier to absorb enemy fire. I think your little lecture about integrity might have to be rewritten.'

She opened her eyes. 'Your logic is too linear,' she said. 'There are two sides to a coin. Yin and yang. They co-exist.' The eyes closed again.

'Why even release him in the first place?'

'Because that was what you wanted. I was your ally. Remember?'

It had been good to have Lisa by his side. While it lasted. But the only thing that mattered now was getting out of here and catching his flight. Lisa's eyes were firmly closed. Gina was looking around helplessly.

He looked around for the handle and found it near the container door. He picked it up and checked the end. The rusty screw was still firmly attached. It was the only weapon he had.

Handle in hand, he ran back to the dockside. He stood for a moment by the barge. Behind him, Lisa and Gina were tied to the container door. To his left, the two Remus brothers were tacked to their BMW. And in front of him, four male members of the Jingsheng family were still flailing about in Hong Kong harbour.

Also in front of him was Doug Matterling, spreadeagled against the bamboo trellis like Vitruvian Man. On a barge packed full of explosives.

And Brennan had one flare left.

He transferred the handle to his left hand and felt for it in his pocket. It was still there. A detonator that could blow this scow into the next millennium. And Matterling with it.

69

Wednesday evening
  Hong Kong

THE GREEN TARPAULIN overlapped the gunwales of the barge and was secured with straps, pinning it to a row of hooks riveted to the metal hull. Brennan turned the handle so the screw faced outwards. He smashed the handle down onto the tarpaulin. The screw pierced it easily and he pulled it several feet across the material. It made a satisfying tearing sound. A gash appeared. He made another cut to form a cross and pulled at one of the flaps. Beneath, the hold was packed with brown boxes.

'A thousand kilos,' he said, looking up. 'A thousand kilos of festive fireworks under you. How does that feel?'

Brennan tore open one of the boxes and pulled out a yellow tube covered in Chinese writing. He tossed it up at Matterling. It bounced harmlessly off a bamboo pole and rolled back down the tarp, but Matterling recoiled.

'Now all we need is something to start the show.' Brennan

climbed onto the barge. He took a few steps onto one of the wooden boards.

Matterling's eyes darted from side to side. He looked towards the BMW.

'Something like this perhaps,' Brennan said and pulled the hand flare out of his pocket. 'I think you know what this is, don't you? You being a nautical man and all.' He held the flare in front of Matterling's face. 'How about I jump ashore, set this little bastard off and throw it back for you to catch?'

Matterling smiled at his bound hands. 'Quite the comedian, eh? Now you're not chained down. But you'll never be free. If anything happens to me there will be a heavy price to pay. It will be your burden. For the rest of your life.'

'You're the one who's crossed the line,' Brennan said. 'It was your choice to threaten my family. You're consumed by it. The torture. The traps.'

'There are no limits on what I need to do. I'll get my revenge, whatever it takes. You of all people should know that.'

Matterling was surprisingly cocky. He was either too arrogant to acknowledge the danger he was in or too confident that Brennan would let him go. Or perhaps he was too sure that his minions would somehow bust out of their bamboo trap and roar to his rescue. Brennan glanced at the BMW. The Remus brothers were still hanging like puppets and scowling in his direction. No chance of them interfering any time soon.

'Your revenge? I'm not the one you're after.'

As they stared at each other, the shouting from the water became more urgent. The splashing had subsided but some of them should have managed to get a hold on the dockside. It was too high to climb but there should be something to cling to. Brennan jumped off the barge onto the dock and turned around.

'I've got a choice to make, Doug. But it's not going to be that difficult.'

Matterling looked at the tender tied to the side of the barge.

Brennan was sure he saw a shadow of panic flick across Matterling's narrow face. The powerful outboard on the tender's transom was revving purposefully, drowning out the shouts from the water.

Brennan was still holding the flare and he grasped the orange cap. Matterling's eyes flashed from the tender to the flare to the BMW and back to the flare. Slowly, he looked up and focused on Brennan.

'I said that I'd underestimated you, Mike Brennan. But that's not quite right. I always knew you *could*. I just never thought you *would*.'

The cold seeped into Brennan. He had never killed anyone before. Not directly, not like this. Perhaps indirectly, by voting with millions of others for a war-mongering politician going after his next election win. But never like this.

Doug Matterling had threatened his family. He had sent a paid thug into Brennan's house to threaten his wife and child. Threaten and more. Who knew how far Matterling would go in his drive to torture? That inexorable instinct to hurt and maim and twist the knife as far as he could.

Brennan knew they were now bound together. The two erstwhile business partners, intertwined like a double helix. But only one of them could survive. There was no choice. He could not free Matterling from the bamboo frame and hope that somehow they could go on with their lives and pursue their separate goals.

There was a price to pay.

'It satisfied me, you know,' Matterling said. 'I liked the planning.' His voice was distant and dull but still robust enough to cut through the noise of the outboard. 'And the trap. The inevitable punishment for bad behaviour.' He was looking past Brennan and not talking directly to him. 'There's no more satisfying sound than trapdoors closing.' He suddenly focused on Brennan. 'I love the moment of realisation. When they realise what's happening. That my plan has worked. That I have control.' He grinned. 'That moment at the creditors meeting. You remember that, don't you? When I produced the Radix file?'

Brennan remembered. It was one of the vivid, grisly moments

that had played and replayed so many times in his head when he was at Ford.

'I loved that. Much more than the money. That never really meant much to me. I'd always had money, ever since I found out where Amah kept the house allowance. She knew what I was doing. But she could never tell, could she? Not after I told her that I knew about what father was doing to her.'

He'd started young, Brennan thought. Real young. He looked at his watch. There was still enough time to catch his flight. Even allowing for a couple of minutes to admire the view when he got to the bluff overlooking the harbour.

'At least I got to control the process. Even if it would never change the result. The destiny that is due to me.' Matterling was talking to nobody in particular.

Brennan's fingers gripped the flare's orange cap.

'A destiny of justice. That is my right.'

Justice? What crazy concept of justice was Matterling hanging on to? Did he think that it was the same as revenge? A revenge that was never going to happen.

'What about your destiny, Mike? I wonder what's been decided for you?'

Whatever it was, it was sure to be better than Matterling's life without revenge. A life of damnation.

'I think that it will be a noble ending, don't you? It will have to be. To make up for the destruction you've left behind you. All that misdirected anger. You're a simple man who's been hiding behind that mask of conviction and creativity.' His eyes narrowed. 'Plus, there's the futile attempts to change my destiny. The two deaths today would not have happened if you hadn't decided to do what you did.'

The cap started twisting under Brennan's grip. He couldn't be distracted now. The picture of Parfitt and Evans sprawled lifeless across those dinghies had been burning into his brain since it happened.

Evans had made his choice to throw his lot in with Matterling.

But Parfitt? That was the one that had really shaken him. That was the one that Brennan really had to rationalise in order to keep his focus. He just had to remember that it was Parfitt's reaction in that moment which had proved to be fatal. He had hesitated. Hesitated badly. It was a mistake that Brennan was not going to repeat.

He ripped the cap from the flare and it fizzed into life.

Matterling's eyes bulged as they homed in on the orange smoke starting to spew from the plastic tube. He seemed to have suddenly realised what was about to happen. Then his face froze with fear. His mouth was half open, his thin lips stretched tight.

There was no more talk about justice and destiny. Raw fear had taken over from rhetoric. Brennan stood still for a moment as the smoke billowed out and drifted towards the barge. He suddenly saw Matterling for what he was. Or more for what he wasn't. He was a killer alright, but he wasn't a fighter.

The smoke started to obscure Matterling and Brennan wanted a few seconds just to think through what he was doing. But he didn't have the luxury of more time to plan. He had to finish the job.

He dropped the flare through the hole in the tarp onto the open box of fireworks. The smoke intensified in the enclosed space and the hole in the tarpaulin acted as a ragged chimney.

Then he untied the stern lines from the barge. It started to drift away from the dockside. The power from the tender was enough to get it moving and Brennan tugged at the stern lines to aim it towards *Kamakura*.

Once he was satisfied that the barge was on course he picked up a length of rope he had carried from the container and quickly tied a bowline to form a large loop. He dropped the loop over one of the free bollards and threw the rope towards the men in the water. Several hands emerged from the murk to grab hold.

A muffled bang came from the departing barge. The first firework had gone off.

Brennan raced over to the Mini and jumped in. The attaché case was on the passenger seat. He pressed the start button and the engine burst into life.

The car was still pointing towards the highway. Lisa and Gina were still lashed to the container door and the Remus boys were still hanging by their thumbs. Lisa's cousins were starting to emerge from the water, bedraggled and exhausted.

He checked his watch again. He would phone Sarah from the airport. He pulled away and drove the short distance to the security cars. Another car was parked across them. It must belong to the Jingsheng clan. He jumped out of the Mini and quickly ran around each car, puncturing their tyres with his handle.

As escaping air hissed around him he jumped back into the Mini and accelerated hard. He climbed the narrow ramp leading back onto the highway.

The highway ran alongside the docks and then curved around to the left, towards Lantau Island and the airport. He could see the massive cranes of the container port ahead. The traffic thickened as it approached a long bridge. He moved to the left-hand lane and peered across the water. He opened the window. He could hear the fireworks starting in earnest. There was a muffled boom and a louder crack and then the screaming of a rocket, which lit up the sky above the dockside.

As he headed along the highway, the sky filled with colours bursting around each other, the detonations increasing in intensity. A few cars pulled over onto the hard shoulder and people emerged to watch the unscheduled display. Brennan pulled over as well and jumped out of the Mini. The fireworks zipped off in random directions. Hundreds of white crackers showered the sea below and vivid flower-bursts corkscrewed towards the heavens. A giant pall of white smoke drifted towards the cranes.

He jumped over the low barrier and scrambled down a grassy bank at the side of the road to get a better view. Through the smoke he could see *Kamakura's* dark shape waiting silently at anchor. The barge was heading directly for it, a multi-coloured fireball moving steadily through the water. From this angle he could just see the back of the bamboo frame, with Matterling tied to the other side.

The barge reached *Kamakura*. It nosed down the far side of its hull. The dark hulk of the hull blocked his view of the barge. There was an eerie silence and the sharp smell of spent fireworks drifted up the hill.

Then it was suddenly as bright as day. Everything was lit up with a dazzling orange light. Through the fireworks, Brennan could see flames climbing high into the air. The sound of the explosion caught up a moment later. Like an enormous bomb going off. The sound of *Kamakura* being blown sky-high. A giant boom that rolled around the harbour and off into the distance. The ground shuddered.

He ran back to the car. The other onlookers looked bemused, unsure of what they were seeing. No one could have survived such a blast and the fireworks were still going off. Brennan wondered if there would be any trace of Matterling left. He hoped not.

As he headed for the airport he felt completely calm. Even though he knew Matterling was right—there was going to be a big price to pay. His life had changed again. Irrevocably. But he had taken control of his destiny. That was complete.

Hong Kong was behind him and he had left a lot there. Including the anger that Matterling had been going on about. The anger of a simple man. The anger of a father who had failed to protect his child, not just when Joe had got into the house but much further back than that. Back to when he had let Matterling bring down the agency.

Matterling was right again. That anger should only have been directed at one person. And that was himself.

70

Thursday morning
   London Heathrow

BRENNAN PASSED through the open doors at Terminal Three
arrivals and headed past the waiting meeters and greeters waving
their name boards over the barrier.

As he scanned the. myriad of black and yellow signs, looking for
directions to the taxi rank, he glimpsed his own name from the corner
of his eye. It was in neat lettering on a large board. He wasn't
expecting anybody to pick him up. Probably another Mike Brennan.
But he had to make sure.

The lady holding the board was dressed in a stylish black overcoat and he noticed her dark stockings and black high heels. She
contrasted with the rows of mainly male, mainly shabby, drivers lined
up awaiting their passengers.

'I'm Mike Brennan,' he said. 'But I don't think it's me on your
board.'

'Hong Kong? Bearer?'

Brennan nodded and raised his eyebrows.

'Then it is you.' She lowered the board and extended a gloved hand over the barrier. 'Carmel de Souza. Pleased to meet you.'

He stared at her, temporarily speechless. He had spent a big chunk of the flight home thinking about her and her involvement in Elba. He had also been working on a plan to get to meet her when he handed the bearer share over to Olson. The only image he had to work with was the tabloid shot of her in the San Francisco garden. She was just as elegant in person.

Carmel was studying him, waiting for him to respond. His ruminations on the flight had led him to just one conclusion. That she was the architect of the murder of her husband, Victor.

He reached across the barrier and took her hand.

'The pleasure is all mine,' he heard himself saying. 'This is a surprise.'

She smiled. 'I wanted to thank you in person.' She looked down at the attaché case in his right hand. 'I hope you had a pleasant flight.'

'Gloriously uneventful, thanks.'

She had not been the only woman in his thoughts since he had left Hong Kong. There were two others —Lisa Richards and Sarah Brennan.

The reason for Lisa's involvement still didn't seem right. There was something else going on which needed to be resolved. All he had was a very vague theory. This could be the time to test it.

As for Sarah, he had been working on a plan. The only problem was that she was going to hate it.

He had spoken to Sarah from the airport and they were both fine. Cara remembered the fight as a bad dream. Sara had been shaken up but was unharmed and fully recovered from her short sedation. She was angry with herself for being duped and furious that she and Cara had been dragged into this mess. Brennan had told her that Matterling was behind Joe's intrusion and that it had been designed to taunt him. There had been no intention to cause Cara harm but Matterling had wanted to show how vulnerable they were. He had told her why he had been in Hong Kong, that he had collected the bearer share and was flying back to London that night. He had not said anything more about Matterling, but he would tell her the whole story when he got home. By the time he had finished, she had calmed down. But there was still a lot of explaining to do.

Carmel led him out of the airport to a sleek black Audi, which she had parked on the VIP floor of the car park, nearest to the arrivals lounge. As Brennan levered himself into the passenger seat he wondered whether he should hand over the share now or wait until he met Ken Olson.

Carmel smiled cautiously at him. Hardly the smile of a murderer, he thought. He did not feel in danger. There was a fragility about her that overcame his natural wariness.

'Ken asked me to give you this,' she said.

She withdrew a white envelope from her coat pocket. She handed it to him and he opened it carefully. He took a quick look at its contents, resealed it and put it in his jacket pocket.

That's dealt with that, he thought and handed over the attaché case. The banker's draft in the envelope was exactly the amount he had been expecting. Drawn to Michael J. Brennan.

Carmel opened the case, glanced inside and closed it again. She slid it under her seat. 'I hope there weren't any problems picking it up.'

'Not really.' Brennan smiled to himself. Nothing that a thousand kilos of explosives couldn't sort out.

Carmel started the car. 'Rush hour is starting. We'll have plenty of time for you to tell me all about it. Queen's Park, isn't it?'

'Thank you.'

He could understand her eagerness to get hold of the bearer share but why not wait until he delivered it to Olson? Brennan was planning to liaise with him later in the day. Unless she was jumping in first. The draft had been drawn on HSBC with no account name to give a clue as to where the money had come from. The amount had been arranged with Olson last Saturday.

She turned and smiled at him again as they exited the car park. He relaxed. There wasn't anything amiss. Apart from being driven into London by a murderer.

'Fire away,' she said without taking her eyes off the road. 'Tell me all about it. I've never been to Hong Kong.'

Brennan cleared his throat and by the time they reached the end of the M4 spur, he had given her a potted summary. Right up to the point where he and Henry had collected the case from the Central Hong Kong branch of the Singapore Merchant Bank.

'That was pretty much it,' he lied and leant back in his seat, watching her for a reaction. 'Straightforward, really.'

Her lips tightened very slightly. Did she know there was more to the story?

'I'm sorry about your loss. I'm sure that Victor was a good man.'

'A good man but a terrible husband. I felt like I was being punished when I was married to him.'

'But he set up the company shareholdings well, didn't he? Ken filled me in on all the detail.'

She glanced at him. 'Ken did, did he?' She refocused on the road. 'But yes, Victor wanted to make sure the family were looked after. Although this bearer share has caused a bit of trouble.'

Brennan couldn't disagree with that. 'I know that all his shares in Elba were held by your family trust. That must have made things easier when he died. Ken was certainly impressed.'

He noticed her grip tighten on the wheel but needed to press further.

'Victor called it the family assurance policy,' she said, 'where the shares could only be sold if both trustees agreed. A perfectly normal arrangement. You would have set up something similar surely when you were in business?'

'Not the last time. But it's one for the future, perhaps.'

She had turned that around pretty skilfully. But crucially, she had confirmed the fact that Victor's death had passed control of his shares to her.

Something Matterling had said to him now came to his mind again. Something that had been niggling at him. Matterling had said that the bearer share had only become important after he had been *deceived.*

What if Carmel had told Matterling that in the event of Victor's death, she would sell the family holding to him? From Carmel's point of view that would have given her financial security—and conveniently relieved her of her philandering husband. Matterling would have had no compunction in obliging. Perhaps the *deception* had been her failure to deliver on her side of the bargain. But why?

He had to come at this from another direction. 'How has it been for you the past few days? Are the tabloids still chasing you?'

Another tightening of her gloved fingers on the wheel.

'It all seems to be dying down now. Yesterday's news. Although Ken says it'll probably blow up again when the bid for Elba goes public.'

'I happened to speak to Sophie Loretta last Saturday. The journalist behind the San Francisco story.'

Carmel's eyes widened and she shot him a concerned look. 'You did? Why would you do that?'

'To find out who was behind it.'

'And did you?'

'Yes.'

'And?'

'Doug Matterling.'

She nodded. 'I thought so.' Her shoulders slumped. 'It's one of his tactics.'

'He's tried it before?'

'He has threatened to.'

'Can I ask when?'

There was no reason for her to tell him. As far as she was concerned, he was simply a courier. A courier with an axe to grind about his previous business partner.

'Sure. I know it won't get back to him.' Another quick look. A complicit look, this time. 'It was when he was pressurising Victor to sell his shares in Elba. Or rather *our* shares. He threatened to spread stories about Elba running into legal problems over intellectual property. He said that it was our last chance to sell before the shares became worthless.'

'Even though it would devalue Heilong's shares as well?'

'That didn't matter to him. I found that out when I stopped him.'

'How did you do that?'

'I told him we were going to raise more capital from Olson Associates. Which would require considerable due diligence that would refute any rumours of intellectual property problems.'

'Were you really going to do that?'

'No.'

'Clever. But you knew he would persist?'

'Of course.'

Another silence. There was no need for her to elaborate. She had used that pressure to engineer Victor's death. As for Matterling, she had as good as admitted that she knew he was dead.

'He was a big threat to you, wasn't he?' Brennan said softly. 'Doug Matterling.'

Carmel chewed at her lip before replying. 'To me and my family.'

'You had to take action yourself?'

'You always have to, don't you? To look after your family? No one else will.'

It was starting to rain and the windscreen wipers started their slow sweep. Brennan noticed the gold crucifix hanging from the rearview mirror. 'Apart from God?' he said.

'God will forgive your actions. But you have to act.'

'You know that Matterling's dead, don't you.' It wasn't a question.

A plane flew low over them, making its descent into the airport behind. Carmel concentrated on the road ahead and said nothing.

'She told you yesterday, didn't she?' Brennan continued.

What had seemed like a fanciful theory on the flight now seemed like the only answer. It wasn't Olson who had instructed Lisa. It was

Carmel. Lisa had family in Hong Kong. A family that wanted vengeance. And Carmel had two major reasons to deploy them. One was to ensure that the bearer share was returned safely to London. The other was to ensure that Matterling would never be involved in her life again. As long as he was alive, he was a threat to her and her family.

Yesterday, Brennan had thought Olson was paying Lisa. She had known the amount Brennan would receive. Or the amount *she* would receive. Whoever brought back the bearer share. But now, he realised that it had to be Carmel. Only she would know the figure involved *and* have the motivation to kill Matterling.

Carmel took her left hand off the steering wheel and leant forward a few inches so that she could touch the crucifix, which was swinging gently from the mirror. She held it tenderly for several long seconds.

'He will forgive you, Mr Brennan. God will forgive. You only have to ask.'

Brennan stared at her as she looked ahead. The only way she could have known about Matterling's fate was if Lisa had told her. They must have spoken last night.

'Why did you send Lisa over so late?' he said. 'I could easily have left Hong Kong by then. With the bearer share.'

'There was no need for her to travel at all. Her family were going to protect Ken when he was due to make the trip. She only decided to go when she realised that Matterling had his own protection. She had to find out what kind of threat Remus Security posed to her family.' A narrow smile drifted across her lips. 'Romulus and Remus. Suckled by a she-wolf, weren't they? Families come in all forms. But family comes first. Always.'

'And me? How was I going to be protected?'

As soon as he asked the question Brennan knew the answer. There was no question of protection for him. He would have been a witness and would have had to suffer the same fate as Matterling.

Lisa had been trying to protect her family's honour. They had lost money in BM, sure. But worse than that was the fact that the relationship did not continue. There was no attempt by Doug Matterling to make restitution. Nor by Mike Brennan either but being in prison offered an excuse. Would that have been reason enough?

'Put your street name into the satnav.' Carmel lifted a finger towards the dashboard. 'I'll get you home safe and sound.'

'You must have identified Lisa as someone with the motivation to get back at Matterling.'

As he leaned forward towards the small screen he saw Carmel's lips twitch. He was right.

'So why put yourself in that position?' Carmel asked. 'You could easily have been killed.' She glanced across at him.

He pressed the screen and entered his address. He sat back and closed his eyes, trying to forget that he was being driven home by someone who would happily have had him disappear into the depths of Hong Kong harbour, as long as she received what she felt she deserved.

'I guess that God must have thought I had things too easy. He probably thought I needed a test.'

'He tests us all our lives, Mr Brennan. Otherwise we would never fear for our destiny.'

'I thought that giving in to God's destiny would overcome all fear.'

'I have lived my life in fear. And I can't see that changing. Even though I have now got justice I still don't know my destination.'

For some reason that thought comforted Brennan. Even though she had death on her hands and knew that her God would forgive her. Even though she knew that God was shaping her destiny. But she was still fearful.

'I'm beginning to think that justice can never be complete.' Brennan knew that this would only make real sense when he got back to Sarah. Everything would be much clearer then.

'Those famous scales will never be in balance for very long.' His voice dropped supportively. 'So it's good that you believe you've got yours.'

'I do. After my life of punishment. There is hope now.'

She sounded resolute. Acknowledging the fear but grateful for her new circumstances.

'I can't help but be concerned for you,' she said gently.

'For me?' Brennan's back straightened in his seat. Where was this coming from?

'You know that I know what happened. As a fellow child of God I fear for you. How will you cleanse your soul, Mr Brennan?'

He looked at the stationary vehicles in front of them. It was a good question.

'I don't think I ever will,' he said slowly. 'It's never going to wash away.'

The traffic moved forward and they drove in silence for the next half hour. Brennan felt a bond between them as they pushed their way through the drizzle. They had both done what they needed to do. Now they would both have to deal with the consequences in their own ways.

He would soon be home. Safe and sound, she had promised.

It sounded good.

71

Thursday morning
  London

AFTER FINISHING his second call of the morning Brennan pocketed his phone and took the final few steps to his front door. He
turned the key. A sense of dread coursed through his body. This was
it. His day of judgement. Sarah's judgement of his actions. She had
sounded very distant when he had called her from Hong Kong. In
every way.

He thought about what Carmel had said regarding forgiveness. If
only he were being judged by Carmel's God right now, it would be a
whole lot easier.

The heavy front door swung open and he stepped into the hall
and put down his bag.

'Anybody home?' he called hesitantly.

He heard the sound he had been hoping for. Cara's running footsteps as she came out of the kitchen and down the hall. Her face was
beaming and she jumped up into his arms. She didn't make a sound

but buried her head in his chest. Her blonde curls tickled his chin and he held her as tightly as he ever had. They hung onto each other in silence for a long moment.

Sarah appeared at the kitchen door.

'Come on, Cara. You've still got to finish your breakfast.'

Brennan gently let her down.

'We'll play after breakfast, darling,' he said. 'You eat up now as Mummy says.'

Sarah followed her daughter into the kitchen and Brennan walked to the kitchen door.

'Can we talk? In the living room?'

Sarah made sure that Cara resumed eating and then followed him to the living room. She stood at the doorway and leant against the door frame, her arms crossed. Brennan moved towards her. He tried to hold her but she stiffened under his touch. He dropped his arms and took a step back.

'You did so well yesterday,' he said. 'That axe kick was amazing. My fearless warrior.'

They had talked about what had happened at length during his call from the airport. She hardly remembered the sequence of events, she had said. It was still a blur. Then he had told her why he was in Hong Kong to collect the bearer share. He also told her that the pick-up hadn't been straightforward and had given her a selective summary of events.

'As I said on the phone, I didn't have a chance to think about it. It was only last night that it all sunk in. It was only then that I felt scared.'

She pushed herself away from the door frame and followed him into the room.

'I would hardly describe myself as fearless.'

'But you conquered it when you had to. That made you a warrior.'

She shrugged, unconvinced. 'Anyway, how did you get from the airport? Taxi?'

'Carmel de Souza picked me up. She wanted to get her hands on that share as soon as.'

'That's what started you off on this whole merry dance, wasn't it? That guy falling off his boat and drowning.'

'It was no accident. He never fell. He *was* murdered. Doug Matterling arranged it but Carmel was the one behind it. They had an agreement that she would sell the family's shareholding in Elba to him. He kept his side of the deal by getting rid of Victor, but then she changed horses.'

Sarah's eyes widened. 'Sounds like quite a piece of work.'

'She is. I was lucky not to suffer the same fate. You're suddenly very disposable when you're on the wrong side of the law.'

'Well thank God you didn't. You're home now. Safe and sound.'

Brennan felt a spurt of hope in his chest. Despite the brusque tone there was real tenderness in her eyes.

'Remember how you used to believe that things would just right themselves?' she continued. 'That there was a natural justice underpinning the world?'

He smiled. 'That was a long time ago.' He moved closer to her and took her hands in his. Her arms relaxed and her hands felt soft.

'I shared that belief. All that time ago. I only saw what I wanted to see. I was just like you.'

Was this going to be a good thing or a bad thing? he thought. But he let her go on, this was obviously something that she had been chewing over.

'Before all this happened, all I could see was stability.' Her fingers tightened around his. 'And love. That's all I wanted to see, I was blinkered. The alternative was unimaginable. So I didn't imagine it. But when the unimaginable became reality I had to see beyond. And then I made a mistake.'

'A mistake?' This wasn't sounding good.

'Yes, Mike. I saw you as our saviour.'

He felt himself stiffen.

'A saviour?'

'Seeing you as our saviour was not the mistake. Seeing you as a saviour with my agenda was the mistake.'

'Oh.'

'I was still just seeing what I wanted—needed to see. I made no allowance for Michael Brennan. I couldn't see that you were flawed. That for all your brilliance you were just as flawed as me. And that let Doug Matterling nearly destroy us.'

She moved her hands upwards and held his upper arms.

'You're a strong man, Mike. Recognising your weaknesses is part of that strength.'

She was waiting for a reply. It had been a painful realisation but it had been true. Sarah was right of course. He had feared a summary judgement based on the incident with Joe. But this was a longer-term assessment.

'I should never have let it get that far, I know that. It was down to me. And that's why I had to fix it in my own way.'

'Fix it?'

She sounded on edge again, that sense of determined resolution starting to evaporate. He knew that the two things he was about to say would test that resolution to the absolute limit.

'A lot happened in Hong Kong,' he began. Although he had relayed much of that when he called her from Hong Kong airport, he had left out one small detail.

'Doug Matterling is dead.'

'Dead? How?'

'I killed him.'

Sarah's mouth dropped open. Brennan could not tell who was more shocked, Sarah at hearing it or him at saying it. Words he had never said before and hoped he would not say again. But it was the truth. And he would have to bear it for the rest of his life.

'But how?' she repeated.

'It was a kind of controlled explosion.'

'An explosion?'

'I let him get too close to some fireworks that were going off. A barge full of them, intended for the New Year celebrations. It was like a bomb. You're right, he would have destroyed us had he lived. And a lot of other people too, if he'd got hold of Elba Technology. There was no option.'

'No option?'

'None. It was him or me.'

Sarah dropped her hands into his again and closed her eyes.

'I believe in you, Mike. I really do.' She pursed her lips. 'It's not just because I have to.'

'De Souza led me to him. Matterling was after revenge as well. He was after a revenge he could never get.'

'I don't understand.' She opened her eyes again.

'A childhood trauma. One that he could never avenge. He condemned himself to damnation.'

'You're sure he's dead?'

'Yeah. I'm sure. No one could have survived that inferno.'

'Is that the end of it?'

Cara suddenly appeared and pushed past Sarah's legs. She came into the room and jumped up onto the piano stool.

'Look, Daddy. Look.'

She held up her arm. The gold piano charm bracelet hung from her wrist. She touched it with her other hand.

'No harm, Daddy. No harm.' She grinned up at him as she slid the bracelet off her wrist. She held it out to him.

'You have it, you have it.'

He looked into her eyes. She was pleading with him.

'Might not be such a bad idea,' Sarah said softly.

He took the bracelet and then leant over to kiss Cara's forehead. He squeezed her shoulders as she wriggled into a comfortable position on the stool and opened the keyboard lid. She positioned her hands over the middle two octaves. Then she started to play. She sang as she played.

'Twinkle, twinkle, little star, how I wonder what you are.'

She looked up at him. 'You sing, Daddy, you sing.'

'*Up above the world so high,*' they sang together. '*Like a diamond in the sky.*'

She had been practising. She was playing the chords with her left hand. Brennan's voice cracked as she finished the final four bars.

'*Twinkle, twinkle, little star, how I wonder what you are.*'

They applauded each other at the end and Sarah joined in. She brushed away a tear with the back of her hand. Cara was flicking through her music book to find another piece to play. The dynamic had changed. Now it wasn't just about them. It was about their daughter.

He reached into his jacket pocket and pulled out the envelope. He passed it to Sarah.

'This is no justification, I know that. It's only money. But it does represent my intention to look after this family to the best of my ability. My choice was the right one. Not because of that—' he nodded at the envelope, '—but because I can look Cara in the eye in the future.'

Sarah opened the envelope and pulled the slip of paper far enough out to read it. 'Just for collecting one share?' she said, wide-eyed. 'Not bad.'

She pushed the draft into the envelope and handed it back to him.

Cara tired of searching for another piece to play and swung her legs off the stool. Brennan scooped her up into his arms. He gave her a big squeeze and kissed her on both cheeks before letting her down. She rolled down his arms and ran out of the room.

'I'll go to the bank later,' he said. 'It'll be in the joint account by the end of the day.'

Sarah put her palms on his chest. 'Is that the end of it? Now that you've got your revenge.'

'A justice has been served. And I feel justified in doing what I did. Not sure they're the same thing.'

Sarah frowned. 'Matterling must have friends. Or at least business associates. Who may want to get even with you. And what about the police in Hong Kong? Won't they be investigating?'

'I don't know if anyone will seek retribution. Or if the police will get involved. I can't see any of those criminals wanting that. But I'll have to be careful.'

'Careful?'

'I'll have to keep my head down for a while. And I want you and Cara to go away for a couple of weeks.'

'Go away? Where?'

'Remember that cottage in Skibbereen? The one we used to go to? You were talking about a holiday there.'

Sarah's brow tightened.

'This would be the perfect time to get Cara on the back of one of those ponies. She'll love it. They'll make such a fuss of her.'

'But what about you?'

'I'll stay here.'

She put a hand on his chest and closed her eyes.

'The cottage is reserved,' he said. 'I just spoke to them.' Then, for added reassurance. 'She remembered us.'

'And then what? What happens when we get back?'

Now for the second thing.

'I'll organise that while you're away. I'll disappear again when you return but you'll be safer without me. I'm going to arrange some security.'

'Security? Here?'

'Yes. For a few months, until we're sure there won't be a backlash from Hong Kong.'

'What kind of security?'

'Domestic security. A company will keep an eye on the house and protect you and Cara.'

'A company? Who would that be?'

'You've already dealt with one of their employees. But there are two more who are still able-bodied.'

Sarah stepped back and her mouth opened and closed a couple of times before she spoke. 'But surely—'

'They work for money. Nothing else. And now we seem to have

quite a lot of it. I spoke to their MD this morning and when she heard that she'd just lost her biggest client she became very amenable. We're going to discuss terms over the next few days.'

'No, Mike. No. I can't believe you're saying this. God knows what that monster would have done if I hadn't come in. There's no way I'm going to let him into my house again'

'Look at it another way. If they're not working for us then they could be working against us. We've got the opportunity here to get on the front foot. They probably won't be needed anyway.'

'But you're talking about them being in our house, aren't you? Protecting us?'

'Exactly. That's what they would be doing.'

'But how could we trust them? And who is this MD anyway?'

'Their Mum.'

'Their Mum?' Sarah's voice rose with incredulity.

'It's a family firm. Mum and three sons.'

Sarah spun on her heel and turned her back to him. She stared hard out of the window.

'Isn't there anybody else we could use?' she asked eventually

'I'm sure there is. But I don't happen to know anybody else at the moment and if we don't act quickly Remus Security might be used against us. Again.'

'So that's what they call themselves?' She was still looking out of the window.

'You won't even notice them. We'll give them the spare bedroom and there'll be one keeping watch outside at any one time. They'll be like ghosts.'

'And where will you be?'

'Not far away.'

'Like a ghost?'

'I'll keep materialising.'

Just then Cara ran back into the room and threw herself against Sarah's legs. She hugged her knees and swayed gently against them.

Instinctively, Sarah leant down and put her hand on Cara's head. They swung together for a few seconds.

'I'm sure that you've thought this through. You're the one who's been dealing with these characters. I'll have to agree. But only on one condition,' Sarah said slowly, her fingers running through Cara's hair.

'Name it.'

'The one who came into the house...'

'Joe.'

'Whatever. He's never to come in here again. He can do outside patrols or whatever they're going to do. But he's never to step foot inside here again. Understood?'

'Understood.'

He moved closer to her again.

'Things will settle down. I promise you.'

Sarah nodded slowly and then smiled. It was a smile that told him she had made her judgement and the scales had tipped in his favour.

He put his arms around her and she rested her head on his chest. Cara extended an arm around his knees as well. She pulled them closer together. It felt good. He had not felt like this with them for a very long time. Since before all the problems with Matterling had begun.

'Being apart again is such a high price to pay. For all of us,' Sarah murmured. Then he felt her shudder softly in his arms, struggling to hold back the tears.

'Why does it have to be like this?' she said quietly, not wanting Cara to hear and to start asking questions.

'I don't know. All I know is that what I've done can never be undone. But as long as we're together again one day, properly, it will be worth it.'

There was a long silence as the three of them held each other. Even Cara sensed the moment and was still.

Brennan squeezed the charm bracelet which he was still holding.

'I never thought of myself as a vengeful person, you know,' he breathed into Sarah's hair.

She moved her head back.

'You're not. You're the least vengeful person I've ever met. Just one of the most unforgiving.' She paused. 'To yourself.'

He had to agree with her. Now that he knew the truth he just had to figure out how to use it. To make sure that his family would never be put in danger again.

'That's been your real struggle, hasn't it? That's been the war you've really been fighting.' She smiled as she said his words back to him. 'My fearless warrior.'

They held each other in silence again, both with their own thoughts.

'How long will it be for this time?' Sarah broke the silence.

He pulled her closer.

'As long as it takes. We'll absorb the blow and come out stronger. That's what you used to say to me. The world no longer has to harbour Doug Matterling. It's not that high a price.'

The shuddering stopped. He felt her gather strength.

Then he thought back to the heavy black lettering on the ceiling of that terrifying cell in Belmarsh. All those days and weeks and months ago. Before the burden. That simple proclamation:

It's Only Time.

REVIEW THIS BOOK

If you have enjoyed *The Bearer* I would be most grateful if you could take a moment to post a review on Amazon. Just a sentence or two would be great. Reviews are so important for a book to get noticed.

The next book in the Mike Brennan series is already in the works. If you would like to be kept up to date with developments then please subscribe for my occasional newsletter. The link is below.

You may also contact me through the website – I really enjoy hearing from readers.

Thank you

Frank

frankmcilwee.com

ABOUT THE AUTHOR

Frank McIlwee studied Philosophy at Sussex University where he started writing stories. He has held a number of finance roles for companies in the UK and the USA. He has also been a freelance financial journalist and photographer. More recently he has undertaken training assignments for the UN in South Sudan and Myanmar. He lives in West Sussex, England and South East Asia.

f facebook.com/FRANKMCILWEE.Author

Printed in Great Britain
by Amazon

44875530R00272